The Truman Nelson Reader

The Truman Nelson Reader

Edited by William J. Schafer

The University of Massachusetts Press   *Amherst,* 1989

Copyright © 1989 by
Truman Nelson
All rights reserved
Printed in the United States of America
LC 88–14701
ISBN 0–87023–647–4 (cloth); 648–2 (pbk.)
Designed by Patricia Douglas Crowder
Set in Linotron 202 Aster
Printed by Thomson-Shore and bound by John Dekker & Sons

LIBRARY OF CONGRESS CATALOGING-IN-PUBLICATION DATA

Nelson, Truman John, 1912–
    The Truman Nelson reader / edited by William J. Schafer.
      p. cm.
    Bibliography: p.
    ISBN 0–87023–647–4 (alk. paper). ISBN 0–87023–648–2
(pbk. : alk. paper)
    I. Schafer, William John, 1937–   . II. Title.
PS3564.E477A6 1989   88–14701
                                                    CIP

British Library Cataloguing in Publication data are available.

Contents

Introduction   vii

Fiction: *The Themes*   1
   The Sin of the Prophet   3
   The Passion by the Brook   62
   The Surveyor   101
   God in Love   142

Essays: *The Variations*   153
   On Creating Revolutionary Art and Going Out of Print   160
   The Liberator   177
   Thoreau and John Brown   195
   W.E.B. Du Bois as a Prophet   216
   The Torture of Mothers   230
   No Rights, No Duties   239
   The Conscience of the North   254

Interview   271
   Truman Nelson: An Interview with Shaun A. McNiff   273

Bibliography, *compiled by Garrison Nelson*   293

Acknowledgments   301

Introduction

I've almost made up my mind to cast my lot with the Negroes. They're the ones that are living an inch at a time. They're not worried about another ten cents a day but about how to get out from under the lash. They're moving, rebelling, running away from their bondage, flaunting their misery in the faces of the smug. We call our factory workers hands. The Negroes have no hands, they are in chains. Our hands can fight, carry a gun, vote even if they want to. I've got more respect for the black people. Unfortunately it is written on the iron leaf of fate that progress comes only by revolutions, not gradually, and comes only in great convulsions and not from patient plodding. If you want a spot to stand on, to move the earth, find the man who is being crucified, who is on the cross today.
—Theodore Parker, to George Ripley, in *The Passion by the Brook*

During the 1950s, in the deep double shadow of McCarthyism and the Cold War, Truman Nelson wrote three historical novels reaching a century back to a great decade of climactic controversy and action, the 1850s. This epoch, called by Nelson's mentor F. O. Matthiessen the "American Renaissance," was the zenith of nineteenth-century American radicalism, focused in the fight for abolition. Nelson's novels—*The Sin of the Prophet* (1952), *The Passion by the Brook* (1953), and *The Surveyor* (1960)—sketch the development of radical consciousness from the communitarian experiment of Brook Farm, through The-

All citations from Truman Nelson's novels are to first editions (page numbers in parentheses): *The Sin of the Prophet* (Boston: Little, Brown, 1952), *The Passion by the Brook* (Garden City, N.Y.: Doubleday, 1953), *The Surveyor* (Garden City, N.Y.: Doubleday, 1960). Other quotes are drawn from Truman Nelson, "On Creating Revolutionary Art and Going Out of Print," *TriQuarterly*, no. 23/24 (Winter/Spring, 1972): 92–110, and from "The Conscience of the North," *Freedomways* 1 (Fall 1961):259–74.

odore Parker's radical ministry, to John Brown's guerrilla warfare in "Bloody Kansas." They form a fresco of the great age of radical social thought in America and a guidebook to our revolutionary heritage in its last, most brilliant manifestation.

Nelson, a self-educated, stubbornly individualistic writer and a committed Marxist radical, wrote to communicate the possibilities of revolution inherent in the American idea, our right of revolution guaranteed by the Declaration of Independence. The three novels are the most intelligent, meticulous, and profoundly dramatic historical fictions by an American in this century. They convey the turmoil and intellectual ferment of America in the age of Emerson, Hawthorne, Melville, Thoreau, Garrison, Parker, and John Brown. They also vivify the complex sociopolitical history of that period through dramatic characters. Nelson's achievement is major but has gone almost unacknowledged by critics and literary observers, probably because the historical novel is in bad repute with modern literary theorists and fiction writers. The bad money of sleazy antebellum romances and potboilers built on tushery and pseudohistory has driven the good money of the traditional historical novel from our literary economy.

In a 1973 essay wryly entitled "On Creating Revolutionary Art and Going Out of Print," Nelson examines his reputation (or lack thereof) and concludes sadly that his exhausting effort was probably in vain:

we are all profoundly weary and hopeless about our present culture. The historical novel is a prime form of people's art; it is storytelling, it is example, it is an embodiment of our hidden continuities of hope and rage. It can be very, very revolutionary and uncontrolled by the consciousness-controllers now deprinciplizing and derevolutionizing students in the academic process . . . teaching counter-revolution.

It seems clear that these same people now control the publishing, the publicizing and the criticizing processes with the same iron hand with which they control their students. It is no longer possible to circumvent them by writing revolutionary history in the form of a novel nor is it possible to attain the distribution or viability of revolutionary essays or tracts until they appear somewhere on a "reading list."

His novels deal not with cold facts or abstruse social-historical theory but with frail, fallible men who tried to make America's ideals work, to secure freedom for black people, and to preserve the revolutionary standards of the Union against both the slavocracy and weak-willed compromise. Each novel depicts a mental and spiritual ordeal, the "man on the cross today," in Theodore Parker's phrase. His stories follow the best New England Puritan-radical traditions, in the paradoxical manner of Thoreau, for example; they are cerebral and passionate, austere and humorous, open-minded and sharply polemical. So are the men and women he describes, and he produces them alive and thinking from the dead-cold archives of the past.

In his first novel, *The Sin of the Prophet,* Nelson charted his personal territory as a writer and devised a methodology for his ideas. He aimed to remind us of America's continuing revolutionary heritage, to assemble the facts and ideas of history in convincing human dramas. Therefore, he settled on his first subject, "an event which, in the sharpest way imaginable, presented a view of the crisis at its zenith"—the Anthony Burns affair of 1854. Burns, an escaped slave arrested in Boston, was remanded under the much-detested Fugitive Slave Law back to his master in Virginia. Boston antislavery forces seized the incident to defy the law and existing administration in Washington, and men like Theodore Parker, Thomas Wentworth Higginson, Wendell Phillips, and Samuel Gridley Howe conspired to release Burns from custody at the courthouse. Nelson focuses on Parker as his central character, the "prophet" of the title, and the story becomes a study of radical political theory and practice—the critical transition from ideals to direct action.

The vortex of the story is a meeting at Faneuil Hall, where Parker cannot bridge the gap between theory and polemic and physical action. Set to urge the aroused crowd to attack the courthouse, to free Burns and spirit him away, Parker cannot make the simple, crucial decision, and for the balance of the story he contemplates this "sin" and works to expiate it. Because Parker was a supremely intellectual, verbal man, the story flows on his Hamlet-like arguments with himself and his colleagues. Nelson uses the rhetorical brilliance of the age to great advantage in his dialogue. But fabricating a dramatic structure was difficult, and Nelson sweated to arrive at Parker's agony as the focus of the novel:

I felt that I had evolved a slightly different method of storytelling and one which could live harmoniously within the materialist conception of history. Letting the event itself come first, relentlessly exploiting and dramatizing every connection except those so remote they could not be proved, I found it did establish its own form. The incessant opposition of wills, which seemed at first to knock every attempt at forward motion so much out of line that the narrative appeared to be a vicious circle, soon began to bend under the tension until the motion along the front began to spiral sharply, increasing its velocity until everything collided at the center. My necessary preoccupation with historical elements gave me an active sense of the dialectical process of becoming. To paraphrase Marx . . . as a writer I became supremely aware that it was not my consciousness that was determining the characters and the action in this book; rather, established social existences were determining both the characters and action . . . and my own consciousness as an artist.

In discovering himself and a dialectical method of developing historical fiction, Nelson's progress paralleled that of Parker. Theodore Parker also plunges through intense self-analysis and examination of his principles and those of politics and society.

Parker is heroic, but he is a flawed hero, a damaged leader. His character became for Nelson a classic definition of the liberal in a revolutionary crisis:

> What [the writing of the novel] revealed very sharply was the paralysis of the liberal in the face of a demand for action, for violence. This was the sin of the prophet: that men of learning and sensibility are capable of understanding the physical and political facts of their own existence, yet cannot commit the irrevocable acts needed to transform them. They proclaim what is wrong, but they hesitate to move against the wrong, and really don't want anyone else to.

Thus the story revolves around Parker's struggle for self-awareness, set against the backdrop of the Burns case with its politicking, the rhetoric of proslavery and antislavery factions, the manipulations of the prevailing Democratic Party machinery, and the figure of Burns himself locked away in the "slave pen" and later sent to Virginia for punishment and humiliation. Ultimately Burns is freed—bought out of servitude by abolitionist supporters—but political pressure makes his Boston trial a hollow formality. His rendition under the Fugitive Slave Law Nelson explains in terms of *realpolitik*—the Democrats must remand him to maintain Southern support and bolster their law-and-order facade.

Burns is drawn with great dignity. He is lonely, terrified, and in a desperate situation, but he retains his humanity and refuses to sell himself out, even when he has lost all hope for freedom. The story exposes the white view of black men in Boston—that Burns is a pawn in a political game and also an oddity, marked by his race as outside the human order. One prosecution lawyer admits this to himself as he hears Burns's description read into the trial record:

Up here a Negro is a Negro. Down there he is a dark-complected man and more, a son, a brother, a cousin, a nephew . . . all these are admitted relationships. And there are the unadmitted ones, the mothers, the fathers. They are there too. (48)

Complex problems of miscegenation, interfamily blood ties, psychosexual distortions, and fears of the slaveholding South lurk beneath the legal arguments. Burns's owner has felt alienated in Boston searching for Burns: "in the Colonel's big trumpet nose was the stink of fear, for not too far off was a tight knot of stout Negroes looking at him with the tender bruised eyeballs of hate" (16). Crosscurrents of guilt, rage, submerged fear, and irrational hatred carry Burns to freedom.

Truman Nelson's second study of intellectual history in the 1850s is a prologue or pre-history, a long flashback to Brook Farm as an experiment in radical communitarianism in 1845. In *The Passion by the Brook*, Nelson develops the story of George Ripley's attempt to create an ideal Fourierist city of man. Nelson felt pressured by his own time to deal with the *positive* creativity of American radicalism:

Because I wrote, and still write, only for use, I felt that the only way to fight McCarthyism, which then threatened to destroy the entire American radical heritage as completely as the monotheism of Ikhnaton in 1354 B.C., was to form collectives and communes to create loving communities where political insult and slander were simply meaningless and all life self-sustained. I felt there was a need for a book about communes.

The Passion by the Brook describes other members of Theodore Parker's generation and their impulse toward order and building— the other side of the coin from the right to revolution, the necessity for resistance to unholy demands of the state. Insofar as Brook Farm successfully demonstrated the potential of men and women to live in harmony under absolute equality, Nelson deals with radicalism in Eden. Brook Farm ultimately failed, and he shows that its collapse is more complex and interesting than cynics of its day (and ours) would admit.

He centers his complex drama around Ripley as the Fourierist leader and tries to make the principles of Fourierism clear and inherent in the structure of the novel itself:

> I decided to drop the complex and laborious event structure [of *The Sin of the Prophet*] and to impose the ideology of Fourier on the novel as relentlessly as the Brook Farmers did on their collective.... So, in the writing, I locked their total experience into a rigid form, constructing the book in twelve chapters, each having for its denouement the relationship of the life of the collective to one of the twelve passions which were the master plan of Fourier ... sight, cabals, touch, smell, taste, hearing, variety, familism, friendship, ambition, love, composite. The total exercise of these passions and their interaction, Fourier thought, would make men and women ideal in their relationship with one another.

The novel spans a year, unfolding relationships between extremely individualistic characters at the Farm, tensions that undermined Ripley's structure, misunderstandings, and inevitable lapses from principle. The Brook Farmers included the Boston intelligentsia—transcendentalists, Unitarians, and refugees from the era's prolific evangelical movements—and workingmen seeking to escape the straitjacket of capitalism, plus many others dropping out of standardized American culture. Nelson focuses on Ripley and two newcomers to the Farm, Edgar and Lili Gray, recruits from the uncommitted outside world who introduce intricate social and psychological currents into the commune.

Lili Gray, a Catholic and convent-raised, grasps the communal concept of Brook Farm readily but does not submit uncritically to the discipline as do the more idealistic communards. The other women feel Lili is worldly and trivial because she has brought fine clothes and manners (she and her husband are among the "drones" boarded at the Farm in exchange for rent money, necessary for the commune's economy). Lili has traveled the road of religious discipline before, so she is an ideal observing intelligence:

> all the things Lili had been asked to do were the tasks forced on her at the convent to the tune of rapped knuckles, personal and penitential prayers and many hours spent in disgrace kneeling beside her chair or in a closet for her

many sins of sloth or woolgathering. Her knees still ached at the memory and she always felt resentfully that it had made them bony and unattractive. (69)

Lili is Lilith in this Garden of Eden, the primeval sensual woman who tests Fourier's abstract theories of the passions in fleshly terms. She falls in love with Adam Smith, a naive but determined young communard, and her presence gradually disrupts and transforms the atmosphere of incompetent innocence on the Farm. Her story and the struggle of George Ripley to maintain the commune against internal dissensions and external pressures are fused. As we pass through Fourier's elemental passions, we see the story of Lili and Adam develop from simple flirtation to a complex human bond. The Farm itself disintegrates under factionalism, despite Ripley's heroic efforts to guide it in Fourier's pattern.

The argument revolves on the Woman Question—the concern of Brook Farmers for absolute equality between the sexes, for the liberation of women. Lili, a practical commonsense woman of the world, intuitively understands the issue:

—What can a woman do, if she's not married? said Lili. —She can't go anywhere. She can't get any money. People look down on her. That's the way things are. Women have just got to do the things their husbands ask and keep the home. That's how they get their living. (120)

But the liberating influence of the Farm allows Lili to leave her husband, at least temporarily, for Adam. Meanwhile, Edgar Gray connives to gain financial control over the Farm, to turn it into a money-making capitalist proposition. The story climaxes when the Phalanstery, the great ark-shaped dormitory under construction as the hub of the commune, burns accidentally. The fall of this building marks the collapse of the Fourierist ideal at Brook Farm. Like other dream communities of its day, it founders on the shoals of human greed and misunderstanding, the splintering of a solid group into small antipathetic factions. Yet we see that George Ripley, Lili, Adam, and others have grown; through the experience they have evolved into human beings perhaps superior to Fourier's ideal man.

Fourier's bizarre theories for communal formation have unexpected results. The anticapitalist, egalitarian format fosters independence and intellectual development, but it is too complex to realize on a manageable scale. Nelson uses musical analogies inherent in Fourier's theory as a running metaphor, an accompaniment to the passionate arias and recitatives of the human drama:

> Fourier had been obsessed by music. He had said that the relation of the notes of the scale showed the harmony of the universe. That if Nature could devise pleasant and unpleasant intervals of sound she could do the same with people. Fourier classified groups by notes in a scale of taste and by combining them found that Group G, for instance, would be very discordant with F, would work fairly well with D but, blended with Groups C and E, made a perfect resolution, a major. (76)

The novel becomes a symphony haunted by John Dwight, the Farm's musician, a Beethoven advocate. He plays his French horn and cornet at gatherings, fragments of Beethoven's "Pastoral" and "Eroica" symphonies and *Leonore* overture—appropriate documents of human awakening and liberation. Dwight plays reveille for the Farm, stepping out in the dawn for the sun "to prod [him], the awakener, out onto the puddingstone ledge in front of the Eyrie, to gild the brass lily of his horn as he raised it to his lips and played his morning psalm to his God, the horn call from Eroica, the theme Beethoven called Lazarus Arise" (57).

The musical structure of relationships on the Farm is like a developing symphony or an oratorio for many voices. According to Fourier's theory, individuals in the commune will combine to form a megaman, a social personality: "Fourier states that the minimum for a Phalanx should be 1620 persons. It takes 810 just to make up one ideal man and you must double that to make sure the settlement has the best of all the skills and faculties. This is just a turn in the road, a pitiful trial" (78). Brook Farm is destined never to reach Fourier's magic number, the moment when 1620 individuals merge as cells of a single social organism. But it is already a complex social being, a refuge from the exploitation and misery of 1840s capitalism. Workingmen on the Farm, who practice their crafts for the benefit of the whole group, are restive, but they understand their society's evils from bitter experience. One young man contemplates going to an industrial company town of the era, Lowell, Massachusetts:

> —If it warn't for my pa, I'd have been there long ago. I've seen him cry when the fall was over because he had to spend another lonely winter, he says. I seen him scratchin' out a livin' on another man's farm, takin' leftovers for his

wages. We used to move from one to another when times got bad and the farms got worse. All we ever owned was a few movables. He never had a cent at the end of the year. He's in the poorhouse now. He wanted to come here but he figured best he shouldn't. Too damned old to do 'em any good, he says, but he sent me. He said I'd better myself. (77)

A familiar picture of the Industrial Revolution—ruined land, deserted villages, the aimless exodus of the unemployed. At least Brook Farm created a place to stand, a refuge for these men.

Brook Farm is attacked from the outside, understandably—by Boston capitalists viewing it as a haven for cranks and do-nothings, a madhouse—but it is also eroded internally. The Concord transcendentalists and their satellites are uncommitted to Ripley's Fourierism, cool and neutral if not hostile. Nathaniel Hawthorne demands repayment of an investment in the Farm, forcing the commune into bankruptcy. Even more corrosive are ideological attacks by men seemingly sympathetic to the Farm's ideals. Orestes Brownson appears in this guise, when he preaches a return to fundamental Christianity. Brownson typifies the 1840s peripatetic radical who has sampled every notion, apprenticed himself to every experiment. As a zealous recent convert to traditional Catholicism, he attacks Brook Farm like the serpent in Eden undermining innocence:

—I am no bigot. You may correct me if I am wrong in saying that Fourierism assumes the perfection of human nature, of the essential holiness of man's instincts, passions and tendencies. That evil comes from causes outside of man, which repress his natural passions and prevent them from reaching their full and free development. And since all the faculties of man are designed by God for useful employment, nothing exists in him which is not called upon to contribute to social harmony, to the good of collective man.

After stating this fair and penetrating précis of Fourierism, Brownson skilfully undercuts it:

—Christianity teaches evil comes from within, said Brownson balefully, — from man's abuse of his essential freedom. Long ago man's appetite became depraved, his moral tastes vitiated to the point that he craves the meat that perishes rather than the meat that endureth to everlasting life. (253)

Brownson's influence seduces those wavering over Christian theology, and the Brook Farmers break into the petty factions and denominations that have already rent the outside world.

Brook Farm is a vast embryo struggling to live but dying in the pangs of birth. Ripley is deeply discouraged by the defection of his wife and others to traditional Christianity. He is fascinated by the life-giving example of Lili Gray as a person genuinely freed by the experiment, but she is one of the few Brook Farmers who instinctively understand the meaning of Fourier's collectivization of the passions. At the end, Ripley talks with his friend Theodore Parker, who empathizes but sees the experiment more clearly from the outside than Ripley can view it. Ripley wonders why the oppressed have not flocked to the peace and freedom of the Farm:

> why don't the people help us, the common people that we're doing this for? Are they content to go on living in these dirty rabbit warrens, a hundred thousand souls living without air or light in these slimy courts and cellars, in garrets open to the wind and rain, to rats and insects, all in dilapidation, drenched with miasmas, misery and uncleanliness? Are they all blind? Do they care nothing beyond getting a few cents more a day for their labor? It's evil, it's worse than feudalism. Someday knowledge will burst upon them and they will see the misery their supineness and indifference have cost them. (311)

The question goes unanswered, but when Ripley realizes the dream is gone, he breaks down, and Theodore Parker gives him the only comfort he knows, from Christian doctrine: "A great sob burst from [Ripley's] chest and he turned away and began to weep violently, to surrender at last. Parker took him roughly in his arms and said tenderly, —You fool, you fool, that which thou sowest is not quickened except it die!" (380).

This ends the novel and summarizes Nelson's feelings about Brook Farm and Ripley's effort to realize Utopia—by living and dying, Brook Farm established an example and made tangible the ideals of American radicalism at its first great crisis. If *The Passion by the Brook* is seen as a prelude to the revolutionary epoch of the 1850s and the apogee of the radical action of the antislavery movement, then Ripley's contribution is immense. He first translated theory—very abstract and difficult theory—into direct action. He unified and led individualistic and autonomous people in a community founded on sheer principle and united by ideology rather than social class or economic interest. Brook Farm is the mustard seed in Parker's comforting words, cast onto the barren soil of Puritanism and traditional self-interest and yielding abundant harvest in the later actions of Parker, Phillips, Garrison, and John Brown.

Ripley's Fourierist experiment at Brook Farm bred ideas and inspired American thinkers who disagreed with it or attacked it. It attempted to create enduring reality from pure ideas, to develop community from a theory of psychology and social ethics. Whether or not we comprehend Fourier's outré categories, it was a clear alternative to the brutal world of the early Industrial Revolution, one of the few socialist proposals of the time offering a comprehensive plan for a secular society free of the greed and profit motive. History may judge Ripley's work, like John Brown's, as a failure. Nelson obviously sees Ripley and Brown as heroes whose failures are larger than other men's successes. In the dark labyrinth of American history, flames from the burning Phalanstery at Brook Farm lighted the way for Old Man Brown at Harper's Ferry.

The Surveyor deals with John Brown's career as a revolutionary during the bitter dispute over Kansas's annexation as a slave or free state, in the years 1854 to 1856. Nelson's characterization of Brown analyzes him as an ideologue and workingman skilled in woodcrafting and pioneering. Unlike Eastern intellectuals in the abolition movement, Brown, as a small farmer-frontiersman, was used to action, to deprivation, to repeated failures. *The Surveyor* deals with the Pottawatomie killings which made Brown famous (or infamous) after "Bleeding Kansas," and Nelson decides that Brown's occupation as a surveyor (a disguise often assumed while scouting Kansas and later near Harper's Ferry) led him directly to the strategy of the executions:

Brown was performing his action in the dead of night, on extremely rough terrain, in an area of widely scattered cabins. As surveyor, he did what was occupationally natural to him. He selected his victims from those residing on a survey line running directly north and south, which he could follow in the night by consulting his pocket compass. It was a tactic of great economy of action and he brought it off with complete success.

Similar insights into John Brown create the drama, despite the extreme complexity of the sociopolitical issues.

The Surveyor is a large, difficult novel, difficult because the issues exposed are of a bygone era and because Brown's character is a vast enigma, a freak of history as massive and puzzling as a stone head from Easter Island. But it is a dramatic work built like the earlier novels on repeated confrontations, frontier folk-speech, and political rhetoric. We follow Brown and his sons from the East and fundraising for abolitionist causes to the rugged Kansas frontier and the turbid complexities of grassroots political warfare. Nelson portrays Brown as a human being, an aging man tormented by family problems, failing health, repeated business collapses, and grinding poverty. He makes mistakes, misjudges men and events, and struggles to understand himself and his duty in the face of the monumental injustice of slavery. He is finally persuaded that violence and force are the only answers, the only vindication of the truth of human equality.

Nelson depicts Brown not as the deranged fanatic of some nineteenth-century historians nor as the Calvinist saint of abolitionist hagiography. His Brown is a revolutionary strategist driven to the wall, striking out with the enemy's weapons to crush the monster of slavery. His sons are as committed to the fight as he, but they disagree on the means and opportunities, looking finally to the Old Man for authority. In Kansas, he and his family organize a revolutionary cadre that breaks the civil war through the outrageous example of the Pottawatomie murders. This single brutal action forces in federal troops, who restore order and allow the weak Free State advocates to win by political means. But the desperate, repugnant deed is necessary to demonstrate that the Free Staters will take any measure to prevent the bogus government and border ruffians from winning.

Nelson's portrait is complex and rich, a more complete psychological analysis of the revolutionary leader than any conventional biography. The detailed characterization of Brown, his sons (each a study in motivation of second-generation radicals), factional leaders, and small farmers caught in the dispute makes *The Surveyor* extraordinarily dense. But the rightness of the dialogue and the consistency of the portrait of Brown make it a convincing fiction as well as a self-justifying historical study. The John Brown who emerges is a flawed man, a supremely difficult individual, but no longer the opaque enigma or study in pathology of traditional historians. The barebones simplicity of Brown's speeches ties him to the old Puritan line, a prairie Cromwell forging a New Model Army from starveling squatters and half-convinced radicals. Everyone around Brown has trouble grasping his marrow-deep conviction and his absolute, unswerving commitment to principles. His daughter-in-law despairs and tries to show him the seriousness of his fate, only to be rebuked by his conviction:

—They will bring cannon against you, the whole Army of the United States, and they will kill you.
—I am willing to die for the slave, said the Old Man simply. —But I can no longer brag about it. I have already delayed too long and have no room to boast of either my zeal or self-denial. (357)

The sense of Brown as a man larger than history, larger than the petty politicians and vain schemers around him, informs this novel with a Tolstoyan shape and spaciousness, a flow like the turbulent events it encompasses. *The Surveyor* is a noble pediment to the structure Truman Nelson crafted in his three novels of our prologue to the Civil War. These historical novels form a panorama that traces the rise of abolitionism as it was informed by transcendentalist thought and argument from the 1840s through the 1850s. *The Sin of the Prophet* thrusts us in medias res into a tragic action, the crisis of belief of Theodore Parker, and his struggle to move himself and his peers to the action necessary to confront and defeat active evil. *The Passion by the Brook* is a flashback, a long retrospective meditation on the root sources of the idealism that shaped abolitionism, especially the strong utopian-idealist strain that made it more than a reaction to the cruel fact of slavery. In *The Surveyor*, Nelson closes the arc of his motion, coming to the instant of direct action John Brown took in Pottawatomie, when he decided the executions were justified by the insanity of institutionalized slavery. The novels chart the dialectic between "soft" and "hard" transcendentalism, between the philosophical idealism of the Brook Farmers and the militant brutality of Brown and his impromptu troops.

Truman Nelson was born in Lynn, Massachusetts, February 18, 1911. His father, John Wilson Nelson, worked as a barber, and his mother, Ida Seymour Nelson, was a strong supportive force in Truman Nelson's life. Nelson dropped out of high school before graduation, went to work, and grew up with the hard times of the Great Depression.

As a factory worker for the General Electric Company in Lynn, Nelson became chief shop steward for his union. His involvement with the realities of the labor movement sharpened his Marxist principles with practical as well as theoretical knowledge. An abiding fascination with history and political analysis led Nelson to read exhaustively in the radical writers of early America: Thoreau, Emerson, William Lloyd Garrison, Theodore Parker, Lysander Spooner, John Brown. He used the Lynn and Boston libraries as his university, reading, thinking, and writing on his few days off work.

At age forty, Truman Nelson began to coalesce the wide variety of essential American ideas he had collected and examined. Encouraged by the brilliant scholar-analyst of American culture, F. O. Matthiessen, Nelson wrote his first novel, *The Sin of the Prophet*. When the book was published by the Boston firm of Little, Brown in 1952 and received wide and generous critical acclaim, Nelson left his factory work to write professionally.

After publishing three big novels, Nelson wrote extensively on America's broad and deep radical heritage as a background for contemporary change. He became involved in a notorious case of police brutality from which emerged a charged dramatic book that indicted the spirit and practice of racism in modern America, *The Torture of Mothers* (1965). He assembled the best writings from William Lloyd Garrison's influential abolitionist newspaper *The Liberator* in an anthology, *Documents of Upheaval* (1966). He prepared a handbook of dissent and radical action, *The Right of Revolution* (1968). In these major works, Nelson combined meticulous scholarship with astute analysis and personal commentary, applying the lessons of our past to current political realities.

He also brought the ideas, feelings, and events of nineteenth-century radicalism alive in essays on individual writers and thinkers from William Lloyd Garrison to W. E. B. Du Bois. These essays, which form a set of what Nelson called "variations" on his grand fictional themes, constitute the second part of this volume, complementing and completing the dense dramatic renderings of the novels. The essays, written as meditations over some twenty years, chart crosscurrents of ideas and actions which finally led to the destruction of the South's "peculiar institution" of slavery. They also connect the great battle of the radical transcendentalist-abolitionists with the equally intense struggle for civil rights in the 1950s and 1960s. Some short pieces were "occasional works" commemorating people, places, and events especially meaningful to Nelson, as a bone-bred Yankee with a powerful personal vision of truth and justice in America. In them, he vivifies his nineteenth-century heroes and connects them firmly with our own time.

Truman Nelson returned to John Brown's complex saga in *The Old Man* (1973), a narrative history of the Harper's Ferry raid, Brown's trial and execution, and the meaning of his sacrificial gesture to the bitterly divided nation. He continued to work on the great figures and issues of the period, including a monumental novel on the communitarian radical John Humphrey Noyes, the founder of the Oneida Colony. This epic traces the triumphant development of Noyes's venture in Perfectionist theology, eugenics, and community organization. Nelson's working title was *God in Love: The Sexual Revolution of John Humphrey Noyes*. In his mid-seventies, Nelson probed with his customary vitality and insight to the deepest taproots of our radical heritage and its shaping influence on the continuing American experiment.

This anthology includes an interview by Shaun McNiff, which catches Truman Nelson late in his career as he reviewed his early writing and planned the direction he hoped his career would take in the 1970s, after the turmoil of the civil rights movement and the New Left upheavals in which Nelson was a source of inspiration for many young radicals. The volume ends with a bibliography compiled by Garrison Nelson that brings together all his father's work for easy reference.

The continuum of writing Truman Nelson published over thirty-five years is a map of his personal concerns and convictions. It is also a bridge that links American radical consciousness over the past 150 years. It is at once wonderfully direct and individual, informed by a unique mind and voice, and universal, gathering our collective experience as a nation shaped by imperishable principles and beliefs. His writing emanates from a clear, steady vision of our culture, in its present and past diversity. It embraces the cosmos-wide inquiry of transcendentalism and the tough-minded pragmatic realism that is the obverse of dreamy speculation, the qualities that make (for example) Henry David Thoreau so paradoxical and so quintessentially American.

Nelson's summary of two seemingly incompatible hero-figures of the abolitionist-transcendentalist movement reflects his own qualities of heart and mind: "Revolutions are bloody awful, no one argues that, but things have to be twice that bloody awful to make them work. This was the way things were with John Brown and Henry Thoreau. Both were real men in a real world. You have to take them as that or leave them alone." "Real men in a real world"—the phrase captures most exactly the mission of retelling and reviving our past Truman Nelson has undertaken in all his writing.

Nelson died on July 11, 1987, in Newburyport, Massachusetts. He lived in that old port town the last twenty years of his life in a seventeenth-century house halfway down the hill from the row of proud homes built by the great shipowners, above the harbor where their sailing vessels docked. Nelson was instrumental in preserving the historic harbor area and its warehouses, threatened by the blind "forces of progress" which have leveled the centers of many United States cities. He delighted in the intrinsic life of old places and the weight of history they bequeath us, always conscious of the great New England thinkers and doers about whom he wrote so eloquently. To the last, even while suffering a long, debilitating illness, Nelson worked and wrote on behalf of people and beliefs needing defense.

His active, vibrant personality will be missed by all who knew him. His works remain a monument and a challenge, voicing his insistence on liberty, equality, and justice for *all* Americans. His own words, from another meditation on Theodore Parker, an essay called "The Conscience of the North," recall his personal credo best:

I have revealed to you without restraint my own conscience, formed and activated, I hope, by a long study of the lives and words of our great American prophets. It does not come from the great beyond, from mystic voices or visions, but from men like myself, only infinitely more gifted and courageous. If, reading their words and the brave promises of my country's founders, I ignore the contradictions between them and the ground rules of our national life, day by day, I would be committing a sin against my own senses, against the light that is in me. If I accepted these gross disparities between man and man all around me with complacency, I would be committing the greatest sin, that of hypocrisy, which blinds man to his own failures and gives him a false idea of his position and purpose in the world.

To the end, Truman Nelson carried his clear vision and his courage before him, leaving us a rich heritage of ideas distilled from the voices of history which were the most powerful music to him.

William J. Schafer
Berea College

I Fiction

The Themes

The Sin of the Prophet

Truman Nelson's first novel opens his chronicle of the abolitionist-transcendentalist saga in medias res, with the first major crisis of conscience in the movement—the Anthony Burns case of 1854. The narrative follows the band of Boston abolitionists—William Lloyd Garrison, Thomas Wentworth Higginson, Charles Ellis, and Theodore Parker, the great radical preacher/orator. Parker is the prophet of the title, and the sin is his failure to make the decisive leap from theory and rhetoric to direct action.

The novel, as Nelson has described all his work, is "thesis-driven": it focuses on the political and psychological dilemma in which Parker finds himself when he is confronted with a complex drama, the attempt to remove Anthony Burns from Boston to Virginia under the rule of the hated Fugitive Slave Law, an attempt Parker and his peers oppose. Nelson constructs a drama of terse, tense scenes that pile up voices and actions of the abolitionists and their enemies, political hirelings of President Franklin Pierce, who view Burns as a pawn in a game of appeasement for powerful slaveowners in Congress. The voices wind into a taut fugal pattern, a swirl of ideas, statements, and emotions echoing in and around the great Boston Music Hall that serves as Parker's church. The final scene of the novel, aptly called a coda, is a quiet conversation between Parker and Burns—the eloquent, impassioned minister-rhetorician and the former slave he has saved from a return to servitude. They stand before a tall statue of Beethoven, the archetypal composer of anthems for human liberation,

From *The Sin of the Prophet* (Boston: Little, Brown, 1952), © 1952 by Truman Nelson.

while an organist rehearses "the wild racing treble which comes near the end of Bach's Fugue in D Minor."

Music and musical motifs bind Nelson's novels, reminding us of the poetry and passion investing the often highly intellectual language of transcendentalism. We recall Emerson, Thoreau, Parker, Ripley, Hawthorne, and Brownson as dry, cerebral creatures pasted against an austere New England background. Nelson's fiction brings them alive with all feelings intact and intelligible. These characters are "realized," as musicians say of work lifted off the score and driven into the ear. One of the most memorable scenes from *Walden* is that of Henry David Thoreau drifting in his canoe across glassy Walden Pond, playing his flute to the moon and the night and himself, a little night music as eloquent as any persuasive passage from his writing. Nelson catches this musical soul of the movement in the structure and texture of his first novel and writes an oratorio as stately and monumental as any by Handel. Theodore Parker, thinking of Anthony Burns and his agony, sings to himself "Despised . . . rejected," the great aria from Handel's *Messiah*, which marks the turning point of Christ's passion. The desperate music, Parker knows, is a buoy for the spirit.

Thus the intellectual, social, and political content of the novel is interwoven with a sense of music and poetry and high human drama. Theodore Parker is driven by his feelings, his instinct for justice and compassion, to defy the law, as Thoreau was driven in 1846. When Parker addresses a crowd wound to defiance in Faneuil Hall, he waits (with the rest) for a signal, an impetus, that will lead the crowd to the Boston Courthouse to rescue Anthony Burns by force. The mission is confused, quasi-abortive, farcically misfired. Parker blames himself for his lack of decision, his inability to translate his passion and the crowd's desires into a simple, headlong act.

This is the sharpest horn of the dilemma upon which the abolitionists were impaled. Parker and his comrades had for over a decade exhorted, persuaded, and taught the necessities of liberation in speeches, pamphlets, newspapers, and sermons. A crisis of union was imminent, the time for talk and negotiation nearly over. Parker understood Garrison's motto, "resistance to tyranny is obedience to God," but the act of resistance must be more than internal, spiritual, and individual. Time had come to assert the unfinished American Revolution. As the crowd hangs fire, Parker recalls that his grandfather stood on Lexington Common and fired the "shot heard round the world." But there is no simple gunshot, no exclamation point to his speech. Parker cannot bring himself to use the brute violence of the slave-owners and politicos he opposes.

The Burns case drags on through tangled hearings and trials. But Parker learns. Anthony Burns is (ironically) *bought* out of slavery. He has not been rescued by the sheer moral force of righteousness. Parker confesses this to Burns in the end, as they stand in his music hall-church:

—This is my sin.... Besides the felony against our bodies the event did something bad to my spirit. I hated the tensions and disturbances created by the weak being driven to the wall. And I must confess thinking it a pity that people so ignorant and degraded should be the means of tearing this nation apart ... this because of my resentment at being forced from my chosen role as a scholar and philosopher and being unable to finish and publish my book. I thought you were all too speechless and submissive, forgetting that your story can only be told in outbreaks and revolutions ... forgetting that such times gave the brave men who wrote the Old Testament the terrible truths, judgments and revelations that others dared not tell.

The freedom in the events of 1854 is not the technical freedom granted one lost, confused slave but the understanding by Theodore Parker and his allies that they must move to action to defeat the active evil of slavery.

From *The Sin of the Prophet*

The Sin of the Prophet *is broken into two sections: "Book One: The Event" and "Book Two: The Judgment." Book One is divided into chapters called "waves"—indicating the rising storm tide against the general evil of slavery and the specific injustice of Anthony Burns's imprisonment and anticipated return to bondage. We enter the narrative in "The Fifth Wave," at a meeting in Faneuil Hall, the ancient "cradle of liberty." Theodore Parker is to speak, planning to incite the audience of radical abolitionists to free Burns by force.*

Higginson counted the steps from the Courthouse to Faneuil Hall, stabbing the ground with his umbrella as he walked. It was a good thing to know. Parker would ask him that when the new plan was put.

It was further than it looked, because the door faced toward the Harbor and away from Court Square. He cheated a little, his legs were longer than most, and as he neared the end of the trail pace he quickened his stride in his excitement and continued at a dogtrot up the stairs to the Hall, over the market stalls. He stepped inside. He knew he should stay there awhile and calmly weigh his plan all over again, but the place looked small as all public places do when there are no people there and it depressed him. Could this contain the plan, he wondered? The white walls were chaste and the broad-arched windows under the columnaded gallery had a cold, aristocratic look, as if they looked out on some duke's park or a squire's greensward. The room was cold and chilling. It was a sterile mausoleum, freshly and slickly enameled like an elegant chowderhouse at a fashionable resort. He drew back upon the landing, waiting for the fish he had to fry.

A great many people went in before Dr. Howe arrived. He listened carefully to the new plan.

—But we have a resolution to offer tonight which calls for a meeting in Courthouse Square tomorrow morning.

—Couldn't we drop it? pleaded Higginson. —Those resolutions were just tentative. We didn't know what we were going to do this afternoon. We had no real plan.

The doctor paused, doubtfully. He looked into the hall. Already the rostrum had been taken over by Father Lamson, a windy eccentric with a long beard and a dirty white robe. And Abby Folsom, the celebrated flea of conventions, was hopping up and down on the floor in front of him with her interminable bleat of—It's the capitalists, the capitalists . . .

—Well, said the doctor, —I don't think it would be wise to mention the attack tonight in the resolutions.

—No, no, Doctor. It's to be a complete surprise. Its strength lies in that, don't you see?

—We're probably the ones who will get the surprise, said the doctor.
—But if the others agree I'll join with it.

He hurried into the hall and up onto the stage. He wasted no time in ejecting the barefoot Father, who backed, still speaking, down to the floor where he was greeted with cheers and the doctor was soundly booed.

Captain Bearse was the next one up the steps and he loudly rejected the plan as the ravings of a madman. —At sea, at sea, he bellowed as he strode into the hall.

Then Higginson heard the deep bray of John Swift's baritone coming up. —Yes, yes, said Swift, without a moment's hesitation. —I'm sure it will work. The Courthouse is definitely going to be open tonight. We can be in one door and out the other before they can say Jack Robinson. Unless the jury up there comes in with a verdict . . . but it's a homicide case and they're still far apart on it.

—We'll plan the attack then, as soon as it's dark.

—As soon as it's dark, said Swift in calm confirmation, as if the night came at a clock-tick, like a curtain down over a window.

—And you'll stay by the door in case anything goes wrong? said Higginson.

—All right. Good luck, said Swift, feigning a calm and soldierly presence, although his heart was beating so wildly and his excitement ran so high that after he had stood awhile by the door he forgot the special reason he had to remain there and went up into the gallery where he could be heard better when calling out the signal.

Dr. Bowditch came in and said he'd go along with whatever Parker wanted. And now there were only two men left to sound out. Higginson devoutly wished that Phillips would come up the stairs first. He was sure he could handle him and that he wouldn't ask a lot of questions as Parker always did. The people were coming now in a stream. It was odd how you couldn't reckon on the public. The reaction of the committee hadn't counted on this great turning-out. Tom felt proud when the Worcester men came puffing up the stairs.

—Sway the crowd, he told them. Mill around, and when the alarm comes shout To the Courthouse, to the Courthouse! as loudly as you can and don't let anyone put you down.

—Looks like the old cradle is going to rock tonight, said one of them, as he stepped his dedicated way into the hall.

Parker came alone. Phillips was still over at the lawyers' building talking to Richard Dana. He had been walking for a spell down by the wharves. It was an open-and-shut day and the air was moist. His chest had hurt some and seemed tender to his breath. He thought it was from the dusty air in Tremont Temple all morning and afternoon. This happened a lot, this soreness, but he didn't think it was pulmonic because dampness was bad for that and made it worse. This trouble he had liked the dampness, and was soothed by it. Still, he had to lean heavily on the railing before he got to the top. He wished he had gone home for his supper and got the strength of hot food in him, but the sight of Tom standing there with that look on his face made him glad he hadn't and made his headache come back.

—Well, Tom, he said wearily.

—Martin Stowell, the man I told you about, suggested that we attack the Courthouse tonight.

—Impossible. We haven't got the forces.

—Look inside, said Tom. —It's jammed to the roof. We have two hundred men from Worcester alone.

Parker took a step to study the crowd. Tom caught him by the arm.

—There isn't time to count them, Mr. Parker. I've got to get back to Court Square right away. At the height of this meeting, we'll have the element of surprise in our favor.

—You've surprised me already, Tom.

—I know, sir. But I think we ought to forget all about this committee business for once. All we have proved this morning and this afternoon is that nobody among us can take an order and carry it out. I've placed myself under Martin Stowell and I'm going ahead with it.

—Going ahead with what?

—The attack. We've got a man at the meeting who's going to announce, as soon as it gets dark, that a mob of Negroes are attacking the Courthouse. Then everyone here will run to the Courthouse. It's simple, like all great plans. Howe likes it . . . I've just talked to him . . . and so does Bowditch.

—Run up to the Courthouse? From here? Parker slightly underlined *run* with a verbal edge. —That would be some chore for me right now.

—It's only four hundred and ninety strides, any able-bodied man can make it if you light enough of a fire under his heels.

—Who's going to light the fire . . . Phillips?

—We can't find him. You'll have to do it. It's very simple: You start your speech just as it starts to get dark. Then when it's pitch-black the signal will come. You put a strong motion to adjourn the meeting to the Courthouse. We'll do the rest.

Parker tried to assess the plan. It was almost too simple to weigh. Speech, interruption, motion . . . There was nothing there to quibble about.

—You see the others . . . he began somewhat lamely.

—Yes, yes, said Tom. —They know, and Phillips will be told. I'll see to that. What's the alternative? Tom went on. —Shall we postpone the meeting and go through the whole thing again? Shall we wait until the Courthouse is filled with troops, as it will be when they hear of the crowd this affair has drawn? Shall we send my men back to Worcester with nothing but a good dose of oratory under their belts? That isn't what they hired a train for. I know the committee decided on something quite different and you may think it wrong to depart from their decision, but there's no time to argue, I must have your answer.

—Don't push me Tom, said Parker, somewhat nettled. —I'm fully aware of the difference between strategy and tactics. The doubt arises from your oratory which is quite a strong dose in itself. As one preacher to another, I'd like it better if you convinced me in cold blood.

—Cold blood? How can I manage that at a time like this?

—This is the best time to manage it, I assure you.

Tom felt obliged to turn away from Parker. He took one or two deep breaths, fiddled with his collar and then turned with his hands outstretched, palms up, hoping Parker would not notice his trembling thumbs.

—As one preacher to another, he said slowly, —in terms of purest transcendentalism, and repeating the lesson I learned at your knee, I will leave the matter up to your conscience. You say it is infallible and will always decide rightly if the case is fairly put before it. . . . Will you make the speech? Will you send the mob?

In the pause that followed, the sound in silence, Tom knew that Parker was hoist with his own petard and heard the yes, yes before it was spoken.

The committee had sought for a man not regarded as a hothead or a partisan to chair the meeting. Thomas Russell, a former mayor of Roxbury and a judge in the Police Court, filled the bill nicely. He opened the affair with proper dignity directly after Parker took his seat beside Robert Morris on the platform. On Parker's right sat a member of the Governor's Council, Albert Browne of Salem. Phillips's seat was still empty after Russell had got beyond his opening remarks.

—Once I thought a fugitive could never be taken from Boston. I was mistaken. The slave catcher boasts he will take his man in the shadow of Bunker Hill. We have made compromises until we find that compromise is concession and concession is degradation. When we get Cuba and Mexico as slave states and the . . . foreign slave trade is re-established . . .

Here Phillips slipped quietly into his chair. He looked over at Parker and nodded affirmatively as Parker rolled his eyes at the huge crowd. The great clock, given by the schoolchildren of Boston, now held Parker's gaze until the long black hands seemed to stick in one spot and he looked away. He felt like a schoolboy, unprepared and anxious about his lesson, hoping he would be called on last or not at all. He saw in the crowd many members of his own congregation. Would they make a mob? A mob to him had been a gang of iron-brained bigots taking vengeance into cruel drunken hands. But mobs usually met and stewed in secret and the door to the hall was open and people were passing in and out unmolested. Is a mob a free-will offering? Is it the people voting with their hands and feet? He swapped seats with Robert Morris to have a word with Phillips. He meant to ask him about the attack, but first he spoke of Dana.

—Judge Sprague refused him a writ of replevin, whispered Phillips.

—Naturally. They've got no one to serve it anyway. Was he downhearted?

—A little. He says he should have got it *valeat quantum*.

—Oh, hocus-pocus, said Parker indignantly. —Does he mean to try the case in Latin? I'm glad Charles Ellis is working with him. Has he agreed to that?

—Finally. But not until he had asked Rufus Choate.

—He must be out of his head, sputtered Parker. —Choate is an advocate of rogues and scoundrels. With him on the case, the spectacle would be about as uplifting as a bullfight.

—*Sh*, said Phillips. —Dana only admires him for his great talent.

—I don't care if he's a genius. His whole life has been treason to justice. He called the Constitution a set of glittering generalities.

Robert Morris poked him to keep silent and he switched to his own seat.

When Russell concluded his long speech, there was no mob. Mr. Bird of Walpole had begged for a chance to say a few words. He wanted to say a few words about the way the newspapers of Boston were handling the case. Mr. Bird was as waspish in his way as the newspapers had been on the other side of the case, and it was agreed that the point he had to make was worth while.

—I'm really glad, really awfully glad to see so many of you here tonight. Glad because I know that at least you people will hear the truth and not have to depend upon those servile tools of the slave power. I am referring, of course, to those great organs of pusillanimity and hypocrisy, the newspapers of Boston.

—I want you to know that they refused to print a denial of a report that the slave wanted to go back because his master was so kind. They were willing to lie for nothing but must be prevailed upon to tell the truth by being paid for it.

Mr. Bird wiped the sweat off his brow. He had a querulous, intimate, high-pitched voice and spoke rapidly without pause. It was a relief to hear him run on after the rolling stops and pauses of Chairman Russell. Mr. Bird could go on all night if he wanted to, without glancing away once from his listener.

—There are many mean men in Boston and I had the pleasure of telling one of them that he was a mean, sneaking dog. It was one of the editors of the *Traveler*.

—I hope you people believe me when I tell you that the man held at the Courthouse told Wendell Phillips that to say he wanted to go back was an unmitigated lie. I drew up his statement in the form of a certificate and carried it to the office of the *Traveler*. I asked if there was time to get it in.

Mr. Bird stopped here and gave a dry bitter laugh.

—I thought, of course, that it was news, and that time was the only question to be raised.

—I was then told, to my great amazement, that there was time to get it in but that it must be paid for at the rate of one dollar and fifty cents. Well, after I had paid the clerk for it, one of the editors came in and I told him it was a mean, sneaking concern. So just be sure you pay little or no attention to what appears in the papers about this affair. Remember they are all run by doughfaces, wearing the print of their master's knuckles and the traces of their spittle on their faces.

Soap and water don't wash it off, nor your hot tears either. They have worked hard for infamy and they have got it.

He waved his hand to the crowd, shook hands with Parker and Phillips, and started to push through the crowd to the doorway. He was wanted at home and he couldn't stay any longer, but it had felt good to get that much off his chest. He got many a slap on the back on his way out.

Dr. Howe came forward now to read the resolutions. He did not drone them out as many do but lined them out as if he were saying, Take them or be damned.

The time has come to demonstrate that no slaveholder can carry his prey from Massachusetts.

That which is not just is not the law, and that which is not the law should not be obeyed.

It is the will of God that all men be free. We will as God wills. God's will be done.

No man's freedom is safe unless all men are free.

The response was good. They were loudly cheering each resolution with rising fervor. The galleries, the window sills and even the anterooms were congeries of men and women, dressed as though for church.

A lamplighter was going about the hall, touching the gas jets with his torch. One flowered into flame directly beneath the place where John Swift was sitting in the gallery. He looked down into it until his eyes saw suns. He turned to one side to blink them out and when he opened his eyes, the windows looked black with the coming dusk outside.

The last resolution Howe read was *Resistance to tyrants is obedience to God*, and it made the hall rock.

John Swift looked into the gaslight again and then struggled to his feet.

—Burns is in the Courthouse, he cried. —Is there any law to keep him there? If we allow Marshal Freeman to carry away that man, then COWARDS should be stamped on our foreheads!

There were no seats on the floor, the people were standing and it was easy for them to face around and look up at him. He choked up with stage fright and grasped at the railing for support.

—When we go from this cradle of liberty, let us go to the tomb of liberty. Tomorrow Burns will have been there three days and I hope tomorrow to see in his release the resurrection of liberty.

He couldn't stop talking. The people kept looking up for him to say more and the thing wasn't working out the way it had been explained to him. He didn't know how to finish off and get the attention of the people back to the platform.

—The resurrection of liberty, he repeated, then said falteringly: — This is a contest between slavery and liberty . . . and I am now and forever on the side of liberty.

He sat down. The people kept looking up for a moment or two, enjoying the side show, applauded and turned stolidly back to watch the stage.

Parker was listening with amazement. Was this the signal? Was this the man, was this the voice? But what did he mean about tomorrow? Was the plan changed? He looked at Howe. Howe shrugged his shoulders to show his confusion. He looked at Phillips, who was rising to speak. Phillips stepped unemotionally to the rostrum.

The dusk was creeping through the square now and Higginson thought it safe to saunter casually to the door near the Marshal's office, the one they were going to use for the assault. He gave a start as a man lurking in a nearby doorway stepped out at him.

—Is that you, Martin? he said.

—Yes, Mr. Higginson, said Stowell.

—Where are the others? They should be here by now.

—I don't know. I rounded up about fifteen and they promised to be along about dark but they haven't come.

—Perhaps they're over at the meeting . . .

—The door is open, said Stowell, bending his head in its direction; —we won't need to use the timber. I've got it hidden in the excavation over there.

Higginson fell into an uneasy silence. He remembered a fire that had burned a house in Cambridge and how he had envied some Southern students who were the focus of great applause for bringing an old man out of the building while he and another boy had risked their lives much more to bring some preserves up from the crumbling basement.

—Perhaps we ought to go over to the hall, he said. —The more of us there, the more support there'll be for our plan. We'll have to do some tall 'lectioneering from the floor to get these cold roast Bostonians on the run.

—Let's wait until it gets a little darker, Stowell said; —I'd like to sneak across the street and put a wedge in that doorjamb, just in case.

—Fine crowd we have, Higginson said in a discouraged voice. —When the boys come to town they just can't keep away from the bright lights and the pretty girls.

Stowell laid a cautioning hand on his arm as four men came toward them, up the street. They stopped. They were Negroes.

—This is all I could get, Mr. Higginson, said Lewis Hayden. —And they're all my cousins at that.

—Good, good, said Higginson. —We've got no one.

—There's two white men up the corner said they'd help out a little, said Lewis. —I'll try to keep out of the way so's not to get you folks in trouble.

—Oh don't mind that. Mr. Parker was just trying to relieve you from responsibility. We were just about to go down to Faneuil Hall. We're going to put a wedge in that door over there.

Stowell held his hand up in front of him. The darkness lay like a deep stain in his palm. He reached into his pocket for the wedge. It was a briar pipe, a huge one, an inch and a half in diameter, the heavy curving sort small men often smoke. He fondled it in his hand, ready to make a dash and thrust it under the hinge.

But then the slow *clop-clop* of the lamplighter's wagon came into the square, and he reached from his platform to touch into incandescence the tip of the iron post not twenty feet from where they stood and not five feet away from the open door.

—It's too late, it's too light, said Martin Stowell.

—It's too late, it's too dark, said Higginson, thinking of the order of business now coming up at Faneuil Hall.

Phillips stood with such imperturbability that Parker felt sure he had been mistaken about the signal. —We have, said Phillips, —up to now, had all the press, the pulpits, the prejudices and political arrangements of the country against us. But as of today, I am happy to report the city government is on our side.

He held his hand up to lull the applause. —We haven't much time. Tomorrow is to determine whether we are ready to do the duty they have left us to do.

The crowd applauded. Parker wondered at this last, but thought perhaps Wendell was covering up the new plan, to insure spontaneity.

—There is now no law in Massachusetts, and when law ceases, the people may act in their own sovereignty. I am against squatter sovereignty in Nebraska and against kidnaper's sovereignty in Boston. See to it in the streets of Boston you ratify the verdict of Faneuil Hall that Anthony Burns has no master but his God.

—You may think that this is a bloody doctrine, but we have every weapon that ability and ignorance, wit, wealth and fashion can command thrust against us. We speak for over three million oppressed Americans who have no voice but ours to utter their complaints and demand their justice. We have no weapon but truth. That, and the honor of Boston. A Boston which might become soon a creature of the South, an anteroom to that great brothel where half a million women are flogged into prostitution; where the public squares of half the cities echo to the wail of families torn asunder at the auction block. All of our rivers have closed over Negroes seeking in death a refuge from a life too wretched to bear. Men skulk along our highways and though guiltless are afraid to tell their names, and tremble at the sign of another human being. Within two years two such men have been captured in Boston, Pathway to Hell.

He paused amidst the cries of—Shame! and the cheers, as the warp and woof of the crowd pulled tight. They were not quiet but rustling as the page they had lived by, up to now, turned over and a new set of rules lay on the opposite: that good citizenship was a snare and a delusion, bad citizenship was honor and a compulsion. That right was wrong and wrong was right.

—See to it, Phillips said, half-turning away from them as if he were giving afterthoughts, —see to it, as you love the honor of Boston, that you watch this case so closely that you can look into that man's eyes. When he comes up for trial, get a sight of him and don't lose sight of him. There is nothing like the mute eloquence of a suffering man to urge to duty. Be there and I will trust the result. If Boston streets are to be so often desecrated by the sight of returning fugitives, let us be there that we can tell our children that we saw it done. There is now no use for Faneuil Hall. Faneuil Hall is the purlieu of the Courthouse, tomorrow, where the children of Adams and Hancock may prove that they are not bastards.

The crowd was roaring now and Parker felt as if he were in the hub of a great wheel. Phillips's speech had been hot and bitter; but then, they always were. He had heard him say as much, even more, to a meeting of the Cordwainer's Union in Lynn with an attendance of eighteen, at a rally to get subscriptions for the *Liberator* so Garrison's youngest boy could get a new pair of shoes. But this was a big crowd and it was whirling, and he had to guide it into time and space. He had to roll it to the Courthouse, or to the Revere House after Suttle, or perhaps to T Wharf where the steamer lay. He had to wait for a signal that he didn't really understand, from a man he didn't know. He had to wait for a signal that might have already sounded. He was not sure whether he had to hold them back or set them rolling. The crowd was calling for him now. They weren't to be cheated of hearing Parker, signal or not. Nor would they have left before Phillips had ended. Eloquence was dog-cheap at these affairs, but Yankees never shied at a bargain.

—Fellow citizens of Virginia! . . . Parker's greeting was answered with a roar. It was loud and friendly with a laugh deep in it. He pointed his arm at them like a farmer prodding a bull with a pitchfork to test his mettle. He bent his head to hide a smirk and the lamplight bounced off his baldness and ran around his steel-rimmed specs. He gripped with his heavy farmer's hands the edges of the desk, as if they were plow handles, and braced his feet wide in the furrows and arched his back as if there were reins around it. He looked out at them with Yankee cussedness, as if saying, I'm going to whip you out of the hall but hold your hosses boys until I get the plowtooth deep in the ground.

—Fellow citizens of Boston, then . . . The roar started again but he stopped it with a brusque, impatient chop of his whip hand.

—I come to condole with you at this second disgrace heaped on our city. A deed that Virginia commands has just been done in the city of John Hancock and a brace of Adamses. It was done by a Boston hand. It was a Boston man who issued the warrant; it was a Boston marshal who put it into execution. They are Boston men who are seeking to kidnap a citizen of Massachusetts and send him into slavery forever and ever. It is our fault that this is so. Yes, we are the vassals of Virginia. It reaches its arms over the graves of our mothers, and it kidnaps men in the city of the Puritans, over the graves of Samuel Adams and John Hancock.

There were cries of—Shame, shame!

—Shame! So I say, but who is to blame? There is no North, said Mr. Webster. There is none. Mr. Webster stamped his foot and broke through into the great hollow of practical atheism which undergulfs the state and church. Then what a caving-in was there! The firm-set base of Northern cities quaked and yawned with gaping rents. Slack men fled, as doves with plaintive cry flee from a farmer's barn when summer lightning stabs the roof. There was a twist in Faneuil Hall and the door could not open wide enough for liberty to regain her ancient cradle. Only soldiers, greedy to steal a man, themselves stole out and in. Legal quicksand ran down the hole amain. Churches toppled and pitched and canted and cracked, their bowing walls all out of plumb. Colleges, broken from the chain that held them in the stream of time, rushed through the abysmal rent. Harvard led the way, *Christo et ecclesiae* in her hand. There is no Higher Law of God, no Golden Rule, quoth they, only the statutes of men. And a prominent merchant of Boston said to his fellows that if any men would assassinate Mr. Phillips and myself, it should be declared justifiable homicide.

The crowd laughed and he laughed with them. It was one of his favorite quotations. But then he stood rigid again. Time was ticking by. The brightness was falling from the outside air and he had to make them ready for the signal.

—Yes, the South goes clear up to Canada. There is no Boston today. But there is a Northern suburb of Alexandria; that is where Boston is, and you and I are fellow subjects of the State of Virginia.

Now some of them were getting riled, and there were many shouts of—No! No! Nay! Some of the Worcester men were taking too seriously the affront to Boston. He pointed toward the *Nay*-ers, looking insolently at them. One tall farmer looked him right back in the eye.

—Take that back, the farmer said.

Parker held his gaze until the man got red in the face.

—I will take it back when you show me the fact is not so.

The outraged farmer looked as though he were going to climb onto the platform and take a swipe at Parker. But his friends began to talk to him and a little knot of men began to isolate themselves from the rest. Parker hoped devoutly that the signal would come from them. He gave the rest of the crowd another flick of his lash.

—Men and brothers, he said, then paused insultingly. —Well, brothers at any rate. I have heard hurrahs and cheers for liberty many times. I have not seen a great many deeds done for liberty. I ask you: Are we to have deeds as well as words?

There were more cheers and cries of affirmation, but nothing about going to the Courthouse. He waited until the silence became embarrassing. Then he had to start building again.

—Now, brethren, you are brothers at any rate, whether citizens of Massachusetts or subjects of Virginia. I am a minister. Fellow citizens of Boston, there are two great laws in this country. One of them is the law of slavery. That law is declared to be a finality. Once the Constitution was formed to establish justice, promote tranquillity and secure the blessings of liberty to ourselves and our posterity. Now, the Constitution is not to secure liberty. It is to extend slavery into Nebraska, and when slavery is established there, in order to show that it is, there comes a sheriff from Alexandria to kidnap a man in the streets of Boston, and he gets a judge of Boston to issue a writ, and a Boston man to execute that writ.

There were more cries of—Shame, shame! But still they stood there looking up at him. He strained his eyes, shading the light above with his hand, to see if there was anyone at the back of the hall trying to attract his attention. How long must he be impaled on this shaft of doubt? He looked back at Phillips and Howe. They were tranquil. Not by the turning of a hair did they help him solve his terrible irresolution.... He must talk, he thought. There's been a delay; the plot discovered.... Something must be stuck.... He was now so nervous, he could not stand at the desk but had to walk up and down.

—Slavery tramples on the Constitution. It treads down states' rights. Where are the rights of Massachusetts? A Fugitive Slave Commissioner has got them all in his pocket. Where is the trial by jury? Watson Freeman has it under his marshal's staff. Where is the great right of personal replevin which our fathers wrested several hundred years ago over in Great Britain? Judge Sprague trod it under his feet. Where is the sacred right of habeas corpus? Deputy Marshal Riley can crush it in his hand, and Boston does not say anything against it. Where are the laws of Massachusetts forbidding state edifices to be used as prisons for the incarceration of fugitives? They too are trampled underfoot!

He paused again. . . . You fools, you fools, where is the signal? . . . He was tired. He didn't want to talk any more. He was repeating himself. He was whirling and whirling around, still like a hub, but the wheel was off the ground. He began again. Outside he could see the last light fading from the sky.

—These men came from Virginia to kidnap a man here. Once this was Boston. Now it is a suburb of Alexandria. At first, when they carried a man off from Boston, they thought it was a difficult thing to do. They had to get a mayor to help them. They had to put chains around the Courthouse. It took them nine days to do it. Now, they are so confident that we are citizens of Virginia that the police have nothing to do with it. I was told today that if any man in the employment of the city meddles in this affair he will be discharged without a hearing . . .

To the watchers in the square the open door was like a live thing. It moved slightly from time to time in the wind with agonizing deliberateness, sometimes as if someone were closing it and then again shifting further ajar, beckoning, inviting. The moment for the onrush of the mob was past due, and the tension becoming unbearable.

—I'm going to fix that door, said Stowell grimly, taking his pipe out of his mouth and knocking out the ashes, —light or no light.

—We'll all go, said Higginson nervously. —There's no one in sight and one of us might be able to get inside and hide.

—I don't think . . . Stowell began to object.

—There's no one around, Martin, said Higginson. —They're all at the meeting, the attackers, the defenders, everybody but Anthony Burns and us is at Faneuil Hall tonight.

Stowell shrugged and the six men began to cross the brightly lighted street. Lewis Hayden stopped short in alarm as they got half over. He had seen a figure at the other end step out from the shadows behind the City Hall. —It's Officer Tarleton of the City Watch, he said. —If he sees me, our goose is cooked.

One of his cousins ran quickly to the lamppost, shinnied it and broke the glass with his fist. In the plunge of darkness Officer Tarleton turned his back on them and shook his watchman's rattle for help. Ike Creen, one of the Courthouse deputies, who had been watching their approach from a basement window, ran upstairs. Just as they got to the steps, he shut the door in their faces. They heard the bolt slam into place.

—The beam, the beam! shouted Higginson. —We've got to get the beam!

The man on the platform turned his head anxiously right and left, pointing his ears toward the applause, not drinking it but rejecting it, hoping to hear in its dismaying dissonance the clear tonic phrase of the signal. His tired scholar's eyes, now beginning to burn in the unaccustomed glare from the battery of lamps overhead, tried to pierce to the back of the hall and up to the gallery. He could hear scattered bursts of response to his thrusting challenges, but it was only crowd comment, as set and static as the Amens at prayer meeting.

—I say there are two great laws in this country. One is the slave law; that is the law of the President of the United States, it is the law of the Marshal and of every meanest ruffian whom the Marshal hires. There is another law, which Mr. Phillips has described in language such as I cannot equal and therefore shall not try. I can only state it in plainest terms. It is the law of the people, when they are sure they are right and determined to go ahead.

The applause was louder, firmer and the crowd began to press toward the stage. Groups swept into the corner, flanking him. There was no passage, no way at all to get through to the door. He felt like saying, Press not so upon me. He decided to end this miserable speech, the worst he had ever made, with its repetition and scraps from older, better ones, and the rough improvisations used to bring the pot to boil too soon; a speech that revealed, to all who knew him, an unhappy division in his mind and a basic reluctance somewhere behind it.

—Now, gentlemen, I say there is one law, slave law. It is everywhere. There is also another law, which is also a finality, and that law is in your hands and your arms, and you can put it in execution just when you see fit. Gentlemen, I am a clergyman and a man of peace. But there is a means, and there is an end. Liberty is the end, and sometimes peace is not the means toward it. Now I ask, What are you going to do?

—Shoot, shoot! someone yelled, louder than all the cheering. There was a quick moment of cold silence, a shocked intake of breath. Then a wild roar began. The man who had cried out for blood was set upon by some earnest Nonresistants, and the whole meeting began to curdle, swirling little rings formed where there had been rows and in the midst of each of them was a Worcester man crying, —Shoot!

This wild digression from the platform came as a relief to Parker. He wanted to think a bit. He had suddenly and almost unescapably come upon a moment he had spent his life preparing for. His grandfather had cried *Shoot* on Lexington Green and put his country in a position that could only be resolved by a bloody revolution. Had he maneuvered Boston into the same position over slavery? Should he take up the cry and say, Yes, shoot, shoot! Take your guns to the Courthouse and shoot down Watson Freeman and the pimps and drunks and thieves and bawdyhouse keepers befouling the seat of Boston justice? . . . Could he?

—No, no, he shouted at the crowd, his voice overpowering them. —There are ways of managing this matter without shooting anybody. Be sure the men who have kidnaped a man in Boston are cowards, every mother's son of them, and if we stand up there resolutely and declare that this man will not go out of Boston . . . then he won't go back, and without shooting a gun.

There was a roar of applause at this, the Worcester men were gasping, silent, waiting for their second wind.

—Now I am going to propose that when we adjourn it be to meet in Court Square tomorrow. As many as are in favor of the motion will raise their hands.

—Tonight, tonight! shouted the Worcester men, and they pressed forward angrily, trying to pull down the upraised hands. Some booed. Some were for going to the Revere House for Colonel Suttle. Parker was appalled at the faces wrestling towards him, glistening with sweat and urging their bloody course, waving their guns and cursing.

Parker clung to the desk for support. The noise was pointed at him, falling on him like fist blows. The windows now were unfriendly, not opening out like eyes but sending back splintery reflections of the hard lights and the turmoil below him. He stepped back and looked around for the rear door. Then he realized, with a sickening certainty, that there was none. The only door was up there, at the back, and there were wild beasts between him and the only opening. He became afraid. They were all in a trap. Marshal Freeman could send six men to block the door and hold them here all night. It was not like his Music Hall, where this trapped, writhing centipede could have spread its legs in any direction out of forty-two doors.

—To the Courthouse! To the Revere House! . . . Tomorrow, tomorrow! came the cries, equal in force.

He knew he had failed. That night Faneuil Hall had been a cannon packed tight with human grapeshot and wadding and he was to be the powder in the breech. But the man with the slow-match had held his hand too long, and the shot would scatter and spend itself long before it reached the Courthouse. And now it was no longer a weapon pointed at wrong, but an untidy closet, and he was an old pair of shoes at the bottom, smothered with rag-tag clothes and cast-off fripperies.

He stood helplessly watching members of the Vigilance Committee, panic-stricken by the suddenness of the squall from the west, butting and buzzing through the crowd, tugging at the lapels of their partisans, trying to trim ship and get back on the charted course.

—Tomorrow, they hissed, —the plan is tomorrow.

The Worcester men pressed on, shouting—Tonight, tonight! until he began to cough half-strangled. He clenched his fists and raised them in choked appeal. If there had been a passage through them, he would have gone then to the Courthouse and smashed the door with his hands. Instead he stood, half-dazed, coughing into his handkerchief, while the agitators leaped and bayed at him, contending like dogs for withheld meat, demanding his approval of their plan.

Wendell Phillips could stand it no longer. He knew Parker was sick. He knew the racking cough was shredding away lungs cursed, in spite of Parker's denials, with the family consumption which New England had planted in the blood of its pioneers. He put his arm around Parker and told him to sit down. Parker leaned against the warmness, a tired swimmer sinking in sight of land after a long pull. He took his chair.

Phillips was severe with the crowd. His grimness quieted them before he spoke.

—Let us remember where we are and what we propose to do. You have said tonight that you will vindicate the fair name of Boston. Let me tell you you won't do it by groaning at the slave catchers at the Revere House, by attempting the impossible task of insulting them.

—What about the Courthouse? someone yelled.

—If there is a man here who has an arm and a heart ready to sacrifice anything for the freedom of a man, let him do it tomorrow. If I thought it could be done tonight, I would go first. I don't profess courage but I do profess this: when there is a clear possibility of saving a slave from those who are called officers of the law, I am ready to trample any statute or any man under my feet to do it. I am ready to help any hundred, any fifty, or twenty-five. But wait until daytime . . .

—We'll leave the lights on, Wendell dear, came a raucous voice.

Phillips ignored him.

—The vaults of State Street are with us for the first time, fellow citizens. We can muster enough people tomorrow to block the street from the Courthouse to the Harbor. You should believe it when a radical like myself affirms it.

This drew more abuse. —You sound like you had State Street in your pocket, Phillips.

In the laughter came another taunt. —What's your definition of a radical, Wendell, a member of the Merchants' Exchange?

—Ask your own party that question, said Phillips, savagely reverting to his Garrisonian principles. —The best men in the city, and I count that man best who treads the Constitution and the Union under his foot, say this man will not leave the city of Boston.

At this heresy, the men from Worcester, mostly voting Abolitionists, Free-soil Democrats and Conscience Whigs, broke out with thunderous boos. Parker, who had welcomed Phillips's interference as a diversion, a time-gainer, realized that he was now opening up a fatal gulf between the floor and the platform. He dimly felt an obligation to rise and take issue with or mitigate the hardness and finality of this position but his will failed and he slumped weakly back in his chair. . . . How could he stop him now in the face of this abuse, ask him to change his tune or quietly take his seat under this onslaught of challenge? Challenge and opposition was Wendell's bread and meat, his whip, his spur.

Parker put his hands over his face as Wendell, magnificent war horse that he was, hardened his mouth against the bit, threw back his high mane, pitched the mellow, flexible voice into a high piercing scream:
—Do not block their efforts by showing ourselves an utterly useless, harmful, tumultuous, aimless, purposeless mob before the pillars of the Courthouse. It will serve no end but to put our enemies on their guard; only to give the garrison notice, only to rob ourselves of the sympathy of the city. You that are ready to do real work, to sacrifice something for the man, must not be carried away by a momentary impulse to a fatal indiscretion. If your enthusiasm is so transient it will be spent by tomorrow morning, put on your hats and go home!

He paused, and in a silence as sepulchral, thick and listless as the dead air of a tomb, a voice came breathlessly from the back of the hall.

—Mr. Chairman, I am just informed that a mob of Negroes is in Court Square, attempting to rescue Burns. I move we adjourn to there.

Louis Varelli's boys, now deputies of the United States Government, were lounging at the upper windows of the front end of the Courthouse. They heard the music of a military band, coming up from the Charles. It was playing "Wood End," the favorite march of the Boston Voluntary Artillery, as it marched up from maneuvers on the riverbank. They went downstairs to hear it on the front steps, and caught sight of the mob from Faneuil Hall swinging into State Street. It took them only a second or two to retreat into the building and shut the big doors with a clang and hook the chains across.

Higginson and the four Negroes were struggling with the timber as the mob came into the square. He directed his toward the door. Martin Stowell was waiting anxiously for the Worcester men to form behind him.

Marshal Freeman's office was near the door, and he ran out into the corridor calling for help. The door began to creak and bend at the blows, and the Marshal screamed in panic. His small son was with him and he sent the boy for Pat Riley who was playing cards in Tony's room. Riley got sabers up from the basement and passed them out to the guards.

Stowell was trying desperately to channel the mob into formation, but the froth and scum of the meeting had got there first, and all they wanted to do was pick up rocks and smash the Courthouse windows.

Inside, the panic grew. Augerhole came running downstairs with his round knife in his hand. He went to the door, but when he saw the splinters springing like veins from the dark oak he stepped back. The Marshal waved his arms wildly at the door, calling his men. Three of the hardiest—Ben True, Ike Creen and James Batchelder—put their shoulders against it, but the bolt-straps gave way.

Finally it opened and two Negroes and Higginson plopped inside. The truckmen deputies, unaccustomed to swords, began flailing them over their heads without taking the blades out of the scabbards. The Marshal got his free and struck Higginson on the chin. Someone turned the lights up inside and suddenly the stairs were full of men reaching for their pistols. The two Negroes backed out and Higginson, pausing a moment to look at the blood on his hands, was cut off from retreat. Stowell rushed up the steps and fired point-blank from his pistol into the hallway.

Isaac Green felt Batchelder fall against him and then he saw him try to work himself out of the crowd in a curious sidestep like a slow crab. Batchelder was holding his belly in his arms and mumbling and the others parted to let him through. —Right in the guts, someone said. — The shot ripped the bowels out of him.

Marshal Freeman saw him sag and crumple at last and took him under the arms and dragged him into the office. The guards came hesitantly to the door. Higginson, finding himself clear and not understanding the reason for the rush and the terror, stepped angrily to the open door to wave on his rabble army.

One of the deputies, in a strange gesture of decorum, pushed him out on the steps like an unwelcome guest.

—You cowards, Higginson cried to the mob, —Will you desert us now!

But as the movement started to the door, the city police, spurred by the hard thud of the iron tongue in the Courthouse bell, and breathless from running down the stairs from the Mayor's office, began arresting those in front. Martin Stowell managed to hide the pistol in his underwear before they carried him off, and the rest of the men taken in were unarmed Negroes—except for a Harvard student, caught while raising his arm to throw a stone. His name was Albert G. Browne, Junior. His father had sat on the platform at Faneuil Hall that evening.

Inside, the Marshal's guard wall got a good look at Batchelder, now bleeding and dead, and Freeman told them to take up positions on the stairs and draw their cutlasses and cock their pistols.

The guard now was bloodthirsty. They wanted revenge. They were mercenaries no longer for the moment, and they shouted for someone to open the door and let the rioters in, knowing that they could shoot them down like fish in a barrel and even up the score many fold.

Freeman thrust a man away from the door and slammed it shut. The Supreme Court justices and the officials of the court were scuttling down the stairs from the second floor. Freeman, now at the height of his uneasy role as an unwelcome tenant in the house of justice, rushed forward to guide them out as politely as he could, smothering them with apologies.

Colonel Suttle, at that point, was running unsteadily out through the unguarded and unmolested west door, without a thought for poor James Batchelder.

When the Marshal was out of sight down the corridor, one of the guards ran to the door again and swung it open, making it the wrong end of a shooting gallery.

Seth Webb, a young lawyer, darted from the street up the steps and was about to go in. Higginson pulled him back, sensing the ominous quality of the silence within.

Those in the crowd who were shouting and throwing rocks were being arrested. The Negro who had smashed the gas lamp was recognized and borne off to the Watchhouse.

Then, from the dark clump of angry people, came a tall man with a cane. He walked up the steps with deliberation, and thrust the door open to its widest arc.

He turned to the crowd and said, —Why are we not within?

One of the bullies on the stairs fired at him. But the volley did not come, as the man swung back to look at them. In the vortex of that moment his tranquillity was frightening, his long hair shimmered in the back light and he looked like a small boy's idea of God. It was Amos Bronson Alcott. After he found no response behind him or ahead of him, he turned and walked slowly down the stairs and sadly to the silent fringe of the crowd, and then to his home, counting this night a failure.

Dr. Bowditch had seen him start for the stairs and wanted to join him, but he felt the futility of the occasion. The people near him stood idly, truly like spectators. Swift, who had waited for him at the bottom of the stairs of Faneuil Hall and who had made the lung-bursting run to the Courthouse with him, was nowhere to be seen. Bowditch felt the urge to throw himself into the maw, but the sheer nonsense of the affair had brought him to a state of mingled horror and shame. Higginson was standing silently and awkwardly on the stairs by the door. Seth Webb had disappeared. And after Alcott's gesture, sacrifice seemed unbearably self-conscious and vainglorious. Bowditch turned and walked from the scene, burning with shame and hating himself.

For some reason, whether for fear of irritating the crowd or simply because they had their hands full with window breakers, a more expensive item than mere revolution, the police were ignoring Higginson. He stood there, bleeding from the chin and pressed to the granite wall, like a man trapped on a precipice with a crowd gathered far below him waiting for him to fall and splash.

Back in Faneuil Hall, the crowd sweeping down the stairs from the gallery had forced back the people from the main floor and they were caught in a crush inside the doorway. Parker and Phillips were tugging and shoving futilely against the irate citizens at the thick end of the wedge. They tried to insert themselves into small eddies and currents of outward motion a dozen times, but ended up at last blocked and hampered by the listless, sauntering rear guard. People that knew Parker stopped him and asked him what to do.—Go to the Courthouse, he repeated, brushing off their attempts to get a fuller explanation. Howe lingered behind with him, giving him many an anxious glance.

—Go on, get up there, Chevalier! he said. —Don't look at me as if you were taking my pulse; I'll get there. See if you can stop Higginson; this is crazy.

But Higginson was already stopped. The band and the Militia had reached the square, and were greeted with loud jeers by the crowd, who left the Courthouse and clustered around the Artillery with the fickleness of anger.

Higginson broke away from the wall and walked unsteadily up the alleyway beside the City Hall and then to Tremont Street. Behind him he could hear the pad of feet coming closer and closer. It was a chase and he was not equal to it. He was able to summon enough guts a minute later to turn abruptly and face his pursuer.

It was a kindly little man who held something out to him with a timid shrug and said, —Mister, you forgot your rumberell.

The mass of men were walking from Faneuil Hall to the Courthouse. Only the young and wild had gone to the rendezvous in a dead run. Parker had to stop at each corner for a deep breath.

Phillips took him by the arm. —Am I going too fast for you? he asked. Parker shook his head.

—You should carry a stick, said Phillips. —It's fashionable.

—I should carry a long staff and knock at the earth and say *Liebe mutter . . . let me in.*

When they reached Court Square, it was all over. Higginson had bled and gone, and the Volunteer Artillery was still drawn up in the square. Howe ran over to them in great excitement.

—Higginson went ahead with it. It failed, and a man has been killed.

—Watson Freeman, I hope, said Parker.

—No, one of the deputies. The bullet passed under the Marshal's arm. Oh God, we've got to do something . . . re-form our lines. I blame myself for this.

Howe walked quickly away; he caught several people by the arm, urging another attack. But they turned away as the police arrested two more.

—How could Higginson have done such a foolish thing without telling us? said Phillips angrily. —He should have known just announcing the attack wasn't enough.

—Didn't you know about it? said Parker in a slow, dead voice.

—No. How could I? I've been chasing Dana all day. Were you in it? Is that why you kept bringing things to a boil? Why didn't you tell me, why did you let me throw cold water on it?

Parker looked at him with unanswering eyes, frozen stupid in anguish.

Phillips tried to comfort him. —Perhaps it wouldn't have mattered if you had told me. I might have opposed it on scruples. I suppose we'll be blamed by both sides now. I wouldn't like to be in Worcester tomorrow! Let's go. This is a bad Friday, if I ever saw one.

—Bad Friday, repeated Parker, —with me the Pilate to you and the Judas to Tom.

—It was an error of judgment, nothing more, said Phillips. —There is still the Resurrection to come. Richard Dana may save us all.

They saw John Swift wandering around, his head down, hands thrust deep in his pockets, like a schoolboy at a football game, taxed with the losing side. Parker went to him to ask about Higginson and the others. Swift cut him dead. He nodded to Phillips and walked off into the darkness.

A small group of roughly dressed men began to gather about them. Phillips tried to draw Parker off, but he stood his ground looking them all, one by one, in the eye. They were truckmen and their helpers with some toughs among them. They stood looking at Parker and mumbling to one another. The knot became a ring around them and the eyes were all filled with hatred.

—You know what you've went and done, said one, with a thick Cork accent. —You killed Jimmy Batchelder with your gab, you killed him.

—Can't you keep your bloody mouth shut and leave people alone?

—Oh, they'll git theirs, said a high-pitched whining voice, the kind that always puts threats into the third person, —They'll git it someday. Git strung up fer it, fer what they did. And if the governmint won't, thin the people will, and God himself will be glad.

—That's right, that's right, said the voices, and the men took a step nearer.

Parker pulled his arm away from Phillips and glared at them. One lout, after looking to see if he had plenty of backing, stood directly in front of Parker.

—You've killed a man with this night's work, he screamed. —But that isn't all your rottenness. You atheist, you blasphemer, you God-damned son-of-a-bitch infidel!

Parker stepped to the man before Phillips could restrain him. The man jumped back at the suddenness of it. Parker seized him by the arm and the old strength, the strength that could hold a plow with one hand and two horses with the other, the strength that could lift a barrel of cider to his lips, came back to him. The man lifted his free hand to shield a blow and two or three men on the fringe began to walk away, looking fearfully over their shoulders.

—My brother, said Parker, his eyes blazing, —I am not afraid of men. I can offend them and care nothing for their hate or their esteem. But I do not dare, as you do, to violate the eternal law of God, the Father of the white man and the white man's slave. I do not dare to violate His law, come what may. Should you?

The man twisted his arm free with a mighty wrench, looked with awe into Parker's face, and walked quickly away, his toadies stumbling behind him.

They walked by the shattered door of the Courthouse and Parker stooped and picked up a long jagged splinter from the shattered door. He held it a moment in his hand.

Phillips watched him with concern. —Throw it away, Theodore, he advised. —I shouldn't keep it, if I were you. You'll be magnifying it into a relic of the true Cross.

—It may turn out to be that, to me.

He wrapped his handkerchief around it and placed it carefully in his breast pocket. And then they began the long dark walk home, past the groups of scorning men.

But Ben Hallett had the last word that day: had it in the dead spot of the night, in the Courthouse now defiled with its windows looking down on the square with broken eyes and the east door hanging from its hinges, all askew like a twisted mouth.

The Justices of the Supreme Court had been obliged to flee in panic from their deliberations. While they were combing through the snarled evidence against a man accused of killing someone nobody cared about in a spot nobody was sure of, a United States Deputy Marshal, trying to keep a mob from breaking into the Courthouse, had been murdered within their hearing. If he had given way from the door and fought his way back twenty yards or more, he might have been killed in the courtroom itself, before the judge's bench, or been propped up to die in the witness chair giving off irrefutable testimony of the scene and the course of the crime, wordlessly, with his dying.

Ben knew the steelyard of time had swung the balance to his side and he was in the Marshal's office making the most of it. He had seen the attack from the lobby window of a nearby hotel and had gone into the Courthouse as soon as the mob had drawn away to jeer at the soldiers marching into the square.

—Lock the door, he told Watson Freeman, —we've got work to do.

And while he scratched deliberately on sheets of legal foolscap, the Marshal stood with his ear to the barred door, listening for threatening sounds in the corridor outside.

The guards stood around on the other side of the door, still holding shiny new cutlasses in their sweaty hands. They were not in formation or walking post; they just stood there. Some of them talked but not about Batchelder. Two talked of quitting and then did throw down their arms and leave. The others, used to violence and sudden death, just said that they were glad they hadn't rushed ahead too quickly and become martyrs for three dollars a day.

The Mayor, the Chief of Police and three of the aldermen came in through the broken door on their way to talk with the Marshal. The guards did not question them but Watson wouldn't open the door until Ben gave him the word. The aldermen banged angrily and shouted, — Open up, open up!

After Theodore Parker's failure of nerve at the Faneuil Hall rally, the political forces behind Anthony Burns's tragic situation emerge. What was planned as a direct, revolutionary coup now becomes a chess game of opposing political factions. By "The Eighth Wave" of the storm, Boston is in a state of seige by pro- and antislavery partisans, while Burns remains a captured pawn.

The Eighth Wave

Charles Mayo Ellis was not cast in the mold of the great lawyers. He was neither deliberate nor confident enough to build a series of notes slowly and patiently until they rang out all at once like a great chord of truth in the ears of the judge and jury. But his occasional incoherence gave his delivery a driving and unusual verbal tempo and he was a good man to open a case and to cross-examine. He was a mild man outside but in court he spoke with a controlled anger. In appearance he resembled a sheep dog. His thick curly hair began oddly far back on his forehead and cascaded down the back of his neck. Unruly wings of it fell and covered his ears. He had a long flat nose, spatulate at the end, and a long sharp chin, projected beyond it. He was extremely round-shouldered and when he was on his feet he bustled about, always in motion, snapping at the heels of the opposition and gently nudging his own charges into line with the strongest defense.

He began his day in court with a bark. —Mr. Commissioner, we need time. Most of the brief amount granted only a day or two to decide more than a man's life; when, if it involved only his coat, the wheels of justice could not be turned in a month. . . . This case involves novel questions of law but the Courthouse library has been locked up. Access to the Courthouse has been made difficult by the military force. The common avenues are entirely barred and impassable. The labor and fatigue of a hurried preparation have thus been multiplied. Precious as every instant is to one needing it to defend another's liberty, I have lost most of the few minutes of time allotted to consulting my client by being forbidden to ascend the stairway by soldiers with their bayonets pointed at my breast. Still, sir, we must go on.

—We shall offer evidence to contradict that produced by the claimant, evidence upon the facts in issue.

—At the same time we claim that there is no evidence here now that will justify the signing of a warrant of slavery.

—We stand on the presumption, of which you, sir, did well to remind counsel, of freedom and innocence.

Judge Loring settled back. Counsel Thomas shaped his body in the chair for a doze. Such talk of presumptions and freedom and innocence were signs of weakness and a presumption didn't amount to a hill of beans against an affidavit and an admission from the defendant. But Mr. Kerr caught a disturbing note of optimism in Ellis's voice. The Judge had sat back too soon. Ellis began to shake a finger at him.

—You sit there as both judge and jury, betwixt that man and slavery. Without a commission, without any accountability, without any right of challenge, you sit to render judgment. If against him, there is no tribunal that can review it or reverse it. You must proceed without delay, without any charge, on proofs defined only as such as may satisfy your mind. You may adjudge, and your judgment will be final forever.

He dropped the finger but the *forever* still stuck in the Judge's face. Counsel Thomas's doze was shattered forever and the guards gaped at the Judge as though a sentence of life and hereafter had been imposed upon him.

—The question here, said Ellis in a quieter tone, —is your own sense of reason and justice. The mind that is to decide this matter will not fail to weigh all these questions, the greater because of the dangers of its result, and require the claimant to prove his case beyond a possible doubt.

Thomas and Kerr began conferring anxiously. They were disturbed by the bold optimism in Ellis's face. Thomas pushed his chair back and fiddled with some papers. He seemed about to rise. Ellis struck at him.

—The claimant's lawyers have no case. They offer a paper or two which they call a record, one witness and a book they call the laws of Virginia. I design for a time to examine such a case as they venture to present, before proceeding to our answer.

Mr. Kerr got to his feet presumably to ask the Judge to have the defense put on its witnesses, if any, and get on with the trial. Ellis turned to him and said, —Saturday morning we asked for a delay to prepare the defense. The counsel of the claimant, against this presumption of the existing freedom and innocence of the man in the dock, and against his right, dared to say we have no defense to make. Yesterday, at the earliest hour, while we were reduced to gathering our facts as they are putting on their case, the counsel ventured to say the same thing. And now, sir, he rises again to try and strike our weapons from our hands. On what sort of presumption does he operate?

Counsel Thomas pulled Kerr back into his chair. Ellis smiled and went on.

—Sir, I am happy to state that we shall offer proof that this atrocious charge and seizure, made on a false pretense of robbery, have no foundation in fact.

—The slave claimant's attorney said, too, that we have no defense to the case but against the law and that we came here to ask that it should be overridden and the Constitution violated. This, too, is not true. Not only have I never opposed the law but I have done something to stay resistance to it. I stand here for the prisoner, under and not against the law. I shall not shrink from debating the just limits of this bill of 1850. I avow my hatred, as a man and as a lawyer, of the bill. But, in reply to this remark of counsel, I will say that with these surroundings, with this form of seizure, charge, and procedure, in the midst of this Courthouse occupied like a fortress, with counsel detained by steel at their breasts, in a cause where claims are asserted and advocated by armed men, held in a room packed with political partisans, in a proceeding in which the sole law officer of the government, Mr. Benjamin Hallett, dared to dress down the presiding judge ... that if there are persons who do need to be reminded that there is a Constitution and that there are laws, they are not counsel for the prisoner. It is not I.

Mr. Thomas, against his own better judgment, got to his feet and addressed the Court.—Your Honor, these comments on a man who is not here to defend himself are most insulting and hardly relevant to the proceeding. I beg the court to inform the gentleman that the United States Government is not on trial here, and to have him get to his evidence and end this Abolition diatribe.

The Judge regarded him blankly, trying to sift the law out of the injury, seeking for the proper words with which to admonish Ellis. Ellis spoke up.

—Please, sir, I cannot consent that the counsel for the claimant shall hint to me the line of my duty. I judge not of his course. I notice these things only because of his own provoking. I neither commend nor condemn their action. Their own consciences shall judge them.

He turned to Thomas, who was still standing and looking fixedly at the Judge in hope of getting him to call Ellis to a halt.

—One of the slave catcher's counsel, all expected to see here. The other appears in such a case for the first time. He has been a friend of mine. I did not expect to see him here. As for myself, sooner than to lay my hand to the work of aiding in such a case, I would see it wither, and rather than speak one word for a slave claimant, I would be struck dumb forever.

—Your Honor, cried Thomas, —I submit that these remarks are not on the case but against the Slave Act.

—It is my duty so to remark, shouted Ellis, —and I am led to by this constant harping on the charge that we seek not a trial but a triumph over the law.

He went directly to the bench, speaking rapidly and intimately, whipping the tempo up.

—It is highly proper that the mind on the bench, which is to judge of fact and law, should perceive, clearly, everything in the position of the parties involved: the procedure, the circumstances and the results that may tend to disturb its balance. We stand here like blind and helpless wanderers without a single guidepost save the thing in which our dearest hopes are centered, your Honor's mind and judgment. May not that mind fail in the coming ruin!

Between the whipping and the pleading, the Judge was drawn into the vortex of Ellis's intensity. He sat slightly turned from him, looking at him once in a while with oblique fascination. The constant references to his mind and its power and importance gave it a high isolation from his frail body, and he let it float over the courtroom. He inadvertently caught sight of the red-faced belligerence of Counsel Thomas, still on his feet hoping to break the flow of Ellis's argument. He waved him to his seat in a detached manner, not wishing to speak or to depart from the marvelous suspension of the mind. Ellis went on, speaking with incredible swiftness and backing slowly up the aisle to his chair, like a man flying a kite.

—Sir, an attempt to mitigate the severity of this case by calling this trial a preliminary examination has been made and will be made again. Preliminary to what? The examination in Virginia was also a preliminary, I suppose. So shall each tinged with guilt lay this to his soul who acts at any stage. They know better when they say so. The law looks no further. Nothing is to follow. There is no postliminium. This is the final act on the farce of hearings. They know, we know, you know, that if you send him hence with them, he goes to the block, to the sugar or cotton plantation, to the lash under which Sims, who entered the dark portal, breathed out his life . . . and that man is a fool who expects me to believe otherwise.

—Your Honor, unless a case of overwhelming proof is presented, this certificate should be refused. They call one witness and as additional evidence, produced a paper to prove the three facts of service, escape and identity. We claim that it is, on their own showing, a direct falsehood; as we can prove by competent witnesses that at the time of the alleged escape, the person charged was a free man at work in Massachusetts.

—I now wish to call William Jones as a witness for the defense who will prove that, contrary to the sworn statement of the claimant's witness, this man was in Boston on the first of March last, and not in Richmond, Virginia, on the nineteenth day of that month.

When Mr. Jones got to his feet and made his way to the stand, the

Southern gentlemen chuckled and great guffaws burst from the guards.

—Look at the head on him, one shouted. It was an enormous head; like a baby's, rocking on a spindle-shanked body. His hair was not set like a neat wooly cap but sprung like a mass of blue steel shavings from his huge skull. His thin neck was fenced in by a very low white collar and when he turned his head, the collar and the black string tie stayed as rigid as if they were on a tailor's dummy.

Mr. Ellis turned and stared angrily at the mockers, but Mr. Jones didn't seem to mind. He sat in the chair and bowed to the Judge and took the oath in a crisp nasal Yankee voice as salty as a caricature.

Mr. Ellis put the question to him gingerly, wondering all the while if it had been wise to call a colored man for the first witness. After the first wave of amusement, the spectators on Suttle's side lapsed into an attitude of heavy, affected boredom, shifting restlessly in their seats and making the courtroom hum with the low plucking of light banter among them. The lawyers for the claimant shrugged their shoulders and turned their backs as if to say Well, this is the obvious thing.

Mr. Jones testified in his confident twang that he lived in South Boston and that he was a laborer. He knew Burns and had seen him first on Washington Street on the first of March.

This remark brought a slight lull in the obbligato of indifference. Mr. Kerr began to take notes. Mr. Thomas kept his back turned to both Ellis and the witness, but his fat back tensed up under his linen coat.

—I talked to him awhile, about half an hour by the clock, said Mr. Jones, precisely. —And then I employed him to go to work on the fourth day of March in the Mattapan Iron Works at South Boston. We worked at cleaning windows. He worked with me five days.

—Is there any particular reason why you should remember these exact dates, Mr. Jones? asked Ellis.

—Yes, Mr. Counselor. I always believe in havin' everything in writing. Put it in writing, I always say, and nobody'll skin you.

—We'll get him on that, whispered Thomas to Kerr. —That nigger can't write a line.

Mr. Jones drew a little notebook from his pocket. —I can't write myself, Mr. Counselor, he said, —so I went into Mr. Russell's store and asked him to put it down in my book. I agreed to give him eight cents a window, and when he got through with the job, I gave him a dollar and a half.

He looked over at Burns in a reproving way, clucking his tongue dryly.—He said I hadn't settled up with him right. He went to the clerk about it.

—But you had it all in the book, said Mr. Ellis in his brotherly way.

—I had it all in the book. Jes' get things in writing and you won't never get skinned. That's how I know I did go to South Boston to work with him on the fourth.

He gave Mr. Ellis the book and Ellis laid it on the Judge's desk. The Judge looked at it and laid it carefully on the other side of the desk, exactly opposite from the Virginia documents.

Mr. Ellis took his seat. He kept his head down to hide a smile. The opposition table was quiet. Silas Carleton, a policeman who was to be a witness for Colonel Suttle, began to jabber to Thomas. He shook his head toward Mr. Jones. Mr. Jones looked around the courtroom and up at the Judge. He started to get up and go to his seat, but Ellis waved him back.

Thomas and Kerr suddenly turned and faced him with hard and calculating eyes. The Southern students leaned forward in their chairs, staring malevolently. Mr. Jones looked a little puzzled. He didn't know he was being treated with the evil eye. He reached into his pocket, but instead of the dirty bandana which the Southerners thought would come out to claw at the expected sweat of fear springing out on his face, he brought out a pair of old spectacles. They were as thick as a skillet and missing the steel bow on one side, but he adjusted them with great dignity and peered back at them. He stuck his long neck forward and began to grin. Mr. Ellis smiled back at him and so did Theodore Parker, and Richard Dana gave him a friendly nod. With a cocky little shrug, he took them off again and put them away in his pocket. The leaning sorcerers, their evil exorcised, sank back in their seats. Mr. Thomas got up for the cross-examination.

—Now, Mr. Jones, said Thomas with heavy sarcasm. He walked to the witness stand, placed a hand on the rail and swung back to face the rear of the court.

Mr. Jones dove into his pocket again for the spectacles. This time he did not put them on his nose but held them up a good eight inches before his eyes and gazed in bewilderment at Mr. Thomas's back. There was irreverent laughter from the guard at this. For a second or two, Mr. Thomas thought they were laughing with him, but then he turned uneasily and saw Mr. Jones was making him the butt. He faced Mr. Jones squarely, his face reddening. Mr. Jones narrowed his eyes and gave a good look at Mr. Thomas, and then put his spectacles away, sunk back and stared calmly up at the ceiling.

Thomas began to fire questions at Jones; his voice was tight and querulous. Mr. Jones answered him in high-pitched petulance.

Q. I suppose you know the prisoner for years. He was your schoolmate at Boston Latin, wasn't he?

A. Never saw him before that day on Washington Street.

Q. You just walked right up to him, a perfect stranger, and asked him to go to work for you?

A. He spoke to me first.

Q. What day of the week was this?

A. Can't recollect the day of the week. It was about the first of the week.

Q. Whereabouts on Washington Street? I suppose you can't recollect?

A. Just below the Commonwealth Office.

Q. Anyone with him?

A. He was alone.

Q. Dressed?

A. Yes. He was dressed, Mr. Counselor.

Mr. Jones brought out the spectacles at this and treated the groundlings to another guffaw.

Q. How was he dressed, Mr. Jones? How was he dressed?

A. He had lightish pants on.

Q. Lightish pants? Do you consider that a good description?

A. Good enough. It's not my business to examine his dress.

Q. Wouldn't you consider it odd if you saw a man on a March day with merely a lightish pair of pants?

A. He had a coat and cap on and shoes.

Q. What kind of coat and cap?

A. Lightish.

Mr. Thomas decided that Mr. Jones was too shrewd a witness to badger too closely and decided to let him run on a while and then trip him up on some inconsistency of detail. —Tell us a little about your conversation, Mr. Jones.

—Well, he asked me if I knew of anyone who wanted a man to work in a store. I asked him what he could do and he said he could do most anything. I took him from there to Mr. Russell's store and we went from there to Mr. Favor's shop.

Q. Mr. Russell's shop is right there on Washington Street?
A. No, sir. It's in the next street to Water Street.
Q. Are you referring to Mr. Gideon Russell?
A. I don't know, sir.
Q. You don't know. Then you don't know where you were?
A. No. I don't know Mr. Russell's Christian name.
Q. Please answer the question.
A. The Mr. Russell I know keeps a bootblack shop.
Q. Then Mr. Russell didn't want any blacks? Pardon me, Mr. Jones ... any bootblacks?
A. I asked Mr. Russell to put down in that notebook that Mr. Burns was engaged for March the fourth, by me. Mr. Russell put down the black and white, Mr. Counselor.
Q. How long did it take him to put it in black and white?
A. About five minutes. Then we went to Mr. Favor's on Lincoln Street, stayed three quarters of an hour, and then to the apothecary shop under the United States Hotel.
Q. What did you go there for?
A. I went there to fool. I don't know what Mr. Burns went there for.

There was more laughter at this. The fickle guard was beginning to like Mr. Jones. He was a sharp fellow and they hung approvingly on every word he said. Mr. Thomas decided to drop his badgering now that the witness was gaining sympathy, and to pretend boredom at his garrulousness.

—Then what, Mr. Thomas said wearily. —Go on, Mr. Jones. You went to the apothecary shop.

—I fetched up there. I stayed there twenty-five minutes. I next went to Mr. Maddox's on Essex Street. He keeps a clothing store. I know his Christian name. It's Stephen, Mr. Thomas. I arrived there about two o'clock. Had nothing else to do but walk about the city. After leaving Mr. Maddox, I went to see Mr. Bell, the dancing master.

Q. Where did you leave Mr. Burns?
A. He came with me.
Q. Did you have a dancing lesson?
A. He wasn't in. Then we went down Washington to Kneeland Street and then went home to South Boston. It was night when we arrived home.
Q. And where did you dine? This was quite a busy day.
A. I had not dined.
Q. Isn't that strange, Mr. Jones? Two gentlemen strolling leisurely about the town, fooling at the apothecary and the dancing master's, on an empty stomach?
A. I eat but one meal a day and I have no particular hour for it.

Mr. Thomas gave up. He sat down and motioned for Mr. Kerr to take over. Mr. Kerr decided to have a go at the weather.

Q. Was it a pleasant day to walk around in, this March first?
A. It was a little cold.
Q. What about the snow?
A. There might have been snow on the ground but I don't recollect. I don't recollect whether it snowed or rained. It might have rained twenty times. I wouldn't notice it. Mr. Burns stayed with me that night, the next night, the next and the next.
Q. You provided him with a hideaway I suppose?
A. I never expected to see this that I see here now.
Q. Then on the next day . . .
A. On the next day he came to the City Hall with me to see Mr. Gould. I don't know his Christian name. It was between ten and eleven o'clock. I wanted to get employment for myself. I wash windows and do odd jobs around the City Hall from time to time. Then I went to School Street and then went out to the Neck to take a walk and see what I could see.
Q. Was Mr. Burns . . .
A. Mr. Burns was with me all the time.
Q. And the next day?
A. I got up, washed my face and hands and went out to the Mattapan Works to see Mr. Sawyer the boss. I stayed two or three hours and talked about the job and then went home. Burns was with me all the time.
Q. Is this all down in the book?

A. I commenced to work at one o'clock cleaning the windows. Burns helped me. The next morning he went back to work with me.

Q. What about Mr. Burns's clothes? Did he leave them with you?

A. He had no trunk. We worked all day and the next day.

Q. Did you work during the snowstorm?

A. Never keep the run of the weather or the day of the week.

This brought another laugh from the guards. Mr. Thomas took over again.

Q. I suppose when Mr. Burns questioned the amount you paid him, you threw him out?

A. No. After finishing the job at the Iron Works, I took him with me up to City Hall to see Mr. Gould. Don't know his Christian name. There was no work to be done. On the eighteenth day of March, I went to work at the City Hall. Mr. Burns went with me about three times. He made the fire in the boiler for me and then he left and I never laid eyes on him again until Sunday morning when I saw him looking out of the window of the Courthouse.

Mr. Thomas called for a recess and it was given until three o'clock.

After the recess, when the court was in order, Mr. Thomas, in ominous tones, called for Mr. Jones to take the stand again. This time he had some notes on Mr. Jones and felt sure that he could break him.

—Mr. Jones, he said, —according to your last testimony, you didn't see the prisoner again after the eighteenth of March until last Sunday morning, the twenty-eighth of May.

A. Yes, Mr. Counselor.

Q. Were you surprised to see him?

A. No, sir.

Q. You seem to imply here, Jones, that you left him or, rather, he left you. By the by, did you pay him for helping you with the boiler?

A. No.

Q. Then it was another incident where you withheld from the man money rightly earned.

Mr. Ellis objected. Objection sustained.

—I only raised the question, your Honor, on the basis of the witness's own testimony that the alleged Burns questioned him on payment for the window-cleaning job and went to the bookkeeper to see how much he had been cheated.

—What is your purpose, Mr. Thomas? said the Judge.

—To prove the lack of good faith and veracity in the witness, your Honor.

—Very well, you may proceed along these lines. Counsel for the defense may take exceptions which I will consider later.

Ellis sat down, disgusted.

Q. Is it not true, Jones, that you had engaged in a great many suspicious activities even before you saw Burns at the window?

Mr. Dana got up. —Your Honor, will you permit Counsel such carelessness with adjectives? The witness is not capable of answering that kind of question without prejudicing himself.

—No adjectives, if you please, Mr. Thomas, intoned the Judge.

—Yes, your Honor.

Q. Mr. Jones, did you know before Sunday that it was Mr. Burns who had been arrested?

A. Yes, Mr. Counsel. I heard of it first on Thursday. I came into the Police Court and the Municipal Court. They said there was a man arrested and I walked around, but I didn't believe it.

Q. When did you learn the awful truth?

A. One of the officers told me of the arrest.

Q. How did you know it was your former employee, or should I say your free-gratis boiler-tender?

A. The officer described him to me. He mentioned the scar.

Q. Then you suspected he might be the fugitive. Had Burns confided in you the story of his escape?

—Don't answer that, said Mr. Ellis. But Jones ignored him.

A. No, sir, but the officer, Mr. Horace Brown, was employed at the Iron Works when I worked there with Burns and he knew him by the scar. He said, The man that worked with you at the Iron Works the first week in March has been arrested as a fugitive slave. . . . What did you say, Mr. Ellis?

—Nothing, Mr. Jones, said Ellis, smiling broadly. —You've made your point.

—Never mind what Mr. Brown said, shouted Thomas. He glared angrily back at Mr. Kerr who could not forbear smiling at Mr. Jones's hits.

—Yes, sir, said Mr. Jones, —I heard Mr. Brown say he'd speak for himself later on.

—Answer the questions, Mr. Jones, said Judge Loring, but his tone was not harsh.

Mr. Thomas looked down at his notes again. He was filled with rage at the shrewdness of the witness. He lost his temper and began to browbeat.

Q. If you were in such ignorance about this case, why did you call on Colonel Suttle?

A. That was after I had talked to Mr. Brown.

Q. Why did you call on Colonel Suttle? Was it to offer your services as a witness for the claimant?

A. No, sir.

Q. Did you bring your notebook with you to have him set down the terms for favorable testimony? Was it to exact the terms of betrayal of this window washer whom you befriended and hired only to have him go behind your back and question your honesty with your employer?

Mr. Ellis got to his feet again. Mr. Jones pulled out his glasses and looked at him and then motioned for him to sit down. Mr. Ellis did, but reluctantly.

A. No, Mr. Counselor, I went to call on Mr. Suttle to tell him that he had the wrong man.

Q. How did you know it was the wrong man if you hadn't even seen the man confined in the Courthouse?

A. Because Mr. Brown told me that it was the man who had worked for me on the first week of March. Mr. Suttle said his man was in Richmond on the twentieth of March. Then Mr. Suttle's man couldn't be my man, now could he, Mr. Thomas?

Thomas had to sit down and compose himself. He motioned roughly for Mr. Kerr to take over.

—Mr. Jones, said Mr. Kerr. —We're trying to find out why you came to testify for this man. It's a long time since March eighteenth. Surely you didn't go to all this trouble without being sure it was Mr. Burns. Has someone approached you on this matter within the last few days?

A. No, sir. I've had no conversation with anybody about this until yesterday.

Mr. Jones stopped for a moment and sized up Mr. Kerr. Mr. Kerr spoke in a low voice and did not attempt to bully. Mr. Jones spoke slowly. —I couldn't get in to see him. . . . I stood on the opposite side. His head was out of the window. It was on Sunday, near twelve o'clock.

When Mr. Brown told me that my man had been taken, I went nearly crazy. I didn't even know his name until someone read it to me from the papers. It was in the paper too, about when he left Richmond, on the twentieth, it said. I called him John or Jack or any short name that came handy. He was a good boy. I was sorry to lose track of him. I went to the Marshal and asked to see him. The Marshal said he wouldn't even let his owner see him. There I was, knowing they had the wrong man; knowing he was shut up there and I couldn't help him.

Mr. Thomas and Mr. Kerr waited like cats to spring on some tiny betrayal as Jones went on. Dana and Ellis were tense and worried.

—I went to the meeting in Faneuil Hall, and I came from there and stood on Court Street until the mob had left, and then went up to the square.

He stopped, thinking about the meeting.

—Then what? said Counsel Thomas rising again.

—Then I went into the Courthouse.

—On Friday night you went into the Courthouse. Why, Mr. Jones? Why did you go into the Courthouse?

The answer came innocently and as smooth as butter.

—To protect the city property.

Over the laugh, Mr. Thomas bellowed, —And who employed you?

—I employed myself, came gently the answer.

—Did you employ yourself to come here with this crudely manufactured iron-work testimony?

—I came here because I saw a man looking out of a window.

Mr. Kerr took the lead again. He said softly, —You spent quite a lot of time around the Courthouse, Mr. Jones. Why didn't you tell all this at the first examination on Saturday? You might have saved us all a lot of time.

—I couldn't get in the Courthouse on Saturday. The guards drove me away. I stayed by the door until half-past seven Saturday night, and then I came back when the church bells rang on Sunday morning. Then I went to the Revere House to see Colonel Suttle again but he wasn't there. If it hadn't been for Mr. Phillips, I would never have got in. I'd never had the chance to tell you people that you got the wrong man.

Mr. Thomas got to his feet and pointed at Silas Carleton.

Q. Did you ever see that man?
A. Yes, sir. I saw him in the Marshal's office.
Q. Did you have words with him?
A. Yes, I had a few words with him. But I didn't tell him that Burns belonged to Colonel Suttle.

—Your Honor, I object. Witness was not asked that question, said Thomas.

—And I didn't say if I saw him I would advise him to go back.

—Mr. Jones, said the Judge, —please do not introduce comments until you are questioned. On motion of the Counsel, I will rule out reference to conversation with Officer Carleton. Court is adjourned until ten o'clock tomorrow.

"Book Two: The Judgment" is divided into chapters called "ordeals." In this, "The First Ordeal," Theodore Parker attempts to rectify his failure to free Anthony Burns by direct action. As he contemplates the suffering of the former slave, Parker is nearly worn out by his own ordeal.

The First Ordeal

> *Of Bodily Affliction*
>
> And the Lord said unto Satan,
> —Hast thou considered my servant Job?
> For there is none like him in the earth.
> One that feareth God and escheweth evil;
> And he still holdeth fast his integrity
> Although thou movest me against him to destroy him without
>   cause.
>
> And Satan answered the Lord and said,
> —Skin for skin.
> Yea, all that a man hath will he give for his life.
> But put forth thine hand now
> And touch his bone and his flesh
> And he will renounce thee to thy face.

They were going to hang Parker for what he said and the crowds came to the Music Hall that Sunday to see if he'd say it again. Not all of them were sensation-seekers; more people went steadily to Parker than any other New England preacher could draw. There were seven thousand names on his parish register, culled from the unchurched, the unbelieving and the protesting. Strangely enough, the other clergymen hated him for this; the same clergymen who welcomed warmly and set a place at their own tables for the itinerant fire-breathing evangelists who could frighten and exhort these same three classes of backsliders back into the deserted pews.

People came to him who worried secretly about injustice done, whose consciences were violated again and again by forces beyond their power to resist. He took away from them the reproach of silent consent.

On this Sunday morning he followed his usual puritan usage of worship: to read some verses from the Bible and sing a hymn or two. But on his desk was a clump of flowers which was whispered about in the back rows as a proof of his paganism. They were blue flags from the brook that flowed by his father's Lexington farmhouse. And so they were proof, for he had made a special trip for them the day before and taken his shoes and stockings off and waded a bit in the stream, warm and swollen with the rain, and picked the flowers and kissed them and told his wife that they were new words of God.

He tried to be a warm stream flowing from the gulf into the icy depth of New England orthodoxy to touch the cold shores and make them bring forth flowers and sweet hay. He tried to make people throw off their fears and float in the unfamiliar fluidity of speculation; to think in the sanctuary itself and in the presence of the open lids of the sacred Book.

But this Sabbath he was too hot. He came hissing like steam into the clear waters, clouding them and raising bubbles of unrest and fugitive force.

—Why standest thou afar off, O Lord? he demanded angrily, reading from the book, —why hidest thyself in time of trouble? The wicked in his pride doth persecute the poor; let them be taken in the devices that they have imagined. For the wicked boasteth of his heart's desire and blesseth the covetous, whom the Lord abhorreth. The wicked, through the pride of his countenance, will not seek after God. God is not in all his thoughts.

He flipped over the pages, nodding his head in agreement with the questioning prophets, like a man listening to an old story from an old friend, both indignant, because an old wound is reopening and an old affliction has been put upon them again.

—How doth the city sit solitary, that was full of people! How is she become as a widow! She that was great before nations and princess among the provinces, how is she become tributary! Her adversaries are chief, her enemies prosper; for the Lord hath afflicted her for the multitude of her transgressions: Her children are gone into captivity before the enemy. . . . Jerusalem hath grievously sinned; therefore she is removed. All that honored her despise her, because they have seen her nakedness. . . . For these things I weep . . . mine eyes are running down with water because the comforter that should relieve my soul is far from me: my children are desolate because the enemy prevailed. . . .

—Judge me, O God, and plead my cause against an ungodly nation: O deliver me from the deceitful and unjust man. O send out thy light and thy truth: let them lead me; let them bring me unto thy holy hill. . . . Why art thou cast down, my soul, and why art thou disquieted within me? Hope in God for I shall yet praise him, who is the health of my countenance and my God.

As he closed the book, the congregation murmured satisfaction. Some of the ignorant among them thought the preacher had written the text himself. All agreed that it was a first-rate description of Loring, Hallett and Marshal Freeman.

The morning service proceeded in decent order. A long hymn was sung to the throbbing of the organ. But the people kept coming in and soon there were no more chairs to set out in the aisles and the latecomers had to stand.

He began his sermon gently, in an easy vein, saving his voice and letting the people who were standing up sag a bit on this foot and the other until they had set their frames for a long hang.

—Within the last few days, we have seen some of the results of despotism in America, which might easily astonish a stranger; but a citizen of Boston has no right to be surprised. The condition of this town from May twenty-fourth to June second is the natural and unavoidable result of causes publicly and deliberately put in action. It is only the first fruit of causes which in time will litter the ground with similar harvests and with others even worse. Let us pretend no amazement that the seed sown here has borne fruit after its kind. Let us see what warning or what guidance we can gather from these events, their cause and consequence. So this morning I ask your attention to a sermon of the new crime against humanity committed in the midst of us.

He stopped and took a drink of water. He could see at least eight reporters scribbling in front of him. He looked carefully around to see whether Ben Hallett was there. He was disappointed not to find him.

—I know well the responsibility of the place I occupy this morning. Tomorrow's sun will carry my words to all America. They will be read on both sides of the continent. They will cross the ocean. It may astonish the minds of men in Europe to hear of the iniquity committed in the midst of us. Let us be calm and cool and look the thing in the face.

That was the message for Ben Hallett, a dagger in his heart. He was not too big a man to stoop to lash his enemies with the scorpions of envy.

—Of course, you will understand from my connection with what has taken place, I must speak of some things with a great deal of reserve and pass by others entirely. However, I have only too much to say. I have had but short time for preparation. The deed is so recent. If some of you find your patience exhausted and standing too wearisome, you can retire, and if without noise, none will be disturbed and none offended.

All smiled at this, the standees most of all. They would be the last to leave. They didn't come there for a place to sit.

—Wednesday, the twenty-fourth of May, the city was all calm and still. The poor black man was at work with one of his own nation, earning an honest livelihood. A Judge of Probate, a man in easy circumstances, a Professor at Harvard College, was sitting in his office . . . and with a single spurt of his pen he dashes off the liberty of a man, a citizen of Massachusetts. He kidnaps a man endowed by his creator with the unalienable right to life, liberty and the pursuit of happiness. He leaves the writ with the Marshal and goes home to his family, caresses his children and enjoys his cigar. The frivolous smoke curls around his frivolous head and at length he lays him down to sleep.

—But when he wakes next morn, all the winds of indignation are let loose. Before night, they are blowing all over this Commonwealth. Ay, before another night they have gone to the Mississippi and wherever the lightning messenger can tell the tale.

—So I have read in an old medieval legend that one summer afternoon there came up a shape, all hot from Tartarus, from hell below . . . but garmented and garbed to represent a civil-suited man, masked with humanity. He walked quiet and decorous through Milan's stately streets and scattered from his hand an invisible dust. It touched the walls, it lay on the street. It ascended to the cross on the cathedral's utmost top. It went down to the beggar's den. Peacefully he walked through the streets, vanished and went home. But the next morning, the pestilence was in Milan, and ere a week had passed, half her population were in their graves and the other half, crying that hell was clutching at their hearts, fled from the reeking city of the plague.

—I know a great deal about this plague. I sat in the pesthouse itself and watched increase of appetite growing by what it fed on. While I sat in the Courthouse, my own life was threatened. Friend and foe gave me public or anonymous warning. I sat between men who had newly sworn to kill me, my garments touching theirs. The malaria of their rum and tobacco was an offense in my face. I saw their weapons and laughed as I looked the drunken rowdies in their cowardly eyes.

—The wickedness began with the Commissioner. He was not forced into that bad eminence. He went there voluntarily. The soldiers of the Czar execute their master's tyranny because they are forced into it. The only option with them is to shoot with a musket or be scourged to death with the knout. If Mr. Loring did not like kidnaping, he need not have kept his office. But he liked it.

—I never thought him capable of committing this wickedness. I have seen him sometimes in the Probate office and he seemed to have a pleasant face, fit to watch over the widows and the fatherless. When a bad man does a wicked thing, it astonishes nobody. When a good man deliberately, voluntarily, does such a deed, words cannot express the fiery indignation which it ought to stir up in every man's bosom. It destroys confidence in humanity.

—The wickedness began with the Commissioner. It was to end with him. He is sheriff, judge, jury. He is paid twice as much for condemning as for acquitting the innocent. He is now the embodiment of Boston justice.

—Why did Loring do all this? He knew the consequence that must follow. He knew that there were men here who will never be silent when wrong is done. He knew the Fugitive Slave Bill had only raked the ashes over fires that were burning still, and that a breath might scatter the ashes to the winds of heaven and bid the slumbering embers flame. Still he dared send another citizen of Boston to be whipped to death.

—Look at Marshal Freeman. I know nothing about him other than that he is a Boston man. He arrested the man on a false charge and threatened him with violence if he should cry out. He kept him in secret and made the Courthouse the property of the slave power.

—Look at the men he employed for his guard. He dispossessed the stews, bawding the Courts with unwonted infamy. He gathered the spoils of brothels; prodigals not penitent, who upon harlots had wasted their substance in riotous living. Pimps, gamblers, the succubi of slavery. Men that the gorged jails had cast out into the streets. Fighters, drunkards, public brawlers, convicts that had served out their time, waiting for a second conviction. Men whom the subtlety of counsel, or the charity of the gallows, had left unhanged. No eye hath seen such scarecrows. He chose fit tools for fitting work. If you wish to kill a man, you buy not bread but poison.

—The conduct of the Mayor of Boston needs to be remembered. He had the police of the city in Court Square, aiding the kidnaper. It was not their fault. They served against their will. The Mayor called out the soldiers at great cost to someone. After the wicked deed was over, the Mayor attended a meeting of Sunday-school children in Faneuil Hall. When he was introduced to the audience, out of the mouths of babes and sucklings came a hiss. At night, the citizen soldiery had a festival. The Mayor was at the supper and toasted the military, eating and drinking and making merry. What did they care, or he, that an innocent citizen of Boston was sent into bondage forever and by their hands? The agony of Mr. Burns only flavored their cup. So the butcher's dog can enjoy himself in the shambles while the slaughter of the innocent goes on around him, battening on garbage.

—What a day for Boston. The day was brilliant. There was not a cloud. All around us was a ring of happy summer loveliness ... the green beauty of June. The grass, the trees, the heaven, the light . . . and Boston was the theater of incipient civil war. Drunken soldiers, hardly able to stand in the streets, sang their ribald song . . . "Carry Me Back to Old Virginny."

Parker stopped here for a moment. There was another name he must add to maintain the unity of the denunciation. But to name this man would help him and ingratiate him with his masters. He would want to be named. To leave him out would disappoint the people. Parker could tell by their expectancy that they wanted him to get his. He decided to improvise something.

—There is another man; to have him named by me would be an accolade of distinction in his circle. Actually he is not a man but only a type. He does not even aspire to be a man but merely a president. He would be before the people continually. No place is too mean, if only public. No failure disconcerts him. No fall abates his desire to rise. He knows no higher law above his own ambition, for which all means seem just. He often speaks of the flag with tears in his eyes, but does not know what the flag represents. His voice is a demagogue's. Ignorant men are evermore his tools. Not many days must we go back for learning how he uses them. And ignorant he begs them to remain so that he and his kind can control the state and laugh at the folly of the cheering masses upon whose necks he rides to power and fame.

The congregation sat back and shifted into new positions. They laughed a little and whispered knowingly behind their fans and put the tag on the victim. Hallett, of course. Ben Hallett.

—Pause with me and look at the causes of this fact. There are two great forces in this nation: One is slavery; freedom is the other. The two are deadly and irreconcilable foes, and they will go on fighting until one kills the other outright. In the period of the Revolution, when the nation fell back on its religious feelings and developed out of them the great political ideas of America, freedom was in the ascendant. These ideas demanded that all men have inalienable rights; in that respect, that all men are created equal. And that the proximate organization of these ideas would be a government of all the people, by all the people, for all the people. But now fidelity to slavery is the test of loyalty for officeholders. It is the leading ideal of America, the great American institution.

—Why not? There's money in it. It gives money power and political power and these are arguments that even the dullest can understand. Why should we not avail ourselves of any institution to secure money and political power? These are the objects of the most intense desire in America. These are our highest things; marks of our great men. Office is transient nobility. Money is permanent, inheritable nobility.

—So the North barters away the transient for the permanent nobility. The South is weak in numbers and money, but has the control of the Democratic Party . . . rather the South has the name of the Democratic Party, for that is all of it that is left.

—The North has the numbers and the money. What does he care for politics as long as his dividends are insured. His tribune is Webster, who said the great object of government is the protection of property. If the South can hold a man as property against the humanity of the world, he has little to worry about his warehouse of goods.

—He cares not whether cotton is sold or the man who grows it. He will not keep a drink-hole in the slums, only own and rent it. He thinks it vulgar to carry rum in a jug, respectable in a ship. He sends rum and missionaries to the same barbarians. The one to damn, the other to save, and both for his own advantage, for his patron saint is Judas, the first saint who made money out of Christ.

—He is the stone in the poor man's shoe. He asks what is good for himself but ill for the rest. He knows no right but power; no man but self; no God but his Calf of Gold. Through him all the nation says all dollars are equal, however got, each has inalienable rights. Let no man question that. The morals of a nation, of its controlling class, always get summed up in its political action. The voters are always fairly represented.

He paused and felt a restless stirring in the congregation. Here and there a door slammed as some left in indignation. Four faces in the front stared at him in hatred. He caught the eye of Sam May. Sam shook his head slightly from left to right. He laid aside one or two more pages of invective with reluctance and said defensively, —Some men know these things, but the mass of men know them not.

He touched the blue flags at his elbow. The pain in his side was coming back and his throat felt raw again.

—But I think the mass of men know that this is holy ground we stand on here. Godly men laid here the foundation of a republic, laid it with prayers, laid it with tears and blood. They sought a church without a bishop, a state without a king, a community without a lord, a family without a slave. Yet even here in Massachusetts, which first of our American colonies sent forth the idea of inherent and inalienable rights and first offered the conscious sacrament of blood . . . here in Boston, full of the manly men who rocked the old Cradle of Liberty a week ago last Friday, the rights of man were of no avail. United States soldiers loaded their pieces in Dock Square to be discharged into the crowd of Boston citizens whenever a drunken officer should give command. A six-pound cannon was planted before our Courthouse with forty rounds of canister shot, and manned by soldiers who were foreigners before they enlisted.

He looked down at Sam May as though pleading with him to forgive his intemperance and pounded his fist on the desk until his knuckles hurt, trying to divert the pain that seemed to be pulling his heart down into his pelvis.

—At high noon, over the very spot where fell the first victim in the Boston massacre . . . where the Negro blood of Crispus Attucks stained the ground . . . over that spot Boston carried a citizen to Alexandria as a slave and order reigned, fellow citizens of Virginia.

He felt their sharp restlessness again and gave a long pause. He wanted to take a drink of water but didn't dare. He was afraid it would increase the pain in his side. There was something sticking in his throat. It was anger, he supposed, and looked down at his trembling hands. And then he stretched them out to them in supplication. — Forgive me. It's just that I know not how many of you know your own slavery. I know and honor those of you who held meetings and passed resolutions. I know that the newspapers of Boston threatened to cut off all trade with New Bedford. They would not buy your oil; they would have no dealings with Lynn; they would not tread her shoes under their feet. They would starve out Worcester.

—I try to remember and be just. I know that the natural instinct of commerce is adverse to the natural rights of labor. That the chief leaders in commerce wish to have their workers poorly paid so that the larger gain will fall into their hands. Their laborer is a mill; they must run him as cheaply as they can. So the cities of the North are hostile to the slave; hostile to freedom. The wealthy capitalists do not know that in denying the higher law of God, they are destroying the rock on which alone their money could rest secure.

—The mass of men in cities, the servants of the few, know not that in chaining the black man they are putting fetters on their own feet. Justice is the common interest of all men. Alas, that so few know what God writes in letters of fire in the world's high walls!

He paused here and listened. All were quiet again and the four hostile witnesses in the front row had a look of sadness on their hard faces. His voice was tired. He looked down at the sermon again. There were three more pages of statistics and invective. Pages of shame that would have to be trumpeted forth full-voice. He laid them aside and rested his head a moment on his hands, after taking off his glasses and wiping his eyes. He let his anger and his courage slide off his back for a while. He wanted to reveal his doubts, to throw himself on the mercy of the court. He pushed away the rest of the sermon slowly and holding his glasses in his hand, he gazed at them blindly, seeing no one with his worn-out eyes.

—What then are we to do? There are some among us, men whose ideas I deeply respect, who say, Let us divide. Let our erring sister go in peace. Let us live in a free North, and our wicked brethren in the slave pen and brothel that is theirs. . . . But where shall we draw the line? Today it would have to be made north of Boston. The only line I could draw today would be from Bromfield to Winter Street, back of the Lowell Institute and down Bromfield Place. That contains the only politics I can trust. My own and those of my dearly beloved congregation.

He moved slowly and painfully around the desk and stood free of it to one side, supported himself with a shaky hand. And now, no longer upheld by the desk, his body sagged. He let all the vanity pass out of it; let his great chest sink, his waist thicken, his head droop until the shining brow became the flat, pale, naked skull. The people saw their pastor for the first time as an old man. They saw his eyes weak and lost in their deep sockets without the glasses over them that used to glitter in the light like knives, not for effect but to get truth at its lowest for once.

—Let us for a while put up with slavery. Some of our wisest men tell us that the lot of the Negro has improved immeasurably since he was taken from African soil and savagery. Let us concentrate our powers on improving the lot of the workingman and the unfortunate in our jails, asylums and poorhouses. Let us work to expand our country to the far-off shores of Oregon. Let it remain whole and unsevered and let not the black man be redeemed by the white man's blood. Let slavery die a natural death and fall at last, like a rotten limb from the tree of liberty.

—We could do it. Millions of workers and farmers are doing it. We could close our eyes and ears. Some of us do not see a member of the despised race from one year to the next. Our stomachs will certainly agree. There is not one among you who doesn't stand a better chance of getting rich and eating regularly than Mr. Garrison. Our children's need for education and security will strengthen our intentions.

—Then out of the iron house of bondage will come a man, guilty of no crime but love of liberty. He will fly to the people of Massachusetts. So he comes to us a wanderer and we will take him into an unlawful jail; hungry, and we will feed him felon's meat; thirsty, we will give him the gall and vinegar of a slave to drink. Sick and in prison, he will cry for succor and we will send him the Marshal and his evil *posse comitatus*. We will set him between kidnapers and they will make him their slave. Poor and in chains, he will send around to the churches petitions for their prayers. Churches of commerce, they will give him their curse. He will ask them for the sacrament of freedom. They will say, Thy name is Slave. I baptize thee in the name of the Golden Eagle and the Copper Cent.

He pulled himself back to the desk again and put on his glasses and pitched his voice up into sharpness:

—And while they are reviling Thomas Paine . . . who died poor and ailing, and is thus a good example for our new resolve, as an infidel and an atheist . . . they will lay their hands, as Jesus said, on the man who seeks them out. But where Jesus laid his hand on men to bless them . . . on the deaf and they heard; on the dumb and they spoke; on the blind and they saw; on the lame and they walked; on the maimed and sick and they were whole . . . Boston will lay its hands on the whole and free man and straightway he owns no eyes, no ears, no tongue, no hands, no foot, and he is a slave.

He pushed himself up with both hands on his desk and threw back his head and let the words trumpet recklessly through his burning throat.

—Your own body in its functions will deny you this course. Just as your own body must deny the abstention from eating, from sleeping or from marrying. Just as your body will suffer and corrode if all its duties are not fulfilled. So will it suffer if the function of conscience is betrayed and subverted.

—The function of conscience is this: To discover to men the moral law of God. To discover those things that are true, independent of all human opinions. Such things we call facts. Thus it is true that one and one are equal to two; that the earth moves around the sun; that all men have certain inalienable rights. Rights which a man can alienate only for himself and not for another. No man made these things true and no man can make them false.

—Then it is true that a man held against his will as a slave has a natural right to kill anyone who seeks to prevent his enjoyment of liberty.

—Then it is true that it is a natural duty for the free man to help the slaves to the enjoyment of their liberty and as a means to that end, to aid them in killing such as oppose their natural freedom.

—The performance of this duty is to be controlled by the free man's power and opportunity to help the slave.

—The cloud no bigger than a hand is forming on the horizon. It is filled with blood. Perhaps it is not too late to bring it harmlessly to earth. . . .

—What shall we do? I think I am a calm man and a cool man and I have a word to say as to what we shall do . . . today. Never obey that law. Keep the law of God. Next I say, Resist not evil with evil. Resist not now with violence. . . . Why do I say this? Will you tell me that I am a coward? Perhaps I am. At least I am not afraid to be called one. Why do I say, then, Do not now resist with violence? Because it is not time just yet. It would not succeed. If I had the eloquence I sometimes dream of, which goes into a crowd of men and gathers them in its mighty arm and sways them like the elm boughs when the wind is high, I would call on men and lift my voice like a trumpet through the entire land, until I had gathered millions out of the North and the South and they should crush slavery forever, as the ox crushes the spider underneath his feet.

THE SIN OF THE PROPHET   57

—It seems that this eloquence was not given to me. It is idle to resist by force here and now. It is not the hour. It will come. Let us wait our time. . . . It will come. Perhaps it will need no sacrifice of blood.

—Let us call a convention of all Massachusetts without distinction of party, to take measures to preserve the rights of Massachusetts. For this we want some new and stringent laws for the defense of personal liberty, for punishing all those who invade it on our soil.

—Let us call, then, a convention of all the states, to organize against this new master. It is not speeches we want, but action. Not rash action but organized action before the liberties of America go to ruin. Then what curses all mankind shall heap upon us.

—Remember, oh remember, all you who love this union of ours: It will not stand long as it is. It cannot be saved with slavery in it. No compromise, no nonintervention, no Fugitive Slave Bill. No. It cannot be saved in this age of the world until you nullify every ordinance of nature; until you repeal the will of God and dissolve the union he has made between righteousness and the will of the people. Then, when you displace God from the throne of the world and instead of his eternal justice enforce the will of the devil, then you may keep slavery. Keep it forever. Keep it in peace. Not till then.

—The question is not if slavery is to cease and soon to cease, but shall it end in peaceful legislation, as in Massachusetts, New Hampshire, in Pennsylvania or in New York, or shall it end as in Santa Domingo? Accept this law and it will end in fire and blood. God forgive us for our cowardice if we let it come to this: that three millions, or thirty millions of degraded human beings, degraded by us, must wade through slaughter to their inalienable rights.

He stopped and turned away to spit in his handkerchief. He had been talking through a bubble of blood for the last five minutes. He went shakily off the platform and into his retiring room. The forty-two doors of the Music Hall opened and slammed shut as the listeners left. A line formed in the aisle near his door. They were silent. They were frightened. Dr. Howe and Julia went to the line to take their places. The janitor came through the door and beckoned to the Doctor. The people stood aside. The Doctor opened the door and shut it quickly behind him. Parker was bent over the sink. He turned quickly, red spittle hanging from the corner of his mouth, and laid his hands clawlike on his heaving chest.

—The venomous cat that has destroyed so many of my people has fixed her claws in here.

The Sin of the Prophet ends on a musical recapitulation of its multiple themes, as Theodore Parker and Anthony Burns are reunited. Both are now freed, survivors of the storm and the ordeals. A powerful dramatic irony shapes this conclusion: we understand that this storm will rise again more fiercely at Harper's Ferry in 1859, *at Fort Sumter in* 1861. . . .

At last they passed through the Winter Street passage into the Hall and went first to Parker's office. He gave Tony a chair and then began rummaging about behind a row of books. He pulled out a stethoscope, placed the earpieces properly, opened his coat and sat quietly with his legs spread apart, sliding it at random over his chest. Tony watched him, his brow wrinkled over the complexities of this man.

—I have to hide this, Parker said as he took it off, —like a drunkard's bottle. My wife doesn't like to have me do it in the house; and besides I feel a little ashamed of my illness, as if I had wrecked an estate. But everyone must have his lares and penates, his household gods, and it is not my fault that mine are *râles* and bronchi.

He pushed the stethoscope out of sight behind the books. He spoke this time more quietly, hoarding his voice. —My gods are not gods at all but demons, and they are multiplying like rabbits. I suppose you think I do this to cheat the doctor, but I have six of them and although they disagree in everything else, they all say I am in my grave up to my chin and want me to shut up shop and get out of here.

—Perhaps you should, sir, if you're sick.

—No, no, I must work. I must save from waste a few things half done and finish one or two more which no one else can.

Parker was sitting in a somewhat slumped position and he straightened up, painfully arching his back. —When I sit like this, for instance, I feel something sticking together in my entrails. If I told the doctors about it they would call it an adhesion of the pleura and put me to bed for six months. Tending it myself, someday I will take a big breath and break it loose. The whole truth of the matter is simply that I'm a very tired man.

Tony stood up. —I'd better be going, sir.

—Wait, I haven't shown you what I brought you here to see. This way. He pointed out a short flight of stairs and together they walked onto the stage of the Music Hall. Tony lifted his eyes to the sixty-five-foot ceiling, turned them from side to side at the seventy-eight-foot breadth, and then to the back wall one hundred and thirty feet away. To him it was a house ten houses high, ten houses wide and a hundred houses deep, reckoned by the proportions of the rooms that had been around his humble existence.

—It doesn't look like much without the people in it, Parker said.

But the bareness of the huge confined space filled Tony with awe. From the crescent-shaped windows fifty feet up on the wall came great drives of prism-shaped light, hitting the floor in harsh pools while myriad dust motes sped like arrows upward into blindness. As he followed Parker to the preaching desk at the center of the stage their footfalls echoed as if they were in a great deep cave.

—They want me to give it up and take a smaller hall to save my voice. But I will stay here as long as I am a target and then they'll have to carry me out.

Someone was fingering the organ keys. Parker looked back at the screen in front of the organ. —That's Eben Tourgee. He wants to start a conservatory of music here. He'll just play a few scales, up and down, to make his fingers nimble.

The great statue of Beethoven stood in front of the screen. —There is my colleague, pastor with myself. See how firm he stands, the archetype of a man organized for use. So I have tried to be an organizer of matter, or men, into forms of use and beauty. But I have made myself more of a target than a teacher. There is a revival going on and all the orthodox churches have their guns pointed this way, ready to pour concentric fire into this pulpit. They want me to go away, even to die, so that they can say it is God's punishment on me for speaking against a religion whose emotion is fear and despair before God and hate before men: whose ideas are that man is a worm and God a great ugly boot, lifted up to tread him down with endless crush of misery.

The organist was not playing scales at all but incessantly the wild racing treble run which comes near the end of Bach's Fugue in D Minor.

—I have never faltered in this or any other fight except the night your freedom was at stake at Faneuil Hall. Look about you, Mr. Burns; there are over forty doors here. In Faneuil Hall there was only one. If the meeting had been held here I could have led; back there a tide seethed before me and the rescue we had planned. I was out of my depth. I was the one that failed that night and I alone. I have brought you here to show you my only excuse. Forgive me for the trouble you have endured. Here you see the climate that might have saved you.

He unbuttoned his coat again, thrusting out his chest as if he were gasping for breath, to break the constriction inside.

—I'm going out West to Oberlin College, blurted Tony. —I hope to be a preacher. I hope you don't think hard of this. I know my learning is bad. Some people think I could do good in the name of the Lord. I guess even a man as ignorant as me could do some good in the heathen nations, 'mongst the savages?

He paused and looked anxiously at Parker. There was no reply. —I wish I had your power of speech, he said lamely.

Parker's answer was belligerent. —You have a greater power than I have. Not among the heathen but with your own people in the South where such as I cannot hope to go. Your voice comes from the ground, straight to the level of their ear.

He said this with such assurance, such demanding acceptance, that Tony could not help but smile and say in his humble way, —Who knows if the Lord is going to make of me a Moses?

The sweet shrieking pipes held their retarded gust and the organist, finally satisfied with the tempo of his approach, spread reaching hands and feet into the ringing themes that swept over the keyboard in a race. The wide web of sound blew like a wind at Parker's back and he stood erect again filling his lungs, feeling the membranes fighting against the cleavage.

—Then I will take that for your forgiveness, he said.

—Forgiveness? questioned Tony. —Could I harden my heart against a man who has been given the name of traitor for my sake?

—That was nothing, said Parker, pitching his voice against the timbre of the organ. —Let them call me a traitor. We come from a rebellious nation, our whole history was treason, our blood was tainted before we were born. Our creeds are infidelity to the mother church. Our Constitution is treason to our fatherland. What of it? Though all the rulers in the world bid us commit treason against man, and set the example, let us never submit.

He brought his hand down on the Bible on the preaching desk.

—What of the treason of the prophets? Was not Elijah false to King Ahab and his painted Jezebel?

He turned and looked with annoyance at the organ pipes, now massing long unfurling waves of sound that rolled and crashed against the high walls, bounding back in thunder from the fifty-foot cornices. —We'd better wait out the voice of the whirlwind, he said, turning the Bible open to the rhapsodies of the prophets.

Tony looked again at Beethoven. He was unaccountably raised into a measure of exaltation and he wanted to freeze it into his eyes and ears. In his innocence and with his tribal heritage, the bronze god of sound had twice the power of the soft compliant baby god and mother god of his faith. And like was the power of the naked head of the man at his side, round and clear as the skull beneath it, with the flesh wasted away to a skin's breadth. And he was responsive, too, to the themes in counterpoint, as rich and disturbing as the exhortations of the man beside him. Had not the drumbeats of Tony's fathers surpassed these in complexity? When it came to its end, he heard Parker cough.

—This is my sin, said Parker softly, spreading his finger over the pages. —Besides the felony against our bodies the event did something bad to my spirit. I hated the tensions and disturbances created by the weak being driven against the wall. And I must confess thinking it a pity that a people so ignorant and degraded should be the means of tearing this nation apart . . . this because of my resentment at being forced from my chosen role as a scholar and philosopher and being unable to finish and publish my book. I thought you were all too speechless and submissive, forgetting that your story can only be told in outbreaks and revolutions . . . forgetting that such times gave the brave men who wrote the Old Testament the terrible truths, judgments and revelations that others dared not tell.

He spread his legs wider apart, the muscles of his left arm knotted as he took hold of the edge of the preaching desk with his farmer's plowhandle grip. His right hand he stretched toward Tony.

—But if it were not for these things, these events, there would be no Theodore Parker at this desk and no Anthony Burns on his way to Oberlin College. And my hand would not be reaching now for yours, and nowhere, nowhere in the world would there be FAITH IN MAN.

The Passion by the Brook

The Passion by the Brook moves backward from the furor of the Anthony Burns case to the taproots of the abolitionist-transcendentalist movement. The story describes the development of a commune, Brook Farm, 1840–46, in accord with the theory of Charles Fourier. This complex, often fantastic, theorizing was based on the need to liberate human nature from imposed bonds of culture and civilization, to return to the primal passions that Fourier claimed govern proper human life: sight, cabals (we might say "affinity groups"), touch, smell, taste, hearing, variety, familism, friendship, ambition, love, and composite (we might say "gestalt").

The novel is charged with exhilarating cross-conversations by the finest minds ever shaped in America. George Ripley abandons his church and pulpit to found a colony to put Fourier's revolutionary social and psychological ideas into play with Fellow New Englanders, gathering Theodore Parker, Ralph Waldo Emerson, Henry David Thoreau, and other brilliant minds. More important, he enrolls a cadre of more ordinary folk from the region. The story depicts the attempt by these average mortals to live in Utopia as well as the ideological debates by the mighty-browed communards.

The *idea* of Brook Farm may have been outlandish, risible, exotic. The *fact* of life in such a place is charged with drama and subtle crosscurrents, as Nelson shows. The population of Brook Farm is for

From *The Passion by the Brook* (Garden City, N.Y.: Doubleday, 1953), © 1953 by Truman Nelson.

Nelson a cross-section of humanity, the perfect laboratory in which to test Fourier's prescriptions. What will happen when the passions are freed? How will individuals and groups be transformed? What is the *true* experience of liberty? The drama turns around the will of George Ripley, a practical visionary, and around the tangled relationships of the communards. Violence, anger, frustration, joy and love are liberated in equal measure, so the experience is neither tragic nor comic, the end of the commune not simply a "failure" (as it is usually pronounced). Theodore Parker has the last word in the story when he comforts George Ripley, who believes his dream has perished. Parker cites the great parable of learning and resurrection: "—You fool, you fool, that which thou sowest is not quickened except it die!"

Brook Farm functioned as a seedbed for hope and action, understanding and *feeling* the reality of freedom. The men, women, and children who experienced the commune lived on to contribute to the great act of rebellion and liberation that abolitionism helped to effect. They finally freed themselves as they helped free the slaves. The novel uses musical themes to emblemize the soul awakening to freedom: the Brook Farmers in song, hymns, and vespers, John Dwight playing as reveille the horn call from Beethoven's "Eroica" Symphony, "Lazarus Arise." The steps the Brook Farmers take away from the ashes of the burned Phalanstery lead to a resurrection of the souls dead in slavery. Lazarus is returned from death not simply to please Mary and Martha but to prefigure Christ's resurrection—and ours.

If the narrative ends as a phoenix story, it moves as intensely dramatic encounters between believers and nonbelievers under the banner of Fourier. Some feel that liberty leads to license. Others see the commune as rampant hedonism, paganism, secularism, and revolt against New England's stern, overseeing God. Others see the place demonstrating the innate goodness of humankind, an enabling of potential. Theories of original sin, free will versus determinism, grace, and retribution collide. "Soft" transcendentalism, emphasizing growth, progress, and innocence, confronts "hard" transcendentalism, anchored in beliefs in natural depravity, sinfulness, and the striving to overcome predestined limitations. The churchly shun the unchurched. But all are excited and marked by the experience. They have, like Thoreau at Walden Pond, been forced "to live deliberately, to front only the essential facts of life." Like Thoreau, each Brook Farmer is made to "see if I could not learn what it had to teach, and not, when I came to die, discover that I had not lived." Brook Farm was an *adventure*, a pioneering in the true American way.

The novel encloses a large cast of characters and interwoven stories, fugal or quiltlike in effect. A central story is that of Lili and Adam Smith, Nelson's prototypical husband and wife. Lili is passionate and strong-willed, Adam pliable and pragmatic. Their gradual growth is a main thread in the tapestry—they "prove" the Farm's efficacy. They are liberated from the sexist assumptions of their culture, learning to separate love from ownership.

The novel travels on the axis of Fourier's passions, but the dramatic events and scenes are not mechanical—the story is infused with a sense of the life at Brook Farm. The story is an overture to the great triumphs of abolitionism, like Beethoven's meditative enunciations in the overtures to *Fidelio* or *Egmont* that prepare us for a turbulent drama ahead.

From *The Passion by the Brook*

In a polyphonic "overture" to the full symphony of events at Brook Farm, we hear the intellectual, emotional, and spiritual themes of the commune and its shapers. The theory of social harmony is ready in the presence of George Ripley, Ralph Waldo Emerson, Theodore Parker, and other geniuses of the place. In a kind of symposium, they meet to talk and think, before they open the wide doors of experience.

Overture Passional: 1840

They did not wait for the sunrise but set out under the morning star. George Ripley was watching its reflection now in the brook in front of Charles Ellis' farm, squatting in the bowl of the bank. A tossed stone shattered the image briefly and then doubled, trebled and made it myriad in the widening rings of dark water. The plonk startled him although it was not unpleasant, no more than nature imitating the art of the bullfrog's love note. His mouth opened in involuntary alarm. Drops splashed on his face and he could taste the warmness, rich with the lees of bark, roots, and green and brown tendrils. Trussed in his best black coat and off balance, he fell back into a clover patch. He strained to get up but then he sniffed the morning and, surrendering at last to the goodness of this quick trill on the five-toned gamut of his senses, he brushed his cheek against the grass and breathed deeply. The morning smelled like a fresh-cut watermelon.

He pushed himself up with his palms and found his brother in Israel grinning at him from across the brook. He and this man, settled over a small church nearby, were going on foot to Groton, a walk of thirty miles from where they were in West Roxbury. They were going to break the trip with a night in Concord.

His friend took off his hat and sloshed some water clumsily over his face and scalp. It was the middle of August. The sun had clanged a ring of fire the evening before and Parker's head wore the stamp of the fallen disk on its top, for although he was bald at thirty and hated it and covered it up whenever he could, he had been helping one of his parishioners with a stint of raking and grubbing and the scarecrow wore the only hat in the cornfield.

Ripley was a more comely man all around; was more slender and an inch taller, five nine, with square sharp shoulders in even steps from the straight sides of his long face. Parker's shoulders were big and slightly rounded, his skull poked out from them like a moosehead mounted on a beam and, when he walked, they brushed and rubbed against his companion in a succession of friendly pats and scoffing blows. Ripley, at thirty-eight, had all his hair. It set close to his head and swept across a high forehead like a chaplet, giving him a Roman look, the ends curling so tightly that they scarcely stirred in the morning breeze.

They were to journey to a convention called to establish a committee to unite all the sects of the Christian world under one great creed, ending the babel of intransigent and transcendental tongues, a proposition easily laughed out of countenance at any other place or time but New England in 1840.

Both were dressed in solemn black broadcloth, thick and almost impervious to the dust of the road. They scrambled up from the brookside and swung their legs over the moss-flecked boulders of the wall. Ripley gave a final backward look of love to the farm, its two great bosoms of knolls and beneath them the girdle of water with its binding of overarching trees.

Out of West Roxbury they walked some wild lanes to Newton, to meet a colleague, one Christopher Cranch who was to spend a few days with their Concord host. The three trudged along in quiet for a while, speaking only of country things, judging crops and views, stopping in the heat to slake their thirst among questioning cows, relishing their hay-sweet breath and clasping their short necks in the common response of man to the tenderness of their animal eyes.

At noon they stopped on top of a high hill at a friendly farmhouse to eat some pie and milk. As they sat on the granite slab of the well stoop, picking and eating the crumbs from their coats, Cranch reached into his breast pocket and drew out a sheaf of foolscap. He was a handsome, sad man, at first joining nervously in the laughter he generated in others and then provoking it to hide his desperation. His curse was an alternating plethora of gifts. He was a painter, a composer, a poet, could sing, play the guitar and flute, and was a capable preacher and scholar. But he was beginning to sweep away, in a tide of inconsequent merriment, the banks of each of his channels until they merged into shallow waters, fit only for wading.

He had lately composed some caricatures on an essay called *Nature* by their Concord friend. He unrolled them with elation and guilt. There was no scorn or mockery in them. They underlined more than they distorted the phrases out of which they scrawled. Clearly they said two things: that their friend had resurrected a warm body from the cold corpse of the faith of their fathers and that this body was free to proclaim itself and its organs, indulge its senses and even, in a dim way, affirm its passions. They said that the new faith had no throne for a Pope or a Calvin but was fit for raillery and joy.

Ripley found favorites consonant with his mood . . . a hatted, personified eyeball with a tail coat and long insect legs inscribed, —*I become a transparent eyeball.* And a picture of two huge melons in a field, radiant with content . . . one with a human head, arms and legs and a curved happy mouth saying, —*I expand and live in the warm day like corn and melons.*

Parker was bent double with laughter over a picture of Emerson with his nose, long, belled and pierced like an oboe, fingering it and saying, —*This is my music, this is myself.*

Ripley moved quietly behind him to the brimming, dewy-sided well bucket and, in retaliation for the stone cast into the brook that morning, poured a dipper of icy water, flashing like a silver fish in the sunlight, down Parker's neck. Parker shuddered and jumped to his feet. He caught up the bucket and let the water swirl and fly, cutting a bright arc in the air. Ripley tried vainly to dodge it, lifting his feet away from the splash in a rustic dance. Cranch, his laughter high and uncontrollable in his throat, a cackle and a shriek, scrambled for his papers and got out of range. The farm wife, deep in her butter making, heard it as the raid of a hawk on the chicken yard and came bustling to the door with her husband's old musket.

Under the gun and a cold disapproving eye, the pilgrims retreated.

Their mood held, light heads rising from heavy limbs, even into Concord. They found their friend in his wife's garden behind his square white house. There was a slight mist coming up from the mill brook at its bottom, compounding the dusk. He was kneeling by a discarded spade, looking at his foot. His small boy stood beside him and spoke to them abruptly in a high, petulant voice. —Papa dug his leg.

Emerson showed his wound, a gash on the instep, faintly beaded with blood. Cranch started a phrase of sympathy but was choked off in the middle by an unrepressible giggle. Parker picked up the spade to hide his grin and Ripley turned to measure the larkspur. They did it instinctively, for this man seemed to be able to check every affront to his dignity as an act of sacrilege.

Parker, whose mind ran constantly in parallels, or chords, even— every thought, every sensation a multiple one, with its tonic, dominant and subdominant—saw it as stigmata. Ralph Waldo Emerson is the Christ, he thought.

When their friend stood erect he seemed to be on a different level than the others although he had only gained two or three inches in height. His shoulders sloped swiftly like a wine bottle, putting the whole thrust of his statue on his neck and head, which began to turn, in the wind of discourse, with the slow sway of a solitary stand of pines on a high grassy hill. His face was sharp with the tamed Yankee sharpness but his brow and eyes seemed worn and softened by gentle, thoughtful use. His white garden smock was soiled and negligent and fell in equal classic folds over a flat chest and a straight back. He did not join in the banter with which Parker and Cranch tried to discharge their merriment but took advantage of a replenishing pause to ask them into the house to see a new print of Endymion which his friend Sam Ward had given him as a mate to the Aurora Thomas Carlyle had sent as a present for Lydian, his wife. His voice was surprisingly strong. Parker, who was barrel-chested and who could roar like a bull, was somewhat surprised. He had forgotten this, although he had heard him lecture many times. But then he thought of the long column of air that could travel up through the narrow compact body to the high head and of a trumpet before it is turned into its convenient shape.

The picture was on the south wall of the sitting room and they all admired it. Emerson was glad and said he wanted his house to be like a college, pleasurable for all that had affinity with him and not like some he knew which were only refreshment stalls, playgrounds for boys, places where people came like cats to prowl around and use it without reference or communication with its inhabitants.

Before they turned away from the print Emerson remarked that Sam Ward was writing another article on art for the *Dial*, a little magazine they had just launched, of which Ripley was the assistant editor and to which the others had contributed. He said it in a slow, artificially offhand way, moving the name word into the group as a gambit. It was plain he wanted to talk about the magazine.

Parker had other ideas. —He'd better be quick about it then, he said rudely. —A good puff of wind will blow the whole project away. If I ever saw writing on the sand . . .

—For instance, asked Emerson, slightly affronted.

—Who wrote that piece called *Aulus Persius Flaccus?* I'm willing to grant some place to mystics but they've got to use their own well, or at least their own bucket.

Emerson's head turned slightly to the door at the right opening into his study at the front of the house. Parker followed his gaze and looked directly into a pair of hostile, catlike eyes using a few motes of light to read in the darkened room. He got a quick flash of a thin young man slumped carelessly in a chair who silently got up, crossed the straw carpet without a whisper and went out the front door, closing it with a small crack of annoyance, as an animal, made unwary by anger, breaks a betraying stick in the ear of a hunter.

—Oh dear, Emerson said. —That was the writer of the piece you damned, Henry Thoreau.

Parker shrugged and made no apologies. He had more common sense than politeness. Emerson had just finished saying that he did not like people to use his house like a cat and there had been a wild one in his rocking chair.

George Ripley, as usual taking fire from Parker's flint, said bluntly, —I agree with Theodore. It is quite unworthy, I think, of its pretensions.

—Come now, Ripley, said Emerson. —We have no pretensions. No one gets paid. Margaret has to depend on free-will offerings. Everyone has been asking for this kind of a journal. It is its own excuse for being.

—Here's what I mean by pretension, said Parker. —Your entire manifesto was quoted in the puff in the *Liberator*. Parker drew a clipping from his pocket. —*No one can converse much with the different classes of society of New England without remarking the progress of a revolution. Those who share in it have no external organization, no badge, no creed, no name. They do not vote or print or even meet to work together. They are united only in a common love of truth and love of its work. They are of all conditions and constitutions. Of these acolytes, if some are happily born and well bred, many are, no doubt, ill dressed, ill placed and ill made; without pomp, without trumpet, in lonely and obscure places, in solitude, in servitude, in compunctions and privations, trudging beside the team in the dusty road, or drudging a hireling in other men's cornfields, schoolmasters who teach a few children for a pittance, ministers of small parishes of the obscurer sects, lone women in a dependent condition, matrons and maidens, rich and poor, beautiful and hard favored, without concert or proclamation of any kind, they have silently given in their several adherence to a new hope, and in all companies do signify a greater trust in the nature and resources of man than the laws or the popular opinions will well allow.*

—Ah, the pretensions are all put there by Mr. Garrison. He wants them all to gather into the Anti-Slavery party, said Emerson defensively.

—Why not? said Parker. —Now that they've been recognized, they've got to go somewhere. Unless we teach them German and make them Transcendentalists.

Ripley laughed. —I would rather spend that time on our critics. A knowledge of German is no merit but the want of it in those who undertake to expound German theology is an inconvenience.

—Let them teach us plain English, said Parker. —Let the *Dial* have nothing more Roman than its numerals. If only Margaret could forget Goethe and write more paragraphs like that one.

—As much as I hate both praise and blame, I must confess I am guilty of that manifesto as you call it. Now have I got to go somewhere, Mr. Parker?

—Just let me ask you a few questions . . .

—Oh, there is no terror like being known. Look at my library instead. You can find my connections as well in my Wordsworth, Goethe, Shakespeare and Coleridge as in what I think of war, slavery, alcohol, animal food, creeds and what not. I must go and change for tea. You can see I am no hero. I have regard for appearances still.

Parker planted himself squarely in front of Emerson. —I looked in the Boston *Post* and the *Advertiser* and I found the Philistines as wrathy as fighting cocks over the paper. Under their sneering there is considerable uneasiness. They shy at the word *revolution*. They think it might have a bad effect in State Street. Now are you going to follow up this new declaration of independence and give them the horns and hoofs they are expecting?

Emerson held up his hands, warding him off. —You know there is no heretic less able than myself to give an account if challenged and I am sure I would not want to follow up or make good a thesis as general as the one you mean. I delight in saying what I think but if you ask me why or how, I am the most helpless of mortal men.

—You won't be alone. You can take your pick of half a dozen issues. The paper would get a following among the reformers and sell better all around. You can throw Thoreau and Alcott in as makeweights if you get the scale swinging first.

—Let's say it's Margaret Fuller's journal. I can't take the responsibility.

—But you put the question. Are you going to leave her with it?

Emerson was beginning to lose his self-possession. Not in anger, but to him conversation was effervescent. He often surrendered too early and said things and made commitments he later regretted. He looked down at his smock and lightly flicked it, letting its folds spread and fall together. —I cannot work with the common tools of reform. The principles upon which things are built, the church and the state itself, are false and some of this virus enters into even the smallest details of charity and religion. I sympathize with all of them and their enemies are my enemies but I must persist in wearing a robe of inaction, loose and unbecoming though it may be, until my hour comes when I can see how to act with truth as well as to refuse.

After he left, the room was still alive with something. Cranch studied the pictures and Ripley looked at the books but Parker could not be still. He was a headlong man rather than a restless one and he was always poking the chinks of the wall between saying and doing . . . pauses and events. It was an instinct with him. This was the first time he had found this crack in Emerson. It had caught him unaware. He had ascribed the sentiments that he had been probing to Margaret Fuller and laid them to one side in his mind because he knew she could not back them up. But Emerson, who usually made a Pyramus and Thisbe affair out of the most casual face-to-face discussion, had opened briefly. It made him remember the time when Emerson had been execrated by old Quincy Adams as a failure in the pulpit and the classroom, who had started a new doctrine to unsettle all things and place the universe on the laws of attraction and affinity instead of God Almighty. When there was a sharp flurry over his quitting his pulpit and denying the sacrament of the Last Supper. But Emerson had let it blow out without even seeming to lift a finger to gauge the wind and moved out to Concord and made his way decently with a small income and some remarkably veiled and noncombative lectures that were said to make people's heads ache.

But there was always time for a new revelation and there could be no better moment than this one. Parker moved around the room, trying to relate it to this casual house. What had revelation to do with this curled kitten on the red plush sewing chair, the spines of books, as tepidly brown as the rows of paintings in the Athenaeum? In the hallway fire buckets were hanging. Strange furniture for a prophet.

But it was only Parker's mind that could not relate to the house. It was full of spires, grotesque in their ascending from the common earth of their base. It could not be diluted by a mood. It brought its own furniture and facade with it wherever it went. On its horizon was something grandiose, something better men had projected only by accident or in uncontrollable repulsion. He was meditating in cold blood a new religion and a new idea of God.

Ripley was peering into the books, weighing Emerson's taste. On the whole he was disappointed. His own library was richer by half, with more philosophers and scholars; more books in French and German. Dry wine instead of cordials.

When they sat down for tea, Emerson had his wall up again. But there was no small talk or remarks of inconsequence. His withdrawal made small talk a sin and forced out of each exchange a reason for its being. Parker began to perceive that the compactly limpid conversation of seers never remembers the awkward silences in between. But since the wall could not be breached, Ripley decided to leap it and came up with a good, round, swinging criticism.

—I am much distressed about one of the paragraphs in your article on modern literature.

—Good. Good, Emerson said. —I was hoping something would be a little bad. I have been brooding about Parker's remarks. I think he is partly right.

Parker straightened up in his chair and cleared the dishes away from the front of his place, ready for gesturing and table pounding if needed.

—But, Ripley said, —purely in a literary sense. I think there is a decided falling off in the end of your paragraph on the majestic artist. I think when you look again you will find you have not said what you meant to say.

—Oh, really? said Emerson. —Let's have a look at the manuscript. He rose from the table. Ripley joined him and Parker reached again for his half-empty teacup.

—The words *eloquence* and *wealth* thus grouped have rather a bourgeois air, Ripley said as they walked on into the study.

—What about *dreadful melody?*

—That too. You know how I hate prettiness. And *dreadful* has become vulgarized.

The graciousness and serenity of their hosts had plunged Cranch into melancholy. The caricatures were burning a hole in his breast. He wished he had not brought them and hoped devoutly that there would be no reference to them from the others. He turned to his hostess with an excessively flattering remark about her garden, something about the bright flowers in the moonlight. To his dismay she took it up with a sharp contradiction. Lydian had a shrewd turn to her mind. It was factual, trained by her brother Dr. Jackson, an excellent scientist and theorist. Lightly she demolished his vaporings on color under the moon and insisted that he come with her to the garden at once to see for himself the truth of the matter. As he rose to let her pass in front of him, he put his hand on the bulge of papers in his pocket and then, smiling as he followed her, wished he were dead.

Parker decided revelation had shut up shop for the night and went into the study to pay his respects before going to bed. The literary discussion was still going on. Goethe. Goethe again. —You will have to admit, Emerson said, —that he unlocks the faculties of the soul more than any other writer. He teaches us to treat all subjects with greater freedom and to skip over all obstructions, time, place, name, usage and come full and strong on emphasis of the fact. I read little else but his books lately to start my flow of thoughts. Look what he has done with Margaret. He has made her pregnant with artistry.

He looked up startled as Parker came in. In the lamplight he seemed to blush.

Parker smiled. If she is, he thought, it was an immaculate conception and the only one the poor girl will ever have. He held out his hand to say good night, his eyes measuring Waldo again. . . . Yes, you are the Christ but a very sectarian one, with Margaret the Virgin and Goethe the Father. . . .

—Wouldn't you like to stay up a bit and talk some more about the *Dial?* asked Emerson.

—He doesn't believe in faith without works, said Ripley.

Parker picked up a book at random from the table. —I'd like to read awhile, he said. It was a small book titled *The Social Destiny of Man.* Emerson raised his hand suddenly as if he were going to take the book away. But it was evidently an involuntary motion which he disguised by waving in the direction of the hallway.

—You and George are in the room across the hall. I hope you don't mind doubling up in the cannon-ball bed. Oh, you've got Brisbane's book. It's very good. I wrote a notice for it in the *Dial*. Fourier is one of your men and a good one. This is the best thing I have ever read on the evils of society and it even offers some prospects for their removal.

As Parker bathed in the cool water of the night, he felt the wetness dissolve the thought tracks on his tired face as well as the dust of the road from his feet. He vowed to keep himself inchoate on this journey, to force no more, to keep his mind a clean script for impressions, to meditate on the new Christology.

While he read by candlelight in the huge old high bed, he half listened to the voices across the hall.

Fourier, expounded through his prophet Brisbane, spoke loudly enough.

WE ASSERT THAT THE PRESENT SOCIAL MECHANISM IS NOT ADAPTED TO THE NATURE OF MAN AND HIS PASSIONS: THAT IT PERVERTS, MISDIRECTS AND DEVELOPS THEM SUBVERSIVELY AND THAT THE SELFISHNESS, OPPRESSION, INJUSTICE AND CRIME NOW PREVALENT ARE ATTRIBUTABLE TO THIS AND NOT TO ANY INBORN, INHERENT DEPRAVITY IN THE HUMAN BEING HIMSELF. THE BELIEF IN THE FATALITY OF EVIL HAS SUNK SO DEEP INTO THE MINDS OF MAN THAT IT HAS ERADICATED ALL HOPES OF COLLECTIVE HAPPINESS ON THIS EARTH.

A well-known phrase of Emerson's came to his mind with such force that it seemed spoken at the moment into his ear. *All things are moral. Every animal function from the sponge up to Hercules can hint or thunder to man the laws of right and wrong. Every natural process is a version of a moral sentence.*

He laid the book on the thin counterpane and listened intently, wondering if he had heard it concurrently with his reading. But George was speaking now, unintelligibly, his full rumbling voice only a drone bass for Emerson's higher piping. He took up the book again, looking avidly to find other tokens of this correspondence of thought.

Fourier-Brisbane were not satisfied with the old house men lived in. Not only did they condemn it but they had a new set of plans well drawn. Its façade was presented in a frontispiece to the book. It was an elegant etching of a congeries of buildings as urban and massive as the

Vatican. But not set in the midst of stews and kennels as a stepping rock out of the mire of the world but among fresh fields with a clear stream and wooded hills beyond. It was plainly a New Heaven and New Earth, stated as concretely as a land deed: a place to live, an integrated Phalanx by name, a body politic with human attractions for laws, deeming them as irrevocable as the law of gravity . . . a body economic, with a guaranteed yearly dividend of five per cent for those who invested either their capital or their labor. Its destinies were to be guided by people's honest passions instead of their frightened prayers; no hell there, but a simple acknowledgement that God must have wanted men to indulge their passions since He had bestowed them so variously and so strong. And its great incentive to be labor made attractive, since man had to work . . . and had stupidly neglected to make the best of it.

Then he heard George's good solid thrum and rumble saying that every man should do some work with his hands, if only as an example, only to create unity. And then Emerson sounded out in tones very unusual . . . full of excitement.

—Work, yes! Work. If only to prove that the man of genius has no right to retreat from it and indulge himself. That, of course, is our present literary creed. A farm is a poor place to make a living when one is alone but if it could be a means to slough off the nonsense of living for show . . . to make labor such a point of honor that coxcombs will work, even the artist might lose sight of this individuality which lays boundaries around him. Must we accept the new God that is starting up behind the cotton bales, this new monarchy of trade more tyrannical than Babylon or Rome!

This was the first time Parker had ever heard passion in Emerson's voice. He had thought him incapable of it, with his heritage of eight generations of preachers. It was strong meat for a dedicated water drinker, an orderly citizen and a cold man whose natural virtues sustained the very institutions his phrasemaking threatened to destroy.

—Certainly, the voice continued, —virtue has its own arithmetic as well as vice and the pure must not eat the bread of the impure but must live by the sweat of their brow. Otherwise we are as false as those we reprobate. When first we are stricken with some light from heaven we can only see death around us, a dead-alive population, war without end as far as the horizon. But God says, Come out, come out from this death once and forever. Not by hate of death, but by a new and larger life is death to be vanquished. We must obey the prompting of that which is creative, passionate, inventive, prodigal of life and beauty. The power of love as the basis of a state has never been tried. We pay unwilling tribute to governments founded on force. Cannot thousands exercise toward each other the simplest sentiments, like a knot of friends or a pair of lovers?

Parker, not certain whether they were talking about the book or running parallel to it, looked at the etching again and suddenly felt the push and pull of these two heads together in the other room were bringing it to life. It seemed to be being impelled toward him, no longer a grandiose backdrop. Organic opinions were being set forth in his hearing, wrung from the convolutions of two worthy and respected brains and capable of moving the stones of the steel-limned new city of light into place.

Emerson's next words rang out heedless of the sleeping house. —If we do have a new religion, let's not make it a cultus as before but a heroic life!

With this he blew out the lamp and he and Ripley tiptoed out into the hallway on their way to the kitchen. Parker was tense in his bed. He thrust one leg to the floor, thinking in his excitement to go to the kitchen and look into their faces and see if they had made genuine commitments together to begin a new life, to make a revolution. But then he heard Emerson say in a covert, secretive way, —When Jesus bade his disciples not to tell of this and that he would say, Lie low in the Lord's power. Receive this fact onto your mind in silence.

Since a wink is as good as a nod to a blind horse, Parker drew back into bed, biding his time.

Ripley came later into the room and began to undress. Parker had left the candle by the bedside burning but was lying inert. From half-shut eyes he could see a seraphic smile on Ripley's face. A little later there was a soft knock on the door and Emerson came in. He had a towel over his arm and was bearing a basin of water. —I know you want to bathe your feet after your long walk. I should have thought of it before.

Parker watched through narrowed eyes as Ripley bowed his head, almost in genuflection. . . . Ah, yes. Ripley is the Simon Peter and on his church Emerson will build his rock but it will crush it and roll away, for it is the kind that gathers no moss. Then from under his arm Emerson drew a manuscript.

—Here are some more of Alcott's sayings, he said. —I know you and Margaret don't like them either but I wish you'd make a place for them in the next issue.

Move over for the Holy Ghost, thought Parker.

He could see Ripley frowning; see his desire to spurn it.

—Grant me this, said Emerson. —I myself will not be with you very long, I fear. I am so busy with my own work but I would rather trust our material to persons in whose affections I have a sure place than eighty or ninety other contributors.

He tiptoed over to the bed and lifted the candle. But Parker, feigning sleep, turned away from his light.

The reality of Brook Farm was more wonderful and various—and more turbulent and unpredictable—than its founders foresaw. By the middle of the adventure, flesh, mind, and spirit are mixed in their whirling chemistry of real life. The ideals of the dreaming transcendentalists are tested in these few acres of Massachusetts farmland.

—Per omnia saecula saeculorum.

Lili awoke with a start. She heard the Latin words coming through her wall and she thought she was back in the convent. She sat bolt upright in her bed. She was clasped with fear. In the haze of awakening hung a weight of guilt. She had overslept early Mass . . . someone was dying and being given the last rites. She shook her head and thought of Adam as she did every morning now. He was wedged in layers through all of her strata and as the moments cut through her consciousness like a knife through a cake she felt him there like a sweet toothsome filling to be relished at will.

Adam. She shook back her hair, held it to her shoulders and lay solemnly back on the bed. She smiled up at the ceiling and dropped her straw-colored strands over her shoulder. Then she pushed the ends gently with her palms to make them curl up. And then with her eyes closed and her mouth curved in wickedness, she put her hands under her breasts and pushed them up until they stood like domes.

—*Dominus vobiscum. Et cum spiritu tuo. Sursum corda. Habemus ad Dominum.*

Lili shifted to her side and lifted herself on one elbow. The blessing and the response were both said by the same person. It was Charles Newcomb again, practicing the Mass.

She reached under her pillow and took out the sonnet. She needed its reassurance. She hadn't seen Adam alone since the night of the storm. She had boldly taken her place at the Graham table but there had never been a seat beside him and he talked to her no more than to the others.

But as she read it, the invitation it had held before, so avid and grasping, had disappeared. Before it had led from nothing to something and now it led to nothing again . . . or at least to a very ephemeral state of affairs. She read parts of it aloud to drown out Newcomb's dreary, stumbling chanting.

—*Strangely enough, I care not when or where . . .*
Nor do I seek you at set hour or date.

She put it down. It was really quite dreadful. It made a pledge of inconstancy, a bond of chance. The frightening thing was that Adam meant it that way. He was so young, or so crazy, that he would be perfectly capable of never seeking her or claiming her or even wanting her but just waiting until some unplotted mesh of circumstances put them together again alone and in secret.

It gave her a sharp sense of loss or at best suspension. If it had said, *love you till I die* and all that and aroused her doubts by overstatement, it would have been less disturbing. There is always compensation for insincerity. But you can't get around the truth.

She was now so disturbed at the gulf of luck opening up between herself and Adam that she began to pray, wildly, fervently, that something would happen to bring them together soon by the code laid down by him like a sword between them.

Afterward she was ashamed and got up and dressed. She had no barn work that morning. It was past time for it now anyway. George had told her to lie abed to show her independence. That was his salute to the day.

Before she started down the stairs she listened at Newcomb's door. He was still at it. She herself felt somewhat helpless at the moment and at odds with a mystery. She wondered if he had some kind of a household shrine in there, some minor relic, a saint's picture or even a withering sheaf of palms to which she could kneel for a while, and cast up her discontent. She knocked.

Charles opened the door a crack and, seeing her, threw it wide. — *Pax vobiscum*, he said.

She looked at him in surprise. He was twirling a large silver crucifix in his fingers. It hung from his neck by a chain. He was in his shirt sleeves with his wide linen collar open to the chest. His hair was hanging down over his forehead, completely obscuring one eye. Instead of brushing it back he tilted his head over to his shoulder so that the hank would swing free.

—Could you be my choir? he asked with a smile. —For the antiphons, you know.

Lila had to admit that there was something rather fascinating about Newcomb. She could not resist going into his room to see what he was up to. He led her to a table which he had fixed up as an altar. There were four candles burning on it and a missal lay open at a Solemn Mass.

—Do you know any Masses . . . I mean to sing? Newcomb said, swinging his face out of his hair.

—I once went to a convent, said Lili. —But I think I've forgotten everything. At least I've tried to.

—Oh, I don't mean that dreary stuff. I mean like Handel or Mozart. Do you know anything from the Requiem Mass? The Lacrymosa?

—No, said Lili.

—But surely you must know *The Magic Flute*, it's priceless. You remember the *Largo al Factotum*. Newcomb began to sing it in an uproarious squeak.

Lili looked over at the altar. There was a huge bowl of roses there and he had spread some of the petals in a pattern around the edge of the water-soiled cloth.

—Oh yes, said Newcomb, stopping short. —Where were we? He put his finger on the missal. —Uh-huh. At the wine.

—Are you going to become a Catholic?

—Perhaps, said Charles with a shrug. —In my fashion.

—What is your fashion?

—Everything for beauty's sake. You see, I've already made improvements. He picked up the bowl and waved it about. —For incense the natural scent of flowers. I believe God made flowers celestially and that they are covered with heavenly little fairies.

—But the incense is supposed to burn. It's part of the sacrifice.

—Oh yes, I know the Mass is a sacrifice but how much of a sacrifice must it be? I mean, good heavens, the purest incense rising from the holiest altar will form a cloud and smoke up the pictures. I mean, take those of Raphael and Guido. They're priceless. They shouldn't be all smoked up.

—But they won't let you do this, said Lili.

—Who are they? Why should I give in to them? I mean, I say the Mass but I don't believe it. I just don't think but as I go on it seems as if thought takes form within me and stays in my spiritual inworld. It makes me love humanity.

He lifted the rose bowl again. —Isn't this better than smoke dimming my pictures? There you are. Newcomb placed his finger on the picture of Fanny Elssler which was hanging, as he had said, between prints of Saints Francis and Loyola.

Lili turned her head away and wrinkled her nose in disgust. —You should change the flowers or the water. They smell rank.

—Oh dear, my roses are festering, said Newcomb. —Worse than weeds. He opened the window and threw them out with a swish. —I'll get some more.

—Why don't you use flowers of the proper color? said Lili. —The colors change with the Mass, you know.

—That's right, said Charles. —I'd forgotten. I suppose it's red, white and blue for the Fourth, he said, winking gaily.

—I think they take the color of the feast, said Lili. —Wednesday was a feast day . . . The Visitation of the Blessed Virgin Mary. That's white.

—How lucky you are to know these things, said Charles. —Sometimes I wish I knew more but then I have to agree with Goethe that only faulty knowledge is creative.

He reached for his coat and put it on. —Would you like to come with me for some new flowers? he said.

Lili said yes and helped him on with his coat. She pulled down his sleeves with a motherly gesture but his gaunt wrists hung inches out of them anyway. She decided she liked Newcomb. He made her feel sure and confident. Perhaps something could be done with him after all. Perhaps he could fill a certain place.

When they got out of the house she turned in the direction of the greenhouse.

—No, said Charles. —Not man-made flowers. These must be secret and innocent. It just occurred to me that those roses were nourished with manure. Awk.

He spat disgustedly. —How could I have done such a thing? They were so beautiful but growing from a dungheap actually.

He began to walk rapidly over the hill and down to the swamp on the backlands. —We must find some small white flower among the ruins . . .

—What ruins? asked Lili obtusely.

—Among the ruins of the sea ages . . . near the sunken rocks or in a cave within a cleft. Somewhere unspecially in nature.

He began to run down the slope and Lili, following, felt a kind of wild pleasure. As he ran through the hummocks, he held out his arms loosely like a child and they jiggled and flapped into elongated forms and contortions saintlike, ascetic and oddly appealing. No wonder, thought Lili, these men with their frail squirmings and white, passionate withdrawals have been in constant flight from the seductions of lusty wenches.

He stopped abruptly and looked over a stone wall at the end of the good pasture land. His face was even more hawklike in profile. But his upper lip was soft and sunken under the great nose and the whole effect was not predatory but sad, as a hawk out of flight is the most melancholy of birds except for his cousin the vulture.

He looked down at her. She had never seen him stand erect before. His hair, whipped by the run and the wind, stood up straight. The bone line of his jaw was darkened with down. His sunken cheeks held purple shadows. He turned his head familiarly to sway his lovelocks and, finding that they were gone, rolled his big, staring eyes slowly toward his forehead. His shoulders drooped again and he held his hands in front of his groin as if shielding it. He was like a wild prophet from the wilderness, living on locust and honey. His body, beneath his clothes, was as familiar to Lili as her neglected prayer book. It was the one in the holy pictures of the saints and martyrs with the bareboned hollow chest, the narrow, square shoulders with one pulled higher than the other . . . the red-lipped wounds on the white-green luminous skin and the crumpled napkin folded over the cloistered privates. And above all the eyes, the veined eyes turned up in the ecstasy of submission.

Lili felt a wicked atavistic desire towards him. She felt conscious as never before of her own roundness and strength and the power and perfume of her flesh. What fun it would be to seize him around the waist and squeeze until his backbone cracked and throw him down on the grass as the men did to the women. She could almost feel him fighting and squirming under her legs, fighting for his virginity. What a sense of power a man must have in a secret place with some frail excited girl reaching for honey and resisting faintly, doomed to succumb to beauty, ready to become impaled on it.

Newcomb, looking down at her, widened his eyes at her calculating look. She had her hands on her hips. Her head was bent back and her high cheekbones narrowed her eyes to fiery slits. She reached out suddenly and seized his slender wrist. She could not resist giving it a little twist. —Oh, said Charles, pulling it away. —You're very strong.

Lili turned away, spread her legs apart and stretched and yawned like a big cat. She had a racing feeling in her. The hot sun seemed to be pressing on her back, urging her on. She threw herself on the grass. —Let's rest awhile, she said. —I feel dizzy.

She rolled slowly back and forth. The sun was drawing up the perfume from her body. The sharp-edged nostrils in Newcomb's arched nose began to dilate. He knelt slowly on one knee and pretended to brush the clover for a hidden flower. She sat up suddenly. He swerved and then stood. She lifted her face and closed her eyes. She felt him move suddenly and she opened her eyes. He was scrambling to the top of the wall. With a frightened look back at her, he leaped to the ground on the other side. His coattails flapped wildly.

There was a long silence. She chewed a slip of grass and then got up. —What is it? she called. —Did you find the flower? She looked coyly over the wall and there he was, thrashing about and nearly up to his waist in a stinking quagmire. —Help, he said. —Help me out.

There was a branch nearby, wrenched from a tree in the late storm.

She dragged it to the wall and pushed it over to him. When he got his hands around it she left him there and ran back up the hill alone. Then she went to the milk room and broke the butter churn so Adam would have to come and fix it before the cream soured.

It was hot near the end of July and the older people were getting fretful and restless. It was too hot for the nightly dances and some of the young people were slipping away to bathe in the Charles near Cow Island. Sophia was becoming greatly concerned with this and she broached a plan to George which he accepted without great enthusiasm.

This was to establish a makeshift water cure down by the brook in imitation of the big one at Brattleboro. Sophia argued that at least it would cool the fevers in young blood and give them something to think about besides the warm and languorous brown waters of the Charles.

So Adam had fixed up a stilt-legged corncrib, calking it with oakum and pitch so that it would act as a tank. With the elevation of its long legs it could discharge a heavy gush of water down the chute with the lifting of a gate.

Mr. Orange, their resourceful neighbor, had run short of hay and was willing to swap a load of ice for some. The ice was melting now in the crib.

Adam had wanted to construct an Archimedean screw to carry water up to the tank but Sophia ruled it out. This, she said, was a wonderful opportunity to organize the children—the little hordes, as Fourier called them—in a useful task. So they were all given fire buckets and, while the eldest stood on a ladder, water was passed up, human-chain fashion, from the brook.

George was rather intrigued with this, after it got started, and was watching with great interest. John Dwight stood by with his horn and Marianne had a banner to reward them with, that they could carry off in a triumphal march after their project was completed.

Unfortunately, Theodore Parker, with his uncanny sense of picking a critical moment to appear on the scene, arrived and stood watching the folderol with the ends of his eyes bent up like a kindly satyr.

George tried to draw him off for a walk but Parker planted his heavy boots and smirked. He was neatly dressed in his broadcloth coat and George had his usual shock of wonder over it, that this man, so rebellious and overflowing, could attire himself daily and consistently in a strait dress of office. Parker's broad and bony face, with the jutting cheekbones, like a fighter's fists protecting the tender sensitive eyes, was clean-shaven to a ruddy patina and exuded a faint scent of bay rum.

George clawed at his own tousled beard, disengaging a furtive snarl, and brushed a strand or two of hay from his smock. He tugged a moment at his torn straw hat, intending to conceal its decomposition by holding it at his side. But he reconsidered this move, thinking perhaps it might wound his friend by calling attention to the contrast between his thick-thatched head and the other's flagrant baldness.

Parker was carrying a sheaf of papers, obviously a sermon, in his hand and he thrust it at George without turning to look away from the goings on. —Read this, he said. —You might want to put it in your paper.

George bent his gaze to it, scanning it quickly so as to make it a conversation piece and so divert Parker from further ceremonies and rituals to come.

The tank was filled. The trumpet blew a flourish. Marianne presented the banner to the youngest child and he took the head of the file and the children marched up to the kitchen for cookies and milk. Then out of the Hive came a half dozen giggling girls, wrapped from head to toe in sheets and shepherded by Sophia. They pressed together under the chute of the crib, shivering and twitching in anticipation of the ordeal to come. Adam was in position up top, ready to lift the water gate at the proper signal.

—What's all this, George? asked Parker with an irritating drawl.

—Water cure, answered George tersely.

—Thank heaven for that. I thought for a moment the girls were wearing bridal veils and you were putting an injunction from one of your predecessors into effect.

—What predecessor? asked George innocently.

—Oh, Sir Thomas More. In his *Utopia* he recommended that a staid and honest matron showeth the woman, be she maid or widow, naked to the wooers.

—I'd like to see that staid and honest matron show you to the edge of that tank and push you in.
—Do you think I need it?
—Certainly. Here you are trying to embarrass me with talk of nakedness just because some uninteresting young girls are taking a cold bath wrapped in sheets. Look at the other people around here. They're completely unconcerned. The carpenters are pounding up there with a full view of the proceedings. The boys are putting hay into the loft. The children are eating their cookies. With all this life around us, all this action and effort, I doubt whether there is one carnal thought.

Parker looked around. What George said was true. The air was full of noisy inattention. When Adam lifted the board and let down a huge jet of ice water on the maidens, falling on them like a cluster of iron balls, their shrieks were unheard in the cacophony of work sounds all around them.

—What do you think of the sermon? asked Parker.

George hated to answer him. Reading the pages had made him melancholy and filled him with a deep sense of waste. It seemed to him magnificent in its way, as Parker's style often was, alive and electric with whipping and pleading, the push and pull of opposite tensions. And all for the sake of a scant hundred persons, many of them adolescents, grouped in a little backwater church here in West Roxbury. And there were hundreds of others like this, over a hundred written every year for less than a hundred listeners. This one was on merchants . . . *the bad ones, who think it vulgar to carry rum about in a jug, respectable in a ship. Who make paupers and leave others to support them. Tell them not of the misery of the poor, they want more jails and speedier gallows. They send rum and missionaries to the same barbarians, the one to damn, the other to save, for their patron saint is Judas, the first saint to make money out of Christ.*

George felt Parker looking at him. He could feel his breath on his neck. He knew he could not evade the question and only postponed it. He flipped over the pages to the end, double-thinking, trying to pass his critique off in a jest. *It is for you,* he read, *who own the machinery of society, to see that no class appropriates to itself what God meant for all. Remember, it is as easy to tyrannize by machinery as by armies and as wicked. Let men not curse you, as the old nobility, and shake you off, smeared with blood and dust.*

A small flick of anger came to him with saving grace. He recalled that Parker not long ago had been asked how the Farm was getting along and his faithless friend had delivered an eminently saucy answer. The exact wording came at once to mind and he turned it skillfully on his dumfounded friend.

—Your sermon in combination with the little church of yours reminds me of a new and powerful locomotive dragging a train of mud cars.

—That's my line, said Parker indignantly. —Where did you pick it up? I said it about you, you know.

—I know, said George. —Faithless friend.

—Oh no. Faithful are the wounds of a friend. Now about the sermon.

—First of all, it is not a sermon. Your text, *As a nail sticketh fast between the joining of stones, so doth sin stick close between buying and selling* . . . This is not from the Bible at all but from the Apocrypha. That will never do.

—As a liberal theologian I . . .

—You are not a theologian, interrupted George. —You repudiate the Trinity, the Devil and Original Sin and reject the plenary inspiration of the Bible.

Parker winced; he was in his own opinion a profound theologian. He would stake his life on it; he was spending the better part of every day studying theology. —What about the content? he demanded.

—The content has nothing to do with it, said George. —I'm not saying that it's not well put. You handle words as if they were knives. They glitter and dazzle, almost charm people, and then they cut to the bone. But what's the good of this in West Roxbury? There's barely three merchants in the whole town.

—Oh, I'm preaching a series in Boston, at the Melodeon. It's just for a while. I can't bear to leave my Patmos in the village.

—How are you being received?

—Well, the first handshake I gave after my first sermon went to a lady who damned me as a heretic in a good set speech. But we're drawing a goodly crowd. The hall is full.

—Why don't you come out from the Church, Theodore? said George bluntly.

Parker flexed himself, giving involuntary testimony of a strong personal struggle. —Because I like to attack and destroy false gods.

George shook his head. —I can't understand how you get by with these ideas of yours. . . . How have you been able to stay in a pulpit as long as this?

Parker laughed. —Every week I preach monstrous heresies. I see my people's faces glow like new-stirred fires. I must confess I don't think they understand me fully. Else they would cast me out.

—But isn't that dishonest? said George. —Isn't that sailing under a false flag?

—Why no, said Parker, nettled. —The truth is there for them to take. What about you here with your talk about the passions? What if people here believed and acted on what you say?

—How do you define the passions? answered George.

—As the old monkish foe. In college I acknowledged them every night by praying to the Lord to free me from my licentious imagination.

—Nonsense. If I read Fourier as you do I could accuse you of lusting after seven wives and concubines because you revere the piety and beauty of the psalms of David.

—Haven't you felt the stormy passions that sweep like a tornado through the heart? When I was courting Lydia . . .

—How long was that?

—About four years.

—We have been courting Fourier only two. Perhaps our passions are still unappeased but they are under control as yours were in your courtship. When our ideas are consummated things may change.

—How long did you court Sophia? asked Parker.

Another jet fell from the ice tank and the shrieks came up again. The girls huddled together, seeking warmth from one another. Sophia, with an iron hand, pushed them apart.

—My regard for my wife was not based on passion but on respect for her intellectual power, her refinement, her dignity and piety.

—You're very lucky, said Parker dourly. George knew he didn't mean it and he was glad. Otherwise his last remark would have been a slur. Parker's wife was neither pious nor intellectual. And many people had expressed pity for him as a husband whose wife could not meet his standards as an intellectual and serviceable helpmate. Lydia was as dainty and beautifully useless as a jonquil, walking always as if she were going to fall and then fall as lightly as a flower on the grass.

Parker began looking around, caught up as always by the activity in all quarters, making his choice over a joke with woodcutters, a political discussion with the cobbler or a few friendly heaves with the boys in the hayfields, when a sudden and compelling silence seemed to fall over the air. The hammers ceased, the children hushed and the girls stopped giggling. They were all looking at the brook.

Lili had kicked off her shoes and was wading there as she did every day. The water was dark in depth but on the surface, between the throbbing basalt shadows of the trees, there were spiral veins of gold. She lifted her skirt as the water grew deeper and her white legs gleamed. She moved vibrantly through the water, shifting and pausing in the play of light and shade as her feet pressed delicately on the uneasy bottom. One hand was gathering up her skirt and the other was holding her hair in a topknot on her head. The angle of her arm was crisp and the body beneath it was tremulous.

—I wish she wouldn't do that, said George.

—Oh, nobody's paying any mind, said Parker gleefully. —But the carpenters seem suddenly to be out of nails to pound and the men pitching hay are leaning on their forks, to test them, no doubt.

Lili's dress was slightly above her knees now and she hadn't reached the middle of the brook.

—Let's hope it won't get any deeper, said Parker.

—There's a hole there, said George. —Up to her thighs. The men all watch to see if she will step into it.

—Don't you love to look at a handsome woman, George? Oh, I love to feel the presence of woman incarnate.

—I think that girl knows very well about that hole and walks just barely around it to tease them. Now why should she do that, Theodore? Do you think that's right?

—That's the marvelous subtlety of a woman's mind, George. They could never be blunt and direct like us. It's a lovable thing, that nimble adroitness. There are some women who advance on you like a regiment of soldiers but . . .

He paused briefly and looked aside. Sophia had come upon them, not at all like an army with banners, but silently, as always, in an almost invisible motion as if her feet had no heel-and-toe action at all but rolled under her tubular dress with mechanical perfection.

—I see Mrs. Gray is making another exhibition of herself, said Sophia sharply.

George jumped.

—It's like ladies' day at the Athenaeum, said Parker. —We all join in the worship of beauty. Beauty is truth and truth beauty, as the poet says.

—Beauty is only on the outskirts of truth, said Sophia. —That's what is wrong with this place.

George toyed for a moment with the idea of punning on beauty being very definitely out of skirts but thought better of it and said, — Now don't get riled at this, Sophia. It's all quite harmless.

—Isn't it about time someone spoke again of the purposes that brought us here in the beginning? she answered. —I, for one, thought this scheme was to remove some of the external obstacles to leading a saintly life. Instead, at every turn I seem to see Mrs. Gray or one of her imitators indulging their own emotions or exciting the emotions of others. They seem to prefer warm baths and spiced wine to the clear crystal spring waters of the spirit.

—What can I do? murmured George. —I can't forbid her the brook.

—You can talk to her, inspire her as you did me of old. She seems very attached to you.

Parker cleared his throat significantly. —Ah, George, have you a Bettine, like the master, Goethe?

Sarah Stearns broke from the clump of maidens and came swathed, shivering and blue-lipped over to Sophia. —Can we stop now, Aunt Sophia, and wade a little in the brook, like Mrs. Gray?

—Certainly not, said Sophia firmly. —You must stay until all the ice water has been used. Then you must walk vigorously about, wrapped in your cold sheets, until you have your crisis.

—But, ma'am, whined Sarah. —Adam isn't up there any more. There's no one to let the water out and we're perishing with the cold. See, he's down at the brook.

Indeed he was, loafing there as if he had no work to do, carefully looking away from Lili, but not enough not to see her reflection in the water. Lili kicked the water once or twice, trying to splash some indignant starlings perched on a slow-sliding derelict branch and turned to come out, her dress falling evenly as the water shallowed. As she got to the bank Adam reached out his arm to help in an offhand way, his back toward her in elaborate casualness, but she ignored it and pulled herself out with a heave on a willow sapling. She looked down with faint concern as the dust clung to her wet feet and Adam quickly unbuttoned his shirt and spread it on the grass for her to tread on and dry herself.

Young Sarah sighed romantically and Sophia remarked that it was the first act of politeness she had ever seen him commit. —He seems to be quite smitten with her, she added.

George demurred. —He's just a boy. She's a grown woman and a married one in the bargain, he said.

—That's just it, said Sophia shrewdly. —You've read chivalrous tales of young minstrels and pages being preferred by princesses while their stalwart lord was off to the wars. I'm beginning to suspect young Adam has, taking his cue from Sir Walter, as he did.

—You're apparently suspecting a lot of things, Sophy, said George gloomily. —They haven't even touched, they haven't even danced together.

But if there was any truth for George in this it was soon canceled out as Lili, with one foot raised to put her slipper on, swayed out of balance and fell against Adam's chest. They could see his muscles tense as he slowly righted her.

—There, you see, George, said Sophia. —I've never observed her that close to her own husband.

—No wonder, said Sarah. —Mr. Gray smokes cigars.

—That's enough, Sarah, said Sophia.

—I smelled Adam's chest this morning and it was delicious. Just like new-mown hay. Mr. Gray smells awful.

—Mr. Smith, called Sophia anxiously. —Would you mind attending to the water again and let the rest of it down on the girls?

—Oh no, Aunt Sophia, wailed Sarah. —Not again.

—You must, Sarah. You have become overexcited lately. I'm quite concerned about you. I've seen many girls in your overcharged state go into a brain fever, acquiring pulmonary sickness . . . or worse.

With a deep sigh Sarah plodded over to the other girls standing in the cold mire and waved her hand disconsolately at the water chute above.

Adam was taking his time about going back. He knelt for Lili's slipper in the grass and put it on her foot. For the first time Lili saw the group watching her. She pushed his hand away in embarrassment.

Parker turned heavily and looked again at the girls at the water cure. They stood in attitudes of abject resignation, their lank hair falling on their unnaturally red cheeks, their feet splayed out from tight-held knees, their backs bent in a hump of anticipated agony. He let a great gruff rush of air out of his lungs, an unphrased statement of disapproval so challenging that Sophia could not resist a defense.

—Don't you approve of the science of Hydrophy, Theodore? she asked.

—It seems to me like a new and fruitful form of martyrdom. Just look at those girls, he said bitterly. —They look like scarecrows in a thunderstorm.

—Let them be scarecrows. I have been called one often enough and I accept the mortification as long as I keep the children from gathering the fruit that poisons them eternally.

Parker reached toward George. —Give me my bastard sermon, as you call it, and let me go along.

George held the papers close to his chest. —No, no, I haven't read it yet. It's wonderful. If you insist it's a sermon we can't print it in toto, but we'll review it and quote most of it.

He turned aside and began to read it more intently, starting from the beginning again. Parker let his hand fall to his side.

—What are you trying to do with these girls, Sophia? he said suddenly. —I thought the object was to produce the Margaret Fuller type of woman here.

—Margaret Fuller has taken the water cure many times.

—Margaret Fuller is not a well woman. But these girls are bursting with health and animal spirits. I see no reason for subjecting them to this torture unless you have some particular reason. One that I suspect but will forbear from mentioning.

—Mention it, Theodore, said Sophia tartly. —We have always been frank with one another.

Parker hesitated. He watched Adam climb to the tank and lift up the water gate. He winced at the shrill cries of the girls as the water fell on them like broken glass. —It looks to me like one of the medieval exercises to preserve chastity, he said fiercely.

Sophia flushed faintly. —You are frank, Mr. Parker. But since you have thrown down the gauntlet may I ask you if there is anything unwholesome in such a device?

—Yes, if it's compulsory, part of a religious dogma, it is. If it is no longer on a natural basis it is no longer moral.

—Why do you say it is compulsory? The girls are not forced into it.

—One was.

—Are you speaking of Sarah? Then she is a special case. Her difficulties are greater than the rest. She has a desire to become a Roman Catholic and she must learn that no human relationship should disturb her mind so as to interfere with her devotion to the will of God.

—I suppose that comes under the heading of broad-mindedness. Do you think she's old enough to know what she's doing?

—St. Theresa, whom she greatly reveres and admires, was a young girl. Sarah wishes to share in her deep experience. She often speaks of the exultation Theresa achieved from the marriage of her soul with her divine spouse.

—Do you really think that it was a spectral man that Theresa was calling to her joyless couch?

—That question I do not care to answer.

—Then what about the other children? Are they to be raised as ascetics? Are they to be chilled off from being true men and true women?

—I have seen many true men and women in our Shaker brethren.

George was looking at the pages of the sermon but was not reading. It was interesting to hear Parker light into Sophy like that. Not that he was disloyal but he felt he might have seemed a little smug when extolling her intellectual virtues a while ago in accidental contrast to Lydia Parker.

Parker was reining himself in. He was getting into dangerous fields, quicksands and mires. He tried to be more deliberate. —Oh yes, he said mildly. —The Shakers have done much good. They seem to have all the things now that you Associationists are contending for. But they are not sounding forth the whole human hymn. They found one or two strings a little difficult to tune and control and they broke them off. The problem of life is to tune and keep all the strings in harmony.

—Oh, I think their music is lovely, said Sophia slyly.

—I was speaking metaphorically. What I mean is that they are attempting to nullify the distinction of sexes.

—We find that in the history of all the saints.

—Excuse me, my dear. But isn't that a great evil? It's bad enough when it is accidental, when a woman cannot marry and realize her deepest need because there are not enough men around. But to deny human nature deliberately . . . that is against God himself, it seems to me.

—Woman should live first of all for God's sake, said Sophia fervently. —Then she will not make an imperfect man her God.

Parker looked over at the dripping girls again, longing to tear whole hog into the question.

—Did you ever see the faces of the women in the Shaker colonies? he asked. —They look so timid, so ignorant and undeveloped . . . clownish almost.

Sophia began her answer but he rushed on. —Is there anything on earth more beautiful than the face of a young girl lit up with instinctive affection . . . with the unconscious joy of a young soul impatient of restraint?

—I wouldn't call Margaret Fuller clownish. She claims no married woman can represent the female world, for she belongs to her husband. The idea of woman must be represented by a virgin.

—I don't remember that passage, he said, wavering a bit.

—I seem to see their faces as tranquil and serene, she continued, —rather than ignorant. And Shaker women exude such a fragrance. Our people emit none, kindhearted as they are. But the bedroom of a Shaker or the cell of a solitary saint is filled with the sweetest odor, filling every nook and cranny.

—You should see the pictures of the saints, as I have, in Rome, he answered roughly. —They look like yella dogs. They hang their heads and wring their hands and go without their breakfasts. They don't sleep o' nights; they make a covenant with their eyes not to look at a maid. On the other hand, the heathens are pictured as plump, ablebodied fellows who did their work manfully, married their wives and begat sons and daughters with thankfulness of heart. I prefer Aristotle and Demosthenes and Fabius Maximus to all the saints from Peter, James and John, down to the last one manufactured by the Roman Church. They had some spunk in them.

—Am I to understand, Theodore, that you have renounced the Christian fathers and become a professing pagan?

—Oh no, I mean I deplore the creatures as they are represented in art. For the actual men I have a reasonable respect.

—I'm sure your congregation will be relieved to hear it.

George felt greatly moved to enter the discussion. But he would have to function as a peacemaker and pour oil. He was beginning to see what was bothering Parker about the Farm. Undoubtedly other people were asking the same questions, wondering if the Associates were surrendering to their experiences and if they were surrendering such experiences to history. It was the same problem he had wrestled with before and put off, feeling that perhaps his own lack of passion made him unfit to judge others. He would tackle it when Sophia went away, to tend to the girls. Or at least tackle Parker.

Parker, at the end of a long silence, risked an amenity. —At any rate, he said, —you seem to be prospering here. I don't know when I've seen so many new faces.

—New faces bring new problems, said Sophia dryly.

—How is my ward doing at the school?

—I'm afraid he is one of the problems.

—What can you expect of a poor lad just out of a heretical home? said Parker, tongue in cheek. —From now on you must expect the products of a base and degraded world . . . if you want any new people at all.

—I'm sure that in the small circle of Mr. Emerson's friends we could have found such workers and scholars as we need.

With a little, cold, half curtsy she moved away down to tongue-lash the girls ten times around the barn or up hill and down dale until a purging sweat broke through icy skin.

George and Parker abruptly swung to face one another with the same combative light in their eyes, happy as boys striding onto a playing field with the women left behind and a bruising game ahead.

—So you have abandoned the Goethean ideal to live out life to the full limits, said Parker.

—Not at all, answered George in quickstep tempo. —We believe man is a real being in a real world endowed with organs to recognize and bring out the actual.

—By heaven, you'd better, boomed Parker. —You've got to warm up to people, old boy. That's all you've got.

—But life hints also at the possible . . . and the possible to us is a life spent without thought of self, where collective interests will take the place of individual interests.

—You can't do that by suppressing the affectional instincts.

—How can man decently exist in close relation to a sick and degraded world, himself degraded and imperfect, without asceticism and self-denial?

—I don't believe man has to be degraded in this world or any other.

—That's pulpit talk, the New Testament form of infantine simplicity. Women are degraded every day by the poverty and the hypocrisy of this world. Every day they are driven into the streets, into lives of open shame. Or commercial marriages wherein the wedding veil conceals a condition for which legalized prostitution is too mild a term.

—What's your answer for it . . . ice-water baths and cucumber sandwiches for the women and the earnest study of Dr. Graham's *Advice on Chastity* for the men?

George laughed. That was a direct hit. —You must have been peeking into our library again. Mrs. Gray's husband is reading it right now.

—Poor woman, I feel sorry for her.

—We have no choice in the matter. This is a Christian country, and we can't offend the righteous and survive. You know if we took any steps to reverse society on this we would be branded as licentious and destroyed.

—Someone's going to try it sometime. What if you had a revelation, backed up by appropriate Scripture, that men and women could press their affectional instincts to their furthest limits?

—Quiet a minute, cautioned George.

They looked up to see Lili loitering nearby. She wanted to speak to George but she was a little afraid of Parker. He smelled to her of the lamp, if not of the sanctuary, and she thought his eyes went right through her, reading her sins.

—Would you like to say something, Mrs. Gray? asked George.

—No, I guess not, she faltered.

—Then it's my loss, and it's Mr. Parker's loss, I'm sure.

Lili nodded shyly. Parker's lips began to curve in a smile. —It's about the little calf, she said. —I'm worried. He won't eat. He doesn't even want any milk.

—Let's go up and look at it, said George and they began the walk to the barn. —Perhaps you could tell us what is wrong, Theodore. We lost our only real farmer when Minot Pratt left this spring.

—Why did he leave? asked Parker.

—Oh, family complications. They were increasing and he thought the children would be too much of a burden to us.

—Didn't the boys pitch in with the work?

—Well, he had another coming and thought he could no longer suffer the inconvenience of his room at the Hive . . . the confusion and disorder that result from our limited resources. It's a difficult place here for a family man. But it was a great loss, I can tell you.

The two men went into the barn. It smelled as hot and dry as if it were on fire or ready to burst into flame. The calf, not more than a few weeks old, had managed to inch itself into a dim corner.

—It's too dark in here, said Parker. —Let's get him out into the light.

He bent over to lift it. —Your coat, said George. Parker ignored this and with a great heave of his massive back scooped up the beast and carried him into the barnyard. He laid him tenderly on the grass and began to examine him.

—He's nothing but skin and bones, said Parker, looking into the animal's mouth and then at his feet.

George, looking down with a face racked with compassion, saw a fly land undisturbed on the great orb of the animal's unshut eye. —He's dead, said George.

Lili turned abruptly away.

The calf's bones settled and seemed to shrink into the ground. Some children, tugged instinctively into the orbit of disaster, gathered around. Adam came. They all looked at Parker as if he might make a miracle.

—I can't see any sign of disease, said Parker.

—I know, said George. He squatted and laid a trembling hand on the dead calf's hide. —He must have starved to death.

He turned to Parker with his eyes stricken with a painful honesty and said, —We needed the milk and we tried to wean him on a kind of hay tea we cooked up.

—You should have used milk mixed half and half with warm water and then thinned it with more water every day. They'll eat soft grains too, corn and bran, if you crush them up with a little clover to keep them loose.

Sarah Stearns came flapping violently around the corner of the barn, almost bent double in her sheet, her face mottled with dust deepening into mud. —Oh, Uncle George. You must come to the pasture at once. Margaret has taken a fit and she's pushing and jumping on the other cows and the bull is pressing against his gate and roaring and stamping. Oh, it's awful.

—Just calm down, Sarah. We're very busy right now.

—What's the matter with the calf? demanded Sarah. —Is it dead? Oh, now I understand, she said tearfully. —The poor mother . . . she's trying to destroy herself with grief. Oh . . .

She swerved off like a bedraggled moth, back to the pasture, the children after her. They could hear her start to wail and keen.

George looked up anxiously at Lili, his face full of shame and guilt. She would not look back at him. He could see that she would not give way now, after Sarah's exhibition, but he shuddered at the thought of the grief and possible wrath to come.

—A foolish young girl, said Parker. —A cow has no feeling whatsoever of the sort she imagines. The truth of the matter is that she's in heat and wants the bull. But if I told Sarah that, George, I suppose your wife would ride me out of here on a rail.

Adam straightened up. His eyes flashed over at Parker. He gave Lili a poke in the arm and began to run in the direction of the bull's domain, with Lili in pursuit.

George braced himself for a swinging rebuke from his friend but Parker didn't say anything but walked away from the calf as if the incident was closed. George felt extremely grateful and took up the thread of their late discussion to force the failure out of his mind.

—You speak of a certain revelation, he said. —Surely then if any group had them it was the early Christians and they were profound ascetics. All through history, wherever the early Christian fervor has been practiced, they have formed both associative and ascetic nuclei. I don't think we have any choice in the matter.

—I disagree. It was the Catholic Church that elevated celibacy to a virtue . . . let celibate priests consecrate an unnatural tendency. It is they who invented such a ghastly doctrine; who say woman is a pollution. The results of which are writ on the obscene face of many a priest.

—May I remind you of St. Paul, Theodore? *In my flesh dwelleth no good thing.*

—He did no service to the Church with that word.

Parker slapped George hard on the chest. —God made no bad thing there. It is full of good things, every muscle is good, every bone is a good bone, every nerve is a good nerve. Do you think God gave us these bodies to nullify the distinction that leads to union and to posterity itself? Trust your own flesh and your own soul . . . there's a spiritual as well as a carnal want in love, you know. Old Paul was sometimes mistaken, even as you and I.

—Jesus himself taught chastity, said George.

—It is difficult to determine just what he did teach. If he did I would not follow him against God. But I'm not sure he did, or that he was the miss-nancyish, whining, canting, head-hanging sort of nobody the supernaturalists make him out to be. That's all in the past, anyway. You aren't here to capture that again, are you?

—Certainly not. But even progressive thinkers, such as Charles Lane, Mr. Alcott's friend, say that marriage and family responsibilities are subversive of Association . . . that the two cannot co-exist. The colonies that have practiced celibacy are the strongest and most enduring, the Shakers and the Ebenezers . . .

There was a sound of feminine panic and around the side of the barn came the whole flock of bedraggled girls, stumbling and lurching in their soiled dank wrappings, and behind came Sophia, the most irate of shepherdesses.

—Go straight to your rooms, all of you, she commanded. —George. I'm reaching the end of my rope with your Adam Smith. He has committed the unspeakable vulgarity of dropping the bars and admitting the bull into the cow pasture.

—Poor Margaret, wept Sarah through chattering teeth. —He jumped on top of her and her back bent right up in the middle.

—Go to your room, dear, said Sophia, putting her arm around the sobbing girl and leading her tenderly away.

—I suppose you think that is an argument for your side, said George quickly. —The very opposite, I say, from the reaction of the girls.

Parker shrugged calmly. —The only argument there is that you are surrounded and pressed upon by the most vital and elementary facts of life. And you must settle them one way or another or you'll have no peace. If you want to be ascetics, you must live like the Shakers, with the most skillful precautions taken against sexual jostling. But if you want the full harmony . . . strike the full chord.

—Say that again, said George. —I just want to make sure of what you recommend.

—I can't recommend a sour and ascetic life, said Parker harshly. — Asceticism is the child of sensuality and superstition and the mother of untold secret sins.

—All right, said George, rejoicing that he had him off balance at last. —You have been coming here and discussing this question for years. As long as I can remember, for some strange reason it has always been you who have taken the most extreme, the most partisan Fourierist position. Away from here you continually attack society as evil and cry out for all of the faculties of man to be acknowledged and exercised. You tacitly agree that this movement with all its superficialities is the only device to bring some measure of happiness and decency to mankind. And still you ask us what we are doing here. Let me ask you a question. What in hell are you doing out there, in the sick, bloated and hypocritical world? What are you doing in the pulpit at a time when the worth of a man is determined by the shortness of his stay there?

—Well . . . you see, faltered Parker.

—Is it finally our ascetism that you object to? said George swiftly. — When our building is finished we can wed and bed lovers off by the score. Will you come then? Shall we set aside a room now for you and Lydia?

Parker was shaken, straining to get on keel again, to gain back the initiative. —I admit the question has to be passed on . . . the evils you speak of are there. . . .

—Then what are you going to do about it? pounded George. —What are you, Theodore Parker, going to do about it?

Parker slapped George apologetically on the back and sidled off to a safe distance of some ten feet. He pointed over in the direction of the village and said sheepishly, —I'm going home, dear boy, and thank God that I was not born to set this matter right.

With a final wave of his hand he set off in a dogtrot to the gate of the Farm.

Well, I have won, thought George, shut him up for once!

But he had no great thrill of victory. It was more like being abandoned than securing a triumph. There was no security or peace in the matter at all . . . nor any gain or certainty in the day. Except for the seed of the bull now growing in the cow.

The Surveyor

The Surveyor describes the greatest crisis forced by the emergent radical abolitionists through the militant acts of John Brown in Kansas Territory in 1856. The story details Brown's past and his evolution into an unswerving activist ready to light the slow match of the Civil War. Brown goes to Kansas to bolster the antislavery settlers under seige by proslavery forces from Missouri.

Brown is an antithesis or alter ego for Theodore Parker, Nelson's indecisive prophet. Largely inarticulate, or at least ineloquent, Brown makes his actions speak through the cyclone of words around him. He is another fierce prophet, but one of the *deed* not the word. The suffering of Brown, his family, and the antislavery settlers convinces him to take immediate, drastic action. His leap of faith is to commit an irrevocable deed in the name of freedom.

Kansas is locked in a small-scale civil war, with Missouri-based "border ruffians" terrorizing Free State settlers. Violence and hardship are the climate of the story—a raw wilderness, with primitive shelters, bitter weather, poverty, hunger and disease. And over all, humans locked in mortal combat.

Like an ancient tribal chief, a biblical warrior leading his clan to battle under Yahweh's shibboleth, Brown uses his five sons as the nucleus of a popular army, a guerrilla force to reinforce the scattered settlers. Brown is opposed by Missouri Senator David Atchison (possibly the most influential man in Washington) and Andrew Reeder, Governor of Kansas Territory. And beyond them, the might of the state

From *The Surveyor* (Garden City, N.Y.: Doubleday, 1960), © 1960 by Truman Nelson.

and the inertia of the status quo. He is armed with surprise, anonymity and invisibility: he and his little band slide through the unmapped wilderness disguised as a surveying team. Brown is "mapping the territory" on several emblematic levels. He blazes a trail for the indecisive masses of eastern abolitionism, and, in the climax of the novel, Brown uses his skills as a surveyor to plot his coup de main, the execution of a group of proslavery settlers for example.

This image of Brown as mapmaker-pioneer thrusts abolitionism into a heroic, uniquely American context. Brown and his sons are the legitimate heirs of the revolutionary heroes of 1776 and of the westering pioneers. A tragi-heroic logic informs the story: Brown and his sons suffer dreadful privations, solitude, anguish, madness, and defeat, until they come to the night of the killings, in which they wield rusted ceremonial swords, armed like bronze-age warriors indicting justice, a justice poetic in several senses.

Brown compares himself to Oliver Cromwell raising the New Model Army, and we recall the iron legacy of militant Puritanism running through abolitionism. Old Man Brown is an image of Hawthorne's Grey Champion, the resurrected spirit of hard-bitten, retributive justice that drove the English regicides to condemn Charles I in a horrific, irrevocable deed. In Brown's logic, only the judicial murder of a handful of Kansas squatters is a statement strong enough to end the deathly rule of the slavocracy. Because he felt slavery was literally death and hell, Brown eschewed his early, deeply felt pacifism and resorted to cold-blooded execution as an ultimate "statement of the deed."

This novel is an overture or prologue to John Brown's final defiant act, the dream nurtured through the bitter Kansas struggle—the raising of a revolt in the slave South, arming and organizing slaves to throw off their shackles. At the end of the novel, John Brown summons his remaining strength for a journey east and south, into the belly of Leviathan, to his Golgotha at Harper's Ferry.

From *The Surveyor*

This excerpt from The Surveyor *is the novel's climax, the culmination of Brown's strategy, the point at which Brown and his small band select and execute their* enemies. *The lethal raid follows a series of armed struggles and defeats for the Free State forces. Brown steps from the arena of political argument and rhetoric into a dark night of direct physical violence. Nelson casts the scene as a stark tragedy, like something from the* Iliad, *men bent on slaughter, carrying old swords. The symbolism, which John Brown has consciously orchestrated, is haunting.*

The Power of the Sword

When he told John why he wanted to take some men back to Pottawatomie Creek, John said, —That is the worst thing we can do, Father, divide our forces in the face of the enemy! —What enemy? asked the Old Man. —We have already let Atchison slip through our fingers.

John, making an effort to remain calm and soldierly, said, —There are Ruffians camping now at Bull Creek. Our plan is to attack them as they come up the Sante Fe road.

—Then we are to let things slide in our own neighborhood?

This got under John's skin. —No, Father, I am only asking you to wait a few hours until we have perfected our plans. Once Robinson is rescued we can put laws into operation . . . make this whole operation in a form that will command universal respect . . . we will have a written constitution and regular courts.

John said this with such passion, amounting to frenzy, that the Old Man was taken aback. All John had to go on was a rumor that Robinson was being brought up to Lecompton to trial along the prairie route, so called, by a Ruffian escort now gathering: it was clear to the Old Man that all the lessons of the immediate past had still not disabused John of his faith in politicians and their horse-trading promises. The truth was, and it was tragic, that his son lusted after legitimacy as much as the rest of them. If a man had a title such as governor, legislator, or judge, or was an officer of any kind, it was all right to go ahead. He spoke to him as softly and winningly as he could.

—John, I won't take more than a half-dozen men. I know you are short of guns, so we will take no muskets and no more than a trifle of powder and ball.

—I don't want you to do it, Father.

—How long do you think the people back there will stand up to an ax at their necks? They will desert to the Ruffians.

John said, pleading hard, —You will break up *this* mobilization if you carry on like this. Think what a disaster that would be! This camp is the only evidence in the Territory that the Free State movement has not been utterly wiped out!

—I don't think a whole lot will want to go back with me when they find out what sort of a blow I intend to strike.

—This is the place to strike our blow. What little we might do down on the Pottawatomie will mean nothing . . . it will never be heard of. The whole movement will collapse and Atchison can proclaim his final conquest.

They were interrupted by Frederick coming up with the swords in a canvas bundle. He was carrying them in his arms like a baby. —What do you want me to do with these, Father?

—Put a good edge on them, said the Old Man, nodding toward Captain Shore's grindstone.

John groaned helplessly and shook his head. —You intend to persist, don't you, Father! Why are you doing this to me? People are watching this quarrel. I am supposed to be in command here.

—That's right, you are right, said the Old Man loudly, looking covertly around to discover that John was correct, they were watching him. He made a little gesture of obeisance and patted John on the arm. But in a low, hard voice under a contrived smile, he said, —John, I told you when we started that I was coming along with a little company of my own. Now you must allow me to do this. You have your theories and I have mine. I am thinking of what happens if Robinson is not brought up this way . . . or if you cannot engage in any military action at all in this area. There has to be an irrevocable step taken somewhere and one of us has to make it.

The sharp rasp of abrased steel shivered the air. John recoiled in alarm. Over at the grindstone the brooding, waiting heat was being bombarded with a hail of sparks as the short heavy sword was being pressed hard against it. John turned to his father with trembling hands, giving in to him. —All right, Father, I know I can't stop you. What are you going to do?

—Summary execution of Cato's court at Pottawatomie.

John shuddered. The whole structure holding together his secret world of right shook under the strain. He put his hands to his ears as the blade screamed against the turning stone.

—You've got to have some kind of a trial for these men. After all, this is the nineteenth century.

—There is no time for that. What do you want me to do, bring all the Ruffians before you with their witnesses and defenses? We will be as bad off as we have been waiting for relief from your friends, those legislative diddlers who have put us in this plight and then run off to get help, or signed treaties of peace.

—How can you keep people's respect if you do this thing without some warrant of authority?

—The power of the sword is authority enough. A trial of these men would be a farce . . . as false as their courts trying us. Do you think we could show less prejudice and mob rule? This is a war, John. They have killed five men and there may be more bodies discovered yet. The military power is now the supreme one in Kansas. Now only the sword can remove this power and give it back to the people to whom it belongs. I will use it with all the tenderness I can manage. Your politicians, your Robinson and Reeder have had trials and bargains for a year now and proved nothing but that tyranny in Kansas is locked on harder than ever. The revolution is the trial now and the only bargain we will strike is on their necks.

No one could stand up against this, John thought. It was like being held in a iron clamp against that grindstone over there. —Who do you want to go with you, Father? he said, in surrender.

—Your brothers seem to have a natural ability for active service.

—No, Father, I beg of you . . . take someone who is hardened to this. There are plenty of roughnecks and bullyboys in this camp.

—I don't understand you, John. I thought we agreed a long time ago that if there had to be any arbitrary taking of life the purest man in the community should be the executioner.

—Robespierre, murmured John numbly. —*The sword of liberty should always be wielded by clean hands.*

—I cannot tell from your tone, John, whether you approve or disapprove of Robespierre or your father.

—Oh, I approve, I approve. I cannot help myself. And I will go and give the handle of the grindstone a few turns to show I am with you in spirit. I know it makes little difference whether the enemy get killed up here or down there or in both places when the fighting starts. But for the sake of the boys I would just like to have some expression that the community is willing to back us up on this.

—All right, all right, said the Old Man reluctantly. —But I can't agree to go exactly by what they say. I have already had it out with them ... now I am afraid they will take all the principle out it and make it seem as if they are using me as an instrument of private vengeance. Men should be killed only for a great cause.

They were walking slowly, meditatively, over to the group at the Townsley wagon now. John said, —I thought you questioned this cause.

—I am taking your word for it, at present.

—Don't put it all on my back ... let's spread the load around a little bit.

Hank Williams and the other men greeted the Old Man with fervor. They had now worked themselves up to the pitch where they looked on him as a savior who could take away all their sins of omission and doubt, empty their hearts of all the murderous desires they had harbored there since the Ruffians' assault began long ago. Hank Williams handed him at once a list on which he had written five names: Henry Sherman, old man Doyle, Allen Wilkinson, Mr. McMinn (foreman of the grand jury), and George Wilson, the probate judge. The Old Man studied it and then, without comment, folded it carefully and tucked it in his waistcoat pocket. A lot of palavering began. Bill Partridge said his cousin Ed had been cornered by one of Doyle's dogs and had killed it to save his own life. George Grant said his sister Mary had nearly been raped by Dutch Bill holding a knife at her throat, but had been saved by Fred Brown, which was news to the Old Man. Some showed warning notices they had received and the full slate of stories was revived of Wilkinson opening all Free State mail for evidence of treason and burning liberal newspapers. There was talk that Dutch Henry's gang should be strung up, they should get the California treatment, their houses should be set on fire and they should be shot down as they tried to escape; all the savage acts against his enemy a man can think of, when he does not have to carry it out in his own person, were mentioned. The Old Man found this unbearably tiresome, making his mission, as he predicted, a cheap act of vengeance, belittling it, and he excused himself to see to his swords. As he walked away, Salmon stopped him.

—Who are you taking with you, Father? he said.
—Why, you boys, if you think you are up to it.
—If we ain't now we never will be, after the texts you have been drumming into us for years.
—No more texts, Salmon. Now comes the trial.
—We're all game, said Salmon. —We know what it is.
—Just remember that I am asking you to do nothing that Frank Pierce would not do if his son or his daughter was being made a slave.

As he walked through the camp toward the grindstone, the other men gave way to him respectfully and somewhat fearfully. He parted groups like Moses did the Red Sea. Later Frederick came and said Mr. Townsley was willing to carry them back with his horses. —Townsley can be our guide, said Fred. —He claims he knows all the slavery men around the creek and has been to all their houses.

The Old Man nodded approval.
—John didn't want us to go, did he? asked Fred. —He wants you to stay with him . . . he is scared.
—John is a big boy now, said the Old Man.

While the Old Man was standing by watching the beautiful shower of sparks from the last of the swords being ground, he was approached by a queer-looking character whom he had been noticing with amusement for some time. He was a dark, slight, very intense-looking young man who had managed to insinuate himself quietly into the fringes of every vital discussion yet held. Most of the time he spent with Theodore Wiener the storekeeper, talking in German. Wiener was a huge, golden-haired man, weighing over two hundred and fifty pounds but carrying it well. The smaller, dark man was carrying one of the old 1812 muskets which the Old Man had distributed at the court demonstration and he began his discussion with a complaint about it in a softly guttural, but clear voice. The Old Man took it away from him and, handling it almost tenderly, said, —Why, this gun is first rate. Men who know weapons would give anything for a fine old instrument like this. Honorably made, every part of it. See how this lock snaps so strong and smart, so that it fills the pan brimful of fire. Every single grain of powder does its work under it. This is a most valuable gun and you'd better be off with it, young man, or I will reclaim it for myself.

Taking hold of the gun, the young man drew the Old Man a little apart from the others and said, in a low voice, —My friend Theodore Wiener and myself want to go along with you, Captain Brown.

The Old Man shook his head emphatically. —I can't take any more, sir. My son is angry at me as it is, for depleting his ranks.

—What difference will it make if two more go? No one will notice.

—I doubt that . . . with the get-up you are wearing, said the Old Man, giving a disparaging look at the man's fancy black felt hat with its waving ostrich plumes, the blue, frogged coat with all its black, shiny buttons. The man drew back, carefully opened a fine black leather cartridge case hanging on his belt, drew out a card and presented it to the Old Man with a curt bow and a clicking of heels. The Old Man studied it carefully, but it was covered with engraving in German script. —I cannot make head or tail of this, he said, handing it back.

—That says my name, August Bondi, Captain, and certifies that I was a member of the Vienna Academic Legion, Captain Zacks' company. This is my uniform and I am proud to wear it, for we fought for our freedom there . . . like you . . .

The Old Man nodded his head, somewhat sheepishly.

—We were all young students from the gymnasiums . . . I speak four languages myself . . . but we were the heart of the revolution. And Captain, we were betrayed by the same sort as these land speculators and stockjobbers up at Lawrence. I would like to go along on your secret expedition and talk to you . . .

—It is private . . . not secret, sir.

—I would to show how our experience in '48 . . .

—I know all about the '48 revolution. I was in Europe in 1849.

—In Austria?

—In Germany . . . I got as far as Hamburg.

Mr. Bondi's soft, slurring accent poured out like heavy, dark molasses as he implored the Old Man. —Then you know what happens in these cases. The city is given up, then the cause rots away from the inside. I stood with a man while he burned the Tabor Bridge over the Danube. It was Robert Blum and it saved Vienna long enough for some of our people to get out. But then he was caught and executed and our people . . .

Mr. Bondi stopped here and gave a shrug expressing nothingness.

—That class that loves money more than the principle, they are the ones at Lawrence. They are more willing to lynch those who try to defend the cause to the last outpost than to fight themselves. They should be taught, Captain Brown, that those who give up decisive positions of the people should be treated as traitors.

—That is another matter, said the Old Man. —Now I respect your position, Mr. Bondi, but I think you could do more good by remaining here and standing by my son. He is going to have an upstream business of it in the next twenty-four hours.

—Take Wiener then, pleaded Bondi. —He begs to go. Look what he has already done for you . . . given so generously of his stock! A thousand dollars' worth and all because of his great respect for what you are doing, Captain Brown.

—Why, I never exchanged a dozen words with the man in my life. I cannot understand a word he says and he cannot understand me.

—He knows you . . . through your son-in-law, Henry Thompson.

The Old Man shook his head. —He still cannot understand me or my orders. You don't realize what we are going into, Mr. Bondi. We will have to work at extremely close quarters and in the nighttime, taking by surprise three or four cabins, strong points, perhaps miles apart. We do not know but what they may be heavily defended and waiting for us. We do not know but what alarms may be given at the first or second encounter and thus made the objects of severe and protracted attacks. I must have the most perfect trust, obedience, and communication from the men about me.

—Take him, Captain Brown. He is a Jew and he knows what this means. There is an old rabbinical saying among us . . . Be'emeth hayah 'abduth Visroel b'Mizraim Ki lom' du l'soblah. The translation is, *The real slavery of Israel in Egypt was that they had learned to endure it.* Six months ago Theodore Wiener was for the South, for slavery, and in his heart my enemy. Now he is my friend, thanks to you. Take him, Captain . . .

—All right, tell him he can come.

The Old Man walked over to the young boy, Bain Fuller, turning the grindstone, and said, —Bain, I am leaving here shortly and after I am gone I want you to start home by yourself and make sure you have witnesses for your whereabouts tonight.

He gathered up the swords, wrapped them carefully in cloth so as to protect the new edges and put them in Townsley's wagon. Owen, Oliver, Frederick, Salmon, and Henry Thompson climbed in and perched along the sideboards. The Old Man spoke to Jason, asking him to keep an eye on his camp kettles and then turned to get into the wagon. An elderly man, grave and disapproving in countenance, and having heard, along with everyone else in the camp, of the Old Man's direction and purpose, spoke to him. —I hope, sir, you will proceed with caution.

—Caution, caution, snapped the Old Man. —Sir, I am eternally tired of hearing that word *caution*. It is nothing but the word of cowardice.

He brushed by the man and, standing on the hub, climbed into the wagon. He gave a bark of command to Townsley, astride the off horse, and the wagon began to move out into the road. Wiener followed on his own pony. The entire camp stood around, cheering heartily and knowingly.

—What did the old geezer say, Father? Salmon asked.

—He wanted us to use caution. *Caution,* he continued, disgustedly. —They would let every bit of manhood be drained out of them, drop by drop, but that is all right so long as they have their infernal bump of caution working for them.

They made good time for the back journey. The roads were drying up in the heat. The prairie was hardening and the Old Man instructed Townsley to leave the road as they got close to their destination and ride on the open land. Near sundown they saw a rider approaching them. It was someone they knew, a Lawrence man by the name of Blood, and he hailed them and rode up close for a chat. —We have no time to talk. We are on most urgent business, said the Old Man.

—What are you going this way for? I must know what has happened in Lawrence. I have just been told at Osawatomie that all the men around here have gone up there to rally against the Ruffians.

—Lawrence was sacked and burned by the Ruffians without any show of resistance, said Frederick.

Mr. Blood shook his head. —I thought as much. I was in Westport yesterday trying to arrange fast transportation back here and the Ruffians were coming in from Lawrence by the dozens. It was like pandemonium let loose, these drunken brutes staggering around in their coal-scuttle boots, stewed to the gills, displaying all their loot and threatening to go back for another strike when that was used up . . .

—Rejoicing in our cowardice, no doubt, said the Old Man.

—Speaking of rejoicing, said Blood, —if one of you lads would pull off my left boot there is something I would like to show your father.

Oliver jumped down from the wagon and obliged. Mr. Blood took from it a paper carefully folded into the heel. —This is a dispatch which came in over the magnetic telegraph just before I left . . . I paid a dollar for a copy and I imagine it was the sweetest music ever tapped out along these southern lines. Listen to this:

TO THE ASSOCIATED PRESS: IMMEDIATELY AFTER THE ADJOURNMENT OF CONGRESS THIS MORNING, PRESTON S. BROOKS OF SOUTH CAROLINA, A MEMBER OF THE LOWER HOUSE, ENTERED THE SENATE CHAMBER AND APPROACHING THE SEAT OF MR. SUMNER, STRUCK HIM A POWERFUL BLOW WITH A CANE, AT THE SAME TIME ACCUSING HIM OF LIBELING SOUTH CAROLINA AND HIS GRAY-HAIRED RELATIVE, SENATOR BUTLER. MR. SUMNER FELL FROM THE EFFECTS OF THE BLOW AND BROOKS CONTINUED BEATING HIM. MR. SUMNER RECOVERED ENOUGH TO CALL FOR HELP BUT NO ONE INTERPOSED UNTIL MR. SUMNER WAS DEPRIVED OF HIS POWER OF SPEECH. SOME EYEWITNESSES STATE THAT BROOKS HIT HIM AS MANY AS 15 OR 20 TIMES ON THE HEAD. MR. SUMNER WAS SITTING IN AN ARMCHAIR AS THE ASSAULT WAS MADE AND HAD NO OPPORTUNITY TO DEFEND HIMSELF. AFTER HIS ASSAILANT DESISTED, HE WAS CARRIED TO HIS ROOM, BUT THE EXTENT OF HIS INJURIES IS NOT ASCERTAINED.

Mr. Blood held up the dispatch. It was a little galley strip. —The Ruffians are spreading this around with great glee. They are sending Brooks a box of prime cigars, filched from the Free State Hotel.

—Don't blame the Ruffians entirely, said the Old Man, standing up in the wagon. —Your friends in Lawrence are fully as much to blame for this . . . with their lickspittle caving in to the Ruffians here. The men who gave up Lawrence and signed a peace should be put to death as traitors. Drive on, Mr. Townsley, if you please.

The wagon pulled away from the astonished gaze of Mr. Blood and was soon lost in the masking glare of the setting sun.

After sunset, the Old Man ordered the wagon back on the road. They crossed Mosquito Creek and then Townsley was told to turn off to the right through a thick screen of timber and in a deep ravine some two miles northwest of Pottawatomie Crossing. It became very dark. The Old Man would permit no fire. They ate some crackers and drank what he considered to be the proper and healthful beverage for soldiers on campaign; creek water mixed with a little ginger and molasses. Soon they were plunged into the deep, double darkness of the ravine, a wild, tortured place. Whenever they took a step, thorn and alder bushes tore and lashed at faces and hands. Outcroppings of flinty rocks and boulders made it impossible to lie out at length without the body being prodded as if on a bed of spikes. But these physical discomforts were as nothing compared to the vast slow hate building in the consciousness of the Brown family. No one said much as they went through the motions of eating and resting under the seal of utter darkness. The Old Man said, —Mr. Townsley, when the moon comes up you will oblige me by guiding us directly to the cabins of Mr. McMinn, Mr. Doyle, Mr. Wilkinson, and Dutch Henry's store, although this last we are all familiar with.

—What about George Wilson? demanded Townsley. —He is the main reason I came along. The son of a bitch has a writ out on me!

—He will be taken care of in due time. The point is that we must not waste movement in unnecessary traveling. We have no time nor have we the forces to go one step out of our way.

—I don't know nary a one of these fellows you mentioned, grumbled Townsley. —How the hell should I know where they live?

—You said back in camp you would be a first-rate guide. You said you knew all the pro-slavery men and had been to their houses and that you had laid out new road hereabouts . . .

—I thought you meant the south side of Pottawatomie Creek. That is my neighborhood; five or six miles below here. There is slavery men as thick as fleas down at the South Fork.

—What do you expect of us . . . that we will sweep the creek?

—Goddammit, what the hell are we here for? Ain't we going to give them bastards the California treatment . . . burn them out or drive them back to Missouri?

—Nothing of the kind, Mr. Townsley. I do not believe in destroying property which could be put to better use. We are here to carry out executions. Surely you know that. You saw us sharpening our swords.

The whole camp was plainly aware that some stern act of retaliation was called for . . .

There was a long, troubled silence on Townsley's part and then he said in a shaky voice, —Swords, what do you mean swords? I reckoned there might be a hanging or two . . .

—There will be no hanging, said the Old Man crisply. —This will be carried out in the most humane manner possible. The same way in which great kings and tyrants have been dispatched.

There was utter darkness here, the Old Man's voice had a disembodied quality to it and Townsley felt a sudden rush of horror and fright. —Jesus Christ, man . . . you mean you are going to chop the poor bugger's head off? Goddammit, count me out of this! I want no part of this night's work.

There was a long, uneasy pause, then the Old Man spoke again, —I find your language very offensive, Mr. Townsley. It goes all too well with your cowardice . . . I never yet saw a swearing, foul-mouthed man who did not lack nerve when facing a crisis.

—I was five years in the cavalry, Brown. No one said I didn't have guts. Jesus, I served in Florida fighting Seminoles and maroons . . . I was under Old Taylor himself . . .

—Then why are you so squeamish all of a sudden? I imagine you hacked off many a head. Was it because you were riding a horse at the time, Mr. Townsley? Did that make the difference?

—We were up against bloodthirsty bastards down there in them swamps . . . bloody half-breeds . . . half of them had nigger blood.

—Then that is the difference, Mr. Townsley?

—Now see here, I am from Maryland and I'd still like to see thugs like Dutch Henry strung up but chopping off a white man's head . . . Jesus, that makes my guts creep.

—There is no difference in the sight of God, He is no respecter of persons.

—Then let Him take care of it, said Townsley. —This ain't human, what you are going to do. Let God do His own dirty work.

The younger Browns held their breath, waiting for the Old Man to blast Townsley for this, but he was not concerned with this side of Townsley but rather with the awful fact that he had no guide now for this delicate operation. He blamed himself bitterly for not being more careful about this and seeing only the fine horses Townsley had to carry them here. He wondered if he could go ahead anyway on the assumption that all these men were appendages of Dutch Henry and would be grouped around him in some fashion. But it was very risky not to know just where to go; he particularly did not want to stray outside the Franklin County lines and it was just here that four counties met in a corner. It would inevitably mean backtracking and waste motion, things he had an obsession against. He had to think this matter out very calmly, hold back all he could and so he began, like a man pondering on a familiar path through the woods, steadied by reflective sights and sounds, thinking through some Bible texts, stalling for time.

—If you would like to debate texts on what God does or does not require of man, Mr. Townsley, I am perfectly willing.

—I'm getting out of here, said Townsley, but before he could get to his feet, the huge paw of Mr. Wiener clamped over his wrist with finality.

—I am always surprised, said the Old Man, —when people do not find it self-evident that we should carry out God's wishes in our own persons. First of all, I think it is generally agreed that God wishes all men to be free and that there is nothing so acceptable to Him as the blood of a tyrant. Do you agree?

The Stygian darkness, the harsh confinement of rough terrain and, above all, the calm, reflective quality of the Old Man's voice froze Mr. Townsley into a state of terror. He was speechless. The Old Man continued; weighing every word. —Mr. Townsley thinks it may be enough to merely drive our enemies off or destroy their homes . . . but if we do that they will still come back, and made invulnerable by their grand juries, they will bleed us afresh. We will be in the same plight as King Ahab in respect to Benhadad of Syria . . . in which Ahab, after defeating Benhadad in two remarkable victories, sent him away in peace and thought he would be grateful for saving his life . . . but only succeeded in having Benhadad hate him the more. The result was that Ahab himself heard the dreadful sentence from the Lord . . . Because thou hast let go out of thy hand a man who I appointed to utter destruction, therefore thy life shall go for his life and thy people for his people.

The Old Man shifted his weight and two small stones began to roll down the slope. To Townsley they seemed like thunderbolts falling on him. The Old Man continued. —Casting my mind back on all victories gained by Israel, I find that they always began with a casting down of the Altars of Baal and the putting to death of the priests who worshiped by inflicting pain on innocent people, like our antagonists of the bogus courts who have already complied in five acts of sin and death.

—What do you want with me? said Townsley finally. —What have you got to prove with me?

—Nothing, said the Old Man. —Only the observation that we must serve God with acts.

—Are you going to punish me? asked Townsley in a shaky voice.

—Certainly not, said the Old Man. —I am glad for your frankness. You might have said you knew, then left us stranded. We will put the whole thing over another day. We are too excited now. Men acting only on hot and active flashes of anger seldom change things or remove the real roots and causes of their troubles.

The Old Man could sense the boys getting very restless over this and then Frederick spoke, —Father, I have been hardening my heart and I feel I can do things now I would not have expected. I never thought that I would have the spunk to kill a man, but when I think of all the animals I have killed, the deers and the birds, frisky little goats, and only for my appetite, I feel that only a man who will not kill *anything* can refuse to kill a man when he is bad and hurting other people. Even the peace people admit that man stealing is worse than murder. They say there is a higher law than violence . . . but the poor slave does not know any higher law than violence, does he? It is the threat of death that enslaves him, the murder of the spirit, only a real death can free him. That is his higher law . . . and ours at present.

The Old Man thought hard about the choice he had to make. He looked up at the sky. It was a black void, not a star showing. He was like Samson, eyeless in Gaza. He might pull down one temple of slavery and lose his own life and the life of his sons in the ruins. Armed as poorly as they were, going up against men accustomed to acting in concert, gathered now perhaps in a nearby cabin, or waiting in ambush along the road, his company could run into self-slaughter. Of course this could happen anyway but still he had the feeling that this error with Townsley was a sign not to make their play tonight. In spite of the boys having their blood up now . . . perhaps because of it.

—In cold blood is the best way, he said finally. —We don't want to hack at human heads like the Ruffians did at Easton, or as Brooks of South Carolina did Senator Sumner in the chamber of the Senate. One swift clean blow as you can deliver, Frederick, at the base of the skull, will do the job. I have some rough notion of surgery and I know that will bring a quick and merciful end. The whole business could be encompassed in a matter of minutes before the subject has time to dwell on the agony of his sins on this earth and his trials hereafter.

—But these men are not dying for their *sins,* are they . . . but for what they are doing for our liberties, this very *minute?*

For a moment, in the darkness, the Old Man did not recognize this breathless voice and then he realized, with a little shame, that it was Owen speaking. He and Owen had very little to say to each other. They worked along together, in silence and remoteness. Once or twice Owen had attempted to interest him in some humorous book he was reading but it angered the Old Man so much to feel that he was wasting so much time on inane, comical joke books and would not give the Bible a try that he just shut off all communication between them. Now he heard the hostility in Owen's voice and it saddened him because he knew the time had come when he needed all his boys and their respect and understanding. He began to speak more softly. As a practical shepherd he had often talked sheep out of running wild with fright. — That is right, Owen, he said, —but we cannot help things with a fiasco, by getting lost, by blundering and being killed ourselves as a result of it.

He lay back himself on the sharp spines of the inhospitable earth but kept talking. —This thing we are doing is noble. It does not require the heat of anger and vengeance . . . no more than Brutus required it . . . or Deborah the prophetess . . . or our own ancestors the Regicides when they signed the King's death warrant. Pagans, Hebrews, and Christians have all struck blows against tyrants . . . it has happened at every revolution and what we are doing here, and what your brother John is setting out to do on the Santa Fe road will place us firmly in the ranks of those acting for the help and not the hurt of mankind.

—There are too many of them, mumbled Owen. —The people are not worth the risk. The Ruffians from Bull Creek may come in, tomorrow . . . a hundred of them.

—When I think, said the Old Man, in a kind of chanting exultation, —when I think of the ample field we labor in and the rich harvest we can bring in, not only for this country but for the world, and this and future generations, I am proud my family is with me as an entire unit. God has honored but few with such opportunities as these. I have been waiting a long time and one day's postponement will not make me lose heart. Still, I will flatter no man into such a venture without him being able to count the cost. So let us sleep on it and if we go forward tomorrow it will be at the prompting of a calm spirit in every one of you.

—About the cost, Father, said Salmon. —Did any of these tyrannicides die in their beds . . . I mean is the cost going to be our lives?

—You young people like to talk about dying. When I was your age I used to feel a strong, steady desire to die but since I have discovered this prospect of harvesting good for other men, I have become not only willing to live but have greatly enjoyed it. Believe me, Salmon, I am now rather anxious to go on a few years more. Now go to sleep, all of you.

Sleeping that night was more akin to smothering. The vapors of heat, the low bank of clouds, the damp mist which rolled like tumbleweed into the bowl-like ravine, pressed on their faces like wet towels. The Old Man woke once and found himself listening anxiously in the dark for horses on the road. He tried to make his way up there for reassurance but after taking a few steps he found it like walking in a damp shroud and gave it up. Now that the decision to wait another night was irrevocable he was plagued that their enemies had more time as well as themselves. He thought of the worst that could happen; dawn and the road crawling with Ruffians who had eluded John's forces. He would still try the executions, he thought, and pondered again the necessity of knowing every foot of the way. There was only one solution, he realized, waking in the vaporous morning. He must make a survey of the ground to be covered.

After breakfast he discussed this with the boys. Frederick knew where Wilkinson's cabin was; he had been there once for mail matter.

This meant he could not go along on the survey. Nor could Henry Thompson, who knew Doyle, nor Salmon, who had hung around the court with Henry the day after the demonstration. Townsley was unreliable . . . Wiener was too well known along this road. No one knew the exact location of Doyle's claim . . . it was somewhere in the Mosquito Creek timber, they thought, after eliminating locations they were sure of. This left only Owen and Oliver to use as a surveyor's crew. Another problem was that his theodolite and chain were at John's cabin, five miles north.

He sent Frederick and Salmon up for these and could not start out until the afternoon on the risky business of confronting his victims. With directions supplied by Frederick he found, close by the road, on a soft roll of clear prairie, Wilkinson's cabin. A short search, and only a few feet from the roadbed itself, located the long piece of limestone which showed the west corner of Wilkinson's quarter section. The Middle Creek timber was north of this, so without setting up his tripod, using his hand compass, he went straight north into a tongue of heavy timber starting to slope down to the Mosquito Creek bottom. Here he found the limestone marker of a full section corner. He set up his theodolite here and put the boys to work with the chain and flag. At the second three hundred feet they struck a patch of forty or fifty stumps where someone had cut off for a cabin. A dog began to bark and he heard a shout. Doyle came walking toward him up from a cabin in something of a thicket. Doyle seemed to be walking unsteadily, as if he were half-drunk, but he had on his greenish frock coat. The Old Man had his panama hat on, which in the dampness of the morning had collapsed around his face almost like cloth. He had the protean gift of concentrating on a *thing* with such force that his personality became merged in it and almost unrecognizable away from it. In this case he kept his eye close to his instrument and every gesture he made was tight and linked with it and his control over the boys, moving them with hand signals, depersonalized them in turn, so that they became only more apparatus. Doyle accepted them at once as government men. —Sir, is that my line you are running?

—What is your name, sir, asked the Old Man, keeping his face tight to the eyepiece.

—James P. Doyle, Section 22, southwest quarter.

The Old Man gestured to Owen to move the flag a little to the left and Doyle said bitterly, —Doggone, mister. What in hell are you doing, giving my timber to Wilkinson? These lines have all been posted last March. What is going on here?

—Just running test lines, said the Old Man, now waving Owen back to the right so that Doyle picked up footage on the adjoining claim. — That's it, man, he said. —Take it from Wilkinson. They're putting in a town here pretty soon and this is going to be the county seat. This land is worth something.

The Old Man took out his notebook and began to follow the regular procedure of putting down field notes. Doyle, squinting over his shoulder, saw him write down, *East on a random line between section 22 & 27. Variation* 10° 24' *E.*, and was duly impressed.

The big dog padded over to Owen and began to nuzzle his leg, his taut, killer's snout butting the calf hard. Owen stepped away and the dog barked. Doyle began to wave his arms excitedly. —Don't move there, mister. That dog is a fancy-bred nigger hound, he can take off your calf in one bite. Down King, you lay down.

The big dog barked a few times in his thunderous voice and then collapsed into a flaccid bag of dun-colored skin. Doyle looked at him fondly and said to Owen, behind a shielding hand, —He minds me now but if someone popped the whip and yelled nigger you would be in trouble, mister. He would run a rail fence to get you.

To the right, the gently rolling prairie began and Doyle looked over and said, —Look there, look there, Old Wilkinson has come out to see what's up. He will throw a fit if he loses a fip's worth of his land.

The Old Man could see Wilkinson, brought out by the barking of the dog, watching them with a hand shading his eyes.

—He may come down to quiz you, mister, said Doyle. —But just remember if he asks you to shave my land a little more that James P. Doyle is as good as constable here, my boy Drury is the court bailiff. We are just as respectable as the Wilkinsons.

Mr. Wilkinson took a few uncertain steps, thought better of it and stopped. —Look at him, said Doyle. —He has a chicken liver in him. He is district attorney here and he ain't got the spunk to come on down here and see if he is losing land. We got all breeds of nigger thieves and gun runners and insurrectionists around here and all he does is keep notes on them, collecting evidence, he calls it. I say he is just a yellow bastard . . . he ain't got the guts to close in on them.

Mr. Doyle raised his voice so that Wilkinson could hear him plainly. —This land won't be worth a hoot in hell till we get shet of them nigger thieves holding their conventions and their midnight councils here. No quality folks will ever come in here with niggers and pay fancy prices 'til we have some law and order.

Mr. Wilkinson retreated a few faltering steps at this and Doyle chuckled. —Look at that, ain't that a mighty small chance of a man? Why us Doyles was better thought of than him everywhere we went. I was captain of the night patrollers back home and I was furnished with a pacing mule. And lots more than that, he continued sadly. — The niggers back home live ten times better than we do here . . . and better than Wilkinson.

Mr. Doyle turned and looked forlornly at his encumbered acres of brush and scrub oak and said, —Ain't nobody here that can plant corn. Back home the niggers did it up nice . . . plow a big field and check it, make a straight row across the field and make a check about two feet square. Then they'd drop the seed in the middle of the square and it would come up as straight as the finger on my hand . . . if it don't the niggers have to eat it then and there, stalk and all.

Doyle's voice had all the lyric plaintiveness of the exile and the dispossessed. The Old Man was getting uneasy; he wanted to break away from the conversation. Watching Wilkinson out of the corner of his eye, he could see him making up his mind to come closer. Doyle squatted down on his haunches and began to chew a spear of grass. He had evidently made up his mind to fend off Wilkinson from using the influence of his office on the surveyor to gain a little of his timber. — Wilkinson has got to get up off his ass and do something right soon. The Buford boys are due back any day now to help us clean up this mess here. Lawrence ain't the only abolition hole needs mucking out.

—Expect a fight? said the Old Man, getting ready to move his theodolite.

—Fight, hell. You can't get them bastards to fight. You always find the folks that take the nigger's part are chickenhearted and soft as shit just like them. I try to tell Wilkinson that.

Owen, his hat pulled down over his face and almost on his hands and knees as he picked up the chain, link by link, was listening very hard to Mr. Doyle. Doyle was watching Wilkinson carefully. —You put a sheet over your head at night when it's dark and jump out at a nigger and by Jesus he'll run himself crazy or dead. Wilkinson claims the Yankees around here are getting ready to jump us; he says he has the names. Bullshit, I say, they are nothing but white niggers, factory-working and shit-kicking farmer niggers and like their brothers they like to sneak away and brag and sometimes they make threats to the court. They got field calls and signals and all kinds of whoops and hollers with meanings to them . . . we know all that.

—Get the law here, he shouted in a bellowing voice. —Let us Doyles get our hounds and our sluts running and a-baying and you'll see an end to this trouble and the sun won't go down on loose niggers and nigger thieves in this precinct.

Owen got the last of the chain. Oliver, who was acting as ax man, was sitting quietly on a large stump just about the right size for an execution block. —Mark that block, said the Old Man grimly and, as Oliver cut a chip out of it for a blaze, he shouldered his tripod and waved the boys another three hundred yards down the line to the east. They were now in good cover. He set up the tripod again, but looking back, he saw Mr. Doyle go genially over to Mr. Wilkinson, doffing his hat with a show of great respect, and the two walked away toward Wilkinson's house. After this, the surveyors, without chaining or sighting, came to Doyle's meander mark at Mosquito Creek. They followed the creek north to the mark of Doyle's north boundary and followed that back to the road.

—I think that was worth while, said the Old Man. Owen was silent with hate. Oliver said, —What about McMinn?

The Old Man grimaced in disgust. —I forgot McMinn. Well, I don't care to risk any more exposure today.

Darkness fell and woke them. It was not yet time for the deed, which needed the full cast of the moon. The Old Man looked up at the Kansas sky. Without the moon in its strength the stars were thicker than anywhere in the world, he thought. He heard the others stirring restlessly but he didn't want any more talk and he let out a deceptive snore. He could sense them settling back in silence as if he had actually admonished them. He closed his eyes and laid there, thoughtless, between waking and sleeping and when he opened them to look up again, the stars were bleeding . . . or they were shooting a single streak of light off to one side as the rising moon dispersed their glow on the near side. It was time to start.

For a moment he lay still, thinking of the long, long road taken to this act and how planless it really was and how out of the way from what he really wanted to do. Yet he had a feeling what he was going to do was right; it was a purpose that hung on and mastered him despite its terrible circumstances. If this had been a carefully wrought plan it could be diverted or corrupted in numerous little ways; it was the other side who worked their will on people by long-standing plottings and gambles and now he, by lying in wait with a will subdued enough not to act until the opportunity came for a decisive stroke, could with a minimum of forces and material create absolute havoc on the camp of the enemy. To your tents, O Enemies, now see to thine own house.

He got to his feet and reached down to buckle on his sword. The others, instantly alert, for they had been restless over the impending ordeal, got up with him. He noticed one was missing, Henry Thompson. —Where is Henry? he asked Salmon. Salmon motioned to a big rock.

Behind it, the Old Man found Henry writing a letter. —What are you up to, Henry? he demanded.

—I am writing to my dear wife, said Henry confidently.

—Mind you take care where you mail it, said the Old Man. —What prompted you to take to the pen at this time anyway?

—These may be my last words on this earth, said Henry, his eyes wide in astonishment that such a question should be asked. He folded the paper very carefully. The Old Man was curious about the letter; he wanted to ask Henry to hand it over to him for perusal but restrained himself.

—I trust it will not uncover our tracks to any great extent, he said glumly.

With the coolness, really the stodginess so prominent in him, Henry said, —I have been sitting here thinking of Ruth and I saw her in my mind's eye and pressed her to my heart.

The Old Man grunted sourly.

—I miss our dear boy too, Captain, and I must say I miss Ruth's society and her advice.

—Do you have any doubts about our mission?

—Yes, Captain, I do. And if I am spared this time I think I had better go home to North Elba and provide for my loved ones.

—How deep do your doubts run, Henry?

—I don't really know, Captain. I have been reading Ruth's letters . . . I really can't express what they make me feel about what is coming. But Kansas is a long way from home.

He shrugged and put the letter in his pocket and took up the sword which had been lying at his side. He stood up, and in his shortness of stature he looked like a small boy. —I'm ready now, Captain. I told her not to write to me any more . . . that I would not be here.

The Old Man put his back up against the rock. —That will distress her. You had best say nothing.

—No. I said, Feel no uneasiness, for I shall be with kind friends. You said, Captain, that we are all in the hands of He that doeth all things well.

—That is what I said, Henry, and I feel it is so . . . but I am troubled about your doubts. Why do you doubt?

Henry looked down at his sword and then said, blurting it out, —I have a feeling that what we are going to do is a sacrifice to Baal. It is a bloodletting and it may not so much be the casting down of his altars as it is laying a victim before it.

He started to walk away, flinching as if in expectation of a thunderous reprimand. The Old Man caught him by the arm. —You must not go, Henry, if this is going to prevent you from standing up to your work.

—You will think I am a coward, which I am not.

—No, Henry. There is a spot in me that flinches from this. All night long the texts have been clashing in my head. God says thou shalt not kill. Christ says love your enemies. But in spite of this evidence there is something in me that will not accept it. My heart gets as hard as a rock and this is a source of despair to me because it is blaspheming God in a way and it is true that if we go on like this there may never be peace or love among men.

The Old Man's grasp on Henry's arm grew tighter, as if he were clinging to him for support. The rising moon threw motes of cold fire on the Roman face. The night, unfolding under the growing radiance, began to glow whitely with the reflection off the rock and slabs of the ravine, cupping the light. The Old Man's metallic voice rang like a cracked bell. —My waters of mercy are choked with muck, Henry, and there is so much clamor in my head to destroy these men that I wonder if God's mercy is only just a fable. God is love, love, I tell myself, but my thought can only rise on the wings of wrath. I go to the Bible, I have for years, hoping to put my anger to sleep with its rocking texts . . . for twenty years I have been trying to ease and chill my blood on this matter but the anger comes on with such noise and strength it could be the Devil himself.

He stopped, looked down, folding his hands in front of him as though in prayer, then broke them apart. —I see the ministers, Henry . . . full of their talk of peace and love. They never risk sin, they never act, they seem to be walking a chalk line, with God steering them from the temptation of anger, but when I see their silence in the face of the sin of slavery, see their silence while souls are sold off for money, the heat explodes in my stomach as if it had burst my bowels out.

—Jesus never killed anybody, said Henry forlornly.

—True, true. He gave himself to be hanged rather than bring on strife. But on the other hand he was marked for the slaughter. David murdered and was an adulterer besides, lusting after strange women. It is a torment to think of these things. I don't know but what I have secret evils in my heart that are just coming to the light. I don't know, Henry . . . but it strikes me that God must think we are very simple to expect Him to do all the work and grub out all the rock from our fields. And to tell you the truth, I am more fearful that I will be made cool than made too hot. Man knows the beginning of sin but he does not know the end and if God means for us to burn away the chaff let us do so. If it turns out that we are wrong; that we are the chaff, then we will be punished. All I know is that a great storm is going to come down that will handle this country worse than people can wonder. This may prevent it. If it is the worship of Baal as you say . . . then let it be the worship of Baal. I have sinned before and will again. The rod of my Father is no stranger to my back.

—Father, said Frederick, coming in on them from behind the rock. —We'd better get going . . . it looks cloudy to the west.

They left the ravine and crossed the road. The Old Man got out his pocket compass and, holding it in his hand, went straight northeast to the point he had noted on Mosquito Creek in the afternoon. Now he set a course directly south and in a few minutes they came upon the path the Doyles used to haul water from the creek up to their cabin. Behind him walked Mr. Townsley, armed, and as intent as any of the others.

They began to come across the evidence of the Doyles' civilization, discarded trash, old bones and broken jars, and the Old Man felt a queer contradictory feeling rising in him, a contempt mixed with compassion for the precarious, hopeless, vulnerable existence that this defilement of the land represented. There was a pathetic little cornfield, choked with weeds and planted among roots and trees. They could not put in a proper field, he mused, that was labor too degrading; they had to hang about courthouses for bureaucratic crumbs, be something connected with the government, even if it meant keeping dogs to catch other men's slaves; being slavery's dogs themselves. — Have your swords ready, he said. —Take care of the dogs if need be.

The cabin was dark and although the intense heat of the day had dispersed somewhat, there was a fetid glow coming from it, the slow warm rot of a compost pile. He closed his eyes and he could feel the cabin standing there, the way a blind man can feel a wall on a sultry day. Tiny little claws of pity began to tear at him. —Go to the door, he said to Frederick, —talk as if you were expected.

Frederick knocked an ordinary kind of knock. They could hear someone moving around inside and then the faint light of a candle glimmered through the chinks. —We are looking for District Attorney Wilkinson. Where is he located? Frederick said.

—Come in, come in! Mr. Doyle's voice rumbled, deeper and more resonant than ever in the languid night. He slid back the bolt and the eight executioners swarmed into the room. The Old Man looked quickly around, seeing what he would expect, chains with padlocks on them, whips, the badly cured skins of small animals such as dogs run to earth. And litter and filth unbelievable in one room, underfoot, on the table: such crazy disorder and so much of it that it seemed a thousand times easier to pick it up than to stumble through it. It was far more than shiftlessness, it seemed like the rack and ruin of humanity itself, as if the living proof of it had sloughed off like dead skin.

Doyle stood holding the candle in a shaky hand, trying to focus on the meaning of this rough entrance, his mouth hanging open. Behind him, drawing back against the edge of darkness was a gray-haired woman whose recoil was so spiritless, her eyes so dead and her whole appearance so drained of her sex and womanliness that she seemed on the thin edge of collapse. With her were children; a dull-eyed girl of fifteen, but physically as robust and germinal as the mother was depleted, two younger boys and an older boy, all these on a huge, ramshackle fourposter bed without a canopy and which had been in a fire and raised its charred posts like trees in a burned over wood lot. The two grown boys slowly and cautiously raised themselves from some piles of old skins and stood blinking in the wavering light, clutching their jeans at their crotches, their rawhide braces dangling loose. Doyle, still befogged with the notion that these men were on a friendly errand, yet finding many awakening, discordant elements there, said in a shaky, self-assurance, —Oh, you are the Old Surveyor. Well, howdy.

He held out his hand and the Old Man side-stepped and said harshly, —We are from the northern army. You are our prisoners.

There was a silence. Doyle's hand began to shake violently. The tiny pool of tallow at the top of the candle began to splash on the flame, sizzling and stinking. Owen reached up and took two shotguns off a rack over the rusty stove, handing them to Oliver. Henry Thompson caught sight of another one under the bed and dragged it out. Doyle's lips began to move oddly. He was trying to whistle for his dog but could not get a pucker from his dry, fear-taut lips. Townsley, a southern man himself, understood this and went out the door. It wheezed on dry, leathern hinges. Doyle threw back his head and in a high, cracked voice he shouted, King, King!

They heard a bark in the distance and then the reverberate howl of a dog running something down as a victim and then the pound and scratch of dog feet coming round the cabin to the door. There was a scuffle, a high, sobbing whine, canine death cries. Townsley had drawn first blood.

—I told you, Jim Doyle, shrieked the woman in a voice startlingly powerful and with a keen edge of rant on it; almost triumphant. —I told you this is what you'd get hanging around the Dutchman's and making them dogs savage.

At this the whole bed started to jiggle and the Old Man, looking over, got the impression that there was abundance and strength there, a terrifying fecundity as sobering as uncovering a lair of foxes and finding the power implicit in the squirming multiplicity of their get.

—Shut up, Mother, ordered Mr. Doyle. The Old Man, pistol in hand, motioned Doyle to step outside. Doyle began to shuffle painfully to the door and when the Old Man looked down at his feet he said, —I got frost sores on my feet last winter. I have to stab them with a knife to get the matter out.

With Oliver and Salmon standing guard in the house, the others formed a threatening ring around Doyle in his dooryard. Doyle looked around instinctively for the rope. There was none hanging from a nearby, convenient tree. The naked swords they carried meant nothing to him and he began to take heart, thinking it was only a warning, or a whipping, perhaps. Out of the house he transformed himself, with familiar ease, from the shiftless father among the dead and living encumbrances he had created, into the public man. His face hardened warily into its customary mask of the bureaucrat. He eyed his captors, sensing indecision.

The Old Man was looking down at Doyle's poor, dirty feet, trying to harden his heart long enough to give the lethal command. You are nothing but a gray worm, he thought, hardly worth the heel of a good man's boot. But you have the means to make other people fear you . . . you have the power of life and death over them, you and your servant the dog. You are strangling a whole race in all its nobility . . . whipping them into groveling, pouring the rotten seed of your loins into the daughters of black warriors and kings . . .

He was startled to hear Frederick's high, querulous voice break the quiet. —Doyle, you are on trial here. Now did you and your gang go to Morse's store and threaten to hang him unless he left the Territory?

—I don't have to answer that, said Doyle, folding his arms over his chest.

—We know you did it . . . we have witnesses.

Doyle looked around and then said with a jeering tone, —You got old man Morse here now? Hey, Morse, you damned, stinking traitor, come out here and say that to my face.

The Old Man was so startled by Frederick's sudden adoption of the judge's role that he had no time to stop him. Now it seemed too late. Doyle's confident assumption that Morse was still around completely changed the picture of guilt. He realized that this deviation from plan could be fatal but he did not dare to stop Frederick; the boys may have discussed this tactic among themselves ... but to open up judicial argument with a man like Doyle, who had sentiently dozed away the best years of his life on the courthouse steps of a dozen southern towns ... —Time is short, Frederick, he said, in a low voice.

—Mr. Morse took such a fright from you bullies that he ran off to the woods with his little boys and he may be dead, said Frederick.

Doyle looked Frederick straight in the eye, sensing the weakness in him, in all of them, and their desire to justify themselves. His assurance that he would get out of this grew apace. —That's nothing to blame me for. Just because he is chicken-livered. He was all right when we left him. You can ask my boys, Drury and Will. They was right there with me. What's all the fussing for? Who was hurt?

The Old Man, his thoughts and resolutions in a whirl, said, —You mind Mr. Doyle. I'll get the boys out here.

He went back into the cabin. Mrs. Doyle was sitting disconsolately at the edge of the bed, her hands folded prayerfully in her lap. The two small children were saying their prayers on their knees beside her. They broke off their Now-I-lay-me's at the Old Man's heavy step and clung despairingly to their mother's skinny arm. The Old Man looked sternly at Drury and William and said, —Go outside.

Muttering obscenities just under their breath, they stalked out, two strong young men, to the judgment ring. The hard pads of their bare feet scuffing across the floor made a sickening calloused scrape, like a beetle running across paper. The Old Man's eyes flickered briefly over the stout form of John Doyle, about equal in maturity to his Oliver. The boy's face was drawn but with an odd glowing expression on it, frightened but fascinated, as if called to this experience. He took a little off-balance step, as if he were going to join his brothers.

—Don't, Johnny, no, cried Mrs. Doyle and, shaking herself loose from the clinging children, she clutched at him with one hand; the other holding the dingy calico gown to her withered breast. She cringed with one side toward the Old Man as if apologizing for her immodesty while her reaching arm, with a detached firmness of purpose, clung to her son. —Don't take him, she moaned. —Don't take my baby. He warn't with them. He's just a baby.

The Old Man left the cabin, carefully closing the door. The Doyle boys were standing beside their father. —Tell them, boys, said Doyle. —We done nothing but throw a scare into old Morse. We was drunk and frolicking a little bit . . . might have chawed him a little mite . . . and the dog took a couple of nips but he was laughing some of the time, now warn't he, Drury?

—That's right, said Drury. —I would take oath on it.

—So if you are giving us a kind of court trial . . . there is a good witness, said Doyle.

The Old Man took off his drooping panama hat and wiped the sweat off from around the band. Standing there in the moonlight, barefaced, his bristling hair slickly tamed into dank locks, his back bending with weary thoughts, he looked like any old farmer stuck with a job beyond his strength already squeezed out between plow handles, beyond a spirit ground just short of dust between sunstroke and frostbite.

Doyle began looking at him with contempt. —I won't even bother fibbing about things to you. But I won't answer no more questions about Squire Morse till he comes to accuse me or his carcass is brought around. Drury, I want you to remember these things and write them down. This ain't the end of this session, by Jesus.

The Old Man, trying desperately to get back on some pivot of action, said hurriedly. —Well, you have taken a hand, haven't you, in bringing slavery men into this neighborhood and you have given information against Free State party members for the purpose of getting writs out on them.

Doyle straightened up and held up his right hand. —God witness, I have done them things. I have welcomed southern men in here because it is their country as much as yours, mister. I am an officer of the court and I ain't doing nothing but to uphold the law by watching folks that are scheming to destroy my country. But they are to be taken care of by the regular courts. We will not even touch one of their cabins unless it is used for a fort or to store guns . . . and then only with writs.

—What about Mr. Morse? said the Old Man.

—Doggone, do you *know* Mr. Morse? He is a no-good son of a bitch. He sells liquor to the Indians. We never shed a drop of his blood or put a mark on him and now hell is busting loose on account of Mr. Morse. Did you know that him and Dutch Henry was as thick as thieves a while back? They was thinking of going in partners on a townsite. Christ, man, you're 'way off the line to break in like this on my wife and my family . . . we don't own no slaves . . . you got no call to bring me to trial except that my politics is different.

—Murder is of the mind, not the hand, said Frederick. —You can kill a man without taking his life, forcing your will on him.

The Old Man stared ruefully into the outer darkness of the woods. Every vesture, every scrap of legality was to be torn away from this act. He wondered if he had better not put Doyle and his sons in the wagon and carry them back to the camp and let them settle the guilt or the innocence of the Doyles and their works. The knowledge that he had about them could not be brought into play here . . . to be used as a shield. He looked at Doyle with a bitter smile.

Doyle took this for a caving in. He was a glib but obtuse man without the least notion of what was blocking the Old Man's responses or first intentions and, of course, could never imagine the personal dilemma confronting his intended executioner. He thought he had talked himself off the hook of these men, weak and infirm of purpose. The Old Man's void of silence was so deep and compelling that Doyle could not stop talking.

—You see things my way you won't regret it, brother. It ain't too late yet for us to make friends. I know who you folks are now that I see the lot of you and I've had my hard thoughts on you as nigger thieves but at least you don't hide what you are, like these sneaking Free-Soilers, skulking around and saying all they want is free soil and meaning to help themselves to my land and Dutch Henry's.

He shook an accusing finger at Henry Thompson. —I remember you and me walking down the road at the time of the election last fall. You declared you'd rather have a daughter marry a hard-working nigger than a lazy white man. I could have arrested you for that . . .

He pointed now at Frederick, his tone half patronizing, half arrogant. —You bought the lead, you big fellow. We know all these things. Mr. Wilkinson knows them. Now you folks are farmers and western men. We'll get along. You won't get nowhere taking part with the Yankees. You can't get the yellow bastards to fight. You boys have the makings of good boys and we Doyles are willing to forget this night....

He held out his hand. The Old Man was far away; probing knowledge and sin. Wondering what would be the worst of it. Wondering if the boys could stand the ultimate knowledge of good and evil he was about to thrust upon them. —Mr. Doyle, he said in a calm voice, —I am ordering the execution of you and your sons as an act of war and a cruel necessity.

Doyle took a shaky step backwards and looked wildly around, finding the sentence as a reality hard to believe, as he had passed it many, many times in threats on other men. Then the significance of the naked swords struck him at last and he gave a small moan of unbelieving anguish and started to faint. He was seized under the arms by Salmon and Oliver. Drury and William, also struck by the almost inevitable collapse suffered by men confronted with ordered death, were taken in hand by Wiener and Henry Thompson, Frederick and Townsley. —Take them up to the stumps, the Old Man ordered, and he began walking the hundred yards or so to the boundary of Doyle's land, pounding his heels into the ground. Owen came with him, holding a sword in his short, withered, and useless right arm.

—Jesus God in heaven, help, help, Doyle was muttering, and the Old Man dropped back to him, thinking of Doyle's mean little life, every act of it circumscribed by its adherence to slavery, and he tried to add some moral splendor to the last minutes of this squalid existence. — Life is a bubble, a leaf, Mr. Doyle, and death is a thing of no great matter in itself. Taking it away from the women and the weepers, it is the same harmless thing your old friend or your old dog suffered yesterday. Tonight millions die with you. It is the least evil of the world; it comes as an insensible and sudden change if we do not sharpen it with fear. Death hastens only to a fearful man. Remember, Mr. Doyle, that God chastens every son He receives and no one knows on this earth but what you are far more worthy in God's sight and loved more by Him than I am.

—You God-damned hypocrite, said Doyle. —You bloody psalm-singing hypocritical bastard taking me out to cut me down and saying prayers over it. If I am so good to God why don't you let me be . . . ?

—Because I am going to meet your tyrannies head on and one of us has got to go under . . .

—Hypocrite . . . whited sepulchre . . . butcher . . . holy butcher, snarled Doyle, now being literally dragged along with his toes trailing in the dirt. —Crazy bastard, don't know you are damned in hell for this . . .

The Old Man answered this hotly, out of the corner of his mouth. — You are getting my blood in a corner, Mr. Doyle. I know well enough your lives may be the only thing standing between me and the devouring flames but I am also aware that good and evil are so tangled up in this world and so woven together that neither of us can ever sort them out.

They had come to the place of the stumps and the Old Man gestured to the big one that Oliver had marked for a block in the afternoon. He continued talking to Mr. Doyle, to take his mind and Doyle's off what was coming. —If Christ was brought down and made to die anew I could not stand by. I would kill the Pharisees and I will not stand by now and see your kind and your dogs and your slow fires killing black Christs. I am a warfaring Christian, God help me, and you may have reason to thank yourself that you are going to eternal glory with God and I am going to the eternal fires of hell. But you are guilty, nevertheless, in my eyes and you are to be put to death in an instant without suffering, and if this is murder I will settle it with myself. Frederick!

Frederick took his place as headsman by the stump and Drury Doyle was brought to it as first victim. He was in a state of near coma and they dropped him to his knees and his head fell forward on the stump. —Blindfold the others, said the Old Man quickly.

—No, no, said Doyle. —I want to see men. I want to shake somebody by the hand . . .

The Old Man lifted his sword, the agreed signal, and then Frederick raised his sword. He looked down at Drury's head lolling on the stump and caught the smell of his human sweat and tears. —No, no, I cannot do it, he cried.

He began to stagger away to a small copse of trees. Owen and Salmon stepped quickly to Drury's side and with a high, keening cry, Owen shifted his sword from his bad arm to his left and brought it down on Drury's head. The blow glanced off hard skull. Owen grimaced from the shock to his hand and took the sword awkwardly in both hands and brought it down again. This time Drury grasped the blade and Owen had to wrest it free. He brought it down again on Drury's head and this time Drury had his arms crossed over it and the sword cut across both of them and they fell, and Owen raised his sword the third time and brought it down with a groan. Everybody heard it hit the hard, obdurate skull, and Salmon knelt quickly and thrust into Drury's belly and it was all over with him. They took his body away and laid it down, and then moved William to the block. He was moaning piteously and moving his head, and Owen first cut his neck a glancing blow and hit again, striking hard skull and Owen turned and hurled the sword into the air, a high arc of bloody steel flashing in the sky and walked away. Salmon closed in and finished off William in the side.

The Old Man went after Owen and when he caught up to him Owen said, —What are we doing, Father?

He was sobbing dryly. —What is happening, Father?

—We are executing.

—But why . . . such little people . . . they are rabbits . . . I can't see why we should be afraid of the likes of them.

—If you don't know now I cannot tell you . . . if you cannot hate the slaveholder's dog worse than the slaveholder! Worse than the slaveholder I hate the white slave serving him . . .

—Then why don't you kill them?

—I have my own work. I am giving orders.

—Are you sure you are being honest about this, Father?

—Perfectly, said the Old Man, with icy calm. —But I don't think you are. You are as bad as Townsley. If you were up on a big fat horse with a monkey suit on and some fat general ordered charge and you rode down some poor Mexican or Indian defending his home with a stone ax or a pitchfork . . . you would lop off his head with a saber cut and consider yourself a great hero. And the ladies would kiss you and you'd get a medal and wind up in the White House. I suppose that's the *honest* way of doing this . . . for hire.

This hit Owen like a shower of cold water. He stood looking dumbly at the Old Man. —Pick that up, his father ordered, pointing to Owen's sword in the grass. Owen did so. In a moment the other six came over from the stumps. The Old Man looked at Frederick. He was white and dazed, he moved like a sleepwalker but when he felt his father's eyes studying him he gave a sad-eyed smile of consent. The Old Man now looked sternly at Salmon, whom he realized was the boy with the most iron in him. —We took care of old man Doyle, Salmon said.

There was no thought in the Old Man's mind that they would not carry the thing through, so they started up the gentle roll of open prairie to Wilkinson's, still heading directly south by a compass line. The Old Man approached with care. If there were elements of a Ruffian posse arriving they would stop here sometime or other for their writs. The house was dark and there were no horses but one standing there. Here again the Old Man had to make a decision about his forces. He put Frederick and Mr. Wiener in the road with two of the shotguns picked up at Doyle's and with the rest went to the cabin. For his own peace of mind he did not want to go in this time and undergo the assault on his sensibilities just suffered at Doyle's. He decided the best thing would be to lure Wilkinson out. In that case, even if Wilkinson had visitors stopping over with him, once he was in hand he would be a hostage against a counterattack.

As they passed the cabin window a dog inside began to bark. Mrs. Wilkinson, sick with the measles, woke up. She nudged Allen Wilkinson awake with a hard elbow into the ribs. —Allen, did you hear that noise . . . ?

—Yes, yes, murmured Allen sleepily. —It's only some people coming up the road.

He dropped off to sleep again but the dog kept on barking and Mrs. Wilkinson heard the scrape of boots and then a knock on the door. —What is that? she called, her pulses pounding with the added thrust of the fever. No one answered. She dug her elbow again into Allen's ribs. He roused himself and rubbed his eyes, lazily and unafraid. There's someone trying to get in, she said. —I know it is the abolitionists.

—They are fifty miles away, he said. —I know what this is; now don't get all het up.

Salmon called out, trying to simulate a southern drawl. —We want to know the way to Dutch Sherman's place.

—Oh yes . . . it is just down the road a half mile or so. You can't miss it. It is right at the ford. The first house you come to is Judge Wilson's office. Go beyond that . . .

The Old Man gave Salmon an impatient dig and Salmon said, —We want you to come along and direct us.

—All right, all right, said Allen submissively. —Just wait until I put some clothes on.

—You're not going out now and leave me in this condition, said Louisa Wilkinson furiously. —Here I am in a fever and in a wash of sweat. What if I should need water?

—I'll only be a moment, said Allen. —These men require directions. I am expected to help out.

—You help your wife and your family . . . that is your great expectation right now. Leaving a sick wife and two small children to go off in the night with some Ruffians drinking over to Dutch Henry's. We've had enough of that . . . too much.

—They are not at Dutch Henry's but at Mr. Harris', that is why I must guide them.

—No, no, said Mrs. Wilkinson, starting to whimper. —You have been the worst man in the world since we moved here!

Allen went regretfully to the door and said, —I can't find my clothes, boys, but I can tell you just as well from here . . . they are not at the store but at Mr. Harris'.

Outside the Old Man motioned for his men to fall back for a consultation. —This proves they are up to mischief, said Salmon.

—We shall have to gain entrance to the house, said the Old Man. They went back to the door and he said, in a low, penetrating voice, into one of its cracks, —Are you on the side of law and order and ready to take action against the northern armists?

—Yes, gentlemen, Allen answered, —I am district attorney here and also the postmaster. I am a member of the Territorial legislature. When you see Dutch Henry he will vouch for me.

—You are our prisoner, cried out the Old Man in a terrible voice. — Open up.

There was a long silence and then Wilkinson answered, abjectly, — Wait, gentlemen, I will get a light.

—Don't open, don't open, said his wife. —What is the matter with you?

—I have to, said Wilkinson, his hand shaking as he lighted the candle. —I have to humor them.

He slid the bolt and the Old Man, Salmon, Henry, and Owen stepped in with drawn pistols, leaving Townsley on guard outside against more dogs. The dog in the house retreated, yelping, under the bed.

Wilkinson stood in the center of the room with the candle held high, as if he were protecting his head. The light fell garishly on his tousled pale hair, spearing out from the exact center of his crown like a doomed dandelion gone to seed and waiting for the decapitation of the wind. —You may ask me anything, he said, in his strangled, knotted grunt of a voice. —I have only done my duty according to the law. My wife is ill and helpless, otherwise I would gladly go with you to the Shermans' and straighten things out. If anyone has done wrong hereabouts . . . doubtless you are thinking of what happened to poor Mr. Morse . . . and I promise you I had nothing to do with it . . . I will take any action you recommend.

The Old Man looked at him in abhorrence, although he was perhaps telling the truth. He would draw writs to arrest his neighbor Doyle and then turn around and draw them to execute those who arrested Doyle; he was conveniently hinged like that, another born bureaucrat of the same breed as Doyle and could serve both sides with the same solemn inaccuracy and frantic cowardice. He did not want to bandy words with this jellyfish blob in the candlelight; there was little time left and Wilkinson's fears were putting our voracious tentacles which could suck resolution out of the strongest. —Have you no other men about? the Old Man asked, and Wilkinson slowly shook his head and looked at him with the ultimate fear, which casts out all loyalties and obligations and is completely truthful.

He ordered a search made for guns and a rifle and a powder flask was all they could find. Salmon went to the corner where the post office pigeonholes were and started to go through the mail matter and look for warrants. The Old Man motioned him away, no longer wanting to risk marring the austerity of the deed itself. —But it's evidence, Salmon said. —Come away, I said, ordered his father.

—Let Allen stay with me until I am better, wailed Mrs. Wilkinson. —He will not run off; I will not let him. He will be here tomorrow or whenever you will call for him.

The Old Man looked coldly at her. She was a fine figure of a woman and her illness had only increased, it seemed to him, her intense vigor and alertness. The children were asleep on the other side of the bed and he could not make them out. —You have neighbors, he said finally.

—So I have, said Mrs. Wilkinson. —But they are not here and I cannot go for them.

—It matters not, said the Old Man.

She turned angrily to Allen and said, —Well, why are you standing there? Why don't you get ready?

—I can't find my boots, he said. —It is damp out.

—You'll need no boots, said the Old Man. —Come along.

The Old Man stopped at the door and said, —Does Mr. McMinn live hereabouts?

She measured hard glances with him for a second or two. Then dropping her eyes, she said, —He lives on the next plain to the east, near the Lykins County line.

Outside the Old Man turned to Townsley saying, —Get his horse.

They took Allen down toward the road, southerly, in the direction of Dutch Henry's. Frederick and Wiener came to meet them. —Frederick, said the Old Man, —you go back up to the house and take the saddles I saw up there.

He did this to get Frederick away from the execution scene and Frederick went up with alacrity. —Oh, you're back, said Mrs. Wilkinson, as he came in. —Now you must stay with me.

—I am here for the saddles, said Frederick, moving clumsily around, getting them out of the corner.

Mrs. Wilkinson leaped out of her bed and threw her arms around Frederick's waist, pressing her hot full-fleshed body hard up against him and saying in a throaty, passionate whisper, —Stay with me, stay with me! I want you to stay with me!

Frederick struggled against her. —I can't, I can't, he said weakly, despairingly, overcome with her wanton desperation. —They won't let me!

—What are they going to do with Allen? she demanded.

—Just take him a prisoner to our camp.

Mrs. Wilkinson let go of Frederick's waist and threw her arms around his neck. —Stay with me. You've got to stay with me.

Frederick swayed with her, laying his cheek briefly against her enfolding, entangling hair, then cast her off. He took the two saddles by their horns and stalked out of the door.

While he was gone, Wiener took over as executioner. Allen Wilkinson knelt down in the road and Wiener tried to dispatch him with one blow but again the unhappy sword hit the hard bone of the obdurate skull and this time Henry Thompson had to come in to deliver the merciful thrust to the victim's heart.

Wilkinson's body was left by the road with no attempt at concealment. And now, the longest and most dangerous approach had to be made to what was probably the occupied headquarters of the enemy. There was another section separating Dutch Henry's from Wilkinson's. It belonged to a man named Wightman. He had been on the bogus grand jury but not on Williams' list of the condemned. The Old Man was disturbed with the problem of McMinn, the foreman of the jury. He was a marked man but his claim, as Mrs. Wilkinson had confirmed, lay to the east and dangerously near to the Lykins County line, perhaps over it, and the Old Man's subtle mind had long since appreciated that so far, everything they had done had been in Franklin County, nominally under the jurisdiction of a court now effectively decimated. Perhaps by abstaining from carrying out the decision in respect to McMinn, he could oblige those who were so concerned about caution; perhaps not involving those living in Lykins County, at any rate. He decided to give up on McMinn and finish off this severe and dreadful night with Dutch Henry.

He was very tired now and very conscious that he had subjected himself and his party to one of the worst ordeals that any human could ever endure, no matter how many times it had been brought off before under the most hallowed and sanctified shibboleths which civilization had flung around the killing of men by one another. Perhaps it would have been better if there had been some fighting back, but there was not. It was a successful ambush or surprise attack and only the most nonsensical sentimentality would regret that it had not been palliated by a bloody struggle between both parties with men killed on both sides.

It was easy traveling down the road to Dutch Henry's. The saddles had been left beside the road to pick up on the return trip. The cabins were all dark but one and Dutch Henry's gray Indian pony was tied at its corner. When they got here, in spite of his common sense, the Old Man felt that he had to burst in on them without dissembling tactics, he was sick to death of those who died like animals in the slaughterhouse. This time he left Frederick, Wiener, and Townsley standing outside and with the rest of the boys, he burst into the cabin, surprising four men playing cards around a rough table. They looked up only briefly and a woman got out of bed and began to fuss around a stove as if to prepare a meal.

—We are from the northern army, said the Old Man. —I advise you to surrender. There are more of us outside. Put your hands on the table, all of you.

This was complied with readily, under his pistol, and Owen began to search the room for weapons, finding two rifles and a bowie knife and some ammunition.

—Where is Dutch Henry? demanded the Old Man.
—He is out, said Mr. Harris.
—Who are you? demanded the Old Man.
—My name is Harris, I live here, he said.

Here the Old Man was presented with another set of problems. There was one more man to go, one more on the proscribed list, and he had set his mind with a resolution of an epic quality to make five for five on this night and gnawing at his consciousness was the death of the younger Doyles and the whole anarchical nature of the deed, which could be carried out only by the most delicate balancing of the mind on one side, or the most gross and uncontrolled madness on the other. He decided to put some questions to the four men here and finish it all up as justly as possible and he motioned for Harris to step out.

Joining him in the dooryard, he said to him, —I am going to put some questions to you and if you answer them now, you will not be troubled.

Like a strong clock running down, the Old Man put these questions to Mr. Harris, who swore with his hand to heaven that he would give honest answers. —Have you had any hand in bringing the pro-slavery men in here to butcher and burn out the Free State men along this creek?
—No.
—Have you taken a hand in guiding or giving supplies to the men that have just now sacked Lawrence?
—No.
—Have you ever done any Free State man harm because of his political belief?
—No.

—Were you with the party that attacked Mr. Morse?
—No.
—Then you can go back in the house, said the Old Man. —But tell me first, how can you live here, Mr. Harris, among these bullies and drunken, traitorous scoundrels?

Mr. Harris shrugged in self-depreciation and said, —Dutch Henry pays good wages, the best in the Territory. He lets me have this house and my found. . . .

The Old Man waved him wearily away and the next man sent out for examination said his name was Glanville. He was from Ottawa Creek and had come down to purchase a cow. He answered no to all the questions and the Old Man let him go back into the house, with a weary shrug, after suggesting that Glanville was down there to report the Free State rally in his neighborhood.

The third man was Mr. Wightman. He said he had come to purchase a cow and the Old Man said, —Is that the same cow Mr. Glanville is here for? Are you going to share it, living twenty miles apart?

Mr. Wightman looked sheepish and the Old Man said, —It is true that you live up on the next claim, isn't it, Mr. Wightman? And you are not here to buy a half of a cow but to make mischief against the Free State men?

Mr. Wightman vigorously denied this and his guilt seemed clear but the Old Man could not get Mr. Doyle out of his head, wondering if he was still alive and suffering from the inept death blows so tragically flawing this episode of pain. He waved Mr. Wightman back into the house in an almost perfunctory way. The other men were watching him closely now. —Salmon, he said, —are you sure you finished up with Mr. Doyle?

—Yes, said Salmon. —I saw to it myself. He is dead.

Then Dutch Henry's brother, the fourth man, came out and Mr. Wiener began to stir in anger at him. The Old Man put his first question to Dutch Bill, knowing the answer; that he had threatened Mr. Morse, that he was a fearsome bully and brute who had held the Grant girl against the point of a knife, who had held the ax at Morse's neck and threatened blood and destruction to dozens of Free State settlers, but a great lassitude and anguish overcame him and his voice faltered. Dutch Bill began to answer him in a thick stream of German and Mr. Wiener, who had held back the fact that Dutch Henry had attacked him and threatened to kill him in his own store, indicated that he wanted to take over the questioning. The Old Man agreed and told Salmon to take charge. He turned away and mounted Dutch Henry's pony. He galloped back up the road again to Doyle's claim. At the place of the stumps, he came across the bodies, and then saw, in the cruel moonlight and with unspeakable horror and self-loathing, the results of the humane death he had planned, knowing that now people would say of him that which he hated and dreaded more than anything, that he had mutilated these bodies. Perhaps they were stunned by the head blow into unconsciousness, he thought defensively.

He turned away from them, accepting what he had to and went to look at Mr. Doyle. In his weariness and shock, he could not see a stunning or terminal wound on Mr. Doyle. He drew his pistol, and risking the alarm he had used the swords to avert, he put a reverberating shot into Doyle's forehead. Then, reaching down for his pulse, he found the body cold with long-present death and he felt, for a moment, an ignoble, exculpating joy that he, himself, had not killed anyone this night.

The morning light was breaking, the darkness disappeared. Riding south down the road, he met his little company returning from their final errand. —Where is Henry, why is he missing? he questioned, slipping off his horse to walk beside them.

—He went over to Osawatomie to mail a letter to Ruth, said Salmon. —He said it wouldn't take long.

The Old Man groaned. —We have been walking all night with the Devil, and this goes to prove it. Matters couldn't be worse. Salmon, you and Oliver go up to the Doyles' cabin and see if they have any horses out back.

The weary, bloodstained, blood-tainted men came at last to their place of concealment and stumbled down into the dawn-bleak pit of slabs and boulders. Frederick held back, crying out, —I don't want to go down there to jostle among the rocks any more. It's like a spoiled graveyard down there ... struck by lightning or split open by an earthquake with all the filthy bones mixed up with broken headstones.

—*Stone Dead is no enemy*, said the Old Man, in cryptic answer. —Now if I were offered a thousand dollars for a tear, I could not sell it.

God in Love

The last large work Truman Nelson undertook was *God in Love: The Sexual Revolution of John Humphrey Noyes*, a novel he planned to cover the fascinating story of the nineteenth-century theologian, social prophet, and charismatic founder-father of the Oneida Colony. Nelson saw Noyes's sexual/gender revolution as the logical climax to his series of earlier novels outlining the radical abolitionist-transcendentalist movement.

Theodore Parker, Wendell Phillips, Ralph Waldo Emerson, William Lloyd Garrison, Henry David Thoreau, and John Brown all represented a liberation movement that ultimately freed black people from the massive evil of chattel slavery. Noyes was a prophet who preached the liberation of women—and, therefore, men too—from the cultural slavery of sexual and gender typing, repression and oppression, and the erosive miseries of the unexamined family life: unwanted children, dangerous pregnancies, sexual dysfunction, and the separation of a whole erotic life from a possible social life.

John Humphrey Noyes (1811–1886) began his odyssey with the theology of Perfectionism—the belief that Christ liberated humanity from its original fallen condition: his sacrifice brought us the promised Kingdom of Heaven, in which we still live, free of guilt and inherent sin. Preaching this subversively optimistic heresy, Noyes was led to consider sexuality not as the burden, curse, or stigma sometimes reflected in Pauline or Calvinist theology but as a vital physical

From the unpublished novel *God in Love*. Reprinted by permission of W. W. Norton, Inc., New York.

and spiritual expression of self, the completion of humanity and communion of souls—and bodies. Noyes moved boldly to understand the psychology and physiology of sex, to envision a community of men and women who could experience a total and authentic "sexual revolution"—in the 1840s!

Truman Nelson saw Noyes's prophecy and struggle in parallel with the work of Theodore Parker in Boston, George Ripley at Brook Farm, and John Brown in Kansas. All worked with fevered intensity to free humanity of burdens, errors, and ancient curses embodied in contemporary society. Nelson also recognized in Noyes's story the roots of America's "sexual revolution" of the 1960s. The highly successful experiment of the Oneida Colonists, who flourished in their utopia for over half a century, left a legacy of social and genetic studies still significant—the first real trial and understanding of eugenics (which Noyes called "stirpiculture").

In his last debilitating illness, Nelson was unable to complete the epic of Noyes and his family of love, but he did trace Noyes's early years, through his important discoveries of "male continence" (a yogic process of contraceptive sex), "mutual criticism" (the psychosocial therapeutic analysis of colonists), "complex marriage" (the shattering of monogamous ties and the establishment of sexual relations between multiple partners), and other basic radical principles of his society. *God in Love* shows us the genesis of Noyes's remarkable work and vividly portrays this genius of love and sexuality.

From *God in Love*

The following excerpt is the apogee of Noyes's early planning and organizing, the moment in 1847 when Noyes leads his first small band of Perfectionists toward the promised land of bliss and equality between the sexes. The bulk of the novel traces Noyes's growth as a social and spiritual leader, his trek from his student days as a seminarian to his leadership of a growing band of committed communitarians. We see him about to strike out into terra incognita, a new settlement on Oneida Creek with a new agenda of social action. The journey begins in New York City, but it will lead to a community free from the shadows and fears that Noyes saw in his corrupt social order. It is also a movement from slavery to uncharted freedom, symbolized by the statue of the Greek slave, the sensuous nude sculpture lighted dimly behind the banqueters.

To the Hall of the Greek Slave

Harriet Holton Noyes—granddaughter of a former lieutenant governor, niece of the town's leading lawyer, wealthy heiress, always of the best people—lay in her lonely bed in the house on Christian Square. It was late, but town roughs gathered on the steps of the church across the street, after an evening's drinking at Black's Tavern, where they shouted threats and lewd remarks at the Noyes residence. The sheets were icy cold, and she sadly remembered the warmth of her husband's bare body, lean and flat but radiating heat like a poker just drawn from the coals. She felt she was plunged in a pool of icy water, a baptism of utter fear. Rumors were strong that tonight the mob would rise and come against them, hurting, tearing their lives asunder, perhaps even burning them in their beds. Her clothes were carefully fixed on the chair beside her, her stockings on the top. Little Theodore was beside her along with the little tin trunk that carried Noyes's papers.

She tried to banish fear from her mind by thinking of a retreat (and they had a little money for this) where they could go and just study and read and talk and dream systems that did not have to be put into practice. Her body began to warm the bed, and she thought of the time when Noyes was "discovering" Male Continence. He had assumed she had slept through most of this, but she had not—she was awake as much as he was, and it was wonderful, and of course would never be repeated.

She thought of George Cragin and his gentleness. He never made demands on her as John did. He was the gentlest, sweetest man in the world. And he had had to flee in the night with Mary and the three children. They said the Cragins only missed arrest by minutes. And now she didn't know where they were. Nor had she heard anything from John: Larkin Mead had "advised" her that this was perhaps—or very probably—because he was in jail and couldn't write. He said no matter where Noyes went, if he espoused any of his ideas (and he would), he would end up in the city prison.

She got thinking of the letter George had written her and John's strange reaction, which she now understood, in terms of the immense care and attachment she had demanded of him, which he had given without complaint. No wonder the thought of a separation, or the diversion of another love, bothered him so much. And then she remembered another letter, a note Noyes had left in her care, telling her to give it to George. She had thought he meant George Cragin, and he was gone, but then she realized that it was for Young George. He had been left as their spokesman. She was still too bashful to stand at the desk at the Chapel and carry on the meeting. And the next morning was Sunday.

She jumped out of bed, found the letter carefully placed in the bureau drawer. She opened it and left her room to bring it to Young George. It was very important. She was dumbfounded to see a candle burning in Young George's room. He was packing, about to leave. His wife was not there. She was relieved at this.

Shortly after the Proclamation of the Kingdom of God in Putney, Noyes had married off his young brother and young Mr. Woolworth to the Campbell girls, Helen and Emma, in their early twenties. They were Acksah's daughters and had been brought up in the faith. Young George had desperately wanted to marry a beautiful fifteen-year-old named Lucinda Lamb, but her father had threatened to sue—and was now suing—them "for enticing Lucinda away to the serious injury and expense of her father." George had resented the fact that his powerful brother gave in to this intimidation.

George's young face was milk white in the candlelight, and when he saw his brother's wife, he said, "Now don't try to stop me. Helen has given me all the tongue-lashing I need at the moment."

"Why are you leaving?"

"Simple. Larkin Mead told me tonight the attorney general is getting ready—is drawing papers—to arrest all the men in the Community for gross lewdness and offenses against chastity, morality, and decency. Larkin says that's from the ninety-ninth chapter of the revised statutes of the State of Vermont."

"Why don't you read a chapter from Saint Paul? He never ran away."

George looked at her and then down at his bag, his face flushing. "Maybe my brother should have read it. He absconded. He ran away."

"Who told you that?"

"Larkin Mead. And Helen says it's all over the village that he did."

"I can only think that girl is possessed by an evil spirit. It tears at her every day. She gives her tongue full liberty to talk about your brother and his 'delusions,' as she called them."

"He shouldn't have absconded. That's what started everything."

"It was Larkin Mead who forced him to go away. He went to Brattleboro to give himself up for imprisonment, to draw the fire away from us. Your brother carried to Brattleboro a written proposal to surrender himself to the law, without bail, on condition of peace for the rest of our society. Larkin convinced him that if he did that, they would kill him in jail, like they did Joe Smith, and then turn on us and destroy us, root and branch. He went away to save us from the barbarians of Putney. You should be ashamed, George."

"Well, Mr. Miller put me up to it, really. He said I must consult with John about what to do with the paper. The vigilance committee busted in on us yesterday. Dr. Campbell kicked Mr. Miller in the shins, and then they presented us with resolutions as long as your arm, saying we had to shut down the paper. And they want their answer in writing. . . ."

She opened the letter and handed it to him. "There is your answer in writing. In your brother's writing."

He brought it nearer the candle flame and read it carefully:

To the Putney Community. The best thing I can do for you now is to give you our position as seen by my standpoint. My desire is to see things as God sees them, hating the fire-eye of fanaticism on one hand, and the fish-eye of unbelief on the other. We have drawn the issue deliberately and no one directly concerned makes any complaint. Because we have initiated a new and splendid theory of sexual rights and relations and proved our power of healing, we have discovered the governments of this world positively forbid the social state of heaven. They will never yield this to us of their own accord.

However, on to practical matters: As to abandoning the testimony that the Kingdom of God has commenced, or acknowledging that we have done wrong, that is out of the question with me. I shall cheerfully suffer the spoiling of goods or imprisonment or death rather than bend in that way. I cannot concede to friends or enemies the right to stop my mouth or muzzle our press permanently, or for any great length of time. The threat of losing two thousand or ten thousand dollars will not deter me from speaking what justice to God and man demands. Yet I shall not brave public opinion in such a way as to put the Community in deep peril and if we cannot publish in Putney . . . God will find another place for our press. I would prefer to stop it altogether, if it is under restriction, and all of you are threatened.

George's face brightened noticeably. She said, "I want that read in the Chapel tomorrow. Please to omit the last paragraphs." George read them buoyantly to her:

Dear Harriet: It seems hardly right that I should leave, even for imprisonment, while you are battling the storms of Putney. But I thought my presence with you would only increase the fury of the storm. There are certain people, you will know who I mean, that you might quietly ask to leave, not because of their offensiveness but because the Pharoahs of Putney in their broad-cloth coats who rule the Tavern mob are crazy with fear that they will come on the town for support. Do this delicately. Be kind to Sissie. Experience has shown that she needs an atmosphere of faith. Her friends could cause her death by driving us away and breaking up our assembly of tender spirits. Putney is not up to the times in religious and revolutionary progress.

I remember with love and pride your attendance at the Lairdsville and Genoa Conventions with me. You helped prepare doubting men and women to face the furnace prepared for them, as Shadrach, Meschak, and Abednego faced the furnace of Nebuchannezzer . . . and pledge to Bible Communism their lives, their fortunes, and their sacred honor. I think of you now as the mother and the representative of our Community in my absence. Don't let public opinion scare you . . . nor keep you from any communication which God manifestly approves and directs.

Your true lover
John H. Noyes

The next they heard, there had been a note from Noyes handed Mr. Miller at the store by a drummer from New York City. It asked Mr. Miller if he had enough generalship to bring the whole party to New York through the whirlpools of the railway stations and to "keep the children on the cars at momentary stations." They were to gather at the Hall of Power's Greek Slave.

The Hall of the Greek Slave Noyes was talking about stood on lower Broadway in New York City. Some enterprising showman had got hold of a copy of Hiram Power's *Greek Slave*, the nude marble depiction of a beautiful young Christian girl taken prisoner by the Turks and about to be sold off at a slave market for some lucky pasha's harem. Her wrists were encircled with manacles and her left hand was chastely placed to cover her mesial grove. The purity of the white marble, her plight—which right-thinking Americans saw as symbolic of the chattel slavery of the blacks—made her nudity acceptable, and the

Reverend Orville Dewey, one of the moral masters of the nation, found her "Clothed all over with sentiment, sheltered, protected by it from every profane eye."

Not everyone saw it exactly like this, including Noyes himself, who loved nudity and felt that the real loss of the Garden of Eden came when Adam and Eve (who were *not* ashamed so long as they were one) "became two, and were ashamed." Then began evil-eyed surveillance on the one hand and morbid shrinking on the other—and then *shame* and *personal isolation*.

Not everyone, to be sure, saw the Greek Slave as Noyes did, but in any case it was a very popular show, and the exhibitor could afford to close the exhibition hall during the evening with its heat and lights shut off. Noyes rented it cheaply. It was located over a popular restaurant and the heat from its kitchen made the hall comfortable. Noyes had tables set up in a square arrangement, the familiar square mandala of his New Haven days. He told the people he had invited that their *Convention* should be a marriage, not an exhibition, a private though not secret gathering, so they could lay their foundations in quiet without provoking the ridicule and animosity of the dogs and swine that rule the press and public opinion.

When the people came, carrying lamps or candles, the soft light of each increasing illumination made the body of the Greek Slave blossom and glow, and the greetings and movement of people gave a wavering, nebulous light so at times the marble woman seemed to come alive while shadows, shifting and deepening irregularly, sometimes cast highlights on breasts, swelling flanks, sleekly dipping thighs. Some were so bold as to bring their lights to the statue itself and move the lights to animate the figure, as the prehistoric people in the caves of France had moved their crude lamps of animal grease in front of the cave drawings to make their animal gods come to life in their worshipping eyes.

Noyes began the meeting sitting directly under the Greek Slave, flanked by his wife on his right, Mary Cragin on his left, Acksah next to her, and Sissie to the right of his wife. He talked at first about Putney: "... where the social theory I intend to discuss tonight was first developed in a *Society* of *Inquiry*. From this school of Believers in Holiness we advanced from community of faith, to community of property, community of households, community of affections.

"While these movements were going forward, the Putney Community, being located in the midst of a New England village, and, of course, surrounded by religious jealousy, was exposing itself more and more by the development of its revolutionary social principles to the indignation and intrigues of its enemies. Public excitement rose against the prominent members to a tumultuous pitch. It became evident that the only peaceable course open was to retire from the village and seek a new location.

"At two recent conventions, attended by most of the people I see here, in Lairdsville and Genoa in the state of New York, it was resolved that we would from now on devote ourselves to the establishment of the Kingdom of God, that it would have an external manifestation, and that we would train ourselves in its principles and put ourselves in conformity to them, as soon as possible.

"We felt the leading principle should be the complete renunciation of all forms of and claims to private property. This would take place in a domain in central New York, which we have already acquired from Mr. Burt, sitting over there. Stand up, Mr. Burt."

Mr. Burt jumped up to take a bow, but the applause was so great he could not forebear saying a few words. "At the close of the talk, Mr. Noyes took from his pocket a small bag which contained five hundred dollars in five-dollar gold pieces and gave it a whirl on the bed, saying, 'I offer this as my contribution to a New York Community.'"

Burt sat amid more applause, and Noyes continued. "It consists of one hundred and sixty acres in a secluded valley on the Oneida Creek, between Utica and Syracuse. It is now occupied by a sawmill and affords power for a grist mill, machine shops, and the like. It has been paid for in full."

He paused here, but he did not reveal that the money Horatio had advanced him (really for getting out of town and ceasing to be an embarrassment) had gone for this payment. He concluded, "There are two ordinary houses and two log cabins at present on the site, and there is plenty of lumber and machinery to construct a Mansion House for our Heavenly Association."

There was more loud applause and cheerfulness all around at this opening. Then he plunged into the difficult part. "This report would not be complete without a full and frank discussion of the relationship of the sexes and their reconciliation with God and each other, which is the principal reason for us coming together. I have prepared material under other heads—Labor and Finance, Arrangement of the Household, Religious Exercise, Common Table, Education—but these are all moot until we examine the core of our belief, as originated by John H. Noyes, while a member of the senior class at Yale Theological Seminary. It was called the Doctrine of Perfect Holiness, or Perfectionism, and it went from theory to practice at Putney, Vermont, and will be embodied at Oneida Creek.

"These theories were first given in the *Battle Axe Letter*, and from the time of its publication I felt that I was called, even under the heaviness of penalties, to defend and ultimately carry out the *Communism of Love.*"

He could sense some of the men getting restive and looking nervously around. Some couples, on the other hand, began holding hands. An argument broke out between a couple. He waited. Finally the man got up and left. His wife, after an uneasy moment or two, left to follow him. The man came back and took away his lamp. Other couples began to move on this, leaving and taking their candles or their lamps, and the glow on the Greek Slave grew noticeably dimmer.

"The theory of absolute Communism of Love, has never, as far as I know, been broached in the world. The Primitive Church left on record only the negative doctrine of no marriage in the Resurrection. And the only positive theories of the sexual relation I know of are 'affinities,' which is really marriage. The Resurrection in the highest sense of the word—the rising of the soul and body into union with our divine nature, the regeneration for which we wait—will only come with the advent of what we refer to as sexual freedom."

There were more defections. He paused calmly to let little flurries of argument rise and resolve and noted that most disputants were men, who sometimes literally dragged their wives away.

"By this we do not mean Free Love, as it is sometimes called. With us there is no freedom to love today and leave tomorrow, freedom to take a woman's person and keep our property to ourselves; nor freedom to freight a woman with our offspring and send her downstream without care or help. Nor does it mean freedom to beget children and leave them on the street or in the poor houses."

He paused again as two couples, standing indecisively beside the exit, decided to come back. Their lamps were out and they did not relight them. Some others left. The Greek Slave was now no more than a collector of shadows.

"We have discovered, through our experience at Putney, that our communities must be distinctly bounded and separated from outside society, even as the ordinary family is, with its intimacies. The tie that binds us together is as *permanent* and *sacred*, to say the least, as marriage. For it is our religion, and we will receive no new members who do not give heart and hand to the Community, for life and forever."

This caused the largest mass exodus. He had come down hard on the words, *permanent* and *for life*. He added, "Whosoever will take the trouble to follow our tracks from the beginning will find no forsaken women or children by the way.

"We have found the way to make love *free* is to purify the mind and let in the light. To clear away the vile, debasing associations that usually crowd around thoughts of the sexual organs and their uses. We substitute true and beautiful associations. The union of the child with its mother in nursing is not base but lovely, even sacred in the imagination.

"Sexual intercourse is *more* lovely and sacred! Instead of thinking of it as lust, vice, and woe, it is as easy—and truer to God's will and our own natures—to associate it with the Garden of Eden, with the Holy of Holies, thoughts of purity and chaste affection, joy unspeakable and full of glory. The wisest of men expressed this joy in a great song of love."

No one was leaving now; attention was rapt. He moved back a little and his head and shoulders hid the manacled hand of the Greek Slave. Her upper body—although shrouded somewhat in the insufficient light—gave off a sensuous gleam from her perfect face and breasts.

"With pure minds and hearts we may approach the sexual union as the truest Lord's Supper, a more perfect symbol than eating bread and drinking wine. To sup with one another is really more sensual than to sup with roast turkey and chicken pie. Pure thoughts are surely better than the shame that envelops the whole sexual department in filth and darkness, even in the minds of those who would be thought of as intelligent and refined. Is there a Christian who will deny that the Bible constantly associates ideas of heaven with sexual intercourse? See Isaiah, chapter sixty-two, verses four and five. See Matthew, chapter twenty-two, verses two and four, chapter twenty-five, verses one to twelve. And Revelations, nineteen, seven, twenty-one and two, nine, et cetera, et cetera."

He paused a moment but felt his best ending was this citation of chapter and verse. His theme could not be defeated on those. He looked at his wife and said, "Harriet, there are eighty-seven people here for our first supper, including myself. Can it be managed?"

She rose and smiled, "We have enough for five hundred." The thirty men and women of the Putney Community got up and went to the back door of the hall opening on the stairway to the restaurant kitchen below. In no time at all, it seemed, they came up the stairs carrying huge platters of corn beef (slabs as big as tombstones), heaping piles of glistening white potatoes, squash, pumpkin, cabbage, rutabaga, carrots, onions all silvery, beets in their rosy glow, all the majestic architecture of the New England boiled dinner, literally the fruits of their summer of unrestricted love. All the preliminaries and joinings of Complex Marriage had been carried out in the field and woods beyond. There were no rooms set aside for this purpose, and Noyes frowned on open affectional displays. It was all done with glances and jostling and working together in the fields, among the corn and growing things, exchanging the hoe handle, chopping weeds side by side, sweating and glowing and loving in the smell of the hot earth and the dim leafy forest and the pine needles and the sun-warmed rocks and under the mating of the tall pointed firs and shadowy oaks.

Noyes drew from his inner pocket an apron, put it on, and began distributing the plates. He put them nearer the statue, and the people had to move together and bring their lights, and the Greek Slave began to glow again with all the effulgence of the bright moon above the Putney fields and forests.

When they were all seated, and the steam still rose like incense from the food, Noyes said, "I don't usually say Grace, but I must point out that there *is* grace here. With this good food and God's help, may we create a resurrection society, so the people of the world will have the peace, the vigor, and the vitality of a true Resurrection!

"Oh, Lord, give us this day our daily love. . . ."

II Essays

The Variations

Truman Nelson's essays cover a broad spectrum of topics and ideas that stem from his commitment to radical thought, feeling, and action and from his self-assurance as a literary artist. In these meditations, Nelson amplifies and analyzes the sources of his historical fiction. He also suggests courses of radical thought and practice in our own times.

In "On Creating Revolutionary Art and Going Out of Print" (1972), Nelson looked back at his accomplishments in his historical fiction. The survey is judicious, beginning with a premise, Nelson's realization that "a revolutionary morality is inextricably woven into the expanding network of the world's advance and that it already runs its course through the American fabric with a greater purity and continuity than anywhere else." Nelson reviews his creation of the three historical novels, their public reception, and the current state of writing, publishing, and reading in the United States. He concludes that our literary culture has increasingly become dominated and narrowed by a combination of purely commercial interests (writing as "commodity," readers as "consumers") and a straitened academic concept of literature (writing as "syllabus," readers as "students"). The essay defines Nelson's position as a radical historian, thinker and artist outside the fashions and modes of mid-twentieth-century literature and criticism.

In surveying the abolitionist-transcendentalist pantheon, Nelson always sees near the apex William Lloyd Garrison, the tireless editor-propagandist of *The Liberator*, a newspaper that for thirty-five years was the loudest voice in America against the colossal evil of slavery. "The Liberator" (1966) presents a survey of Garrison's life and accomplishments. While literary artists and politicians of 1830 to 1860 are often extolled and credited with the force of abolitionism, Garrison is overlooked. A humble—but brutally effective—*worker* in the movement, whose words and personal actions literally *forced* America to deal with the "problem" of slavery, Garrison seems an improbable hero. Nelson notes, "Garrison today is denied both logic and moral power. His exaggerations, his high poetry, his inability to adjust to political expediencies, have created a current judgment that he stated the obvious at the top of his voice too many years and too repetitively to be taken seriously as a major prophet." The paradoxes of Garrison's ideas and actions abound: he was a pacifist inciting direct action against authority, a thinker who was repeatedly physically assaulted for his beliefs, a self-educated working man who inspired the greatest writers of his age, an optimist who graphically described the vilest sin and evil. Nelson brilliantly resolves these paradoxes, summarizing Garrison as an effective, practical catalyst of revolutionary abolitionism: "He did not go away and construct little models of a new form of society which tried to screen out all humanity's ugliness, error and cruelty. He took man as he was, with all his sin and darkness on him, and tried to ignite in him, by the abrasive power of statement, conviction and sacrifice, a flood of cleansing light."

"Thoreau and John Brown" (1966) is a masterly conjunction of apparently contradictory characters and ideas in the history of the abolitionist-transcendentalist movement. Nelson examines the doubleness of Thoreau's character—the loner-individualist versus the social revolutionary–political visionary appalled by the evil of slavery. Using John Brown as a measure, Nelson shows how Brown's actions and final martyrdom galvanized Thoreau. The careful argument reviews Thoreau—usually described as a wispy romantic figure, an eccentric or a gifted wastrel—from a new perspective. Nelson meditates on the tragic wound in the American spirit and polity that John Brown cauterized through his sacrificial actions. Nelson describes Thoreau's immediate empathetic response and moral self-identification with Brown: "Thoreau shouldered and put along with for the rest of his life, the full burden of his responsibility and affinity to John Brown's revolutionary morality; to the tragic waste, the straits, the conspiracy, the killing, the tenderness, love and sacrifice, the whole diapason of upheaval that lesser men find so abhorrent." The meditation on both characters is a major contribution to understanding American literature and history through the minds of two of the central actors in the drama of the mid-1850s.

Truman Nelson's interests also reach into our own times, and in considering the amazing career of a major scholar-historian-writer-theorist in "W. E. B. Du Bois as a Prophet" (1965), Nelson reviews the after-history of abolitionism. Du Bois is for Nelson the exemplar of the scholar as prophet, the activist-intellectual: "The world of W. E. B. Du Bois was the world of color, and its people the majority of all the earth's people. I think of him as WORLD MAN ONE. No man ever moved within a wider bracket of humanity." The essay recounts DuBois's long, honorable career as an advocate of black pride and industry, his visionary sponsorship of the African Congresses, his historical commentaries, a long lifetime of brilliant work "to organize intellect, black intellect, black articulateness, to countervail forever this degradation [of racism], this sullenness that is taken for apathy or ignorance and which destroys the psyche far more than guilt over a sudden act of violence ever will." Nelson ends with Du Bois's shameful indictment on subversion charges in 1951, when he was in his eighties. Nelson rightly calls this absurdity a "tragedy," an effective ploy to frustrate and silence the most able and articulate black activist of the twentieth century, America's ignoble attempt to disown one of its most gifted native sons.

In 1964, Nelson became involved in a case known as the Harlem Six—the arrest and abuse of young men during the civil unrest of that "long hot summer." He transcribed taped interviews with the young men, their friends and families, creating a document dramatizing institutionalized racism in operation, revealing its devastating effects on the lives of oppressed people. *The Torture of Mothers* (1965) was first printed by Nelson himself, under his Garrison Press imprint. When it was excerpted by *Ramparts* magazine in 1966, it gained a wide reputation as a living statement on revolutionary change. Nelson's commentary on the eloquent testimony he collected is a gloss on the *facts* of racism as a corrosive condition of life for most black Americans. In documenting the treatment of this one case of injustice and active oppression, Nelson demonstrates the depth and permanence of racist attitudes and practices, the failure of U.S. society to dispense—or even approximate—"freedom and justice for all." The passion of Nelson's own language is amplified by the counterpoint of black voices he recorded as historic testimony to conditions in the richest country on earth.

Extending his experiences and observations on the struggle of black people for freedom in the 1960s, Nelson wrote *The Right of Revolution* (1968). One section from this study of America's rich revolutionary heritage, "No Rights, No Duties," details the historical backgrounds of revolutionary change, to give context to the work of black activists and to connect the great surge for freedom in mid-1960s America with a long, honorable and *constitutional* right of our people. "There was the Boston Massacre," Nelson writes, "and there was the Newark Massacre. The last took place yesterday, in our time, in our country; the men who carried it out bore our faces, the bullets that found their way anonymously into black bodies were paid for, in part, by us. It is our consciousness, our heritage, vibrating in the air we breathe." With the force of his convictions and the logic of his long study of our radical inheritance, Nelson puts the struggles of black Americans in the twentieth century into focus as the inevitable consequence of our history and principles. He excoriates the racism that subverts justice and demonstrates how the foundations of our polity *demand* the responsibility of individuals and social groups to *change* unjust conditions: "The American black man is a citizen in a rich land, with a citizen's rights and duty to resist, resist all attempts to deprive him of its manifold blessings. Even if he doesn't *want* to resist, he must; it is his duty, as it is the duty of all honest whites to urge him and support him in the process."

Truman Nelson wrote his essays in the 1960s, while he worked with radical causes, traveled across the United States, lectured, and spoke with groups ranging from university forums to small activist committees. Many were first presented as speeches, in the tradition of Emerson's essays. These short, meditative works follow the great themes of his novels as variations, continuations of the thought and feeling he poured into his imaginative writing of the 1950s. As he concludes "The Conscience of the North" (1961), in which he reconsiders Theodore Parker, the prophet of his first novel, Nelson brings the great theme into focus for our century:

We must travel the road to perfectability together . . . to our fulfillment as persons, as citizens, and the road goes in only one direction . . . into a life of principle, under the guidance of ideas, in response to the great and accursed questions of personal independence, the citizen's relation to the state, the right to resistance, the wrong of poverty, racism, and bigotry and the quickening vision of the brotherhood of man all over the world.

This, in miniature, is the credo demonstrated in both the fiction and the essays—the themes of our revolutionary past played out as live variations in the immediate present.

On Creating Revolutionary Art and Going Out of Print

As long as I can remember having any political consciousness at all, I have been shocked and obsessed by the awareness that this is not really a land of the free. Like many other innocents growing up, I began to wonder if the whole complex of libertarian ideas and promises I was told to live by and to defend with my life was not a pious fraud. If I looked on the gross corruption of the rights of man, the ground rules, supposedly, of our daily existence, with unstirred contemplation, I knew I was committing a sin against my own senses, against the light that was in me. If I accepted the disparity in the human condition existing all around me, I knew I was committing the greatest of sins: that of hypocrisy, which blinds a man to his own failings and gives him a false idea of his position and purpose in the world. Pressing forward for some answer to the accursed questions confronting every practicing citizen, I finally began to understand that a revolutionary morality is inextricably woven into the expanding network of the world's advance and that it already runs its course through the American fabric with a greater purity and continuity than anywhere else.

Why, then, was it always blacked out, always denied—historically, juridically, politically? Why were our heroic personalities, the carriers and reinforcers of the lifeline to a future beyond the chaos of a

"On Creating Revolutionary Art and Going Out of Print" first appeared in *TriQuarterly*, a publication of Northwestern University, 23/24 (1972): 92–110; reprinted in *Literature in Revolution*, ed. George Abbott White and Charles Newman (New York: Holt, Rinehart and Winston, 1972).

greedy and irrational society, so denigrated, so deprinciplized that they could no longer fortify the hope that we can establish a rational world of peace and beauty. As the great names came to mind, now on far-off shores, dimly seen, the names of Sumner, Theodore Parker, Garrison, John Brown, Wendell Phillips, Frederick Douglass, Atgeld, Debs . . . I began to realize that these men have been exorcised because they understood and dramatized those crises which came at the peak of the flowering of a young and vigorous capitalist democracy, dramatized them in ways which led to the unmasking and sharpening of the very contradictions which will cause this bloom to fade and flower into yet higher social forms. The savage irony is that the contemporaries of these noble and prophetical men, most of them a hundred years dead, were better prepared to understand the multiple revolutionary crises engulfing the world presently than we are; were better fitted to keep this republic intact because they were less liable, through ignorance and apathy, to tolerate the militarist-bureaucrat assaults on colonial revolutions which could trigger the ultimate holocaust for humanity.

No one talks of this, but somewhere along the line our primary right has been taken from us: the right of revolution, of resistance to any government which is clearly destructive of all other inalienable rights of man. The proof that this is gone and that hardly anything is left of the truth between us and our revolutionary beginnings lies in the things that have been done by the white people to the black people here and all over the world . . . things that have made many of us want to secede from the white race. It is in this area that we find the historical contradictions and conflicts most clearly developed; here millions of oppressed people and the classic "one reactionary mass" generate polar tensions which can only exist in the real world when crisis is at its zenith, when political action and passion is at its most elemental and decisive stage.

My overruling purpose has been to get the greatest number of people to rethink the whole concept of revolutionary morality . . . to keep it alive as a living faith. No one will ever do this, I know, because I ask them to, although the urgency of this demand is attested by crisis after crisis in the daily press. This is a revolutionary epoch but we cannot judge it intelligently by its own day-by-day consciousness, any more than we can judge an individual by his own opinion of himself. So I turned to an intensive study of the period immediately preceding the Civil War, a massive struggle in which, willy-nilly, the fundamental interest of a huge oppressed class was realized. About ten years ago, I stumbled upon an event which, in the sharpest way imaginable, presented a view of crisis at its zenith.

What I had been looking for was a situation in which it was possible for a small number of dissenters to release in one action, uncontrollable explosive forces which could overturn an oppressive social system. It had to be a small group in order that their personalities could be explored with enough depth to invest the affair with a credible human scale. In May, 1854, a fugitive slave, Anthony Burns, was captured in Boston and remanded by a Federal Court, in accordance with existing law, to his master in Virginia. Resistance to this was developed by a secret vigilance committee under the control of some very distinguished men: Theodore Parker, Wendell Phillips, Samuel Gridley Howe and others, ornaments of their age as they would be of any age. They decided, after the exploration of many alternatives, to hold a mass meeting in Faneuil Hall and, at a certain point, to whip the crowd into such a frenzy that they would storm the courthouse in which the fugitive was confined and rescue him by brute force. This would constitute a direct attack on the national government, which was using the rendition of Burns as a pledge to the South that their peculiar institution would be respected and enforced. Some of the men involved in the conspiracy were armed; it was patently a violent and unmanageable plan which could be represented by administration supporters as of treasonable proportions. Great personal drama was provided by the fact that Theodore Parker, the chairman of the Vigilance Committee and the man who would give the word for the assault on the courthouse, was the grandson of Captain Parker, whose shot on Lexington Green had already proven that it was possible for a handful of people to transform revolutionary impulses from potential to kinetic energy. Up to a point, Parker acted with innocence and a sense of righteousness but at the climax, his revolutionary morality broke down; he had a failure of nerve and haplessly betrayed himself and his associates and the heroic design became a fiasco.

Regardless of this unfortunate result, perhaps because of it, I felt that the episode revealed the essence of revolutionary morality, American style, so I tried to write a book about it. A quotation from Thoreau became the ideological matrix for the work. "A very few, as heroes, patriots, martyrs, reformers in the great sense, and *men,* serve the state with their consciences also, and so necessarily resist it for the most part; and they are commonly treated as enemies by it." The question then arose as to what form the book would take. To be truthful, I did not decide in advance on any form but began to set down the pre-incidents just as I thought they had happened. My first problem was to put the reader back at a stage of the event where he would not be directly conscious of what was already known to him historically, so that he would have to grope with the characters involved for the solutions necessary to advance along the chain of circumstances leading to the climax. This, I felt, would force the reader to share some of the darkness and the ambiguity the actual characters had in the beginning, some of the agony and effort of other humans striving to understand their situation and attempting either to rise above its perils or to extract from defeat the full values of a bitter and tragic experience. Michelet calls this process "humanity creating itself." I then discovered that this method created confusion in those used to reading history strictly as a series of causes leading to effects, ignorant of the elements of interaction, of contradiction . . . of dialectic. Here I had to make a choice of simplifying, perhaps stereotyping, the ascent to the climax in the hope that in its emotional shock the reader would feel, even though he did not know, all that had happened (however, the more I considered this easy way out, the more abhorrent and cowardly it seemed to be) . . . or utilizing the discoveries of historical materialism to show the truth of the way things are and to recreate it as the nature of an historical event requires it should be . . . a "conflict between many individual wills, of which each again was made what it is by a host of particular conditions of life. Thus there are innumerable intersecting forces, an infinite series of parallelograms of forces, which give rise to one resultant, the historical event. For what each individual wills is obstructed by everyone else and what emerges is something that no one willed."

It was obvious that I could not make the story I wanted out of "an infinite series of parallelograms of forces." And yet I felt it was important that people should understand the peculiarly will-less motion of history. My prior experience as a writer had been as a highly unsuccessful playwright and I began to wonder if I could not utilize some of the direct perceptions of character, action and settings which adhere even to the written form of drama to solve the dilemma of developing a humanly compelling narrative line from "an endless host of accidents." There is a certain amount of stability and predictability about individuals themselves; if their immersion in the event could be made visibly plausible, I thought perhaps the reader could carry each scene intact in his mind as a picture and be able to keep the pieces in a dramatic alignment as the event developed organically, regardless of its inevitable contradictions and delays. But this meant that I would have to make a contained little drama, with its own little denouement, out of every connective incident in the event—a prodigious, an impossible task.

Again I went to historical materialism for the answer; reading in Marx's *Eighteenth Brumaire* that: "Nineteenth Century revolutions criticize themselves constantly, interrupt themselves continually in their own course, come back to the apparently accomplished in order to recommence it afresh, deride with unmerciful thoroughness the inadequacies, weaknesses of their first attempts, seem to throw down their adversary only in order that he may draw new strength from the earth and rise again more gigantic before them, recoil ever and anon from the infinite immensity of their own aims, until the situation had been created which made all turning back impossible."

The impacted drama of this protean vision of humanity creating itself really hooked me, gave me an appetite for the impossible. Moreover, it was obvious that to attempt to evoke the smallest segment of this concept as formal history would not work; for one thing, there was not a sufficient sum of empirical data available to present the characters and scenes as would be necessary for formal provable history. Furthermore, to do the job right, the disciplines of art forms would have to be utilized. Themes would have to be picked up symphonically, dropped and picked up again at intervals. The artist's eye would have to be used with its sensitivity to aspects of coloration and composition. Every mutation of ideology, of character, of taste had to be striven for, while the author's viewpoint had to constantly change focus from a close-up of an individual to the movement of this or that contending group and then to a field of vision wide enough to let the reader catch a glimpse of the whole panorama of the front. Only an egomaniac would attempt such a task . . . an egomaniac or a citizen obsessed with the need for a restatement or reaffirmation of the indigenous nature of revolutionary morality.

Working through the total data of the Anthony Burns case, I found that fortunately it took place in a very compressed time scale and was, therefore, easy to manage chronologically. Furthermore, the characters involved were prodigious writers and talkers and had made public or private statements upon every conceivable matter on which opinions might be asked. This made it possible to reconstruct their diction to a fairly close degree. And by presenting the event as it happened, with the chronology intact, it was possible to avoid those erroneously invented incidents or ideas which mar a work of art by falsifying the psychology of the characters.

While this work was in process, I was working and also functioning as a union steward at the General Electric plant in Lynn, Mass., six days a week. I had to write on Sundays only. It was a dreadful ordeal but I was greatly helped by the late Professor F. O. Matthiessen, who, although I had no passports to the academic world, not even a high school diploma, gave me the advice and encouragement that I had to have. Under his perceptive and tolerant eye, the book began to emerge in a bastard form, neither history nor fiction; its frame of reference best explained as an attempt to deal directly with the social superstructure under pressure and in line with Marx's insistence that differentiation must be made between the economic base, which can be determined with scientific accuracy, "and the juridical, political, religious, aesthetic, or philosophic—in a word, ideological forms wherein men become conscious of the conflict and fight it out."

Parker was a great man, willing to admit his failure and to pay for it. He was indicted by the courts for the rescue attempt and in a magnificent defense said this, again, through me, under the nose of McCarthy: "Let them call me a traitor. We come from a rebellious nation, our whole history was treason, our blood was tainted before we were born. Our creeds are infidelity to the mother church. Our Constitution is treason to our fatherland. What of it? Though all the rulers in the world bid us commit treason against man and set the example, let us never submit!"

Despite the book's failure on many levels, I felt that I had evolved a slightly different method of storytelling and one which could live harmoniously within the materialist conception of history. Letting the event itself come first, relentlessly exploiting and dramatizing every connection except those so remote they could not be proved, I found it did establish its own form. The incessant opposition of wills, which seemed at first to knock every attempt at forward motion so much out of line that the narrative appeared to be a vicious circle, soon began to bend under tension until the motion along the front began to spiral sharply, increasing its velocity until everything collided at the center. My necessary preoccupation with historical elements gave me an active sense of the motion inside the characters, the moments in the dialectical process of becoming. To paraphrase Marx again, as a writer I became supremely aware that it was not my consciousness that was determining the characters and the action in this book; rather, established social existences were determining both the characters and action . . . and my own consciousness as an artist.

What it revealed very sharply was the paralysis of the liberal in the face of a demand for action, for violence. This was the sin of the prophet: that men of learning and sensibility are capable of understanding the physical and political facts of their own existence, yet cannot commit the irrevocable acts needed to transform them. They proclaim what is wrong, but they hesitate to move against the wrong, and really don't want anybody else to. I have Parker trying to explain this failure in the last paragraph of the book: "This is my sin. I hated the tensions and disturbances created by the weak driven against the wall. And I must confess thinking it a pity that a people so ignorant and degraded should be the means of tearing this nation apart . . . this because of my resentment at being forced from my chosen role as a scholar and philosopher and not being able to finish and publish my book. I thought you [the slaves] were all too speechless and submissive, forgetting that your story can only be told in outbreaks and revolutions . . . "

When the book came out it had a good critical reception, but as it was in the high tide of McCarthyism, two of the largest wholesale distributors refused to handle it because it had the picture of a black man and a white man on the cover, which made it a communist book. Because I wrote, and still write, only for use, I felt that the only way to fight McCarthyism, which then threatened to destroy the entire American radical heritage as completely as the monotheism of Ikhnaton in 1354 B.C., was to form collectives and communes to create loving communities where political insult and slander were simply meaningless and all life self-sustained. I felt there was a need for a book about communes.

In that marvelous period of American history when every honest artist was ignited again and again by the struggle to abolish slavery, there was also one to abolish capitalism. There were over eighty communes established. Their economic basis was very shaky, but all of them completely understood what Marx wrote in *The Holy Family*, that capitalism brings about "the divorcement of existence and thought, consciousness and life." They knew that property, capital, money, labor and the like are far from being figments of the mind, but they are all the very practical, objective products of their own alienation, which therefore must be abolished in a practical, material way; so that not only in thinking, in consciousness, but also in his mass existence, man should become human.

The problem was which collective to choose to write about. After much research I decided to write about Brook Farm, in West Roxbury, Massachusetts. Perhaps the most famous, but always written about tritely because the historians persist in dealing with it in its early, transcendentalist phase, instead of later, when it was worked out from a blueprint by Charles Fourier. Georg Lukacs says of Fourier, "Despite the fantastic nature of his ideas about Socialism, and the ways to Socialism, the picture of Capitalism is shown with such overwhelming clarity in all its contradictions that the idea of the transitory nature of this society appears tangibly and plastically before us." The people at Brook Farm expressed their repugnance at the brutality and stupidity of capitalism in the early 1840s, felt it was transitory and tried to build an alternate form of society to replace it. I decided to drop the complex and laborious event structure and to impose the ideology of Fourier on the novel as relentlessly as the Brook Farmers did on their collective.

Charles Fourier was unquestionably one of the greatest of all satirists ... Marx considered him the most brilliant ... but his positive guidance system for the replacement of capitalism was to "utilize the passions now condemned, just as Nature has given them to us and without any way changing them. That is the whole secret of the calculus of Passionate Attraction."

Again I decided to use "real" characters who could be historically validated. The reality of their experience could not be wholly organic and personal because they were all acting under the externally imposed structure of Fourierism. They had to accept it and live with it every day. So, in the writing, I locked their total experience into a rigid form, constructing the book in twelve chapters, each having for its denouement the relationship of the life of the collective to one of the twelve passions which were the master plan of Fourier ... sight, cabals, touch, smell, taste, hearing, variety, familism, friendship, ambition, love, composite. The total exercise of these passions and their interaction, Fourier thought, would make men and women ideal in their relationship with one another.

The leading character had to be a Unitarian minister, George Ripley, who one morning stood up in his pulpit and said, "I cannot witness the glaring inequalities of condition, the scornful apathy, the burning zeal with which men run the race of selfish competition with no thought for the elevation of their brethren, without the sad conviction that the spirit of Christ has well-nigh disappeared from our churches. Any defense of humanity is considered an attack on society. When a minister cannot show by his words and works that he is hostile to all oppression of man by man, and that his sympathies are with the down-trodden and suffering poor, I feel it is time to look at the foundation on which we stand and see if it does not suffer from some defect which threatens its destruction."

Ripley is a good man, now forgotten, and I do not regret that I revived him and his magnificent failure at Brook Farm, but in comparison with the drama inherent in a genuine revolutionary crisis, Brook Farm is pretty small potatoes.

My thoughts were drawn back to the failure of Theodore Parker at his moment of truth and I began to look for a man who would not fail when the chips were down and would meet his tyrannies head on. The question arises whether it is possible for a man to control or surmount a revolutionary act of violence which he himself has ordered and carried through without becoming so corrupted by it that he does lose, finally, his revolutionary morality. Meanwhile, the decade of the futile fifties began to develop a universal image of man as a helpless bundle of inexplicable ganglia, straining toward status, appetite, repletion and togetherness like a plant to the sun, with no more judgment, discrimination or control over his destiny than a puppy dog. The followers of Freud began to occupy the commanding heights of criticism and editorial taste. But there is more than one Sigmund Freud and the older and wiser one said, in *Moses and Monotheism,* after affirming the will-less nature of the historical process, "But we must keep a place for the great man in the chain, or rather the network of determining causes. His nature is not as important as the qualities by virtue of which he influences his contemporaries ... done in two ways, by his personality and the ideas for which he stands. The great man is the image of the father; the decisiveness of thought, the strength of will, the forcefulness of his deeds, belong to the picture of the father; above all things, however, the self-reliance and independence of the great man, his divine conviction of doing right which may pass into ruthfulness."

Every American with a fair knowledge of history has to read this with a shock of recognition ... a name sounds in his ears with the attack and timbre of a horn call ... JOHN BROWN. Here is a man who compressed into his personality the whole image and conflict, the whole consciousness of his time, and then brought it to an end, after dying the death of a Socrates, a Jesus, with a titanic apocalypse of fire and blood such as this country had never known. Somehow he was able to work on the mass emotions of his day with the same impact of fear, pity and exultation with which the great Greek dramatists used to shock and delight the citizens of Athens in its great days. But old John Brown was a real man in a real world. He killed and got killed, and always, incredibly always, for principle. There is no question that he is the finest example of pure revolutionary morality produced in this country, perhaps in any country.

It is almost impossible for a writer of my mold of mind to describe the point-to-point solutions of his work in process. With my decision to do a book about John Brown as a Great Man came a warning from the man who will always be my editor, regardless of who publishes my books: Angus Cameron.

" . . . as long as a single dramatic episode is employed, the reader does not miss the suspense of the novel. Now there is little suspense in John Brown if a considerable portion of his life is taken for a novel [I had decided to tell of his Kansas adventures], because we know, or we think we know, that he had a monolithic character, almost without contradictions. Brown's career was not a self-contained narrative like the Anthony Burns case. Of all your writing in this new form, I find it viable when you are telling a story which contains, historically, its own form . . . beginning, middle and end, but find it difficult when the material doesn't. It is then the book is neither fish or fowl."

Characteristically, I ignored this and went ahead anyway and was wrong in the end, wasting over two years of intensive effort and having to junk a complete manuscript of a 500-page novel. My error was that I thought by putting back all the wonderful truths about Brown taken out by the latter-day deprinciplizing historians, and representing him as the man Emerson and Thoreau knew and celebrated, I would have a good book.

I was wrong in many ways. I had Brown figured for an anarchist, which he was not. I ignored his religion as something related exclusively to his time and not motivational to him. I thought I could pin the entire story on the executions or murders he had carried out at Pottawatomie . . . which I thought were in simple reprisal for five men killed by his enemies and, in anarchist terms, "propaganda of the deed." In building up a historical justification for this act, I had to include long stretches of approach which I thought were significant but which were really only background and without any organic life of their own.

I wish I could say I had this or that moment of dazzling revelation where I saw the truth and everything "started to jell," but it was nothing like that. In 1954 I went out to Kansas and poked around Brown's sites and the papers in the Kansas Historical Society. I knew I had got it all wrong and that I had to start all over again. By this time, the advance money on the book had run out.

If there was any one turning point in my mind, it was the deep realization that what went on here was revolutionary and could be ultimately explained if I could only somehow penetrate to the historical motion underneath. I knew it could never be explained by a single episode or a single outstanding character, and that rather than a one-act play, as *The Sin of the Prophet* had been, this was a four-act drama of titanic proportions.

Stumbling and fumbling along, I came across some hard evidence which allowed me to begin the drama with some sense that I was entering a believable totality of human history. There was a letter at Duke University from David Atchison of Missouri, the active agent in the Southern cabal to control the western territories and enter them into the Union as satellites, to Jefferson Davis, then Secretary of War. This was my first real benchmark.

"Sept. 24, 1854. Dear Davis: We will before six months rolls around, have the Devil to pay in Kansas and this State with the Negro thieves. They are resolved, they say, to keep the slaveholder out and our people are resolved to go in and take their 'niggers' with them. We are organizing to meet their organization. We will be compelled to shoot, burn and hang, but the thing will soon be over."

I had to find out everything about this invasion and boil it down to elements of action and passion in personal interplay. There was, alas, in the congressional report on *The Troubles in Kansas*, 1,206 pages of the lists of every settler in Kansas, their allegiances, their claims, their points of origin. There was the sworn testimony of their conflicts or collaborations with the various Missouri invasions. Using this for a mere starting point, I read everything available, finding the richest pay dirt in bound volumes of the *New York Times* and *Tribune* for 1855 and 1856, in my personal possession.

My next springboard was the opposite tension of what happened in the Free State resistance movement, which had agreed, in June, 1855, "to take all steps necessary to throw off the tyranny imposed upon us and form a provisional government for ourselves." There was a genuine revolution in prospect, which was changed into a "legal and peaceful one," then changed back in the face of a third Atchison invasion in May, 1856. Then, according to the diary of the former Territorial Governor of K.T. (Andrew Reeder), deposed, and going over to the Free State side:

" . . . the plans of the enemy are well laid, if they are allowed to pick up our leaders on these treason indictments, they could then take our people and break them down in detail and destroy our party. We resolved to make an open, organized resistance and to make it as effective and justifiable as it is already righteous and just, we must do it under the forms of a state government set up against the Territorial, and make the issue of force and blood in the best way we can."

That was the Free State policy around May 19, 1856. On May 24, under attack from 3,000 Missourians, it collapsed, and Brown's "Pottawatomie Policy" took over. This was discovered only after unearthing some forgotten records of a Territorial grand jury carrying out the pro-slavery master plan of indicting for treason the Free State leadership in Brown's neighborhood. Brown's policy was the bloody but enormously effective one of executing, without trial, the D.A. and some prominent members of a Territorial court . . . which plunged all other Territorial courts into such a panic that they could not go on with Atchison's and the South's grand design for the conquest of Kansas.

I will mention a final piece of evidence. There has been some awareness, historically, that Brown's deed of darkness at Pottawatomie was political, but there was an unsolved contradiction in that one of his victims was not a court official and that he had not killed the foreman of the jury . . . in short, the choice of victims was not fully consistent with political assassination. I felt I had the answer to this when I studied the original surveys of the township in which this took place. Brown was performing his action in the dead of night, on extremely rough terrain, in an area of widely scattered cabins. As surveyor, he did what was occupationally natural to him. He selected his victims from those residing on a survey line running directly north and south, which he could follow in the night by consulting his pocket compass. It was a tactic of great economy of action and he brought it off with complete success.

Naturally, I can only give a few highlights of the germinal discoveries which allowed me, I felt, to gain control over the massive complexities of the Kansas struggle. I finally boiled it down to as near as I could come to a formal narrative line in which the fusion of historical and human events began to take hold with the unity which life shows, but which is seldom achieved, or even understood, in either history or fiction.

David Atchison of Missouri, the overlord of the Southern expansionists, had led thousands of armed Missourians into Kansas at the time when the political forms of a virgin territory were to be determined by the popular vote of the settlers. By the familar tactic of seizing and controlling the election apparatus, Atchison successfully swung the plebiscite to the pro-slavery side and the permanent government of the Territory was established in such a way that it was not possible to alter its pro-slavery character by democratic means. The Free State organization decided to set up a complete rump government to actually overthrow the Atchison cabal . . . although it was not to be put into operation until appeals had been made to an ostensibly sympathetic House of Representatives in Washington. The House was petitioned to reject the Territorial government, as established by force and fraud, in favor of a Free State, based on a rump election which proved that the majority of settlers were not pro-slavery. Like all revolutionary movements, this was a very complicated sequence of events, full of betrayals and opportunisms.

John Brown, then in Kansas and living with his sons, committed the so-called Pottawatomie Massacres in May, 1856. The generally accepted authority for this period, James Malin of the University of Kansas, explains the killing of the five men who were not slaveholders and had not molested any of the Browns personally, as "the explosive self-assertion of a frustrated old man . . . a means by which he might enjoy untrammeled authority and restore his confidence in himself." Professor Malin, and all the other professors who have consistently accepted his findings, ignore the revolution in process in Kansas in 1856 and that John Brown's bloody act of tyrannicide was its culmination and turning point.

Why this obvious conclusion has been evaded is somewhat strange. Perhaps it is because the traditional concept of tyranny is the oppressive government imposed by a single ruler. But modern tyranny is more often an institution, a system of impersonal pressures exerting arbitrary power. Brown's victims at Pottawatomie were all members or partisans of the pro-slavery court at the precise time when it was using its undeniable powers to indict all anti-slavery settlers as traitors. His assault was on tyranny as a system.

The two factors for re-establishing the connection were Brown's religion and politics. It is admittedly difficult to explain his pure Calvinism against the image now persisting of the Calvinist as a naysayer so everlastingly permeated with guilt over man's depravity that an enlightened conscience recoils in disgust from any justification of the doctrine.

Nowhere in Brown's expression do you find this rat-hole darkness and despair, the notion of God as treating man as a worm under his heel was completely irrelevant to him. Thoreau said of him, "No man has appeared in America, as yet, who loved his fellow man so well and treated him so tenderly." Brown was a "Calvinist" who so disbelieved in the "innate depravity of man" that he fought to free men often chained up like ferocious animals, who put guns in their hands and depended upon them to act toward their late oppressors with justice and mercy.

Actually all Brown took from Calvinism was its revolutionary cutting edge and its revolutionary righteousness. With it he could explain why he acted without consciousness of guilt, against the law and against the system. When in a dialogue with those who did not need God-talk, he was quite divested of his religious idiom. When he did use it, it was because, as Donald Freed pointed out, the Bible provided radicals with an acceptable vocabulary of dissent which "allows one to take extreme positions when required and yet not cede an inch of humanism or patriotism to the status quo." Whenever John Brown's revolutionary morality came into conflict with his Calvinism, it was the Calvinism and the Bible and the fear of God himself that went down, and the revolution that prevailed.

Parenthetically, in the latest book about Brown, touted as "the first based on original research to appear in sixty years," Brown is presented as a "violent old Calvinist who always exhibited a puritanical obsession with the wrongs of others and punished them with an Old Testament vengeance." Needless to say, this book was received with high praise from the critics, including the super-liberals of the *New York Review of Books*, and will inevitably become the "taught" book about John Brown for the next decade or so.

John Brown's politics were concise, revolutionary, quick with innocence and righteousness. He simply believed that slavery was unconstitutional and that the founding fathers, after carrying through a liberating revolution, could not possibly have sentenced a class which had fought by their sides to eternal bondage. His theorist was the great and neglected Yankee thinker, Lysander Spooner. Spooner, the platform writer for the RADICAL ABOLITIONIST PARTY, claimed it was the constitutional duty of every citizen to go to the rescue of those enslaved; that not to was to connive at their enslavement.

He wrote that "A government, so powerful and so tyrannical as to restrain men from the performance of these primary duties of humanity and justice, ought not to be suffered to exist." To those who claimed that the democratic process allowed evils to be corrected by legal and peaceful means, he argued that once the first act of tyranny has been allowed to be enforced against the people, those in power are capable of preventing its repeal by forbidding discussion and dissent and can then impose a whole chain of oppressive laws. He said that government knows no limit but the endurance of people and their revolutionary right to resist by force when the other alternatives are closed off to them.

It was a convention of the RADICAL ABOLITIONIST PARTY which financed Brown's trip to Kansas with a wagonload of arms. It seemed obvious that he had a full awareness of political programs and that all his acts, however irrational they seemed to be, related to cold-blooded cerebration . . . (Although, as Thoreau pointed out, he never bothered to explain himself, nor had he any "organ advocating his cause.") Where Brown differed from most libertarians was that he felt that those who destroy the inalienable rights of man should be punished for it, swiftly and to make an example.

Brown's story had to come out of a matrix of months of reverberating alarms and incidents, crowded with false starts, threats that ended nowhere with plots and conspiracies that were outright crimes, ranging from the White House to the lowest of frontier post offices, in which the fate of the nation swung like a pendulum between solution and self-slaughter. I felt again that no "history" could achieve the reflected reality, the "mimesis" that should tear at the emotion of the reader; that the wholeness of it had to be felt, the peripheral whirlpools of senseless violence closing in, the sense that every alternative to blood-letting was being played out; . . . that only the "charging" of the facts and conjectures with the intangible energies of an art form could make it work.

It worked for a little over a year . . . it took six years to write . . . and then *The Surveyor* went forever out of print, to join the two other novels in the living-dead limbo of living authors whose works are dead. They were not regarded in any realm of academia as containing any usable truths. I like to think this is because of their explicit and insistent revolutionary content but this is not really true . . . what had happened was that the political-revolutionary-historical novel was phased out of the American literary scene. No one pretended to take it seriously anymore. But it was a genre which, in the words of the great critic Georg Lukacs, "portrays the totality of history, and makes it a mass experience . . . makes it possible for men to comprehend their own existence as something historically conditioned, for them to see in history something that deeply affects their daily lives and immediately concerns them."

It is difficult to pinpoint the reason for this. Perhaps we have become too decadent to either write or read them. Trotsky says, "Literature without the power of great synthesis is the symptom of social weariness." Certainly we are all profoundly weary and hopeless about our present culture. The historical novel is a prime form of people's art; it is storytelling, it is example, it is an embodiment of our hidden continuities of hope and rage. It can be very, very revolutionary and uncontrolled by the consciousness-controllers now deprinciplizing and derevolutionizing students in the academic process . . . teaching counter-revolution.

It seems clear that these same people now control the publishing, the publicizing and the criticizing process with the same iron hand with which they control their students. It is no longer possible to circumvent them by writing revolutionary history in the form of a novel nor is it possible to attain the distribution or viability of revolutionary essays or tracts until they appear somewhere on a "reading list." The only sensible suggestion on this matter comes from Lenin. "The first thing to do is deprive capital of the possibility of hiring writers, buying up publishers and buying newspapers, and to do this the capitalists and exploiters have to be overthrown and their resistance suppressed."

The Liberator

1

When Garrison issued the first number of the *Liberator* on Saturday, Jan. 1, 1831, he flung into the consciousness of his countrymen an assertion so grandiose, so fixed and tempered with the personal certainties of a self-fulfilling prophet, that only the historical Jesus Christ can serve as a comparison figure for him.

He was going to destroy a going economic system, a political institution and way of life, thought and belief so deeply rooted in the national character that it is still (unanswerably) predominant.

And he was going to do all this with the *word*, "through the foolishness of preaching" as he called it, and with the methodology now referred to as "nonviolent, direct action" which he virtually invented.

His forces were to be the slaves, who had no arms, no communication with one another, and who could scarcely get out from under the master's lash long enough to pray: the free Negro, at that time even more ineffectual, despised and rejected than the usable toiler in chains, and the American woman. This last was perhaps the most hopeless and stateless of the three, not really knowing her own plight but feeling her frustration and slavery in oblique ways.

Over and over again Garrison used the innocence, the vulnerability

Reprinted from the *Boston Sunday Globe*. Published in three parts: "The Pacifist 100 Years Ago" (September 18, 1966); "Pacifist, Moral Crusader, Newspaperman" (September 25, 1966); and "Man of Peace Finally Accepts Solution of Force" (October 2, 1966).

and the moral power of women. They acted with such devotion and fearlessness in the early stages of his thirty-five-year struggle that he had no doubts that they would help him transform the world. They supplied, more than any other group, the funds to carry on, although the first years of the *Liberator* were almost entirely supported by free Negroes. But the women kept warm the kitchen of the cause; they fed it through all the leanness and downright attrition of the unquiet years.

The slave and the free Negro knew there was "something in it" for him; the woman learned, after a while, that she also could be transformed. This was Garrison's great message and promise: that he had the transformation factor; that he could give renewal.

A highly perceptive disciple, Maria Weston Chapman, put it this way:

It has been objected, in the past years, that our power to effect any change was so *little*, that it was absurd to exercise it. It is now objected that our power is so great, that it is dangerous to exercise it. That the slaveholders will be angry—and what will we have then—disunion, division of the church, civil war, etc., etc. We reply, there is something of more consequence than man's impotent wrath. The revealed command to 'come out on the Lord's side' must be obeyed, and the civil war, disunion, and division of the churches are left at His Almighty disposal. We sometimes, but not often, hear it said—it is such an odd, unladylike thing to do.

We concede that the human soul, in the full exercise of its most Godlike power of self-denial and exertion for the good of others, is emphatically, a very unladylike thing, We have never heard of this objection but from the sort of woman who is dead while she lives, or to be pitied as the victim of domestic tyranny. The woman who makes it is generally one who has struggled from childhood to womanhood through a process of spiritual suffocation.

Garrison's treatment of the Negroes was slightly different: he did not think so much of freeing them as of getting back for them the freedom they had already earned and were defrauded of after the Revolution. His major attack was based on the revolutionary contradictions inherent in the whole canon of the American statement of purpose.

Wendell Phillips said the antislavery cause owed its ultimate success, if you want to call it that, to Garrison's forgetting that he was white; and because he could look on the great questions posed by the church and state as a Negro looked on them.

Usually when he talked about race, he said *our race*, i.e., the human race.

In the name of God, who made us of one blood, I demand the immediate emancipation of all those who are pining on American soil. I make this demand not for the children merely, but for the parents also, not for one, but for all, not with restrictions and limitations, but unconditionally.

I assert their perfect equality with me, and not until by a formal vote, the people repudiate the Declaration of Independence and brand Washington, Jefferson, Adams and Hancock as fanatics, and place themselves in a position of colonial subserviency to Great Britain, will I even bother to argue the question of whether the slaves have the rights of citizens as fully as any white born in New England.

This was his whole argument, his whole life, beautifully simple, beautifully ethical and, in the long run, the only possible solution to the American Dilemma. Yet he had to wake up every morning for thirty-five years and feel in a rage about it and raise it over again for a nation so blind, and a people so dehumanized that it took a bloody war to resolve it. If he could only have gotten people to change roles, to change their skins inwardly long enough to look around them and see what frauds they were with their Christianity, their Liberty and Justice for all.

"Suppose," he said in 1839, "that by some miracle, the slaves should suddenly become white. Would you shut your eyes upon their sufferings, and calmly talk of constitutional limitations? No, your voice would peal in the ears of the taskmasters like deep thunder: you would carry the Constitution by force, if it could not be taken by treaty; patriotic assemblies would congregate at the corners of every street; the old Cradle of Liberty would rock to a deeper tone than ever echoed therein at British aggression; the pulpit would acquire new and unusual eloquence from our holy religion."

But how then, did Garrison himself become "black," in the terms of this total commitment? He was born in Newburyport, Dec. 12, 1804. His father was a sea captain and a drunk and abandoned his wife and three small children when Garrison was less than three.

Garrison's sense of woman's capacity for self-reliance must have developed here, for his mother, in utter poverty, went to work as a nurse and a shoe worker. Both occupations were shifting and precarious, and she had to keep the children farmed out to relatives, themselves so poor that it was Garrison's ignoble task to carry table scraps home in a tin pail from the charitable back door of a Newburyport mansion.

He got to know early about subsisting on back door handouts and about being "placed" with families so near to chronic hunger themselves that they would watch sourly every mouthful the little stranger put in his mouth. He learned about the dreary chores and odd jobs, usually as hard to get as to do, with which he had to justify his child's existence at the table and under the roof. He learned to read and write between chores and had a few years in grammar school, up to the age of thirteen.

At nine he had to learn to make shoes and work at it, in Lynn. At ten he went with his mother to Baltimore, to work at odd jobs and pull his weight in the family. At eleven he had to go on his own back to Newburyport, to "finish his schooling": really to earn his keep in another poverty-stricken family, a trifle better off than his mother in Baltimore.

He was then taken on as a cabinet maker's apprentice in Haverhill, where he existed under bonds of legal slavery and from which he planned and executed an escape as desperate as any chattel slave, was caught, brought back and given a grudging quittance from a nine-year unpaid bondage. Then it was much harder for his mother to "place" this boy in some decent proximity to a table and a bed, but he had a stroke of luck at last and got apprenticed in a newspaper office. He was now fourteen and fate had decided to settle with him with reasonable alacrity. His hands took at once to the manipulation of type: he was a born mechanic and before long became one of the fastest compositors in the trade.

There was a natural development from setter to writer and editor: the roles were not artificially separated then. He could set type as fast as he could talk or write and from then on he set, edited and wrote little newspapers of a humanitarian bent with a degree of skill and sagacity which allowed him, finally, to take on the *Liberator* with a concentration on content like a piano virtuoso whose battles with digital technique have already been fought and won. And the content was, of course, the racist exceptionalism underlying American life; what he came to feel was the devil in the plump, wholesome, democratic American flesh and that he, with a touch of his worker's hand on the composing table, could exorcise, forever.

It is a little sad to think of this man of twenty-four feeling the impact of this great wrong, and thinking, because of his rearing in the Baptist faith, that all he had to do was to call it to the attention of his Christian country with clarity and power and then there would be instantaneous mass conversions, as in a revival.

There would be a great awakening, and the people would see light, as he had, in a sudden revelation of their sin toward their brother. He had undergone this conversion from accepting the idea of gradual emancipation to the awareness that gradualism was in itself a sin.

This "immediatism" became his trademark, but instead of igniting a searing flash of revelation in the hearts and minds of his fellow citizens and Christians, the response was that he was trying to plunge the South into a blood bath and destruction . . . that if the slaves were freed, they "would rise and cut their masters' throats." The power of the fear came with the unspoken acknowledgment that the slaves had a moral right to do this, in response to the treatment meted out to them, and that this is what white Americans would do under the same circumstances.

To offset this he had to retreat a little from the Declaration of Independence and put forward the Sermon on the Mount, and so he was whipsawed between these positions for the next 35 years, trying desperately to combine them, or reconcile them—a process that had his own nature fluctuating wildly between these extremes, between red-shotted darkness and chaos, and a calm, pure effusion of heavenly light.

But he was one of the men of the world who have to try to transform humanity without the use of force. This was his true center of gravity and his attempt to abolish one of America's oldest institutions, racism, in terms of moral suasion, forced him to an ideological eminence unsurpassed in the western world.

In a way, Garrison was the last great evangelist and a great Christian in the word's true sense: he demanded that all who called themselves Christian, should literally live like Christ. He would not let them wallow in the unforgivable sin of racism and human exploitation and slaughter. He wanted to convert them, to make them say they were sinning against their brother. He imitated the function of Jesus in stirring up strife, in evoking reaction and hostility, in driving himself toward martyrdom. The Abolitionist Revolution thus brought forth a New and an Old Testament prophet—Garrison, and John Brown.

The most persistent and logical protests against his harsh language came from the Unitarians, the fixed liberals of their day. Their clergymen realized uneasily that the sense of sin Garrison was invoking was not the Calvinist doctrine and dogmatism that their humanism must resist, but true sin coming with consistent cruelty from one human toward another, and having nothing to do with intellect, education and surface gentility. He made the Unitarians face what their theology virtually denied, that educated, ethically cultivated people can act with cruelty every day, and what is more, can allow it to become institutionalized.

The true, sad splendor of Garrison's vision of man was that he felt that every revolutionary program he offered had an excellent chance of being adopted by the millions: by everyone who called himself a Christian. He asked no more of anyone than that he accept the moral system of the Prophet Jesus. He was always unhappy, and often physically sick during the times when his ideas took great leaps forward, bringing the inevitable alienation and misunderstanding. And he was unhappy when he had to create mobs (actually he invented the moral mob of the passive resistants) and to use mass hostility against himself to publicize some segment of advance being pointedly ignored. In the end he always surmounted this alienation and the enemies he deliberately created, but it took a terrible toll from him.

As the years passed and he began to realize that his program of moral suasion would not be allowed to work except through the persuasion of terror, his terrible pendulum-like swinging between the extremes of love and hate increased. His problem was how to work on the white South's fear of upheaval, to keep threatening it by predicting it without ever having to go through with it. It reduced him to the absurdity of saying in effect, Love God and man in His image or He will kill you.

But it was the daily confrontation of this ambiguity that made Garrison the most seminal of American thinkers and the *Liberator* the most fascinating historical document of its time. The tensions it tried to solve, the push and pull between moral suasion and denunciation between violence and nonviolence, brought to its pages every expression of political, religious, philosophical, societal and revolutionary utterance erupting in the golden age of the American Renaissance, the forcing ground of Emerson, Melville, Whitman, Thoreau and even Hawthorne, who was not above reading it, while Thoreau's family were regular subscribers.

2

There is no question that the period of 1861 to 1865 was our richest in the expression of the great emancipatory ideas and the only one in which a clear trajectory of a profound moral cause can be seen in its relationship to all other factors in national life.

What makes William Lloyd Garrison's newspaper *Liberator* unique is that it presents on one hand the mind of a prophetical genius whose vision of universal peace and love remains yet unattained, if not unattainable, and on the other repeats every position taken by his detractors.

People, glancing through a few copies and being struck by some marvelous thrust of invective and truth, hitting and demolishing whole edifices like a battering ram, think, this is great, but how can you go on like this? Once it is said, that's it, and how could this man go on like this for thirty-five years? In a total, roughly, of 7,080 pages!

He was able to because he made it—as it was subtitled—*The Spirit of the Age.*

It began with the Nat Turner Insurrection, anticipated and fortified the Transcendental upheaval against the established church, published more material on the Utopian Colonies of the early 1840s than any other periodical, reflected with favor the turbulence of the labor movement beginning to coalesce under the pressures of the early depressions, smoldered fitfully in the hot winds from the Texas, Manifest-Destiny expansions, and rose to a great climax with the entrance of the towering figure of John Brown, attacking the national sin of slavery with the cold ferocity of the Prophet Samuel hewing Agag to pieces before the Altar of God.

And he was a world man. The motto on his paper was *My Country Is the World, My Countrymen Mankind.*

He felt the salt in the air as the rough tides of the European revolutions came hurling on the shores of the Americas, bringing the foamy, salty effervescence of other people nobly daring to be free. The nationalistic divisions of language culture were becoming as fluid as these tides. "The whole firmament," he exulted, "is tremulous with light!"

It was out of this revolutionary matrix that he was able to make William Lloyd Garrison, an unemployed printer with hardly a scrap of formal education, just out of jail for committing the greatest sin in his occupation (inciting a successful action for libel against his paper), with no family or political connections, and no money whatsoever and with his social status described by one of the Boston clergy as that of a "low-lived, ignorant, insignificant mechanic, connected with no church and responsible to nobody"—the incarnation of the greatest moral crusade this country has ever known.

How did he do this? With acts, with nonviolent, direct actions from principle. He did irrevocable deeds—deeds the establishment had to deal with or lose face—public acts of defiance which had to be utterly ignored or punished with a finality which would prevent repetition. He performed this brilliantly on a stage where the establishment could do neither. They had to enter, publicly, and attack him head on, and with the built-in futility which comes out of all attacks on passive resistance, so that he always won the right to fight another day.

This is the organic pacifist tactic. Perhaps there were too many other days in the next thirty-five years. This long, slow building of the perfectibility of man usually becomes the perfectibility of me. Wendell Phillips once said, "My friends, if we never free a slave, we have at least freed ourselves in the effort to emancipate our fellow man."

Yet Garrison was never doctrinaire about this; some of his most ardent supporters, including Phillips, were not pacifists, and they stayed with him over the years, taking his judgment as final on most controverted points. He had a clever way of absolving his followers from his more extreme position. He would say this or that form of cooperation with government was "sin for me" and thus save them from associative guilt.

Phillips well realized the skill with which Garrison let his individuality bear the brunt of counterattack, saying, "Saints do not march in regiments, and martyrs do not travel in battalions; they come along once in an age. You cannot create an anti-slavery sentiment so durable, so unrelenting, so vigilant that the government cannot outwit and undermine it. Consequently the only way you can save the slave is to arrange political circumstances so that there will be no such government in existence."

Certainly, someone arranged the United States government of 1776–1862 out of existence. Perhaps Garrison did do it. Lincoln said of the emancipation which completely altered the major compromise of the Constitution, "The logic and moral power of Garrison and the Anti-Slavery people of the country and the army have done it all."

Garrison today is denied both logic and moral power. His exaggerations, his high poetry, his inability to adjust to political expediencies have created a current judgment that he stated the obvious at the top of his voice too many years and too repetitively to be taken seriously as a major prophet. But this fearsome energy, this keeping up of the demonic clang of dissent, is in itself a form of genius. Men as uncomfortable to be with as Garrison offer only two solutions; you have to suppress them or you have to take away the logic of their arguments.

If you cannot do either, they will come at you with their arrogance, their humorless impatience, all the annoying traits that are the mint marks of the prophet and the revolutionary and which give them their creative tension; which are the frets that keep them on tune. They come at you, saying self-righteously, we cannot suffer fools gladly, and their anger against you is usually correct.

Sooner or later, if the hammering is kept up long enough, they develop a metallic essence so pure, of such moral density, that it drops like a plumb line into the consciousness of all those around, probing the unmeasured depths of reality. And if they find a wound there, they also bleed, and get a whole nation to bleed with them.

Garrison's raging reality, his open wound, his flowing blood, came from a single source: his hatred of racism. His catechism was simple:

Negroes were enslaved, hated, feared and dehumanized "because they were black." And how he bled! This creativity, pouring out of his anguish over what was happening to somebody else, was proof to his followers that the fullest renewal, the sweetest redemption, the most resurgent euphoria, comes out of the revolutionary experience, whether on the humble scale of defending some remote incident of chaos and change, or participating in a revolutionary event with the majestic and solemn fervor of a John Milton.

His first assault on the slave power was to print, while working in Baltimore for Lundy, a gradualist abolitionist, a libel on a fellow townsman of his in Newburyport [Massachusetts].

This was one Francis Todd, who, like many other New Englanders, used his ships to transport slaves along the coast.

Garrison attacked the hypocrisy of the North which claimed to have washed its hands of slavery, although it was obvious that the difference between the criminal foreign slave trade and the lawful domestic one was minor, and in some instances, the latter was worse.

Todd got a judgment against him, Garrison was imprisoned in Baltimore, gaining the trust of the free Negroes of Boston and actually of the whole North, as the first white man to put his body on the line for them. His blunt attack on Northern racism, the subtle and demoralizing forms of segregation which are not supported by law but which rot out all hope of participating in simple human advance, reads truly and well today. It was the free Negroes who gave him money and support to start the *Liberator*. This certainly was an effective beginning for a nonviolent, direct action movement.

His next step sent the pendulum in the other direction. The Boston Negroes had a hero and martyr named David Walker who had published, from an obscure old clothes shop on Brattle St., a pamphlet calling for the slaves to insurrect and kill their masters, whenever there was a chance that they could win.

Garrison's subscribers or sustainers insisted that he comment on it. He could not say it was bad, naturally, for Walker had been mysteriously killed on the Boston streets a year before, and the rumor was that he was assassinated by Southerners. He had "depreciated its spirit" but thought it "one of the most remarkable productions of the age." Finally, he had it reviewed at length by a sympathetic associate, with all its revolutionary incitements and exhortations in full view and put with a tolerance and skill just short of open advocacy.

Shortly after this, perhaps because of this, he was invited to address a Convention of Free People of Color in Philadelphia. He said there what few or no whites had said before: "I never rise to address a colored audience without feeling ashamed of my own color, ashamed of being identified with a race of men who have done you so much injustice and who yet retain so large a portion of your brothers in servile chains."

He went on from there to offer them his whole life and work, pledged to give the slaveholders and their apologists as much uneasiness as possible and along with this threat of incitement, developed the linkage of the Negro cause with the contemporary French, Polish and Belgian uprising.

So it was not at all strange that when Nat Turner, only two months later, led a slave revolt in Southampton, Va., in which some sixty white men, women and children were killed, Garrison was blamed for inciting it, in the national press.

An "adjustable" man would have been crushed by this and have run for cover, but Garrison kept the pot boiling by replying to the press attacks so vigorously that people thought more than ever that his protestations of pacifism were some form of revolutionary duplicity. He had the genius to use this excitement, and the curiosity aroused over his presence and personality, to hold the first organizational meeting of the New England Anti-Slavery Society, the first in the United States.

He turned an unforeseen disaster, which could have been the utter extinction of his value as a reformer, into a triumph, saying simply, "If you free them they will have no reason to insurrect." This meeting of attack with more agitation became the basis of his method. Every advance he made for the cause came out of some awful turmoil and upheaval, usually instigated by him, which raised the accursed question so starkly that people of conscience felt a compulsion to join a man who made himself so humanly vulnerable in attempting to make a settlement.

Then he had an agonizing near miss: the terror evoked by the Negroes in revolt brought on a great debate in the Virginia legislature.

The discussions out-Garrisoned Garrison in their frankness about the institution that was bedeviling them, and then ended, as Garrison predicted they would, in a decision to get rid of the free blacks and suppress the slaves with the power and finality of the methods used in Hitler Germany. Garrison published the counter-revolutionary plan of the chief architect of the post-Turner South, Watkins Leigh, which worked, up to the John Brown raid.

In the North, the slaveholders' counter-revolution was carried on under liberal auspices—the American Colonization Society. This was, on the surface, a gradualist emancipatory organization which proposed to purchase slaves and ship them, along with free Negroes, back to Africa. For a time, before Nat Turner, Garrison had been a member, but now his contact with free Negroes taught him that the Colonization Society prejudiced whites against free Negroes by their insistence that the Negroes' "incurable degradation" would never allow them to enter the main stream of American life.

He leveled an attack against the Colonizationists from which they never recovered. By doing this (hell hath no fury like the moderate scorned), he incited the thirty-years' war against him, the mobbings, the slurs, the shutting out from the churches and meeting places: the most fanatical opposition came from this!

His connection with Nat Turner's bloody revolution left him virtually unscathed. Southern legislature had put a price of several thousand dollars on his head, an agent of the Colonization Society "put the finger on him" at a public meeting in Salem, but nobody in the North tried to collect. He gingerly toured New England after the Turner upheaval, advocating immediate emancipation, and discovered to his surprise that he could draw large, nonhostile audiences.

His most effective exposé of the basic inhumanity of the Colonizationists came with his crucial encouragement of Prudence Crandall, a young schoolmarm, to open an institution for Negro girls in a small town, Canterbury, Ct. Some leading Colonizationists (the same who were insisting that Negroes were too ignorant to remain in the country) met this high-minded attempt to correct this by trying and imprisoning Miss Crandall, passing laws forbidding her family and friends to see her: shops were forbidden to sell her provisions, public transportation would not carry her or her pupils, her house was smeared with excrement, pelted with rotten eggs and stones every night for nearly two years, and finally set on fire.

Garrison's angry report of this got him indicted for libel again in Connecticut. He went to England a jump ahead of the sheriff and there attacked the Colonization Society and the United States itself with a fury so outrageously intense it becomes laughable.

He returned home to more mobs, set up a National Anti-Slavery Society, forever agitating, agitating, forever feeding the Word into the fiery furnace of consuming change. His role had become so threatening and so powerful (societies were forming at the rate of one a day) that Harrison Gray Otis and other dignitaries took him to task in Faneuil Hall as actually destroying the basis of the American Revolution itself, or at least the contract between the States that came out of it.

3

William Lloyd Garrison, early in the anti-slavery movement, received a sharp warning that his method of moral suasion—and ardent pacifism—had to fail in the end.

Boston civic leader Harrison Gray Otis said truly in his Faneuil Hall speech that no matter how peacefully organized and operated, the Garrisonians constituted a revolutionary society.

Of the Garrisonian movement, Otis said: "It would change the civic policy, it would give political power to them in all places where they (the unenfranchised women and Negroes) happen to be a majority of the population."

And it was obvious that the women and the Negroes combined, as they were being combined under Garrison, would in fact be the dominant power in a democratic society.

Otis was really saying the situation was impossible, short of violent overthrow. A few days later Garrison was mobbed in the streets of Boston and nearly lost his life.

Going away for a while after this, in a state of shock, he began to realize that the change he wanted to see could only come through a complete overturn of the present state, church and society, and that in order to do this peacefully, the minds of men had to be changed. He felt it could be done in the existing context of the Christian philosophy and practice.

"Shall we, as Christians, applaud and do homage to human government, or shall we rather lay the ax to the root of the tree and attempt to destroy both cause and consequence together?" he asked.

These dangerous thoughts were troubling him in 1835, and he had thirty more years to go in his chosen task. There is an awful hopelessness about them, about the society he had to work with.

He wrote: "I believe that society, as it now exists, is radically false in its structure—the embodiment and supremacy of all the selfish passions and at war with the rights and interests of mankind—and as unnatural as it is iniquitous. I believe, moreover (for truth and love must finally prevail throughout the world), that it ought to be reorganized, from the foundation to the roof, and must be, before peace and good will can prevail.

"I do not believe, however, that this mighty change is to be effected by any mere external arrangement, or by the adoption of any written creed, however excellent in itself, but by a regeneration of mind and essence of spirit in righteousness which shall turn and overturn all that is oppressive and unjust, until the form of society shall be simple, beautiful, the outward symbol of an inward redemption.

"But this redemption must exhibit itself in a practical manner, and it seems to me must ultimately lead to such an organization."

The organization "alluded" to was a little Utopian-Socialist colony in Northampton, Mass., founded by Garrison's brother-in-law, and whose prospectus seemed undeniably drawn up by Garrison himself.

But this was not really the organization he chose for his try at universal redemption, but the "Non-Resistant Society," for which he was the founding theoretician and had written the "Declaration of Principles." It was to be a world group. "The interests, rights, liberties of American citizens are not more dear to us than are those of the whole human race." They also expected to "prevail through the foolishness of preaching."

This was in 1838 and the following sentiments on civil disobedience should be of interest to all Thoreau worshippers. "We shall submit to every ordinance of man . . . obey all the requirements of Government, except such as we deem contrary to the commands of the gospel and in no case resist the operation of law, except by meekly submitting to the penalty of disobedience."

The entire left wing of the Anti-Slavery Society, mostly women and Negroes, joined Garrison in this, and as he predicted, it brought about a split with the right wing, the clergy and business men, who had begun to feel that there was now a great political future in antislavery, and that the whole problem was ready to be settled by constitutional prose. The Non-Resistant Society as such did not last long, but its complete merging with the Garrisonian Anti-Slavery Society in a few years went unnoticed.

The last phase of his struggle was agonizing, bitterly Sophoclean in its intensity and moral grandeur. From the early 1840s to the 1850s his every appearance was an explosive demonstration against the church and state.

He hammered incessantly on the visible contradiction that everything that is condemned in the white Christian morality—adultery, neglect of the Bible and its teaching, and of the Sabbath, kidnapping, rape, theft, a seizing of the private property that is the fruit of man's daily toil—was not only permitted, but encouraged between the master and the slave.

In his own person he demonstrated that whereas everyone was urged to follow Christ and be like him, no one could really do this without undergoing the most hateful persecution.

His stature became towering and obsidian in its imperviousness to attack. His method now was mainly organizational: to hold together by constant, regular meetings and ceremonies his small extremist group, his revolutionary congregation, and have it act as a saving remnant, as leaven in the great lump of inert dough which was the northern American consciousness, until he could somehow penetrate it to the extent that it would stir and throw off its guilty collaboration with slaveholders.

This revolutionary puritanism led him inexorably to his final tactic, Revolutionary Separatism. In 1843 he proclaimed, in the name of the American Anti-Slavery Society, that conscientious Americans could no longer give their allegiance to slaveholding and racist government, and that a higher allegiance to God, and fidelity to human freedom, "requires that the existing national compact should be instantly dissolved."

He got an amazing number of people to go along with him in this, including women and Negroes, whose involuntary separation from "the Union" already existed (all the women of the Thoreau household signed their names to the formal text of separation).

Three regular and continuing members of the American Anti-Slavery Society protested against this move on the following grounds: "that the abjuration of the Constitution of the United States and the dissolution of the Union, do not seem to us to tend in the slightest degree toward a peaceful abolition of slavery, but rather, to its abolition by force on the part of the free states, thus released from their connection with the South, or by means of a servile insurrection, countenanced and sustained by the North."

This remarkable prophecy of both Gettysburg and Harper's Ferry came from the mind of the Whig historian, Richard Hildreth, one of the signers.

The first phase of its fulfillment erupted in the Kansas Wars of 1856 in which the North and South faced one another behind the sights of loaded guns, and in the Fremont Campaign, and in the emergence of Capt. John Brown who created a new revolutionary presence by showing at Pottawatomie there was one white man willing to kill another of his race solely for being a partisan of chattel slavery.

Out of this ferment and upheaval came distorted, suppressed news of slaves rising in countless frustrated acts of rebellion.

How could the Garrisonians now continue to tell black people not to take up arms after they, the pacifists, had failed in their attempt to equalize the struggle by disarming the whites with moral suasion?

The stress of this dilemma broke through to the base of their organization. To condone violence and arms went against the primary doctrine of the society. Men who had followed Garrison for twenty-five years as the purest man they knew found him equivocating and pettifogging on principles; he had let the organization go smash rather than modify by a hair's breadth. It pierced deeper and created more cleavage than any other controversy. Yet somehow he was able to overcome it. He opened up his platform to abolitionists of a new school—Theodore Parker, Henry Ward Beecher, George Cheever and T. W. Higginson—who talked openly of insurrections and cleaving the heads of tyrants.

He knew he could never deny the Negro what he wanted, come what may. Charles Lenox Remond, a great Negro abolitionist and Garrisonian, found a way of rising above these inconsistencies. "I believe this movement is the only possible way to effect peaceful emancipation. I admit my hopes are not strong that the slave will be emancipated by such means . . . American slavery will go down in blood."

And so it did. Immediate and unconditional emancipation did come, and in the context of the revolutionary separatism which was Garrison's main contribution to the struggle.

When the war came, he supported it, as he supported John Brown. Approving any violence whatsoever broke up the foundations of his deeps, but when John Brown went to the gallows in Virginia he felt that John Brown, dying, lived and that he, living, died.

In a great Homeric defeat, he allowed the moral core of his pacifist movement to disintegrate, because it was, in a sense, befouled by this inevitable violence and blood.

Yet he still felt enough of the Old Testament in him to know *the Lamb must be slain*, and in his own, early prophecies he had cried out that this guilty, racist nation should be rent asunder by a judgment of God.

No man in history was ever presented with a greater illusion of triumph than Garrison. On the last day of February, 1865, the Thirteenth Amendment, abolishing slavery forever, passed the House.

He was again mobbed in the streets of Boston: this time the people touched him with love and pride. The press congratulated him on the transformation of public sentiment, over the years, in respect to slavery, property, and his long rejected doctrine of immediate and unconditional emancipation. Lincoln wrote him. Secretary of War Stanton wrote him. His advice and approval was sought in the highest councils of state.

This triumph, in its deepest sense, could only be ashes in his mouth. He knew, from talking to the ruling junta of the victory, that they were aware that if leniency and concessions were made to the leaders of the rebellion that there would be another military buildup of the Confederacy, and another explosion of pain and death.

"There seems to be one feeling," he wrote in 1865, "that sound policy demanded that fullest justice be meted out to the colored population of the South, whose terrible wrongs had brought this tempest of fire and blood on our land, and upon whose loyalty and valor the chief reliance must be placed in holding the South hereafter to the performance of her constitutional duties."

And how was this to be done? Not with moral suasion, he knew. By the sword must their deliverance be . . . and in the hands of the Negroes themselves. A long period of violence both for and against the Negro was beginning and might not ever end.

He was still a man of love and peace, and the society he had shaped was a pacifist society.

He could not begin again the task of transforming a people to redeem itself by love alone, creating a nation of saints. The cause had to merge, to dissolve itself into the revolutionary demands, however harsh, of the whole people.

Thoreau and John Brown

The accursed question in Thoreau's day, that issue that every man in his time has to make a choice of confronting, or going around, was the peculiar institution of chattel slavery. The personality in which the resistance to it was most perfectly seated was John Brown, the first white American to attack slavery with force and violence on the soil where it existed and with a combined armed group of black men and whites. He went up against this tyranny so that it had to give way to him or he to it, and this, as Thoreau pointed out, "distinguished him from every other reformer I know."

In the midst of the shock waves from Harper's Ferry, a lurid drama which affected the whole American people in the same way the performance of a ritual tragedy used to purge, with pity and with fear, the citizens of Athens, Thoreau also distinguished himself from all other reformers by speaking out in Brown's defense. The chronology of his stand is highly significant. It took place *before* Brown had had his day in court and had aroused the country with that great affirmation of his purpose and character which, like an unexpected flash of summer lightning, made incandescent the acts, meditations and resolves that summed up the totality of his life ... and inevitably made his death a martyrdom.

As Thoreau spoke, the Republican Party, staking its future on a policy of slavery containment, vociferously condemned the deed. The

Reprinted from *Thoreau in Our Season*, ed. John H. Hicks, pp. 134–53 (Amherst: University of Massachusetts Press, 1966).

Liberator, after thrumming incessantly for over a quarter of a century that the slave must be free, called it a misguided, wild and insane effort. On all sides the most liberal people were drawing aside in holy horror, declaring they hadn't done it, or countenanced him to do it, in any conceivable way. "You needn't take so much pains to wash your skirts of him," Thoreau said. "No intelligent man will ever be convinced that he was any creature of yours." But even Brown's best friends murmured that the old man was a little unhinged on the subject of slavery.

Immediately after the sensational and distorted reports of the raid filled the papers, Thoreau's *Journal* began to blaze with anger over the abuse and defamation poured from all quarters on John Brown. He told himself, and later some others, that he knew a little about Captain Brown and that he wanted to correct the tone and the errors in the press and on the lips of his neighbors and countrymen respecting the Captain's character and action. "It costs us nothing to be just," he said. "We can at least express our sympathy with, and admiration of, him and his companions, and that is what I now propose to do. . . . As for his recent failure," he added, truthfully, a little later, "We do not know the facts about it."

The cost of justice to others was not then so high as it is now, with our new concept of guilt by association, but I imagine there are still a few men around who would do the same today for someone in a similar plight . . . defend a man's *character* against common accusations without knowing the *facts*. It was a temperate and fair-minded statement of purpose, but this temperance did not long continue. A few paragraphs later he was proclaiming that the event was a touchstone bringing out with glaring distinctness the character of the government. "I see now it was necessary that the bravest and humanest man in all the country should be hung. If any leniency were shown him, any compromise made with him, any treating with him at all, he might be suspected. And furthermore I rejoice that I live in this age, that I am his contemporary . . . and all in all, it is the best news I ever had."

This is most curious for a man who did not know the facts, a man who had scarcely been known to praise another human being before. Who had spent a lifetime observing with meticulous accuracy the life cycle of a leaf. Who would squat, patient and immobile for hours, to shake hands with a woodchuck. Is it not curious that this fastidious and accurate man should say these things of a man in chains and self-condemned of treason and murder . . . or at least, of killing? If there are any doubts that Thoreau rejected non-resistance and even passive resistance, his position toward John Brown has blasted them forever.

Millions of toiling graduate students have speculated on what Thoreau meant when he said he had lost a hound, a bay horse and a turtledove. There has been little speculation on what is a real mystery, in the light of contemporary value judgments: his considered opinion of John Brown as "a man of rare common sense and directness of speech, as of action, a transcendentalist above all, a man of ideas and principles . . . that was what distinguished him. Not yielding to a whim or transient impulse but carrying out the purpose of a life." How does this square with the Emersonian definitions, or non-definitions, of Transcendentalism in which this revolutionary theology appears somewhat as a "saturnalia of whim," impulse, and the purest individualism?

In many ways, the best description of Henry Thoreau comes in Emerson's marvelously perceptive lecture on Transcendentalism in 1842. I think it really *made* Thoreau. It was nature imitating art. Emerson described the Transcendentalist as believing, first of all, "You may think me a child of circumstances: I make my own circumstance." The perfectibility of man becomes the perfectibility of me. The Transcendentalist is lonely, he shuns society as imperfect, as evil. "He whoso goes to walk alone, accuses the world." Unlike John Brown, he never plans. Everything has to be instinctive and new. "I do not wish to do one thing but once. I do not love routine."

But when he does act, that action can be revolutionary. To illustrate this, Emerson quotes Jacobi, who: "would assassinate like Timoleon; would perjure myself like Epaminondas and John de Witt. I would resolve on suicide like Cato; I would commit sacrilege with David; yea, and pluck corn of the Sabbath, for no other reason than that I was suffering from lack of food. For I have assurance in myself, that, in pardoning those faults according to the letter, man exerts the sovereign rights which the majesty of his being confers on him."

With this sort of eloquence and self-deception Transcendentalism conferred on individualism a morality it did not deserve. For every action based on one man's "sovereign rights" is bound to debase the sovereign rights of another man. Actually, very few Transcendentalists ever acted at all, and this is the reason why they did not: because they knew *all* acts are invasive of others. If they did, sooner or later they had a failure of nerve, and without a real plan which had allowed for this invasion and its reaction, their acts became an exercise in futility. Finally, in combat with slavery, they learned to organize and plan, instead of going by Christ's rule to take no thought for the morrow. They began to realize that Transcendentalism could be more than an exalted private whim, could become a very pure and optative recognition of the highest human potential. Or, as the brilliant modern philosopher Herbert Marcuse put it, in his *One Dimensional Man*, Transcendentalism designates "tendencies in theory and practice which in a given society, 'overshoot' the established universe of discourse and action toward its historical alternatives (real possibilities)."

It was the problem of reaction to the invasion of persons that the Transcendentalist had to face in their assessment of John Brown. Brown tried to get people to do what they did not want to do. They fought back and he killed them. Transcendentalism in theory had such respect for the private character of man it would hardly judge him at all, let alone condemn him to death. Transcendentalism, like pure pacifism, was theoretically based on the supreme dignity of the individual man, which included the supreme inviolability of his body against the physical invasion of bloodletting.

"John Brown," says one of the most noted of modern historians, Allen Nevins, doubtlessly speaking for the majority of his fellows, "was an ignorant, narrowminded, thoroughly selfish egotist, with a vein of hard cruelty and was in fact, insane and fanatically prejudiced, a religious maniac."

"John Brown," said one of his contemporaries many years afterwards in the New York *Sun*, "in Kansas, at Pottawatomie, dragged from their beds at midnight, three men and two boys and hacked them in pieces with two-edged cleavers in such a way that the massacre was reported to be the work of wild animals. If any butcher in New York should hack and slash his own hogs and steers as this man hacked to death these two boys, he would be arrested and imprisoned without delay."

All these things were said, and much worse... that he was at Harper's Ferry to touch off a massive slave insurrection in which every white man, woman and child in the slave country would be in imminent danger of being butchered in the night, in their beds... all these horrible things were being written about John Brown at the precise time Thoreau was saying no man in America had ever stood up so persistently and effectively for the dignity of human nature. "I read all the newspapers I could within a week after the event," he said, "and I do not remember a single expression of sympathy for the seventeen white men and five Negroes concerned in the enterprise."

He was the first. Then Emerson said the gallows holding John Brown would become a cross. Then Theodore Parker wrote from Italy that "A man held against his will as a slave has a natural right to kill everyone who seeks to prevent his enjoyment of liberty.... A freeman has a natural right to help the slaves recover their liberty, and in that enterprise to do for them, all which they have a right to do for themselves.... It may be a natural duty for the freeman to help the slaves to the enjoyment of their liberty, and as means to that end, to aid them in killing all such as oppose their natural freedom."

Parker was a blunter man than Thoreau, and besides he was out of the country, dying in Rome. But could not Thoreau have been in agreement with Parker's revolutionary affirmations? Horace Greeley, in printing Thoreau's incendiary speech (made in Framingham at the time Garrison, on the platform with him, burned the Constitution on a pewter plate), called Thoreau the country's greatest champion of the natural law philosophy, placing him above Sumner, Seward and Chase in this respect. But after Harper's Ferry Greeley had great reservations about natural law in the revolutionary context and said Brown was wrong and the freeing of the slave could come about more quickly and decently by "the quiet diffusion of the sentiments of humanity" without any "outbreak."

How Thoreau pours scorn on this liberalism. "The slave ship is on her way, crowded with its dying victims; new cargoes are being added in mid ocean; a small crew of slaveholders, countenanced by a large body of passengers, is smothering four millions under the hatches, and yet the politician asserts that the only proper way by which deliverance is to be obtained, is by 'the quiet diffusion of the sentiments of humanity' without any 'outbreak.' As if the sentiments of humanity were ever found unaccompanied by its deeds, and you could disperse them all finished to order, the pure article, as easily as water with a watering-pot and so lay the dust. What is that that I hear cast overboard? The bodies of the dead that have found deliverance. This is the way we are 'diffusing' humanity and its sentiments with it."

This is an outcry for the deed, for the revolutionary act. And this is not the first time he did this. I could never understand how writing as full of revolutionary incitements as "Civil Disobedience" can be fed like pap to students without, until recently, causing any noticeable upheavals. It clearly teaches the overthrow of the government. It is subversive under all the present definitions of that very elastic impugnment. He says, "all men recognize the right of revolution" and then adds, "When a sixth of the population which has undertaken to be the refuge of liberty are slaves and a whole country is unjustly overrun and conquered by a foreign army and subjected to military law, I think that it is not too soon for honest men to rebel and revolutionize. What makes this duty the more urgent is the fact that the country so overrun is not ours, but ours is the invading army." What would happen if Thoreau said this today at a Vietnam teach-in? He leaves none of the sacred cows unscathed in "Civil Disobedience," giving a death wound to the democratic process itself. . . . "All voting is a sort of gaming, like checkers or backgammon. . . . "

But something in this essay took the revolutionary edge off it. Its underlying anarchy, perhaps, and individualism. It is so patently a call for individuals to be more so: not to unite against a common enemy with a common program, which is a dangerous thought, but to strive so as to get the State to recognize "the individual as a higher and independent power." But what individual? What *kind* of individual? One can be an individual like John Bunyan and sit in jail for acting against the state and write *Pilgrim's Progress*. Or like Hitler and write *Mein Kampf*. One can be a radical, a severe critic of the status quo in the context of individualism, but you cannot be a revolutionary without connections with like-minded dissenters in the mass, wherever they are in upheaval, and fighting in line with them.

Thoreau submitted meekly to the force used by Sam Staples in placing him under lock and key in Concord Jail. There is no recorded outcry. He sat at the barred window listening to the voices of his townsmen, heard clearer than he had ever heard them before. He called to none of them to rescue him. He felt no resentment against Staples, who was acting according to his individual belief. And when he got out in the morning, it was because, as he complained, "someone interfered," and paid the tax. He had performed an act of defiance as an individualist: leaving others to join him or not at the prompting of their individual conscience, or their inner light. There was no reason, he felt, for him to do as his neighbors did, but by the same token, there was reason for them to do what he did. Thus principle is canceled out. So he remained, in his first encounter with the accursed question, the completely self-orbed transcendentalist-individualist, marching to the drum he heard, in the direction his inner self laid out. And if your drum beat leads you up against the State, do not step aside, the monster can only block your body, your senses. Let them lock the door on you if they will, your thoughts will go marching on, and they are really all that is dangerous.

In his next great polemic, spoken at the Anti-Slavery meeting at Framingham, July 4th, 1854, he shows, I feel, profound revolutionary growth. He sees now that it is not only the uniformed and formal state which functions as a repressive force, but that the church and press act upon our minds in the same way the state confronts our bodies. Twelve Massachusetts men were in jail in Boston for attempting to rescue a slave, Anthony Burns, on the eve of his return to his master in Virginia under the terms of the Fugitive Slave Law. These men, incited by Wendell Phillips, Theodore Parker and Samuel Gridley Howe, and led by Thomas Wentworth Higginson (who escaped arrest), had broken down the door of the Boston Courthouse where the slave was confined and had then been driven off by deputy sheriffs. One of the deputies was killed. The men, five of them Negroes, were accused of murder, or arrested for murder. The grand jury had not yet indicted them. They had acted.

American historiography has been so adept in recent years, in cutting our sinews to our own revolutionary past, and the New Critics so successful in exorcising every vestige of "statement" and politics from our "literature," that not one reader in a thousand knows what Thoreau was actually talking about in his Framingham Speech, aptly titled "Slavery in Massachusetts." Thoreau was angry; he was intemperately furious because the twelve men who had tried to rescue the slave with axes and meat cleavers were still in a Massachusetts jail and no one was trying to get them out. This is what he meant by *Slavery in Massachusetts!* All the Massachusetts liberals wanted to talk about was something happening a thousand miles off in Kansas. Thoreau compared the assault on the courthouse to the action at Lexington Green.

Instead, this time, of being anti-state, he complains that although he had read recently of a state law making it a crime for any officer of the state to detain a fugitive slave, this law had been broken. And although a writ of replevin had been secured by the slave's sympathisers which could have legally taken him from the custody of the Federal Marshal, it "could not be served, for want of sufficient force to aid the officer." He castigates the Governor for not supplying this force. Was that not his duty as the executive officer of the State? He is useless, or worse than useless then, if he permits the law to go unexecuted. Thoreau is now *for* the law, for its physical enforcement at the point of a gun. What was wrong was that the State put its military force into the service of the slaveholder and the Federal Government! He asks indignantly why Massachusetts has been training these soldiers in the arts of violence if they cannot save a citizen of Massachusetts from being kidnapped? Thus, militarism itself is permissible if used for a purpose of which Thoreau approves.

As for individualism, this time he would rather trust to the "united sentiment of the people"; the judge could decide this way or that, his opinion was only "the trammelled judgement of an individual, of no significance, be it which way it might." In fact, the people, *en masse*, should go behind the courts, as the imprisoned twelve did, for "the law will never make me free, it is men who have got to make the law free. They are lovers of law and order, who observe the law when the government breaks it."

Thoreau was speaking here of a specific law, not some vague concept of "natural law." He was saying that the Federal Government had no right to enforce the Fugitive Slave Law against a state statute restricting it and that the men attacking the courthouse were carrying out a proper function of the Massachusetts government. He then offered a concrete program, not for individualists, because it strikes directly at the right of private judgment, editorially speaking. "Among measures to be adopted, I would suggest to make as earnest and vigorous an assault on the press as had already been made, and with effect, on the church." What happens here to the infinitudes of the private man? As a preacher? As an editor? He is a dead duck. "The freemen of New England have only to refrain from purchasing and reading these sheets, have only to withhold their cents, to kill a score of them at once." The editors have kept step with the wrong drum. He feels that editors and preachers, as well as politicians, are wrong because they are totally concerned with "the mismanagement of wood, and iron and stone." And that in combination they act upon the consciousness of the people of Massachusetts until they are brought ignobly to say, "Do what you will, O Government, with my wife and children, my mother and brother, my father and sister, I will obey your commands to the letter."

Against this stultification, this moral paralysis, this slavery, Thoreau utters one of the most violent statements ever written, or spoken before a mass audience: "Rather than do this, I need not say what match I would touch, what system endeavor to blow up but as I love my life, I would side with the light, and let the dark earth roll from under me, calling my mother and brother to follow."

There is no telling what would have happened to Thoreau as a writer and as a man if he had been approached directly after his inflammatory speech by some of the breed of youth we see around today on picket lines, sit-ins, sleep-ins, teach-ins, or traveling perilously to Mississippi or Cuba. If some of these, in the blue jeans and sneakers of that day, had come and said, "Like man we want to enforce the law when the government breaks it," he might have been, in the realm of action, much more than Captain of a Huckleberry Party. At least, for once, he would have had a direct reply to one of his rare collective proposals.

But no answer came to his "Slavery in Massachusetts," and this element of failure must be taken into consideration in explaining some of the misanthropy of the later years. He was always unlucky in his audiences. . . . "Civil Disobedience" ended up in the quietest category of "Aesthetic Papers," and the people he was agitating in Framingham were devout pacifists of the Garrison school, themselves locked in the violence versus non-violence dilemma plaguing and, I feel, paralyzing the civil rights movement today. No one of these had any cannon fuses for him to touch a match to, or any bombs for him to throw. As far as any practical purpose was concerned, their attitudes were as inert and gradual as the politicians who felt that they could redeem the slave ship with its hideous cargo with the oil of compromise and the winds of constitutional prose.

Again and again, after the Anthony Burns case in 1854, the North, largely against "slavery in the abstract," went down to defeat when pitted against the simple-minded racism of the white South. This plunged Thoreau further into a long period of discouragement and despair. He became so weary of the confusion and ineptness of the Northern role in Kansas, and of the American liberal, seized, as ever, by a paralysis of motion in the face of a vast moral problem demanding immediate and drastic action, that he wrote in his *Journal*, "only absorbing employment prevails, succeeds, drives Kansas out of your head. The attitude of resistance is one of weakness, in as much as it only faces an enemy, it has its back to all that is truly attractive."

This sort of comment is generally taken as proof that Thoreau was never aligned with the real radicals and was a writer at heart and nothing but a writer. But its shocking polar bleakness could only come in a great pendulum-like swing from a heart packed with fiery heat over the sins and failures of his society. There are few evidences in literature of a stronger social agony than in the outcry of the shy little man in the green groves of Framingham about the match he would touch, the system he would blow up . . . a statement so outrageous that generally speaking only the most callous demagogue would say it in public, if at all.

His state of mind at this time is clearly revealed in a letter to his English friend, Thomas Cholmondeley. "There has not been anything which you could call union between the North and South in this country for many years, and there cannot be so long as slavery is in the way. I only wish the Northern . . . that any men . . . were better material, or that I for one had more skill to deal with them: that the North had more spirit and would settle the question at once, and here instead of struggling feebly and protractedly away off on the plains of Kansas." In another paragraph Thoreau writes: "I dwell as much aloof from society as ever: find it just as impossible to agree in opinion with the most intelligent of my neighbors."

Here is Thoreau's fatal contradiction full blown. In one vein he wants to arouse, he wants to lead, he wants to help settle the great struggle of his time, by force if necessary, and in the other he proclaims himself an avowed recluse, unable to share a common opinion with anyone. He had become the revolutionary *manqué*, completely at odds with the society around him. But he could not seem to go beyond this. On one hand he was deeply aware of the struggle between will and duty which takes place in the consciousness of the artist who wants to create something incarnate in himself, but is drawn into a common struggle in which he has to be *selfless*. Every writer knows this: if you surrender your being to a Cause, you can't write for a while. Not the way you want to, out of your deepest self. On the other his anger and frustration at the defeat of the Free State elements in Kansas were so acute that he was using his work as a secondary motive, as therapy, which is also fatal to the self-infatuation that high creativity demands. "Only absorbing employment prevails," he says, "drives Kansas out of your head."

His perceptive friend Cholmondeley seemed to feel that the collective, or the *societal*, side of Thoreau was struggling for expression. "You are not living together as I could wish," he replied. "You ought to have society. You should be a member of a society not yet formed. You want it greatly and without this you will be liable to moulder away as you get older. . . . Your love for, and intimate acquaintance with, Nature is ancillary to some affection which you have not yet discovered . . . take up every man as you would take up a leaf, and look attentively at him."

Thoreau had already tried this and it had not worked. He rejected all money and land grubbers out of hand. This ruled out the majority of his neighbors. Men of sufficiently ethical bent were either voting abolitionists and he was opposed to voting, or Garrisonian pacifists, love-alls, whose tendency to "cuddle up and lie spoon fashion with you" outraged him. He liked people who kept their distance and never called him "Henry."

Even casual, harmless conversation, little human byplay, annoyed him. "I would fain walk on the deep waters, but my companions will only walk on shallows and puddles." His friendship with Emerson was turning sour; in his *Journal* he speaks of him with hate. And above all he was stricken with that Timonism that Melville speaks of in *Pierre:* that black despair and hopelessness that comes to a serious writer when a book he *knows* is the best work he will ever be able to perform, falls flat and becomes, in a month or so, stale and unprofitable. He had written two fine books, *A Week* and *Walden*. Both were failures in a contemporary sense. Writing was his work and he wanted rewards for it, all across the board, and it is dehumanizing a writer to say that he does not, or is "above this."

He was keeping on with his journals, doggedly, joylessly. He plowed, sowed and reaped the Concord soil, season after season, casting up, year after year, the same rocks, sods and miniature life, while its fecundity, and his, drained away under the pitiless sun of reality. Like Pierre, perhaps, "at last the idea obtruded, that the wiser and profounder he would grow, the more and more he lessened his chances for bread; that could he now hurl his deep book out of the window, and fall on some shallow nothing of a novel . . . then he could reasonably hope for appreciation and cash."

The few patches of light and heat in these later journals are reflected from his awareness that the Abolitionist Revolution was drawing to its breaking point. It only needed some form of human embodiment; some indestructible man performing irrevocable deeds to make it wholly visible. In these years, or more precisely, in this year of 1857, Thoreau stood, as all revolutionaries do, in that awful limbo between moral suasion and the expressed will of the majority, waiting for someone to be "all transcendental" and supersede the common morality then prevailing: to commit some irrevocable revolutionary act. In short, to embody revolutionary morality.

Shortly after he had received Cholmondeley's letter, a man he could hold up to the light like an oak leaf, and study the transparency and wholeness of his form and function, stepped off the Boston train. It was John Brown, who in Kansas, at Pottawatomie, Black Jack and Osawatomie, had created at last for Abolitionism, a revolutionary presence. He had come East during a lull in the Kansas wars to raise money, guns and men. Brown carried a heavy carpet bag in his hand and in it was a long length of trace chain with the blood of his son rusting on it. John, his oldest son, had been dragged on bleeding feet for miles over a flinty, dried-up river bed in Kansas, by a U.S. Dragoon mounted on a horse ahead of him. His crime was that of accepting an elective office in the provisional and illegal Free State government of Kansas. Brown would throw this chain at the feet of a possible recruit, saying in his metallic voice, ringing with the demoniac clang of the single-minded prophet, "This treatment made my son a maniac, yes, a maniac."

This tall, gaunt, ceremonious man, with the curious mixture of Quaker and warrior in his dress, whose talk had the stately movement of Jeremy Taylor's prose, whose walk, like Mohammed's, was the hard, pounding stride of a man climbing an invisible hill, made his way to the office of the Kansas Aid Society on School Street. In charge there was Frank Sanborn, a young school teacher who lived in Concord, directly across from the Thoreaus' boarding house. "Thoreau," wrote Sanborn in his autobiography, "who had his own bone to pick with the civil government . . . was desirous of meeting Brown." Sanborn took the Captain to dine at the Thoreaus' table. After dinner, Sanborn left Thoreau and Brown discussing Kansas around the parlor fire.

So these two unique men, natural revolutionaries, faced one another that long winter afternoon while the red ashes slowly fell from the glowing logs. Both were surveyors trained in precise measurement, and Thoreau was happy to see that "he did not overstate anything, but spoke within bounds." The story of the encounter from the listener's point of view is well recorded in the *Journal* and the "Plea." Apparently most of the virtues Thoreau had been so desperately looking for in a friend, a cause, a society, rested in John Brown. We know the old Puritan would sooner say "God Damn" than address Thoreau as "Henry." We know of the depth and earnestness of the Captain's talk, mainly describing action that he had initiated and carried through. Thoreau must have looked in awe at the deep blue eyes, as cold as wintry mountain peaks shrouded in blue dusk, and yet with volcanoes burning underneath. He must have thought of what those eyes had looked upon that bloody night at Pottawatomie when the old man ordered the death of five men, put the tender flesh of five unresisting men to the edge of the sword. It was impossible not to think of Pottawatomie in Brown's presence. He never talked like a bloody-minded man but he told Thoreau, very markedly, "It is perfectly well understood that I would not be taken."

Yet there was no real communication between these men and it is curious, perhaps tragic, that there was not. Captain Brown was not so transparent as he seemed to Emerson, who called him "the most transparent of men." Brown was capable of great revolutionary duplicity. He had come to Boston ostensibly to get supplies for the Free State cause in Kansas; actually it was to get control of two hundred Sharps' rifles owned by the Massachusetts Kansas Committee and stored at this time in Tabor, Iowa, to make a direct assault on what Thoreau called "The obscene temple of slavery." In his private judgement he had as much contempt for the fumbling of liberal Northern politicians in their struggle to make Kansas a free state as Thoreau did. But he covered this expediently, while acquiring the money, guns and men he needed for the act which had been the purpose of his life.

Thoreau himself felt, and later recorded, this lack of communication. He had a very curious juxtaposition in his *Journal* for October, 1859. "I subscribed a trifle when he was here three years ago; I had such confidence in the man,—that he would do right, —but it would seem that he had not confidence enough in me, nor in anybody else I know, to communicate his plans to us. . . . I do not wish to kill or be killed, but I can foresee circumstances in which both of these things would by me be unavoidable. In extremities I could even be killed."

Thoreau was wrong in one respect: Brown had confided his ultimate plan to four men that Thoreau knew intimately and two others that he knew casually. The Transcendentalists with whom Brown shared his revolutionary commitment had two attitudes that could bind them to a common cause with him. First of all they believed that the Constitution was anti-slavery in its intent. They felt that the South had usurped power to support its slave system and that the Jeffersonian doctrine that there were "sacred and sovereign rights reserved in the hands of the people, and judged by the Constitution (of England) unsafe to be delegated to any other judicature," gave them the right of a people's revolution against chattel slavery.

In the second place, they had divested themselves of that sterile individualism which still had Thoreau in its coils. They had joined the society that Thoreau's inner consciousness was demanding: a revolutionary society, built up out of the experience process by which an individual, acting under ethical compulsion, withdraws from the mass society around him, and after an existential pause, becomes fused in a common cause to transform the rejected society. This fusion, to a real revolutionary, is irrevocable, and to the death. The morality of the prevailing society becomes obsolete, and a new revolutionary morality takes over. This is a step some Transcendentalists found very easy to take. It is highly compatible with the Emersonian dictum that man himself is the lawgiver.

No one can deny that John Brown was aware of these fine distinctions and preconditions, after reading the letter with which he recruited Frank Sanborn to his side. "My dear Friend, —Mr. Morton has taken the liberty of saying to me that you felt half inclined to make a common cause with me. I greatly rejoice in this: for I believe when you come to look at the ample field I labor in, and the rich harvest which not only this entire country but the whole world during the present and future generations may reap from its successful cultivation, you will feel that you are entirely out of your element until you find that you are in it, an entire unit. . . . God has honored but comparatively a very small part of mankind with any possible chance for such mighty and soul satisfying rewards. . . . I expect nothing but to 'endure hardness'; but I expect to effect a mighty conquest, even though it be like the last victory of Samson. I felt for a number of years, in earlier life, a steady, strong desire to die; but since I saw any prospect of becoming a 'reaper' in the great harvest, I have not only felt quite willing to live, but have enjoyed life much; and am now rather anxious to live for a few years more."

With a similar appeal, the very essence of revolutionary renewal, Brown recruited Thomas Wentworth Higginson, Edwin Morton, and Theodore Parker. None of them ever mentioned it to Thoreau, although Sanborn later became Thoreau's biographer, saw him, almost daily, for years, and although carped at by many academics for his lapses in scholarly disciplines, knew the *man* rather than his literary corpus, much better than his critics are willing to admit.

Edwin Morton had been at Brook Farm as a lad. Like the others, he was a practicing Transcendentalist. He had the greatest admiration for Thoreau and his writings, and was as familiar with them as anyone in the country. While at Harvard he had written a review of *Walden and A Week* so laudatory that Thoreau made a special trip to his dormitory to present him with a copy of *A Week*. In one of Cholmondeley's last letters he sends regards to Morton through Thoreau, feeling that Morton was truly of Thoreau's intimate circle.

Thomas Wentworth Higginson, one of the most voluminous writers and chroniclers of this period, salted almost every one of his works with references to his intimacy with Thoreau. He had married Mary Channing, the sister of Thoreau's often constant companion, Ellery Channing. He also knew Thoreau through Harrison Blake, Thoreau's Worcester friend. Thoreau was a little too hard pan for Higginson, who was the dandy of the movement; he liked to live off the top and be around where the action was. However, he did respect Thoreau's political judgement and in his *Cheerful Yesterdays* he wrote, "During this time . . . my alienation from the established order was almost as great as that of Thoreau's." As for Theodore Parker, the great prophet of Transcendentalism, and a man completely organized for use, he was not intimate with Thoreau, but if he had thought he would be at all usable, he would have recruited him forthwith.

Why then, was it they, and not Thoreau, that the great Captain of Liberty picked for his little army? Why was Thoreau, in effect, blackballed from a society which may have redeemed him from long years of melancholy and despair . . . years of which he recorded, "My life is like a stream that is suddenly dammed and has no outlet: but it rises higher up the hills that shut it in, and will become a deep and silent lake." It was a *society* Thoreau needed; not individual friends. There are few pages in literature more agonizing to read than those in which Thoreau records his broken friendships:

> And now another friendship is ended.
> I do not know what has made my friend doubt me,
> But I know in love there is no mistake
> and that every estrangement is well founded. . . .
>
> I know of no aeons, or periods, no life or death
> but these meetings and separations. . . .
>
> I have not yet known friendship to cease, I think.
> I feel I have experienced its decaying.

> Morning, noon and night
> I suffer a physical pain, an aching of the breast
> which unfits me for my task. . . .
> A man cannot be said to succeed in this life
> who does not satisfy one friend. . . .
> What if we feel a yearning to which no breast answers?
> I walk alone.
> My heart is full, feelings impede the current of my thoughts.
> I knock on the earth for my friend.
> I expect to meet him at every turn, but no friend appears,
> and perhaps none is dreaming of me.
> I am tired of frivolous society in which silence
> is forever the most natural and the best manners.
> I would fain walk on the deep waters,
> but my companions will only walk on shallows and puddles.

This is the dark, sick side of Thoreau's individualism, or isolation, or alienation. It explodes distantly, like some deep fissure in the earth's bed rock, disuniting and leaving forever flawed the wholeness of the terrain above. There were no heaps of brilliant fragments in the last journals to be fused into mosaics as clear and brilliant and indestructible as meteorites for another *Week* or *Walden*. But then came the great drama at Harper's Ferry and two fine fragments left by the visits of John Brown to his fireside became fabricated in the fiery furnace of the day and hour and gave Thoreau a wonderful wholeness again.

He had no time to string together, with a jeweler's touch, a glittering continuity of sentences seen glowing in the density of his minutiae like crystals in a cave. This was no *Walden*, conceived with such broad margins it could take eight years to shape it right. He had to forge this between the hammer and the anvil of desperate hours of chaos and confusion in which everything he had thought and known about John Brown was contradicted and denied in the public press and in the opinions it brought forth . . . desperate hours, even minutes, where a good man's life and immortality were being pounded into a flat oblivion. "I think we should express ourselves at once, while Brown is alive. The sooner the better." He wrote this in a letter to Harrison Blake, asking for a meeting in Worcester where he could speak on The Character of Captain Brown, Now in the Clutches of the Slaveholder. He took eleven days to write his Plea for John Brown. In the first three pages of the address he used material from eleven different pages of his *Journal*.

The most significant element of his transference of his thoughts and words from private to public utterance came in the way he altered the impersonal character of the journal entries. Where he had written *I understand that* . . . , he now said, *I heard him say that.* Or where it read in the *Journal, I have been told he made such a remark as this* . . . from the platform he puts it bluntly. . . . *He said*! He was my friend, Thoreau was saying, proudly, and he may have told me more, trusted me with more, than the government can ever prove.

In spite of this bold, and politically dangerous identification and commitment, his reputation as a "loner," so individualistic he could never *act* in a common cause with anyone, dogged him to the end and kept him out of another society, formed to rescue John Brown from the clutches of the slaveholder. Amos Bronson Alcott, Thoreau's friend and neighbor, was proposing to a few companions that "There should be enough of courage and intrepidity, —in Massachusetts men, —to steal South, since they cannot march openly, rescue him from the slaveholders, the State and United States courts, and save him for the impending crisis. Captain Higginson would be good for the leadership, and No. 64 will be ready to march with the rest." No. 64 was Alcott himself. Thoreau was never asked and Alcott's journal, from which the prior quotes were taken, says indirectly why, a few days later. "It is well that they [Brown and Thoreau] met, and Thoreau saw what he sets forth as no one else can . . . Brown taking more to the human side and driving straight at institutions, while Thoreau contents himself with railing at and leaving them otherwise alone."

Alcott should have known from Thoreau's speech that he was changing: that he was counting numbers at last, first empathizing with the group. . . . "When I think of him and his six sons, and his son-in-law, not to enumerate the others, enlisted for this fight, proceeding coolly, reverently, humanely to work, for months if not years, sleeping and waking upon it, summering and wintering the thought, without expecting any reward but a good conscience, while almost all America stood ranked on the other side, —I say again it affects me as a sublime spectacle. . . . These men, in teaching us how to die, have at the same time taught us how to live. . . . "

And then reaching hopefully for the masses, the millions: "The newspapers seem to ignore, or perhaps are ignorant of the fact, that there are at least as many as two or three individuals to a town throughout the North who think as much as the present speaker does about him and his enterprise. I do not hesitate to say that they are an important and growing party. We aspire to be something more than stupid and timid chattels, pretending to read history and our Bibles, but desecrating every house and every day we breathe in. Perhaps anxious politicians may prove that only seventeen white men and five negroes were concerned in the late enterprise; but their very anxiety to prove this might suggest to themselves that all is not told. Why do they still dodge the truth? They are so anxious because of a dim consciousness of the fact, which they do not distinctly face, that at least a million of the free inhabitants of the United States would have rejoiced if it had succeeded."

There is still individualism there too, but it is no longer permeated with solipsism. It is the revolutionary individualism of man "*coming out* from evil." "Any man knows when he is justified, and all the wits in the world cannot enlighten him on that point. The murderer always knows that he is justly punished; but when a government takes the life of a man without the consent of his conscience, it is an audacious government, and is taking a step toward its own dissolution. Is it not possible that an individual may be right and a government wrong? Are laws to be enforced simply because they were made? or declared by any number of men to be good, if they are *not* good? Is there any necessity for a man's being a tool to perform a deed of which his better nature disapproves? Is it the intention of law-makers that *good* men shall be hung ever? . . . What right have *you* to enter into a compact with yourself that you *will* do thus and so, against the light within you? Is it for *you* to *make up* your mind, —to form any resolution whatever, —and not accept the convictions that are forced on you, and which ever pass your understanding? . . . I plead not for his life but for his character, his immortal life, so it becomes your cause wholly and not his in the least."

Thus, with consummate brilliance, Thoreau sets up the push and pull of the dialogue between the findings and stirrings of the individual conscience and the mass action necessary to carry these findings to their resolution. The shy, woodsy little man who in 1855 told someone that he "suspected any enterprise in which two were engaged together," took on the sole sponsorship, and for a time, the total public defense of twelve traitors caught red-handed. The men Brown had chosen to help him, with the exception of Higginson, had vanished. Gerrit Smith went into an insane asylum. Sanborn and Doctor Howe went to Canada. Parker was already dying in Italy. Edwin Morton went so fast and so far that he was scoffingly referred to as "The wicked flea whom no man pursueth."

And so the stone the builder rejected became the foundation of all who have faith in him . . . and who believe today that he is still the greatest prophet in this accursed racist country where the black man still has no rights that the white man has to respect. The great abolitionists other than Brown have been downgraded for so many years now that they are practically exorcised from the American consciousness. Only Henry Thoreau has remained indestructible, escaped planned oblivion, and that only because of his consummate art. And all who pick up, or are taught *Walden* and *A Week* and are drawn by their magic into the totality of their author's work, come at last to his great plea for a still despised and defamed man who for fifty-six powder-blackened hours, amidst the bloody agonies of his dying comrades and his dying sons, was the conscience of the world.

In his lens-clear view of John Brown, Thoreau came finally to realize that there is an exalted form of individualism which merges into universality and becomes one with it. He expressed this best at the service held for Brown on the day of his hanging. "So universal and widely related is any transcendent moral greatness, and so nearly identical with greatness everywhere and in every age, —as a pyramid contracts the nearer you approach its apex, —that when I now look over my commonplace book of poetry, I find the best of it is oftenest applicable, in part, or wholly, to the case of Captain Brown." The key word here is pyramid, for greatness in any individual can only come when he rises as a symbolic peak out of a broad base below him; when he is literally lifted and held on the broad shoulders of men and women, like-minded with himself, whose common, whose multiple aspirations he embodies in his own selfless, revolutionary presence.

Henry Thoreau shouldered and put along with for the rest of his life, the full burden of his responsibility and affinity to John Brown's revolutionary morality; to the tragic waste, the straits, the conspiracy, the killing, the tenderness, love and sacrifice, the whole diapason of upheaval that lesser men find so abhorrent. He did not safely and sentimentally enthuse over the overthrow or the attempted overthrow of tyrannies distant in time or place while knuckling under to the petty tyranny, the censure and threat coming from the wooden-headed reactionaries all about him, from questioning inquisitors and the policeman's violence that backs them up. Revolutions are bloody awful, no one argues that, but things have to be twice that bloody awful to make them work. This was the way things were with John Brown and Henry Thoreau. Both were real men in a real world. You have to take them as that or leave them alone.

W. E. B. Du Bois As a Prophet

In the beginning the prophet sees pre-conditions, the explosive present and the transcendental future like a man sitting by the window of a darkened room, reading by strokes of lightning. A flash of insight, of foreboding, flares across his consciousness, and then he is plunged back into the confusions and the doubts of the ordinary mortal, groping his way through what may always be a total darkness and incomprehension of his private world and his fate in it. In time the flashes come closer and closer until the world he is destined to illume lights up under his hand with an incandescent glare and he is able to hold its crimes and secrets, its dungeons and despairs, to a steady cleansing glow which crackles and consumes like a forest fire.

The world of W. E. B. Du Bois was the world of color, and its people the majority of all the earth's people. I think of him as WORLD MAN ONE. No man ever moved within a wider bracket of humanity. Early in his life he "made it" with the whites; there were no intellectual prizes nor artistic achievements that he could not have taken from them at will, if he had chosen . . . chosen to be the "exception" whites are reluctantly willing to thrust upward to prove that they are "democratic." He did not want this, ever. Not only because it was morally wrong, and Du Bois was one of the most consistent moralists of all time, but because it was a false notion. The whites permit "exceptions" because they think of themselves with complacent blindness as

First appeared in *Freedomways* 5 (Winter 1965): 47–58; reprinted in *Black Titan: W. E. B. Du Bois*, ed. the editors of *Freedomways* (Boston: Beacon Press, 1970).

the majority, and thus quite safe from being overturned by a handful of alien, inexplicable men of genius from outside, or *below*, where they usually place them.

What a searing lightning bolt W. E. B. Du Bois launched against this false, jerry-built elevation back in 1911. "The coming world man is colored. For the handful of whites in this world to dream that they, with their presently declining birthrate, can ever inherit the earth and hold the darker millions in perpetual subjection is the wildest of wild dreams." But it was a successful dream the whites had, because, as in a dream, they could choose their own landscape and the people in it, and as they moved on in the cataleptic trance of their own skin, they kept always just outside the penumbra of their consciousness, so as to be invisible, the "dark race" and the "dark Continent" from which they came.

I know this is true because I am white-skinned and I was taught not to see Negroes, to avert my eyes and not stare curiously with a child's innocence, at their strange black faces, so as not to embarrass them as they moved quite happily and uncomplainingly in their own subterranean world, so simple and primitive that if they had "work" and some free time to make music and dance, they would never cause trouble to anyone. The very sad thing about this attitude was that it was not intended to be cruel, but highly compassionate, like not staring at a cripple making his contorted way down the street or at some bedraggled tramp or drunkard passed beyond reclamation into a decent, orderly society.

This ethic of "not-looking" was fortified in school where the black man never appeared humanly in the histories, and where such white men who had devoted their lives, as William Lloyd Garrison, or literally given them, as John Brown, to Negro liberation, were themselves ignored or explained away into "madness" or "fanaticism" as the black man was into subhuman inferiority and invisibility.

Du Bois changed all this. After reading him the black presence invades the whole consciousness. Grandeurs of intellect, perception, revolutionary thrust and power become apparent. And so does that ideology of lies which props up those centuries of white "liberalism" in which everything is judged by the words, by its "sentiments" and never by its fruits. In which "liberty and justice for all" means liberty and justice for *some* . . . of the white people, by the white people and for the white people. In which all our talk about the perfectability of a man end with the perfectability of *me* . . . the white, superior me, first, and the black man can wait for the half loaf, or the crumbs, or whatever is left over as "time" settles this vexing problem.

W. E. B.'s first exposure of this widening gap between words and deed, and his first flash of prophecy, came in 1891, at the Eighth Annual Meeting of the American Historical Association. There, surrounded by droves of college presidents, pundits of the most exalted rank, and Henry Adams, he "read a scholarly and spirited paper on the 'Enforcement of the SLAVE TRADE LAWS!' . . . Mr. Du Bois showed that the prohibitory act of 1807 was not enforced . . . the infamous business was continued, for the United States would not permit the right of search . . . Vessels were fitted out for this traffic in every port from Boston to New Orleans. Mr. Du Bois estimates that from 1807 to 1862 not less than a quarter of million of Africans were brought to the United States in defiance of law and humanity."

This burst on the meeting with the impacted force of several years of the most intensive scholarship by a young man of genius, accorded, by his very appearance at this gathering, one of the highest accolades of American pedagogy. It was flung into the faces of teachers, and teachers of teachers, who had, to a man, taught that the founding fathers had been opposed to slavery, and that the proof of this came with the provision in the Constitution abolishing the slave trade, whereupon, according to the popular and still operating American myth, slavery itself would disappear . . . and but for the unexpected invention of the cotton gin, you know how the story goes, slavery would never have persisted in the Land of the Free. Du Bois said, this is utter rot, you abolished nothing with your *ersatz* law, but an honest tradesman's approach to the selling of men, woman, and children like meat in the market.

And he had to sit there, amongst his peers, on probation toward being human, whilst the President of this upper, upper elite of American scholars, William Hirt Henry, said in his inaugural address, "as regards the African race there is little to lament (about slavery) in comparison with the great benefits slavery conferred on the slaves. From a state of barbarism it raised the race into a state of civilization, to which no other barbarous people have ever attained in so short a time. The late African slave is now rated by our government as superior to the American Indian and to the native of the celestial Empire of China, and is intrusted with the highest privileges of an American citizen."

Just hear this: "our government" writing its Nuremburg laws some forty years before Adolf Hitler, setting up its racial ladder and looking down, then and now, from the topmost rung. It was not precisely there that Du Bois launched another one of his prophetical lightning bolts but I can well imagine the thunderheads collecting over this obscene complacency and condescension by the best brains the country had been able to gather together. The bolt came later. "This is the modern paradox of Sin before which the Puritan stands open-mouthed and mute. A group, a nation, or a race, commits murder and rape, steals and destroys, yet no individual is guilty, no one is to blame, no one can be punished. The black world squirms beneath the feet of the white in impotent fury or sullen hate."

It was this impotent, this virtually silent fury that reoccupied his early years of prophecy. Frederick Douglass, Charles Lenox Remond, Henry Garnett, were gone as spokesmen of the race. He stood alone against American racism, the worst in the world, buttressed and concealed as it is by the best, the kindest, the most advanced consciousnesses the country can produce. What he had to do now was organize intellect, black intellect, black articulateness, to countervail forever this degradation, this sullenness that is taken for apathy or ignorance and which destroys the psyche far more than guilt over a sudden act of violence ever will. In itself it was a stupendous task, a one-man-directed Renaissance, but his greatest opposition came from within the race itself.

No one knew better than he the great potential of the black race. His profound historical sense (for the prophet is an historian above all else) drove him to find the evidence to reverse the whole historical canon, deliberately falsified, which pictured the Reconstruction period as proving that the Negro was not competent to rule himself. After the Civil War, "Industry gave the black freedmen the vote, expecting them to fail, but meantime to break the power of the planters. The Negroes did not fail; they enfranchised their white fellow workers, established public schools for all and began a modern socialistic legislation for hospitals, prisons and land distribution. Immediately the former slave owners made a deal with the Northern industrial leaders for the disenfranchisement of the freedmen . . . the freedmen lost the right to vote, but retained their schools, poorly supported as they were by their own meager wages and Northern philanthropy."

"Northern philanthropy," by controlling the money bags, forced upon the Negro a failure of nerve, convincing their leader, Booker T. Washington, that all was lost and that the Negro school and college had to be used as a saving remnant . . . and these schools to be mainly work-training schools. Washington and his lieutenants began to retreat and to even cringe before the white avalanche of ridicule and abuse which swept away or buried their will to resist. Du Bois could not contain his anger at this. He did what every prophet must do at some time or other, turn on his own people when they are wrong, when they are suicidal. With the cruelty of the light beam of a doctor's exploration of some putrid sore in the secret membranes, he showed them what they were becoming by not resisting at all levels the pressures of reaction.

He was a master at rediscovering and correctly analyzing the hidden continuities between events and trends which seem to have no surface connection. Booker T. Washington's retreat into proving the Negro's case by his ability to "work hard and save," his tactic of trying to shrink a great race into a mere petty bourgeoisie while they were still standing and struggling as *men*, did just what Du Bois predicted it would—brought on increasing spirals of suppression and degradation, coming full circle after the election of Woodrow Wilson, in the resegregation of the Capitol itself, and culminating, in the country, with a foul wave of lynching, terror and newly enacted racist law, nearly as bad as in slavery times.

Du Bois wanted them to fight, every day, for everything the white man had, right across the board. He called for an education that was a real education, not mere job training, and those jobs of the menial sort. Work was not education—education was the development of power and ideal—the source of art, of understanding. Work was too often to the Negro only a way of being used. He wanted black boys and girls to storm the heights held by Beethoven and Rembrandt, by

Shakespeare and Pasteur. Why not? Du Bois was no diplomat, he drove a hard truth. Nor was he a pacifist; nor did he ever want to shed "our" blood before "theirs."

"Let no one," said Du Bois in 1913, "for a moment mistake that the present increased attack on the Negro along all lines is but the legitimate fruit of that long campaign for subserviency and surrender which a large party of Negroes have fathered now some twenty years . . . only the blind and foolish can fail to see that a continued campaign in every nook and corner of this land, preaching to white and colored, that the Negro is chiefly to blame for his condition, that he must not insist on his rights, that he should not take part in politics, that Jim Crowism is defensible, and even advantageous, that he should humbly bow to the storm until the lordly white man grants him clemency—the fruit of this disgraceful doctrine is disenfranchisement, segregation, lynching. Fellow Negroes, is it not time to be men? Is it not time to strike back when we are struck? Is it not high time to hold up our heads and clench our teeth and swear by the Eternal God we will *not* be slaves and that no aider, abettor, and teacher of slavery in any shape or guise can longer lead us?"

In 1913 and 1914 Du Bois' flashes of revelation began to fuse and stay lit and the pages of *The Crisis* for these years are one great coruscating glare. No wonder, said Du Bois, the sly Mister Dooley said the black man was "aisily lynched," they had made themselves the mudsills for the western world; when their wives were called prostitutes and their children bastards, they smiled; when they were called inferior half-beasts, "We nodded our simple heads and whispered, 'we is.'" When they were accused of laziness, they shrieked "ain't it so." They laughed at jokes about their color, about their tragic past and their compulsions to steal chickens. And what was the result? asked the prophet. "'We got *friends!*' I do not believe any people ever had so many 'friends' as the American Negro today. He has nothing but 'friends' and may the good God deliver him from most of them, for they are like to lynch his soul."

Then came World War One and his great soul was torn from the plight of his own people to the suffering of the world. He had to think now of all men. He went to Europe . . . "Fellow blacks," he said, "We must join the democracy of Europe," for there he found the dirty race hatred of America did not exist. He became aware of the Russian Revolution: that it was the one saving remnant of the bloody war. He went to the Soviet and said, "If what I have seen with my own eyes and heard with my own ears in Russia is Bolshevism, I am a Bolshevik!" Coming back to the United States he was in an agony of soul over what it did to his people, seen clearly from distant shores. "*It lynches . . . it disfranchises its own citizens . . . it encourages ignorance . . . it steals from us . . . it insults us . . . and* it looks upon any attempt to question or even discuss this dogma as arrogance, unwarranted assumption and treason."

It was the great American tragedy of this period that the rising tide of radicalism, of socialism, had little in it for the Negro. The revolutionary impulse which permeated the America of the thirties, for instance, was based on the trade union movement; the sit-down strike, the hunger marches, the action in Detroit on picket lines and in occupying factories. But the Negro was invisible there, too; he tagged along, but no one for a moment let him put his hand on the lever of mass power. Du Bois knew sadly that when he saw the Union Label on anything, it was almost always a sign that no Negro had worked on it. He knew all the arguments for unity of black and white . . . but why did so many unions, such as the International Typographical Union, exclude every Negro, with very few exceptions, from membership, no matter what his qualifications? This was unbearably tragic to him, for he understood more than most men that the people, the workers, give the world the homes, the bread, fulfill every human need out of their toil and devotion, and in turn, do all the fighting, suffering and starving. He has a mythical old Negro put the matter this way. "If what *you* [capital] gives us gives *you* the right to say what we ought to get, then what we gives *you* gives us a right to say what *you* ought to get; and we're going to take that right someday!"

He realized with the ultimate political sophistication that all workers were disenfranchised in respect to the wealth and power they create and felt that the workers should determine the policies of all public services through owning them themselves. There was no question about him being a socialist (he had joined the Socialist Party in 1904); but when he looked around him and saw, over and over again, the black man being excluded from trades or held down to the lowest grade of job, and heard on the other hand, the radical parties extolling the organized Union as the vanguard of the revolutionary class, he cried out in anger and frustration, "Black brother, how would you welcome a dictatorship of this proletariat?"

It is a sign of the true prophet that although he cries out in the wilderness and into the unheeding voice of the whirlwind, he wants to gain the hearts and minds of all men . . . he wants to join the millions: he is not in the least exclusive. Over and over again, by pleading, by flogging, by toil and example of the very highest order, Du Bois tried to lead his people into the promised land of equality and fulfillment. He created a Negro intelligentsia, poets and exhorters who sometimes equalled and occasionally surpassed him in their denunciation and awarenesses of their white oppressors.

Obviously there was no majority for them here on American soil, but in the world, and particularly in Africa, there was a spiritual majority which could buoy them up and sustain them as they moved their frail, despised twenty million souls against the towering mass of white indifference and actual oppression. Du Bois tried to make them feel the confidence of being in a majority. "Most men in this world are colored. A faith in humanity, therefore, a belief in the gradual growth and perfectibility of men must, if honest, be primarily a belief in colored men." But where could he demonstrate this perfectability? Where but in the home place, the motherland! His prophet's instinct told him that Africa could be the great base for the transformation of black people everywhere.

He brought this presence to black Africa's table, scraped bare and gouged and splintered by white imperialist greed and looting. First, in 1900, there was a "Pan African Conference" in London, called by a West Indian. There were only thirty people there, among them Du Bois, and it had no roots in Africa itself, but it was a beginning. Then, after the Allied victory in World War I, hearing the pious disclaimers of the victors that they wanted, not blood and loot, but only "self-determination for all nations," Du Bois went to Paris to ask Wilson why he could not begin with the self-determination of the African colonies held by the defeated Germany. This is the way of the prophet; he demands the transformation of flowery words into solid fruit.

This idea was greeted with official indifference and in the press with scornful laughter. "An Ethiopian Utopia, to be fashioned of the German colonies, is the latest dream of the Negro race . . . Dr. Du Bois's dream is that the Peace Conference could form an internationalized Africa, to have as its basis, the former German colonies, with their 1,000,000 square miles and 12,500,000 population . . . to this, his plan reads, could be added by negotiation, Portuguese and Belgian Africa . . . within ten years, 20,000,000 black children ought to be at school . . . " (Chicago *Tribune*, January, 1919).

Du Bois organized a congress around this idea, to sit simultaneously with the Versailles Conference, enlightening and rebuking it, showing it the way to real peace, with an example of the nonexploitation of people.

The official American reaction to this was made clear in a typical State Department release to the press. "It was announced recently that no passports would be issued for American delegates desiring to attend the meeting." But it was already taking place, with Du Bois at the head of the table. The resolutions passed, the plans offered, came fresh baked from the warm ovens of his capacious brain; they may have sounded Utopian, but they could have been the bread of life to a hungry, stirring, re-borning continent.

Resolved that: the African land would be held in absolute trust for the native and they would have effective control over all acreage they could develop.

That: capital and investments be regulated beyond its power to exploit the native, revokable at any time, and its profits taxed for the complete social and material benefit of the native.

That: Labor would not mean slavery, and its conditions proscribed and regulated, humanely, by the state.

That: every native child should be taught to read his own language, and that of the trustee state, that all who wished would have higher technical instruction, that all who wished would have the highest cultural training, and all who wished would be trained as teachers.

That: the natives would be allowed, at once, to resume their participation in their ancient forms of local and tribal government, that this participation, when education and experience permitted, would be extended to the higher offices of the state until Africa was ruled totally by the consent of Africans.

This was "Utopia" for the white world. Well, you can hardly blame them for this . . . they haven't made it; obviously the natives of this land of the free have not effective ownership of their own land, they have no "higher" technical or cultural education that is *free*, the state does not protect them in the least, from the exploitation of Capital and investments . . . nor is it ever possible, under present conditions, for anyone but a millionaire, or the hired creature of a billion dollar corporation, to "extend" his political participation to the "higher offices of state."

This ideological base was fortified and armed, again and again, by African Congresses coming in 1921, in 1923, in 1927, coming to a climax in 1945. Much of the expenses of these congresses were paid for out of Du Bois' pockets, although he had to subsist on the meager earnings of a scholar and editor.

Someone else is telling the story of the African revolution and his part in it, but it is part of the making of a prophet to record all his triumphs and failures, and by the stupendous irony of time, just at the moment when Kwame Nkrumah heard first the locks open on his prison door, and walked then into the office of the alien Governor of his occupied country, to hear, then, himself asked to form the first free government his country had known since their enslavement by imperialist England, Du Bois heard the clank of an American prison door, opening to close him in.

The time had come when he had to face his mob. It was the whole country, it was the government, the courts, the press, the Congress, the F.B.I., the State Department, the Justice Department, all bearing down on him with a malignancy that would seem insane, except that motives had at the core, the central truth that he, with his wisdom and prophecy, was threatening their overthrow. That lynch mob of the rotten center, which goes by the name of "law and order" and "security," had decided that because he had been on a committee to achieve nuclear disarmament in a world on the brink of self-extinction, that he was an agent of a foreign power and subject to a fine of ten thousand dollars and five years in jail.

When he heard of his indictment in February of 1951, he was aghast at the presumption, at the disgrace. "Never in any single year has the frustration and paradox of life stood out so clearly as in this year, when, having finished some 83 years of my life in decency and honor, with something done, and something planning, I stepped into the 84th year with handcuffs on my wrists." He felt that this was the utter rending of the fabric of his work; that all his achievements were blotted out as he stood, as the government's lynch mob made him stand, in open court with handcuffs on his wrist, when they put him into a medieval cage with human derelicts, when they fingerprinted him, searched him for concealed weapons and performed all the other barbarous acts of insult that people, presumed to be innocent before trial, have to endure when they fall into the hands of the police.

His arraignment took place in February, 1951, his trial in November. So the lynch mob ran at him for six months, screaming at the top of its lungs that he was an agent of Russia and that some well-proven treasonable activity on his part had brought him to trial. It was at the time of the Korean War, which was traitorous to resist. He was retired on a small pension and had very little money. He had to raise cash for his own defense in an agonizing series of talks and pleas to groups all over the country . . . this great man, this giant who had crushed the grapes of liberation for a whole continent, had to go around raising handouts for his own defense. For a long while he could not wholly understand why this was happening to him: he knew he was innocent, he had never taken, never seen any money or support for his committee from a foreign power. But then between the hammer and the anvil of the process experience, he began to renew, in its final essence, the revolutionary impulse that was deep in the marrow of his life.

He realized that he was on trial as a criminal because he had been the most prominent American in the circulation of the Stockholm Appeal, which said, "We consider that the first government henceforth to use the atomic weapon against any country whatsoever will be committing a crime against humanity and should be treated as a war criminal." He did not know, but he might have sensed, that the U.S. Government was meditating the use of atomic weapons against the people of Korea, people of color like himself. As the war went on and the immorality of American policy in Asia became clearer he realized why he, although other people were on trial with him, was singled out as the real culprit and why it was always said of him, in the newspapers, that he was a Negro. He felt that his persecutor's "real object was to prevent American citizens (particularly those of the Negro race) of any sort, from daring to think or talk against the determination of big business to reduce Asia to colonial subserviency to American industry, to reweld the chains on Africa, to consolidate U.S. control of the Caribbean and South America; and above all to crush Socialism in the Soviet Union and China. That was the object of this case."

More and more he became conscious that this was a war against people of another color, akin to his own, and that his towering presence as a Negro nuclear pacifist was extremely embarrassing to a government using Negro troops against other colored people . . . "worst of all is the use of American Negro troops in Korea. Not only is this bound to leave a legacy of hate between the yellow nations and the black, but the effect on Negroes of America, in a sense compelled to murder colored folks who suffer from the same race prejudice that they do at home, to be dumb tools of business corporations, this is bound to result in the exacerbation of prejudice and inner conflict here in America."

His defense cost him $35,150 dollars, and it was all for nothing; the case was dismissed after some days of trial, without ever going to the jury. The government had no case, said the judge. And the protests from countries all over the world who saw the condemned man as a giant among dwarfs, bore down on a nervous and uneasy State Department. So his only punishment for his innocence and truth was six months and more of agony as an indicted criminal, begging literally for his life . . . for who stays long in jail, or in life, at the age of 83? The state was wrong, but who punishes them? "A nation steals and destroys, yet no individual is guilty, no one is to blame, no one can be punished."

After his trial, after the establishment of his innocence, he was still tainted in the eyes of the rotten center, the lynch mob. The soaring crescendoes of the African liberation movement exploded like fireworks. White pundits from Minnesota, from Walla Walla, from everywhere and anywhere but Africa, came in droves to TV and radio to "explain" the African revolutions. Across the river from the tower on the Empire State Building lived the man who had prophesied it and helped make it. Nobody asked him; nobody put in a ten-cent phone call to have him explain it. Now he was in exile. America acted as if he did not exist. Great countries outside wanted him for their honored guest; a few colleges dared listen to him briefly, but all that damned-up wisdom and experience had no outlet into the mainstream of American life.

This was the final tragedy. The prophet silenced: isolated by petty defamation, by suspicion, by officially contrived alienation. Oh the waste of this! His country wasted him as some great natural resource is wasted; like a mountain wasted for a carload of ore, a forest splintered to make newsprint for the publication of trivia and lies. Wasted as Frederick Douglass and Garrison were wasted; Nat Turner and John Brown. Du Bois could have been greater than any of these, if only by the sheer longevity of his presence amongst us. If only because he embodied in his person the whole process experience of the American Negro from the time he was freed until now ... and in his intellectuality and integrity, in his selflessness and lack of race chauvinism, gave to his own people a sense of their own attainable human grandeur, and to the whites an inescapable reminder of their racial shamelessness. When will the people learn to cherish their prophets, to defend them with their lives, to let them be heard, to *make* them be heard? When will they realize that wasting them like this means in due time, the tragic waste of themselves, or their sons sometimes, perhaps always, on bloody battle fields where their young blood and promise runs out into the unremembering earth!

The small, nobly erect and intact figure began to bend a little from weariness and pain. This enforced silence was for him, a damned defeat. But then he had his final triumph ... greater than Moses, greater than all the prophets. There are few moments in history more moving than when Kwame Nkrumah, in all the erectness and power of a young manhood that had wrested a new nation from a continent thought to be eternally dark and despised, and filled it with effusions of light, came to the old man and said, "Father, we want you to come home."

And so the great prophet returned to the land of his ancestors, to walk its bustling streets, full of the buoyancy of people living a life of revolutionary promise and advance, seeing in the faces of passersby the reflected glory of his presence. He died there, and the cold sea rolls between us now. He was my great man and I miss him, but the indestructible terrain of his life and work, his writing and prophecy unites me with him, and transmits his warmth, as the stony bed of the ocean valley carries warmth and unites Africa to these troubled shores.

The Torture of Mothers

How can I make you believe this? This is what is blocking the long outcry in my throat, impacting the anger and frustration until I too become dumb and sick with the gorge and glut of my own indigestible fury. Even keeping my voice down, even speaking to you in a whisper, my breath staggers and halts under the weight of this monstrous wrong.

Perhaps if I said the victims were guilty, in some small way, I could get you to suspend your disbelief. Perhaps I could get you in that region where all humanity can merge in a common sadness over human hurt . . . there beyond all the rules of innocence and guilt that man has made. Very well, three boys, all black, and two men, one black and one white, did interfere, or did interpose, in a questioning or resistant way between the police and some supposed wrong-doers.

It is important to know that this happened in Harlem and was, therefore, a *racial* incident. Our sensibilities act differently when that word comes into play. White teenagers, college boys on a spring rampage, on panty raids, beach sleep-outs have now made an American tradition out of assaulting police, turning police cars over and setting fire to them. When we read about this we settle back with an indulgent shrug and dismiss it from our minds. One scarcely bothers to read what the punishment was for these acts against the state . . . we know in advance that it will be light and easy, a mere admonishment.

From *The Torture of Mothers* (Newburyport, Mass.: Garrison Press, 1965), © 1965 by Truman Nelson.

But when it concerns black against white, when it is racial, we cannot see the fun in it. It frightens us. We suddenly see the snarl on the tiger at the other end of the tail these same police are holding for us. We tell ourselves hastily we do not want the black people of Harlem to be slaves . . . but we do like them to be a little servile. After all, we are all a little servile to the police. Of course, we want the black men in Harlem to be servile and stand quietly by while their brothers and sisters, their children, are being beaten.

Somehow, we do not really believe this is happening. How could we, in God's name, *know* that this happens and expect these citizens and men to stand by without interceding by word or gesture while little kids not yet in high school are kicked and cuffed and beaten over their heads with clubs until they are bleeding? We do not see this, we do not hear this, because if we did, we too would bleed, because when a man has a conscience, and it is real, and active, and free, then it bleeds in times like this. Sorry . . . I am starting to raise my voice.

The incident, now known as the Harlem Fruit Riot, is described in the *New York Times* from the retrospective date of May 29, like this: "On April 17, about 75 Negro children on their way home from school overturned some cartons at a Harlem fruit and vegetable stand, and what might have been a minor incident grew into a riot."

On April 19, the *Times* carried this story slightly different: "The defendants, four youths and a man, were involved in a free-for-all on Friday afternoon, after they allegedly overturned a fruit stand at 368 Lenox Avenue, near 128th Street."

The difference in the two stories is important. The May 29th story is the police version which never fails to disfigure the most simple occurrence with errors of fact, nor to compress within the tiniest compass of its utterance some form of malignancy. The truth was that there were three boys and two men. The men, Fecundo Acion, a Puerto Rican seaman forty-seven years old, and Frank Stafford, a salesman, had no conceivable reason for overturning a fruit stand and pelting the proprietor with fruit, as they were charged with doing. The three boys, Wallace Baker, nineteen, Daniel Hamm, eighteen, and Frederick Frazier, sixteen, were definitely cleared by the proprietor, who told the police they were not at his store.

The police say the five they arrested made the incident into a riot.

The five they arrested say the police made it into a riot. The case has just come to trial in the courts. We are still left with the explanation of the arrested five, who charge the police with gross brutality. The police denied the charge but refused to elaborate. "We will not dignify the charges," one official explained. But the defendants tell their stories with a passion that confers a dignity on them beyond the power of the police to dismiss stories that do not all fit together like links in a chain but are more like rays of flashing, searing light, illuminating a landscape of pain.

First Frank Stafford: an American prototype, thirty-one years old, a family man with two kids and a nonworking wife, plays a good game of basketball on Sunday; a salesman, hits the sidewalks of Harlem with a neat attache case and a peddlers license; goes in and out of houses, stores, beauty parlors, offering ladies' hosiery, men's socks and shorts, flowers in the springtime, horns and favors at New Year's time, anything to decently support his family . . . an American prototype, except that he's black.

April 17, in the afternoon, he came out of 110 129th Street. Mrs. Evelyn Johnson had wanted to buy some of his stockings, but he didn't have her size and he told her he'd be back on Monday if she'd wait. She said she would if he'd be sure to bring back the exact shade she had picked out. Frank was going to call on another customer at 166 129th, and then go to the Jolly Day Store. He had nine boxes of stockings in the case he was carrying in his hand. When he got to the street he saw many people, many police, little boys running. In the windows people were standing and staring out. But there were more police in the street than there were people in the windows. And the police had their guns out and the people on the sidewalk were shouting, "they got their guns out, they got their guns out." And the people in the windows drew back for fear of getting shot at. The police were pointing their guns at the roofs. Frank got down two houses beyond Evelyn Johnson's and then his life abruptly changed.

Frank Stafford

They had this kid in between the cops.
So I spoke up and asked them, Why are you beating him like that?

You all going to take him on to jail.
You don't have to beat him like that.
Police jump up and start swinging on me.
He put the gun on me and said get over there.
I said what for?
Then one hit me on the back of the head from behind.
I tried to protect myself,
Moving in towards the one that was in front of me.
I tried to fight, but it wasn't useful, because there was
   three of them.
I was in the Series, I was in the midst of three policemen.
Then one hit me on my right shoulder,
And when I turned to my left there was a cross blow,
You know, a swing crossways.
He hit me up side of my eye.
Then all the pain like a crack ran through my whole head.
The best thing I could do then was fold up
And try to protect myself on the ground. . . .
They took me upstairs in the detective office and there
   they started,
Like when everyone else got there, they started beating on
   us.
They came in with oranges and started smashing them in
   people's faces,
Saying . . . you like fruit, you like oranges, well try these.
There were five of us, all handcuffed behind our backs.
It went on for a while. About thirty-five I'd say
Came into the room and started beating, punching us in
   the jaw,
In the stomach, in the chest, beating us with a padded
   club . . .
It's not a blackjack but it's got leather on it
And it's got big stitches on the side and it's about twelve
   inches long.
They just beat us across the back, pull us on the floor,
Spit on us, call us niggers, dogs, animals.
You got what you deserve, these are the things that they
   said to us.

They call us dogs and animals when I don't see why. . . .
There could have been an easier way for the police
To subdue everybody out there that day
Than going through the things we went through,
Beatings and throwing down and kicking and everything.
No one out there had any weapons;
The only ones that had weapons was the police.
They could have used other methods stopping what was
    going on.
But the police don't have no like for us, black people in
    general.
The way they handle this, that proved they don't have no
    like for us,
No respect.
The way they did this, really they didn't have to do it like
    this.
They was like more or less afraid.
I don't know why they should be afraid of anyone out
    there.
They have everything on their side.
They come in a drove with clubs, guns and everything
    else.
No one else out there has no weapons.

Daniel Hamm

We got halfway up the block and we heard a police siren,
And we didn't pay much attention to it and then we heard
    children scream.
We turned around and walked back to see what happened.
As I got closer to the corner I saw this policeman with his
    gun out
Waving it at some young children and with his billy in his
    hand.
I like put myself in the way to keep him from shooting the
    kids,
Because first of all he was shaking like a leaf
And jumping all over the place,

And I thought he might shoot one of them.
So I stepped in his way to keep one of the kids from
 getting hurt,
Trying to find out what was going on . . . and he turned on
 me.
I tried to get out of his way,
But as I ran and got in the middle of the street,
A patrolman apprehended me by the neck, flipped me
 over,
And put his knee on my chest. . . .
We went to the precinct and that's where they beat us
For nothing at all.
They like turned shifts on us,
Like six and twelve at a time would beat us,
And this went on practically all day we were at that
 station,
They beat us till I could barely walk and my back was in
 pain.
My friends they did the same till they bled.
All the time they were beating us they never took the
 handcuffs off. . . .
They don't want us here.
They don't want us . . . period!
All they want us to do is work on these
Penny ante jobs for them . . .
And that's *it* . . .
And beat our heads in whenever they feel like it.
They don't want us on the street
'Cause the World's Fair is coming,
And they figure that all black people are hoodlums
 anyway
Or bums, with no characters of our own.
So they put us off the streets
So their friends from Europe, Paris or Vietnam—
Wherever they come from—
Can come and see this supposed to be
Great city.

Mrs. Hamm

I didn't know anything about this.
They didn't call me.
When I saw him he couldn't pull up his pants,
He had a blood clot on each leg.
But they didn't bother to call me.
I had went to the precinct to see about him
And see about the other boy, Fred Frazier,
'Cause I knew his mother was working at the time.
And they wouldn't let me in the precinct.
They told me he would be in court nine o'clock tonight
And made everybody in front of the precinct go away.
When I was there it was lined up with policemen
Stopping people from going in.
That night when Fred Frazier's mother came home
She had to go to the hospital to sign for him,
For twelve stitches in his head.
They kept them overnight,
Then they were bailed
And charged with incitement to riot and assault.
Danny told me they beat him all night
And how they called more ones in to help.
His hands looked like they stuck pins in them.
I know it's unbelievable but it's the truth. . . .
You just have to fight back the best way you know.
'Cause when I saw this it was unbelievable.
I mean I just couldn't believe it.
I kept asking him are you sure, are you sure, because . . .
Well, I saw the blood clots and the bruises,
But I just couldn't accept a police would do a thing like
    that.
I just couldn't accept it.

Wallace Baker

I seen some little boys picking up fruit from the ground,
So they start coming toward One-Twenty-ninth and Lenox
    Avenue.

So I seen three policemen running over there
And grab one between his legs
And get ready to hit him with a stick.
So I ran over and tried to stop him.
And two of them jumped on me and beat me for nothing.
Then they put me in the car, handcuffed to Danny Hamm.
In the car they were beating the brother
For having his hand on the door,
Hitting him on the hand with the blackjack.
And when they got us to the precinct station,
They beat us practically all that day,
And then at night they took us to Harlem Hospital to get
 X-rays.

Mrs. Baker

When he got home Wallace told me
They're beating us all night . . . every shift go off and one
 come on.
Oh God!
How they step on their hands . . . handcuffs behind their
 backs.
People won't believe it.
But I could just look at him and tell practically all what
 happen to him.
He still has the blood clots on his legs
They never tell me the charges on him.
I don't know what it was.
How could he know for what reason
If one group go off and another group walk in
And they say what did he do?
And then they start beating on him, took turns beating on
 them,
And they continued all night . . .
Call them dirty dogs, black dogs,
Everything they called them.
For them to beat them like that.
Even one of them had the nerve to spit in Wallace's
 face. . . .

They don't have to have a reason,
And I don't think there's nothing you could do.
They is the law and the law is always right.
You can stand up and they can shoot you down.
They in the right and you in the wrong.

No Rights, No Duties

Thomas Jefferson, when queried about the authority, legal and otherwise, for his revolutionary assertion that people have a right to overthrow their government under certain conditions, said:

All its authority rests then on the harmonizing sentiments of the day, whether expressed in conversation, in letters, printed essays, or the elementary books of public right, as Aristotle, Cicero, Locke, Sidney, etc. . . . it was intended to be an expression of the American Mind.

It was just as plainly understood by the founding fathers that all government is a contract, and if it gives no rights, or even diminished rights, you owe it no duties. What allegiance, really, can this government demand of a group commonly known as *second-class citizens?* The same is true of *paupers* and *minors*. They are never given the equal protection of the laws. The poor are confined by economic attrition in slums where violations of housing and health codes are carried on with impunity every day. They could not exist as slums, otherwise. The minors, healthy young boys under voting age, are forced into an involuntary servitude in the military establishment, which demands of them that they kill or be killed in countries far away for purposes which they consider irrelevant to the point of madness. As minors, they have no rights that a legislator needs to respect.

The American people as a whole, even the affluent, seem to have lost control over their own politics. They know that faceless men at the

Chapter 3 of *The Right of Revolution* (Boston: Beacon Press, 1968), copyright © 1968 by Truman Nelson.

levers of power in the Pentagon can throw a switch to oblivion for the world without even considering asking for the consent of the governed. Many of us are finally getting this straight in our heads, but they have got to us lower down and made us political eunuchs. We are so squeezed by our "responsibility to the free world" that we cannot have a free thought but what we are warned that the whole "free world" will go down if we act on it.

Political emasculation is not our only organic change. The simple facts of the Newark rebellion reveal that the total organism of American life is rotting faster and faster into putrefaction. The stinking decay grows in our guts, and when we try to cure it, they break in our hands. One of our most sacred rights, that of the individual, *individualism*, forsooth, is now debased and swept away with the full connivance of the elected powers.

The crimes, if any, in Newark, were carried out by individuals. A few armed men, estimated by the police as not over ten men, with names, personalities, and motives of their own (men feeling perhaps, that they owed no more duty to this government than the Irish did to the British Government in the beginning of their revolution) fired at our police and our soldiers. A whole people was punished for this. Mortal punishment in a rain of fire went sweeping into the apartment houses and killing the innocent.

It is nowhere known for certain if any snipers were killed by the police, and it never will be known because the police have moved into simple warfare where the trajectory of function is to find the locus of the enemy and flush him out with firepower. And to act, with the greatest immediacy, not against a suspected individual, but against a flawed totality. Thus our nationalism has reached its apogee. No longer can a man stand and bargain with his government over the extent of his rights and duties, his innocence or guilt, as our forefathers did, even with their God.

This new point of view, the consciousness now formed which demands that we punish collectively for individual guilt, we are acting out all over the world. The most important task assigned to us as a nation, the leading and generating fact of our lives, is the war we are carrying on in Vietnam, a war against a total people, wherein it is a routine function to bomb and burn a whole village because it is suspected that one or two of the active enemy are located there, or have always lived there.

How can we think that in performing this, which even our apologists characterize as a cruel and *dirty* war, that our actions will not stain through our whole consciousness and benumb and degenerate us in our wholeness and make us act toward ourselves as we do toward others?

The fact is, what the rich man does to the poor man, what the landlord does to the tenant, what the merchant does to the consumer, what the boss does to the worker, what the policeman does to the suspect, what the jailor does to the helpless criminal in his power is only a local reflection of what we are doing as a nation abroad with our armies. And as the merchants, police, judges, landlords, bosses, jailors increase at home, while our soldiers escalate their presence abroad, so does the scope and intensity of their action against their victims.

And all the time we are told that to suffer this is part of the *duty* we must pay for our *rights*. That these acts which they say they perform only as a cruel necessity are saving us from being the victims of evil men, somewhere else, or evil systems, over there . . . who will only use us for their gratification. That if they let up for a moment their heavy-handed control of our lives, it will provide the vicious and unprincipled a chance to oppress the innocent. So, although some individuals may question some of the acts performed by those in power . . . they must continue to rule us for the greater good.

This means that they, our overlords, are all virtuous, all compassionate, all understanding public servants who took up the cross to suffer and sacrifice in carrying out their tasks and duties to us . . . that it is their duty to curtail our rights because they are carrying out a responsibility to law and order and the greatest good.

We, on the other hand, have to accept their acts of usurpation and control as our *duty* and promise on our oaths that we will unquestioningly obey their commands as spoken and enforced by their myriads of overseers, spies, interrogators, and whippers-in, from the President to the local draft board and social worker. And cheerfully recognize their rights to the lion's share of our daily labor so they can carry out their duty to control us with a maximum efficiency and have a gracious surrounding in which they can unwind, after a wearisome day of holding us in an appropriate system of checks and balances.

And we must carry out, proudly and cheerfully, our right to mark, every four years, a cross beside some names printed on a ballot . . . names of men either completely unknown to us, or only too well known as scoundrels, windbags, and embezzlers who have lived all their lives on the public payrolls and prospered well beyond the million mark. And although we know, from the experiences of ourselves, our fathers, and grandfathers, that regardless of the inane speeches they utter, promising change, they will do the same as the men in office before them and before them and before them, and they will plead the same crises of the Republic, plead the same urgencies and imperatives about the obscene Vietnam War of 1967 as they did about the obscene Mexican War of 1847, and in about the same words.

We must also perform the right and duty of serving voluntarily in the courts, and sitting in judgment on other frail humans; knowing that by the time the government prosecutor and the government judge get through with the case we will still not know much about the guilt or innocence of the accused or be able to do anything about it if we did. All we have to do is be the face of the rubber stamp which the clerk pounds on the face of the man on trial which says, The people find you guilty and sentence you to prison and torture for your life's duration.

And finally, we must always consider it part of our rights and duties that, no matter how decent, how politically and economically advanced, how humane, gentle, and loving we know people in other nations to be, and no matter if the cause they are fighting and dying for is to overthrow the yoke of centuries of exploitation and despotism, we must be prepared at a moment's notice to look on them as deadly enemies threatening the very foundations of our homes and be prepared to burn them, starve them, torture them, kill them, and do the same to all others who do not regard them as deadly enemies because of government fiat, even though these others may be our own sons, brothers, fathers, lovers, and friends. Laws, lawmakers, or law-enforcers who do this are not to be considered laws, nor lawmakers, nor law-enforcers, and should be resisted as any usurpation or usurper should be, at all times.

The self-evident American right of revolution lies in this: that an unconstitutional law is not a law. An unconstitutional law can be defined, in revolutionary terms, as one against the people en masse, and for special privilege. It should be just as opposable when it is against *a people*, living within the confines of the United States. It is thus clearly not agreed on by all the people.

An officer of the government is as any officer "of the law" only when he is proceeding according to law. When he is killing a woman in an apartment house that may or may not be the location of a sniper, he is not acting in a lawful way. The moment he ventures beyond the law he becomes like any other man. He forfeits the law's mantle of immunity and protection. He may then be resisted like any other trespasser. A law that is palpably against the peace and security of all the people, such as all the racist laws on the books of the southern states, laws limiting the rights and privileges of privacy and movement of the blacks in the northern states, the laws against the Indians in the western states, and those against the poor in all the states, is really not a law at all, constitutionally, and is thus void and confers no authority on anyone, and whoever attempts to execute it, does so at his own peril.

Common sense, the conscience of the mass, will tell you if this doctrine is not valid; then anyone with police power can usurp authority, and sustained by these unconstitutional laws, can treat people as he pleases. Many have already done this, are doing this, and still we wonder why we can't get these usurpers off our backs. A self-proclaimed "law-making body" or "law-enforcing agency" can beat, rape, torture or kill at will—as such bodies do now, in Mississippi, and have for over a century—and the people have no right to resist them. It simply does not make sense. The best of our founding fathers wanted the law to make sense . . . wanted a "government and policy on such plain and obvious general principles, as would be intelligible to the plainest rustic. . . ."

The true revolutionary, then and now, holds that the Declaration and the Constitution contemplate no submission by the people to gross usurpation of civil rights by the government, or to the lawless violence of its officers. On the contrary, the Constitution provides that the right of the people to keep and bear arms shall not be infringed.

This constitutional right to bear arms implies the right to use them, as much as the constitutional right to buy and keep food implies the right to eat it.

The Constitution also takes it for granted that, as the people have the right, they will also have the sense to use arms, whenever the necessity of the case justifies it; this is the only remedy suggested by the Constitution, and is necessarily the only remedy that can exist when the government has become so corrupt that it can offer no peaceful solution to an intolerable way of life.

It is no answer to this argument on the right of revolution to say that if an unconstitutional act be passed, the mischief can be remedied by a repeal of it, and that this remedy can be brought about by a full discussion and the exercise of one's voting rights. The black men in the South discovered, generations ago, that if an unconstitutional and oppressive act is binding until invalidated by repeal, the government in the meantime will disarm them, plunge them into ignorance, suppress their freedom of assembly, stop them from casting a ballot and easily put it beyond their power to reform their government through the exercise of the rights of repeal.

A government can assume as much authority to disarm the people, to prevent them from voting, and to perpetuate rule by a clique as they have for any other unconstitutional act. So that if the first, and comparatively mild, unconstitutional and oppressive act cannot be resisted by force, then the last act necessary for the imposition of a total tyranny may not be.

The right of the government "to suppress insurrection" does not conflict with this right of the people to resist the execution of laws directed against their basic rights. An insurrection is a rising against the law, and not against usurpation. The actions, for example, of native fascist groups can be demonstrated by their own public acts and statements to be designed for privilege for themselves and to be defamatory and oppressive to other groups among the people. The black people don't want the police to shoot into white working-class apartments either.

The right of resistance to usurping laws is in its simplest form a natural defense of the natural rights of people to protect themselves against thieves, tyrants, monomaniacs, and trespassers who attempt to set up their own personal, or group, authority against the people they are supposed to serve. It is the threat of the power of the people to remove them by force that keeps officeholders from perpetuating themselves. Not that they are any worse than other men, but the rewards are great and most of them act as though they were trying to discover the utmost limit of popular acquiescence to their self-exploitation and small tyrannies. In sum, if there is no right of revolution there is no other right our officials have to respect.

By no means am I saying that this is the prevailing concept of our organic law among the leaders and pundits of the country. Although they might, if pressed hard enough, give lip service to it. Arthur Schlesinger said in the *Atlantic Monthly* that the American concept of the right of revolution was the greatest idea we have given to the world:

First and foremost stands the concept of the inherent and universal right of revolution ... proclaimed in the Declaration of Independence: the doctrine that "all men are created equal ... possessing inalienable rights to life, liberty and the pursuit of happiness" with the corollary that governments derive their just powers from the consent of the governed and that therefore the people have a right to supplant any government "destructive of these ends" with one they believe most likely to effect their safety and happiness. True, the history of England provided precedents to the men of 1776, and the Age of Enlightenment supplied intellectual support; but the flaming pronouncement, followed by its vindication on the battlefield, made the doctrine ever afterwards an irrepressible agency "in the course of human events." Europe was the first to respond ... A series of revolts overturned, or strove to overturn, illiberal governments through most of the Continent, and hastened popular reforms in other lands to forestall popular upheavals. These convulsions all had their internal causes but in every instance the leaders derived inspiration from America's achievement of popular rule, as well as from its freely expressed interest in their similar aspirations.

"The Declaration of Independence is our Creed," Supreme Court Justice Douglas said, in an article on "The U.S. and the Revolutionary Spirit." He said we should not be afraid to talk revolution and to voice our approval of it. He tells us to become the active protagonist of the independence of all people. Go up against the darkness and pain of continuing feudalism. "There is a political feudalism where a dynasty has the trappings of a parliamentary system but manipulates it for the benefit of a ruling class ... Revolution in the twentieth century means rebellion against another kind of feudalism ... economic feudalism ... the United States should promote democratic revolutions against these conditions of economic feudalism."

Going back, we find John Locke's dictum, in his essay on government, that when the natural rights of man are violated, the people have the right and the duty of suppressing or changing the government. "The last recourse against wrongful and unauthorized force is opposition to it."

It is the massiveness of the display of force against them that has brought the black people to their revolutionary flash point more than anything else. They know, as soon as they hear the sounds of masses of police sirens that their little insurrection, or their little rebellion, or their small act of resistance will turn into a massacre, not of the enemy, but of themselves. But yet they go on resisting until the local police sirens are replaced by the clank of tanks, or personnel carriers; the clubs, the police revolvers are superseded by bayonets and death-spitting machine guns. And still their exultation grows, an exultation that is absolutely inexplicable to the whites, seeing them surrounded by the massacre of their own people. Sartre speaks of this; of how the Frenchmen of the Resistance never felt freer than when they were under the attacks of the Nazi S.S. How the more they were condemned to silence, the more they felt that they were approaching liberation.

These rebellions by the blacks are a minority action: they cannot succeed militarily, and nobody thinks they will. The whole process is a *telling* revolution, a way of stating something buried under centuries of apathy and indifference far worse than omnipresent opposition. A *Life* magazine interview with a black sniper reveals this. He is not trying to kill cops and Guardsmen. When they are struck down it is by accident. He is trying, he says, to tell "our people we are here." And in the process, "the firing of five or six shots in the air is enough to draw cops thick as fleas on a dog and still give time to get away." Then the people take what they want.

But it is much more than that: the black insurrection–white massacre method of telling revolution is in some ways comparable to the Buddhists burning themselves to tell of their to-the-death commitment to their country's revolution.

I always felt that an enormous amount of time, money, and effort was wasted in the last years of the civil-rights crisis, while the leaders, black and white, were trying to convince the American black man that he was really a downtrodden Hindu, a palpitating mass of ingrained and inborn submission, a victim of a caste society which stretches back, almost to prehistory. The Hindu, or to be more specific, the followers of Gandhi, were victims in a land so impoverished and barren that a lifetime of starvation was, and still is, their common lot . . . a land where living is so hard that men want a God so they can hate him as the father and ordainer of their degradation.

The American black man is a citizen in a rich land, with a citizen's rights and duty to resist, resist all attempts to deprive him of its manifold blessings. Even if he doesn't *want* to resist, he must; it is his duty, as it is the duty of all honest whites to urge him and support him in the process. Why should he have been urged to go through all this Hinduizing to regain the rights he already had in 1776? He was here then and fought alongside of the whites out of the same revolutionary morality, for the same revolutionary rights he is dying for right now . . . the idea that men before the law are exactly equal and that no man can take away these equalities except as forfeiture for a crime adjudged and confirmed by ancient and democratic due process.

Legally he has always had these rights. They were taken away from him by force and fraud. When the racist laws were written and enforced and then upheld finally by the Supreme Court of the United States, it was the lawbreaker and should have been resisted. The black man did resist these racist laws, but in vain. Police, militia, Federal troops beat him until he went down, over and over again, a victim of blood and violence, his land looted, his home burned, his daughter raped, his son lynched, his babies starved, his progeny for generations suffering automatically the same fate.

When he was finally handed the weapon of "soul force" he tried it; no one can deny that he honestly gave it a try. But we are living in a lunatic society, a racist society that will never stop hiring cops and soldiers to beat him until he stops them . . . or we stop the hiring. If we say the black man is a citizen, then he has a clear duty to resist tyranny and dictatorship, legally and peacefully if he can, forcibly if he must. He is the birthright possessor of the same rights we have. He cannot give them up if he wants to. He was not born to be a victim to test the longevity of our desire to oppress him.

Take a good look at the *Life* magazine for July 28, 1967. Look at it before it lies dog-eared in the dentist's office, or slides to oblivion in the trash trucks. Before the eyes of one of its reporters and cameramen, a police cruiser drew up on a littered street, surrounded by stores so gutted and debased that they are simply valueless: they are not stores anymore, they are piles of trash. A twenty-four-year-old black man took a six-pack of beer from one of them. He saw the cops. He had been arrested before, so he ran.

A yellow-helmeted cop with a shotgun leaped out of the cruiser. He aimed the gun with *his kind* of all deliberate speed and shot the black man dead ... for a six-pack of beer! And the spreading pellets from the murderous blast tore their way into the soft flesh of Joe Bass, Jr., a black shoeshine boy, twelve years old, with nothing in his hands. He was struck in the neck and the thigh and fell bleeding to the pavement, his eyes open and staring straight ahead, his body almost finding a restful embrace in the dirty asphalt.

The Newark policeman, his shotgun still at the ready, turns away from the murdered Billy Furr, the looter of a six-pack of beer. There is no anguish in his face, his mouth is relaxed, almost soft as he reaches into the side pocket of his blue shirt for a cigar. The story is told accurately and compassionately, even to the point of telling how when little Joey was struck down fifty sobbing black men and women tried to get to him, to help him, and were clubbed back by a small squad of police with rifle butts. But the name of the murderer in the blue uniform shirt is not reported. And it is possible he will never be known, and his face will be forgotten, for the police in this country, when they are acting against the black people, are usually faceless and nameless and omnipotent, infallible and unpunishable, like Yahweh.

There was the Boston Massacre and there was the Newark Massacre. The last took place yesterday, in our time, in our country; the men who carried it out bore our faces, the bullets that found their way anonymously into black bodies were paid for, in part, by us. It is our consciousness, our heritage, vibrating in the air we breathe.

Let us examine again the rules we live by ... the life, liberty and pursuit of happiness guarantees. These rules say, if these guarantees are not forthcoming . . . "that whenever any form of government shall become destructive of these ends, it is the right of the people to alter or abolish it, and to institute a new government."

Certainly, no one in his right mind will deny that this form of government has been highly destructive to the life, liberty, *et cetera* of the black people. This, above all things, is self-evident. The black people are still in a social, economic, and political bondage. After a great war was fought to free them, they are not free. There is no excuse for the brute fact that our parliamentary system has not been able to bring them into the mainstream of American life. Not only that, their story can only be told in times of upheaval and self-slaughter. And even after these take place, the only comment made on it, or the only ones asked about it, are old crocks like Senator Dirksen, someone who is supremely irrelevant to what is going on, anywhere, and who yet is considered one of the two or three leading spokesmen of our government. All he can say is that we, the whites, are "getting impatient with this disregard of law and order." This fact alone, that Dirksen is speaking for it, shows the complete idiocy and futility of the Congress.

We say over and over again that the solving of the race question will take time, but there is no excuse for this. We establish new forms of government because it took too much time before, in the old form, to resolve an accursed question of human suffering. New governments are not to create a continuation of the same wrongs and social stultifications that made the new form a bloody imperative. We have had long enough . . . enough, enough to see ourselves as white-skinned racists creating and maintaining a society where some get all the good of it while others deeply suffer . . . where the good of one comes out of the evil put upon another . . . where we exist in a prison of our white skin as inescapable as that of our black neighbors. What we do to the black people, daily, makes me want to secede from the white race! It makes me, down deep, hate myself, and my color. All decent whites, especially the young whites, abhor having to bear the burden of racist guilt their fathers have placed upon them.

And they hate white racist America and their own fathers for sustaining it, for stealing from them what should have been a birthright of human brotherhood, alienating them from young blacks by white cruelty to them, in their white image. For setting up impassable barriers between young whites and young blacks, areas of suspicion coming from a constant betrayal. They want to clasp hands with the blacks, if only in admiration of the dignity, patience, and restraint they have shown up to this breaking point. If we let them alone they will offer them love and support for their bloody struggle to rise to a level of liberation and privilege which whites accept as due to them by their birth alone.

And we adults: we hate white racist America because it has blocked out of the culture of our time the unfettered expression of the wisdom of a people to whom the meaning of life has had to be privation, suffering and alienation, but who have lived, somehow, with moments of ecstasy, with spurts of infectuous and inexplicable joy. White racist America makes me ashamed of my own country, which not only presents to a vibrant, revolutionary world the complacent facade of a sluttish society whose mass ideal is the unlimited consumption of all possible goods and services . . . but has lost all of its revolutionary virtues in an hour when the darker people are finally climbing into the light, and are forced to seek elsewhere the encouragement which some of our revolutionary fathers meant for us to bestow upon mankind. And in the losing of this revolutionary virtue, we have turned despicably into our opposites and are murdering revolutionaries all over the world.

And all the time we are doing this we are telling the little white children, and some of the little black children, that Abe Lincoln said in 1848: "Any people anywhere being inclined and having the power, have the right to rise up and shake off the existing government, and form a new one that suits them better. This is a most valuable and sacred right, a right we hope and believe is to liberate the world."

And we are teaching high school students, black and white, that Abe Lincoln, the great emancipator, said, in his First Inaugural Address: "This country, with its institutions, belongs to the people who inhabit it. Whenever they shall grow weary, of the existing government, they can exercise their constitutional right of amending it, or their revolutionary right to dismember, or overthrow it."

They tell us that we have this great and basic right, but if we so much as suggest the use of it, we are punished . . . we are imprisoned. So that it serves as an entrapment, a vicious provocation to smoke out radicals and revolutionaries. Why do they say this . . . why do they so piously quote the forefathers and then blame and hurt people under an unforgivable longevity of oppression . . . obviously getting worse instead of better . . . for trying to act under it?

The United States House of Representatives has just demonstrated its imbecility and outright betrayal of the Bill of Rights, which it has sworn to uphold, by passing a bill which makes traveling from one state to another and saying anything that might be, after the fact, twisted into a connection with a riot, a criminal offense. It carries a fine of ten thousand dollars or imprisonment for five years, or both.

It was written by a white racist from Florida and forced onto the floor by the white racist from Mississippi, who said, the insurrections in the black ghettos were "organized conspiracies backed by the Communists . . . if you vote against this bill, what are you going to say when you go home and meet the policeman and fireman who risked their lives, and in many instances, lost them. . . . " As if it was not already clear that the lawless, conspiratorial, rioting element in the community is the police themselves.

This does not mean that the Southern racist congressmen were responsible for the bill. Charles W. Sandman, Jr., a Republican from New Jersey, was one of its most ardent supporters and said the police in Newark had told him that rioters had crossed the Hudson River in buses, were picked up in cars and taken to the center of Newark, where the trouble occurred. There is no proof in existence that this did occur, while on the other hand it is well known that the police will say anything that will develop their own positions. So the bill was passed by a vote of 347 to 70 . . . and they were not all Southern congressmen who voted for it.

This is how we put off, again and again, truth and resolution for some dishonest and shoddy solution. And then we snivel and hurt the helpless when the chickens come home to roost. It was not outside agitators behind the guns of Newark . . . it could be the inflammatory boasts and texts of our daily education. Now they will have to prevent Thomas Jefferson, in the form of his writings, from crossing state lines, for he said: "What country can preserve its liberties if their rulers are not warned from time to time that this people preserve the spirit of resistance. Let them take arms. . . . "

Or if the agitator from New Jersey crosses the line into Pennsylvania, he will find the Pennsylvania Declaration of Rights already there, saying: "The Community hath an indubitable, inalienable, and indefeasible right to reform, alter or abolish government in such manner as shall be by that community judged most conducive to the public weal."

Henry Clay of Kentucky, the Great Commoner, said: "An oppressed people are authorized, whenever they can, to rise and break their fetters."

John Adams, the second President of the United States, said: "It is an observation of one of the profoundest inquiries into human affairs that a revolution of government is the strongest proof that can be given by a people, of their virtue and good sense."

His son, also a President of the United States, said: "In the abstract theory of our government, the obedience of the citizen is not due to an unconstitutional law: he may lawfully resist its execution."

And Henry D. Thoreau, a good revolutionary, an artist of the revolutionaries, said: "All men recognize the right of revolution, that is the right to refuse allegiance to and to resist, the government where its tyranny or its inefficiency are great and unendurable."

In Maryland its Declaration of Rights reads: "Whenever the ends of government are perverted, and public liberty manifestly endangered, and all other means of redress are ineffectual, the people may, and of right ought to, reform the old or establish a new government; the doctrine of non-resistance against arbitrary power and oppression is absurd, slavish and destructive of the good and happiness of mankind."

General and President U. S. Grant said: "The right of Revolution is an inherent one. When people are oppressed by their government, it is a natural right they enjoy to relieve themselves of the oppression if they are strong enough, either by withdrawing from it, or by overthrowing it and substituting a government more acceptable."

And Emerson, talking of affairs in Kansas, when white settlers in 1856 had to knuckle down to racist tyrants and live like people in the black ghettos today, said:

> I think there never was a people so choked and stultified by forms. We adore the forms of law, instead of making them vehicles of wisdom and justice. Language has lost its meaning in the universal cant. . . . *Representative Government* is really misrepresentative. *Democracy, Freedom,* fine names for an

ugly thing. They call it attar of roses and lavender, —I call it bilge water. They call it Chivalry and Freedom; I call it the stealing of all earnings of a poor man and the earnings of his little girl and boy, and the earnings of all that shall come from him his children's children forever. But this is union and this is Democracy, and our poor people, led by the nose by these fine words, dance and sing, ring bells and fire cannon, with every new link of the chain which is forged for their limbs by the plotters in the Capital. . . . What are the results of law and Union? There is no Union. The judges give cowardly interpretation to the law, in direct opposition to the known foundation of all law, *that every immoral statute is void!* If that be law, let the ploughshare be run under the foundations of the Capitol—and if that be government, extirpation is the only cure. I am glad that the terror at disunion and anarchy is disappearing. . . .

Now I submit that somewhere, every day in this country, some schoolboy is reading about these men; that their words, revolution and all, are passing into their consciousness. This being undeniably true . . . how can we stop these dangerous thoughts from crossing state lines, color lines, or lines of any kind? We could not stop them from entering the icy legal mind of Mr. Justice Jackson, late of the Supreme Court, who gave, in 1950, the most concrete modern juridical opinion of the right of revolution based on the Declaration of Independence.

. . . we cannot ignore the fact that our own government originated in revolution, and is legitimate only if overthrow by force can sometimes be justified. That circumstances sometimes justify it is not Communist doctrine, but an old American belief. The men who led the struggle forcibly to overthrow lawfully constituted British authority found moral support by asserting a natural law under which their revolution was justified, and they bravely proclaimed their belief in the document basic to our freedom. Such sentiments have also been given ardent and rather extravagant expression by Americans of undoubted patriotism.

So there it is, deep in the hide of the Republic, and you can talk about it all you want, having a revolution, that is, just as long as it is in a classroom, and you are white. But don't say it, as William Epton did, on the streets of Harlem before a group of silent men, whose eyes have a tiny glow like the stirring of a long-banked fire.

The Conscience of the North

The first thoughts, the first words that come to me on occupying this desk must be in praise, in thanksgiving to, and in memory of the great prophet who gathered this congregation over a hundred years ago. At every occasion at which the human condition, its plight and its potential becomes the question of the hour, the enduring presence of Theodore Parker is evoked in my mind and in the mind of your present preacher, the carrier of the Parker tradition.

It is Theodore Parker who makes it possible for me to stand here and bear witness against the wrong that I perceive. It is Theodore Parker who brings all of you here, week after week, to one of the few places in the country where public crime, official crimes, acts of repression and sickness against the people of the country and the world are dealt with rationally, intelligently and in earnest and whenever necessary, the public punishment of denunciation is meted out. Without this there are many of us who would feel that humanity has fallen into cureless ruin, who would suspect our own unspoken revulsions and dissents and sour ourselves forever out of that faith in man and his perfectibility which saves us from melancholy and malignity . . . and even madness and self-doom.

The reason why Parker could do this and why he could maintain the continuity of his purpose and his strength in the personalities and the purposes of those hundreds of scholars, dissenters, radicals and truth

Originally delivered as an address at the Community Church of Boston, March 12, 1961; first published in *Freedomways* 1 (Fall 1961): 259–74.

tellers who have followed him here is because he founded this pulpit as a place where a man was obliged to deal out to you his life, passed through the fire of his thought . . . still roughly fused by this fire, with all the unground edges of his effort, his confusion and his agony. The example Parker laid down here for others to follow was that conscience was a primary function of man and should be listened to above every other voice.

We used to believe that we could be told what our conscience should accept or reject. It used to have much to do with whether we prayed enough, whether we were obedient, or sexless, or dutiful to our betters or our employers or to a wrathful god who crushed erring man like a worm beneath his enormous boot. Even Parker, who more than any other theologian destroyed this notion that conscience was a kind of invisible concentration camp, put it that conscience disclosed the moral law of God . . . and that God, in turn, was absolute perfection. I don't want to offend anyone here but I must say that anyone who waits for the voice of God to tell him what to do will never hear it.

He may hear some irresistible command that to follow out may bring him trouble and woe, particularly if it enjoins him to attack the vested power of the community or state. It will come lunging out of his deepest consciousness with a divine imperative and it does not really matter who put it there. It is my belief that it is our social existence that determines the consciousness from which these compelling calls to action arise. This is not new, but was stated by another great prophet of Parker's time.

What is or is not the "conscience of the North" is a big and actually indefinable subject. But we do know, by observation and sensation, the quality of the world around us and we do know that there are certain ideological forms existing in the placenta of time and place in which we grow that can make us conscious of vast moral problems and contradictions and which arouse in us compulsions to act on them on one side or the other.

This is what I mean then when I talk about the conscience of the North; its reflection of the life around us. I know that it exists: society demands it . . . there is no real escape from our consciousness of the real world. Wendell Phillips had a very good definition of conscience. He called it the common sense of the mass. But in order to create this conscience so that it will be mature, active and mutually effective, it must be confronted with realities day by day, so that the whole complex of events and contradictions which stir men into action from principle is given concrete expression before our eyes. You cannot get it by listening to Jack Paar, Mort Sahl records or joining the Book of the Month Club. You have to really know the way things are.

One majestic moment of human advance which has penetrated the whole American consciousness, I believe, is the emergence of the new African nations and the evidence it presents that the brutal colonial conquest by the white man of the darker people has come almost to an end. The two great power blocks of the world are frantically courting the Africans; the red carpet is out in Washington and Moscow.

This is all to the good and I applaud it but I still find it somewhat sickening that with all this adulation, all these fervent promises of cooperation, of defense to the death of the liberty, fraternity and equality of the black man ten thousand miles off, a black man trying to buy a modest home in Danvers, Massachusetts, has to go to the courts and invoke the law before he can get the liberty, fraternity and equality which has been his birthright and privilege since 1776, right here at home.

I find it equally sickening to hear all these pious disclaimers of any sympathy with segregation in the South without any concern for the fact that there are segregated schools in Boston . . . schools in which over ninety percent of the pupils are Negroes . . . not by law, but by the unwritten commandment of our business civilization which has forced the Negro citizens to live almost exclusively in the ninth and twelfth wards of Roxbury.

You may feel that it is sensationalism for me to call these schools segregated. But there has been a recent court fight in New Rochelle over this very situation, segregation by school district. There it was legally decided that the Supreme Court in finding that segregated education is injurious to children, laid down the constitutional principle that schools with gross racial imbalance violate the constitutional rights of the children of minority groups.

It is a fact that in Boston the Negro people have made three migrations and in every one of them have been compelled to live together in restriction. They have moved from the West End to the South End to

Roxbury, intact from first to last as an unwanted minority group, while every other ethnic minority has passed into integration with the whole community. It is also a fact of life that the Negro population is increasing, and the problem is becoming more intense, while other minorities are decreasing. By 1940 the increase was 23,000 plus, in 1950, 42,000 plus, in 1960, approximately 55,000.

We all know why these people come here and where they come from. The hope that they had of their children being educated in equality in their southern homeplace because of a decision of the highest court in the land has been answered there by the integration of about 74 children in the first five years, a rate of acquiescence in which it would take nearly eighty thousand years for the two million five hundred thousand children to receive what has always been one of their inalienable rights.

So they come here and find more of the same ... schools crowded with other Negroes, apartments and houses as unavailable to them outside the Negro district as if they were back in Dixie. The segregation is neither open or lawful here ... it is a kind of sneaky, underhanded experience in which they are met face to face with smiles and agreement and cut to the quick when their back is turned ... somehow never being able to prove that they are being kept out of schools, jobs or residential districts but never getting there either. But all the same they are infinitely better off here, for anyone who discriminates against them is not only befouling his conscience, he is breaking the law of his state and should and can be punished.

Nevertheless the glaring discrepancy between what official America is saying to black Africa and what it is doing to black Americans is so shocking, so profoundly evil, so indicative of a split in our national consciousness that I begin to wonder if the whole nation is not insane ... or at least so out of touch with reality, with rational thinking, that some terrible doom is awaiting us, some awful day of reckoning. In April of 1960, the best reporter of the *New York Times* described the conditions which are driving these fellow Americans to tear up their roots of generations and come to us as wanderers, as political refugees, for us to accept with love and compassion.

"Every channel of communication, every medium of mutual interest, every reasoned approach, every inch of middle ground has been fragmented by the emotional dynamite of racism, enforced by the whip, the razor, the gun, the bomb, the torch, the club, the knife, the mob, the police and many branches of the state's apparatus. The difference between Johannesburg and Birmingham, said a Negro who came south recently from the middle west . . . Is that here they have not opened fire yet with the tanks and the big guns."

When I read this or think about it, I wonder how, in good conscience, the American people can think of anything else . . . why they worry about the Soviet or Cuba with this awful cancer eating at our inside! I marvel that we can face the men of color anywhere, in the United Nations or elsewhere in the world, where they are the majority of this earth's people. There is no place in this planet where they have not suffered from the bloody advance and triumph of our white business civilization. W. E. B. Du Bois, the great Negro prophet, said this about it . . . "This is the modern paradox of sin before which the Puritan stands open-mouthed and mute. A group, a Nation or a race, commits murder, and rape, steals and destroys, yet no individual is guilty, no one is to blame, no one can be punished. The black world squirms beneath the feet of the white in impotent fury or sullen hate."

There are many Americans pondering this . . . some fearfully. Some dreading that when the day of reckoning comes and the sleeping giant of color rises in his might and sets things to right, that he will follow our path and mete out justice and rewards according to the pigmentation of the skin.

There are others, and Theodore Parker was one of them, who find a racial defect in the circumstances that the darker people have not risen long before to defend their rights. The answer to that is, they have, but they were suppressed and the history of their uprisings suppressed along with them. When the white man rises up to claim gloriously his inalienable rights under natural law, he is universally applauded by other white men as a liberator, as a saint. The black man's revolution is a bestial, servile insurrection when the white man tells the tale.

When Garrison, here in Boston, was being mobbed by gentlemen of property and standing for saying to the black men, cast off your chains, your masters are thieves, kidnappers and murdering scoundrels with no moral right to enslave you, these same gentlemen were holding enthusiastic meetings in Faneuil Hall to acclaim the glorious revolution in France, the glorious revolution in Greece, in Hungary, in Poland.

Tiny Boston school children were taught to read by the revolutionary texts of Adams, Otis and Hancock, but when the Negro David Walker published his revolutionary tract known as Walker's Appeal, it was instantly and hysterically denounced and suppressed and a year afterward, its author was dead, under mysterious circumstances. David Walker had assured his brethren that they would be free, if not peaceably, then by the crushing arm of power. If they were treated as men, they would use power as men, if as brutes, their triumph would be as brutish as the slaveholder, who had already piled up a debt of unspeakable wrongs against them, wrongs that came back to haunt him in the terrors of the night. As long as the Declaration of Independence remained a living creed in this country, David Walker said, "My color will root some of them off the face of the earth. They shall have enough of making slaves. This country is more ours than theirs, we have enriched it more with our blood and tears."

David Walker in his day felt the recoil of those well-meaning sentimentalists to whom any expression of hate was a vulgar abomination and who said then, and are saying today, that any violence by the Negro in the South will "lose him all his friends." But this did not bother him. "Some will accuse us of a bad spirit," he said. "But I do not care. You should not be astonished that we hate you for we are men and we cannot help but hate you while you are treating us as dogs."

It is a pity that the insidious evil of racism has stained so deeply into our national consciousness that this revolutionary tract written in 1839, of such noble intensity, such fierce pride, such consummate powers of eloquence and intellect, is missing from almost all historical indexes and bibliographies. Otherwise, it is thought highly desirable, in fact it is demanded that our historians remind every other white that this country was founded on the moral concept that resistance to dictators, large or small, or to oppressive laws which stop short of the full scope of dispassionate justice, is our most honored tradition. But the Negro is another matter . . . when he states it he is "stirring up racial hatred," and reopening wounds which have not bled since the merciful stillness at Appomattox.

Then there is another class of whites, and these include many people of honesty and perception, who charge the Negro masses of the deep south with apathy toward voting and claiming full citizenship. This may be true, such apathy does exist. But they are apathetic because we are apathetic. We poison them with our lassitude and disclaimer, for we have the vote already and the implied power over rulers and yet we have let almost as many of our acknowledged liberties slip away by default and indifference as those they never had.

We have been silent when we should have been heard, tolerant and objective when we should have been fighting mad, frightened and secretive when we should have been rising in righteous power to rebuke and punish those who subvert the rights of man for profit and privilege, and so swiftly and totally that they will see that no one trying this again will have the slightest chance of escape.

The past few days have provided shocking evidence of the inability of the liberal whites to protect themselves and maintain a legal resistance to usurpations of the Bill of Rights. The Un-American Activities Committee, whose years of steady harassment of dissenters has now been openly denounced by most of the big newspapers and all of the liberal organizations of this country, has just received a smashing victory over its critics. The Congressman of every person in this audience voted to maintain and endorse it. The six congressmen resisting it were called communist sympathizers on the floor of the house.

Coeval with this, two distinguished white men who have devoted their lives to fighting segregation were summarily ruled against by the Supreme Court on contempt charges and will now have to serve jail sentences for their efforts. The case of Carl Braden was directly related to the problem now under discussion. In the noble dissent of Justice Black it was baldly stated that from now on, "no legislative committee, state or Federal, will have trouble finding cause to subpoena all persons anywhere who take a public stand against segregation...." Furthermore, the decision, says Justice Black, "may well strip the Negro of the aid of the white people who have been willing to speak on his behalf."

There are many well-intentioned Northerners who feel that the white South should not be pushed too rapidly into social change. This is based on the notion that they have a secret gnawing guilt and that this should arouse our compassion ... that somehow this guilt feeling explains away and absolves them of the constant wrong they are doing their colored brethren. I do not believe this guilt exists to a significant degree. The crime of the white South springs from their racist unit of loyalty which, to my mind, places them beyond redemption until they take an honest look at their society and its discontents.

First of all they must wake up to the brute fact that the golden age they hark back to was a slave-holding, slave-breeding, slave-driving hell on earth. They might realize that its image and all the so-called heroes who sustained it with fire and blood, Robert E. Lee, Stonewall Jackson, Jefferson Davis and all the other traitors, are anathema to at least one-third of their fellow citizens at home and the overwhelming majority of the citizens of the world.

Secondly, they must be told that most of us know that when they talk about States' Rights they mean *white rights*. Their continuing horror over John Brown's Raid on Harper's Ferry . . . all the present acts of Negro resistance, the sit-downs, the pray-ins, the trespasses, would be swallowed as a sacrament if performed to protect the purity of the white race. If the Negroes rode as the Ku Klux Klan has, in the night and on an errand of lynching, murder and human degradation, and against their own people, they would be hailed as saviours. There was never a time when the white South did not put racism above every other form of loyalty.

There was very little talk of States' Rights whenever they were able to compromise Congress and the Supreme Court into bringing the power of the Federal Government against the Negro and not for him. Is it States' Rights which tells a man that he cannot send his children to those common schools to which they are entitled to by the law of the land of their birth, because he is colored? What is the political system that prevents colored men and women from voting for the agents that represent them in the government and there form policies to which these disenfranchised peoples are supposed to give their unquestioning loyalty . . . and when called upon, in war time, their heart's blood? The John Brown that is in me, and there is a little John Brown in all of us, once we have been exposed to the greatest Yankee of them all, tells me that this is white rights, it is a form of slavery and that it will never be anything else until everyone in the South can vote and attend common schools.

As for time taking care of the problem, we have all seen the fallacy of this answer; seen with our own eyes Southern mothers of New Orleans, typical young matrons such as we encounter in the supermarkets, solemnly telling their helpless children before the astonished eyes of the world . . . "You don't want to go to school with the black niggers." It is not hard to imagine *these* children telling *their* children . . . that is the exact way it has been carried on since the Emancipation Proclamation . . . these cherished customs of the Old South.

While in the North there is the glaring sin of omission. Look at your children's schoolbooks sometime. You will find that the history of the slave and the abolitionist is never told . . . your children may never know of them unless you tell them. The grand names of Garrison, Phillips, Frederick Douglass, Theodore Parker are barely mentioned and if they are, it is as raving fanatics who started the Civil War as a demented incendiary starts a fire. And so the towering personalities, whose lives could give a child the manliest examples of the courage and breath of intellect so desperately needed today, are withheld from their consciousness. All the values these men thought out and implanted in the living tissue of the republic have been lopped off and in their place we are offered as patriots to be venerated, traitors like Lee and Davis, bigots like Andrew Johnson, drunken hirelings of the rich like Daniel Webster, racists, all of them, who have spread filth on the garment of the American dream of the brotherhood of all.

You will find by your indifference that your children are being taught a false and vilely corrupt version of history, one that deliberately distorts the role of the Negro and feeds the obscene myth of white supremacy and keeps it unnaturally alive in the face of supreme Negro achievement on every side. When they ask the historian why the colored race has slipped back so far after a war was fought to free them so long ago, they will be told that when the Negroes were given full equality after the Civil War, they abused it in an unpardonable way, selling their votes and wandering lazily about, stealing and frolicking in a saturnalia of corruption and bestiality. Furthermore, the men who made this possible, Charles Sumner and Thaddeus Stevens, were not themselves interested in the Negro but were merely fanatic and vindictive Yankee radicals drunk with power and determined to grind a noble, defeated adversary into the dust. The historian Du Bois names dozens of historians who believe the Negro to be subhuman and congenitally unfitted for citizenship and the suffrage. Authority after authority has made it part of our historical canon that the South was right in Reconstruction, the North vengeful or deceived and the Negro stupid. This is not *Mein Kampf* I am speaking of, it is mine history, the texts our children are reading every day.

And so the strong fabric of the American past is torn apart, the threads are snapped that lead back to the best hope man ever had. A whole race is slandered by separation from the continuity of truth.

There might be some slight excuse for these omissions if the actual historical struggle between the sections was being played down to present a united nation to a disorderly world. But the opposite is true. The Centennial of the Civil War is coming in, loud and clear. The best place to read about this is in the *Wall Street Journal*. A whole new industry has been born. The blue chip possibilities of yield are said to be enormous. Disney's Law of Proliferating Profits will come into play: the Civil War Book becomes the TV Spectacular, then the movie, then breaks up into an unceasing downpour of golden fragments . . . the toys, the hats, the uniforms, the facsimile hardware and the new brand names . . . we may see, for instance, the Jefferson Davis Freedom Fighter's Plastic Cannon . . . an exact copy of the one designed for shelling the capital of the United States. The largesse never stops, raining on restaurants, gift shops, motels, gas stations and above all on the cars and roads which will carry the celebrants of the worshipful rights of this American passion play to the shrines that embody them.

As in every successful industry every effort will be made to remove from the product every abrasive element . . . anything that might give offense to the least possible consumer by casting aspersions on his region, his religion, his politics, his home life or his day-to-day assurance that every act of his government or his employer is solely for the purpose of producing the very best state of well-being in the very best of nations. The battle soil of the South will be sterilized to the depth of three generations to remove any suspicions that there was a racial conflict going on there. Everybody will be told that it was really just an exercise of great gallantry between four noble men, Lee and Davis, Lincoln and Grant . . . and that they were, all of them, all-American-Americans laboring under a slight, and still unresolved, constitutional misunderstanding. Thus the pageantry will not be half-safe, but a completely dependable national product . . . both sides separately, but equally righteous in their own Cause.

This is the way it is supposed to be set up but as in all separate and equal formulations, one side is always a little bit more separate and equal than the other. The scenes reprised so far have been largely Confederate. Not long ago we were treated to a backward glimpse of Jefferson Davis taking office as President of a Government based on the wild and tragic phantasy that slavery was to be the perpetual condition of the majority of its citizens. We saw the Southern whites in their broadcloth and crinolines re-enacting this obscenity, while passing by in the streets of Montgomery and looking at them as if they were raving mad, were the colored descendents of the American men and women whom they were struggling to keep enslaved. As usual, the resurrected Confederate heroes acted as if their fellow citizens were not there . . . as if they were utterly invisible.

The next momentous public scene to be revived will be a full-scale reenactment of the battle of First Manassas, a Confederate victory. The resurgence of Confederate interest and ardor in these rites has become so intense that the *New York Times* complained bitterly to the Court in Montgomery that it was impossible for them to get a fair verdict in their libel suit in the atmosphere of this passionate reawakening of the Lost Cause. The irony is that the *Times* has been one of the most avid publicizers of this fumigated and deprincipalized Centennial. Furthermore, they have joined with most of the other mass media in the obvious attempt to rescue the white South from the embarrassment of its resistance to desegregation, playing hard attitudes down wherever possible and making it seem that the white South had excuses for causing delays in treating Americans as Americans.

Neither the *New York Times* nor any other agency has called for counter events to be dramatized as an offset to this triumph of Southern arms. No one has called for a reenactment of the Nat Turner Insurrection in Virginia, really the first scene of the war, although these Negroes were only carrying out the forefather's injunction that RESISTANCE TO TYRANNY IS OBEDIENCE TO GOD. No one has requested the restaging of the rescue of Shadrack the Fugitive Slave by Lewis Hayden and other Negroes from the Boston Courthouse, although this is another beginning of the beginning. And it is absolutely unthinkable that the parade of the fifty-fourth Massachusetts Negro Regiment marching off to South Carolina in 1863, passing the house of Wendell Phillips on Essex Street in Boston, saluting William Lloyd Garrison as he stood there on a balcony with his hand resting on a bust of John Brown, and with the massed bands playing "John Brown's Body," be added to this pageant of dusty death . . . of death and dust made futile by the continued oppression of the Negro.

Many people feel that these ceremonies are harmless and a little ridiculous but I do not agree. Their flagrantly one-sided direction makes me suspect that they are part and parcel of the resistance movement the white South has been carrying on against human rights for a hundred years. These nostalgic mummeries are entered into with such devotion that I agree with what Garrison wrote long after Appomattox. "They are under the Union but not of the Union. They are under the Constitution but not for the Constitution, except as a matter of duress. They are nominally Americans but really Southerners in feeling and purpose. If they could see their way clear to throw off the authority of the Federal Government and to resuscitate their defunct confederacy, they would instantly rise again in rebellion and expel every loyal Northerner from their territorial domains."

There is not much danger of this but there is a very real danger that these tides of bogus sentimentalism engulfing us with tributes paid the old South for its honor, integrity and heroism are being used to bedazzle the rest of the nation out of thinking about, and having a concern over, the shameful foot-dragging going on in respect to desegregation and all the other overdue demands of the American Negro.

But there is another element here far more offensive and degrading than the broadcloth and crinoline glorification of a society of enslavers. This symbol is the flag under which they fought and which will be carried proudly on these synthetic battlefields and entwined in honor with the stars and stripes as the hallmark of these festivities. This is the same flag which the world has seen flying in every shameful and demeaning crisis in this country for the last five years . . . from the march of the White Citizens Council members in force to beseige a public school and spit in the faces of some small, helpless and vulnerable Negro children, to the latest orgy of moronic white racist students on the campus of the University of Georgia. It is inevitably paired with Nigger Go Home signs, and other national obscenities. Before this, the Confederate flag has a long and unbroken tradition of appearing at the time and place of every gross offense against Negro citizens, in the hands of night riders, hooded bigots, floggers, lynchers and burners alive.

Most people seem to be unstirred by such a connection and I cannot figure why. This nation has lately been convulsed with horror over the outbreak of Nazi symbols in many places, but surely the brash persistence of the Confederate flag is as deep a symbol of insult to the Negro as the Swastika is to the Jew, both being standards of a political system which had written into their code of laws that one sort of human was to forever be the prey and slave of another. I can never be made to understand why racism in Berlin is a crime against humanity and racism in Alabama a tolerable local custom, so honored that to defend it, all the libertarian aphorisms of the founding fathers can be brought into play. Nor can I understand why the Confederate struggle for the right of individual states to enslave people because of their color is somehow noble, while there is universal agreement that a German Reich founded on the bleached bones of millions of Jews was manifestly obscene.

Granted that nothing in the world so far can equal the impacted horror of the Nazi racial onslaughts, there still exists the slow horror of the bitter, no-exit life of the Negro in the concentration camp of his skin; without the larger anguish of the deep physical pain and unspeakable death, but full of the day-to-day degradation so eloquently put by John Hope Franklin: the degradation of finding human advance and achievement negated by a black skin, of finding himself mobbed or shot at if he tries to vote, of being shunted into ghettos to be exploited by landlords, of being insulted and driven out of every community of whites, north and south, where he seeks eating, sleeping, or even toilet facilities.

And now I have a very practical suggestion. It is a little more than a century since John Quincy Adams preserved for us the right of petitioning Congress, while he was brilliantly carrying out the political phase of the abolitionist struggle. It is still not too late to commemorate this with a new abolitionist petition which will arouse the same howls of bigot rage from the same quarters that wanted to lynch Adams for his abolitionist petitions. This will focus the awareness of the nation on the sad and significant truth that many members of Congress have a set of loyalties indistinguishable from those who trained the enemy guns at Gettysburg on the Star and Stripes on Cemetery Ridge. We have been too long and forgetfully a country under two flags.

Therefore, Whereas the flag of the defeated and defunct Southern Confederacy is today the most prominent and consistent symbol of forcible attempts to deny citizens their rights: and as it was, and is, the battle emblem of a Negro-whipping, Negro-enslaving, and Negro-degrading society, in flagrant opposition to a democratic form of government, we, the undersigned citizens of United States, demand that it shall not be displayed on any occasion, partially or completely under the sponsorship of the United States.

I am speaking to you from a lacerated conscience in the hope that I can lacerate yours. The purpose of this pulpit is to arouse and organize conscience and to deal with the relationship between man and man and the duties that grow out of this, in a completely honest way. At its best such duties are a labor of love but there are times when hate is evoked.

In the quickening and deepening of the desegregation of the South, a new leader of the Negro people has arisen. He is young and vigorous. He has been tested and found among the bravest of the brave. He is eloquent, his personal life is stainless and he sheds credit on his people wherever he goes. As a reconstructed abolitionist this should be an event of the greatest joy to me . . . I should celebrate his arrival and glorify his name. But, contrarywise, I find his personality and his policy among the saddest stories of this long and heart-rending struggle.

The leadership of Martin Luther King, Jr., was achieved by his developing a position which would be acceptable to large masses of people north and south. He feels that it is an honest and attainable one . . . and it is, indeed, an exact reflection of the limits to which he feels the conscience of the North will support him. But it is unbearably tragic. . . .

His position, as he states it, is this, "The American Negroes must say to their white brothers we will match your capacity to inflict suffering with our capacity to endure suffering. We will meet your physical force with soul force. We will not hate you, but in good conscience we cannot obey your unjust laws. Do to us what you will and we will still love you. Bomb our homes and threaten our children; send your hooded perpetuators of violence into our communities and drag us out on some wayside, beating us and leaving us half dead and we will still love you. But we will soon wear you down by our capacity to suffer. And in winning our freedom we will so appeal to your heart and conscience that we will win you in the process."

People of the North . . . you people out there . . . is that what you want the Negro to go through in order to regain the rights which he had already in 1776? He was here then, you know, and he fought alongside of us. He always had this freedom; it was only taken from him by force and fraud. And do you want him to suffer another hundred years of fraud and force, of beating, bombing and degradation until the heart and conscience of the South gets round to accepting him . . . to loving him? That is a lunatic society down there: they will never stop beating until we make them stop!

There has been enough of this . . . two hundred years of it is enough, enough, enough. Today I cannot look at my colored brother but what I see the ancestral welts upon his back and feel the anguish in his heart! The Negro is a citizen, he has no right to endure this for any reason other than his own survival. As a citizen he has a clear duty to resist tyranny and dictatorship, legally and peacefully if he can, forcibly if he must. He is the birthright possessor of inalienable rights . . . he cannot give them away if he wants to. He is not born to be a punching bag to test the longevity of the Southern whites' desire to beat him!

My friends, I am not afraid to hate . . . or to be hated. Theodore Parker has taught me that any physical violation of the rights of man or of his person . . . which is a sacred thing; the body of a man and woman is a sacred vessel and should not be violated . . . is a crime against all humanity. He who spits in the face of a Negro child spits in my face. Therefore I hate the Southern racists and all their works. I hate them for clapping me into a prison of my white skin as inescapable as that of my darker neighbor. What they do to others in the South makes me want to secede from the white race . . . and what the white-skinned racist does in the North is just as abhorrent. I hate them because they have stolen my own birthright of human brotherhood, alienating me from my blood brothers by their cruelty to them in my image ... setting up impassable barriers of suspicion between me and the people I want to clasp hands with in loving admiration of the dignity, patience and restraint they have shown in struggling upward to a level of liberation and privilege which my kind accept as due them by birth alone. I hate them because they have blocked out of the culture of my time the full expression of the wisdom of a people to whom the meaning of life has had to be privation, suffering and alienation but who have lived with quiet confidence, and far more than we have, with infectious and inexplicable joy. I hate the white South because they have made me ashamed of my own country ... which not only presents to a vibrant world grappling with problems we ignore, the complacent surface of a sluttish society whose mass ideal is the unlimited consumption of all possible goods and service ... but which has lost all of its revolutionary virtues in an hour when the darker people are finally climbing into the light and are forced to seek elsewhere the encouragement which our revolutionary fathers meant for us to bestow on mankind.

Thus I have revealed to you without restraint my own conscience, formed and activated, I hope, by a long study of the lives and words of our great American prophets. It does not come from the great beyond, from mystic voices or visions, but from men like myself, only infinitely more gifted and courageous. If, reading their words and the brave promises of my country's founders, I ignore the contradictions between them and the ground rules of our national life, day by day, I would be committing a sin against my own senses, against the light that is in me. If I accepted these gross disparities between man and man all around me with complacency, I would be committing the greatest sin, that of hypocrisy, which blinds man to his own failures and gives him a false idea of his position and purpose in the world. If I should deny the Negro any form of resistance for which white men have been applauded and venerated, I am acting as a racist. To me they are citizens and men in the old sense, in the revolutionary sense. We have no right to deny them the truths that only upheavals and outbreaks can tell ... the terrible judgments which prove without any doubt that the future and the fate of black and white in this country are indivisible forever.

Humbly I say this, no amount of invited suffering, of passive resistance, will restore to the Negro his inalienable rights. Only the united conscience of the North can do it, standing beside him and supporting him under any circumstances. Now this conscience lies inert, confused and deprinciplized. That is why we need the Negro almost as much as he needs us. We must travel the road to perfectibility together . . . to our fulfillment as persons, as citizens, and the road goes in only one direction . . . into a life of principle, under the guidance of ideas, in response to the great and accursed questions of personal independence, the citizen's relation to the state, the right to resistance, the wrong of poverty, racism, and bigotry and the quickening vision of the brotherhood of man all over the world.

Let us begin our regeneration right now . . . in standing together against the segregationists North and South and crying out . . .

VERILY THOU ART GUILTY CONCERNING THY BROTHER.

III Interview

Truman Nelson: An Interview with Shaun A. McNiff

Truman Nelson is an author, historian and revolutionary whose life's work has been concerned with the integration of art and revolutionary morality. Nelson is a self-taught writer who left the factory at the age of forty to dedicate himself totally to his art. Now sixty-five, he has produced seven books which deal with revolutionary themes together with numerous essays. Although Truman Nelson has been praised by men such as Sean O'Casey and W. E. B. Du Bois for what they perceive to be his major contributions to American art and history, his work has never attracted a large public audience. Nelson, a white man, is interestingly enough better known in the black community whose struggle has been the primary theme of his writing. In his first book, *The Sin of the Prophet* (1952), which deals with the case of fugitive slave Anthony Burns in abolitionist Boston during the 1850s, Nelson prefaces his story with the following statement by Thoreau:

A very few, as heroes, patriots, martyrs, reformers in the great sense, and men, serve the state with their consciences also, and so necessarily resist it for the most part; and they are commonly treated as enemies by it.

Twenty-four years after the publication of that book we see that Truman Nelson has himself joined the company of those men and women of high moral conscience who are neglected by society because of the threatening nature of their pronouncements. Nelson is an artist of great personal integrity who cannot compromise his art and principles to please his readers. Rather, his goal has been one of casting the reader into a process of inevitably painful self-examination.

Reprinted from *Minnesota Review*, n.s. 10 (Spring 1978): 72–86.

Julian Mayfield writing in *The Nation* described Nelson as a genuine friend of Malcolm X and Robert F. Williams and as a man who " . . . is concerned with the state of his own salvation and that of the larger North American community . . . white Americans do not like to be reminded by Nelson of their revolution and the spirit which motivated the abolitionists." George Abbott White of Brandeis University has described how "As an historian Nelson has perhaps embarrassed his colleagues by constantly measuring American past and present against the yardstick of America's revolutionary and libertarian ideals." In a letter to Nelson, Sean O'Casey wrote: "Your work is the pulse the world needs to question its cynical and timid feelings and thoughts, to quicken our hearts to more daring and our minds to greater affirmations of what we ought to say." James Baldwin in his review in *The Nation* of Nelson's book, *The Torture of Mothers*, wrote: "The tone is rare. I have come to expect it only of Southerners—or mainly from Southerners—since Southerners must pay so high a price for their private and public liberation. But Mr. Nelson actually comes from New England, and is what another age would have called an abolitionist. No Northern liberal would have been capable of this book because the Northern liberal considers himself as already saved . . . I think the book is an extraordinary moral achievement, on the great American tradition of Tom Paine and Frederick Douglass. . . . " In response to Nelson's book, *The Right of Revolution*, Conor Cruise O'Brien wrote: "It is very powerful stuff. Indeed I cannot think of anyone else now living who can write fighting prose of this order." And from Conrad Lynn: "You may be the last white man relevant to the Black Revolution."

Nelson's ideas are congruent with those of the nineteenth-century social idealists whom his writings and studies have examined. A native New Englander of what he describes as "old yankee working class stock," Nelson is first and foremost a humanitarian. In studying the lives and writings of figures such as Emerson, Thoreau, Garrison and other New England abolitionists together with his all-encompassing studies of John Brown, he must have realized that the injustices that these men fought against in the mid-nineteenth century were every bit as real and present in the mid-twentieth century. Thus Nelson channeled his historical studies into a more direct political-artistic form of writing which would hopefully be instrumental in changing the minds of his contemporaries. His goals have always been to move society as Dickens and Tolstoy had done, to reconsider its ethical and moral standards. Repulsed by the sins of racism and political oppression, Nelson has harnessed all of his personal and artistic strength to accomplish his task and in this respect he unabashedly considers his art to be prophetic of a better world to come.

Perhaps the most neglected aspect of Truman Nelson is his art. In reviewing his book, *The Old Man: John Brown at Harper's Ferry*, Robert Merideth from the University of California describes Nelson's stunning use of language. The review goes on to say that "He displays as does no other American scholar or writer what it means to immerse oneself in the historically specific situation and to render it with consummate skill and great political understanding ... *The Old Man* reads like *The Andromeda Strain* in not being projection or fantasy." In this respect Nelson's books are characterized by rich and sensual imagery, thorough character studies and fast, penetrating drama. The reader can also see in Nelson's writing a longing to keep these historical realities alive as a testament of the more noble accomplishments of American civilization.

Yet with all of his poetic gifts, Truman Nelson's writing is dominated by the theme of revolution and more specifically, the delineation of revolutionary morality. In describing Nelson, George Abbot White has said that " ... although he would chafe at the suggestion, in his devotion to freedom and the liberation of the spirit through art, tract, life, he is as much a New England 'saint' as any man I have known."

The following interview was initiated by me to explore the roots of Truman Nelson's artistic motivation. I have been intrigued by his ability to consistently maintain his creative energy through very frustrating times. I also wanted to raise more art-oriented issues such as the extent to which personal motives for competency, achievement and self-fulfillment relate to revolutionary ideology; and to what extent aesthetics are compatible with revolution.

Shaun A. McNiff

S.M.: What is the motivation behind your art?
T.N.: My art is concerned with the revolutionary process and this revolutionary art is motivated by a desire to change American society.

Many young people in America with similar goals have entrapped themselves in very egocentric forms of self-exploration. In art you have to get down to a different state of intimacy which is interchangeable with other people. Art is purely interchangeable in that it enables another to absorb the artist. The work of art should not be totally individual in that it should bind people together. Great artists like Milton, O'Casey and others are still important today because they are interchangeable and they do not relate to specifically private and personal experiences. Our culture has killed redemption and revelation, which is a property of great art and something which people need.

I have never attempted a book that did not have a specific didactic motive. There are political motives behind all of my writings in that I have been consistently concerned with the development of revolutionary morality; meaningful action; the rediscovery of history; and symbolic figures.

The didactic artist whose work has an avowed and preconceived political purpose must attain the balance between art and reality. You could say that art is the ultimate reality and agree with Thoreau in that "One must make a fact flower into a truth," but people are trained to base their decisions and their judgments on so-called factual evidence. Now the artist who takes this line of political art is always torn by this dichotomy. I have encountered difficulty with critics and editors who say: "Where does the art end and the fact begin? How much can we believe this?" and I say: "Believe all of this because there is an overruling psychological truth that can come out of my absorption of the total empirical substance that I am transmitting." I realize that the greatest perceptions of mankind are those coming from art more than fact or history.

I know for instance that the picture of the Puritans created by Hawthorne in *The Scarlet Letter* is factually false, unsophisticated and prejudiced but it is the image of the Puritan which has been stamped on the minds of American students for all time. The great teachers of the most enlightened periods have been artists—Sophocles, John Bunyan (*Pilgrim's Progress*), Goya and others. For instance in Goya all of the sacerdotal essences of Spain, which still prevail today, were made visible by him long ago. What happens is that the artist who is intent upon forcing the perceptions of a moment, or an epoch, on his readers/listeners is very dangerous because of the charged quality of his communications which add an unstable dimension to society. The artist, as prophet, as interpreter, is always suspect to the status quo. This is why art is pre-censored or cut away under the guise of objectivity, from the history and functions of people. Think of the academic thesis which is as rigid as a sonnet, in which quotes are confined to a certain length, and the form dictated in advance by the academics so that form and content are totally controlled. Censorship of form is the same as censorship of content—perhaps even worse—because the form dictates pre-censorship—of leaving out and foreshortening the free exercise of the creativity of the interpreter.

S.M.: To what extent does your art express universal truth and to what extent does it express personal perception?

T.N.: We get back here to the validation concept. There has to be a kind of guideline process. What I call "bench marks" so that when you describe an event or an incident, you can cite contemporary reporting of the fact—by an eye witness, preferably. For example, in my book *The Sin of the Prophet*, I dealt with a man who was programmed to send the members of a protest meeting out of a hall and into an onslaught on a building where a slave was confined so that he could be rescued by force. This was to be triggered by a signal from a member of the audience. The signal came and the man did not do it and chaos and a seeming betrayal ensued. Since he was a good man in every way and committed in all sincerity, I can only assume a profound failure of nerve. So we go from event to character. No one can dispute the event, validated by manifold contemporary observers. The question "Why did he do it?" comes into the realm of art.

S.M.: Can you speak about the art involved in the interpretation of this event?

T.N.: This man, Theodore Parker, showed by his actions afterwards that it was not physical fear that inhibited him. Put on trial he said: "I will admit more than the government can prove." Why then did he fail? This is what I call "the sin of the prophet." Let me read to you a statement by Parker in my book.

—This is my sin, said Parker softly, spreading his fingers over the pages. — Besides the felony against our bodies the event did something bad to my spirit. I hated the tensions and disturbances created by the weak being driven against the wall. And I must confess thinking it a pity that a people so ignorant and degraded should be the means of tearing this nation apart . . . this because of my resentment at being forced from my chosen role as scholar and philosopher and being unable to finish and publish my book. I thought you were all too speechless and submissive, forgetting that your story can only be told in outbreaks and revolutions . . . forgetting that such times gave the brave men who wrote the Old Testament the terrible truths, judgments and revelations that others dared not tell.

This as I interpreted it is a conflict with his creativity. He sensed that if he did this, he would be prevented from exercising his own creativity, his own role, and be put in bondage to someone, intellectually, socially and creatively inferior to himself. He was afraid of backsliding culturally into what seemed to him to be the primordial mud.
S.M.: Is that a verbatim quote?
T.N.: No.
S.M.: So where is the art in this passage?
T.N.: The art is that I made it up.
S.M.: Would you say some more about the artistic process in this case?
T.N.: To me it was the final touch on the portrait of a man—all of whose written works I had read, absorbed and worked over in my consciousness for a long period. They fell into line with my summing up of the portrait and I had the assurance that looking back through the book no one could really say that it wasn't true or that it could not have happened.
S.M.: There is then a point where the presentation of historical fact stops and artistic interpretation begins. Your interpretative process seems to be very much like that of the actor in that you recreate the consciousness of another through your own artistic consciousness.
T.N.: That's right.
S.M.: So why does artistic interpretation of this kind have such great historical value? Why do Sophocles', Bunyan's, Goya's and Hawthorne's have such enduring value and permanence?
T.N.: Because objectivity, so called, leaves out the emotional dimension which the artist resupplies. . . . The artist rehumanizes man. Objectivity dehumanizes him. That is the implicit rule of objectivity. So people reject the dehumanization of so-called objectivity and

cleave to and remember rehumanization, that dimension added by the artist from his depths.

The artist does not separate feeling and intellect because one feeds on the other. I am obsessed with the problem of society breaking our historical continuity so that we have to constantly rediscover the wheel. My hope is that it is running underground in people like an undiscovered nerve that I can somehow touch and reactivate a whole system of revolutionary morality—which is also one of my obsessions.

S.M.: It is very much like what Carl Jung described as the "archetypes," the universal and eternal realities underlying all experience.

T.N.: Yes it is but I must admit that I do not read Jung, or any of the psychologists. My discoveries have all come from the examination of human reactions and specific historical events. . . . I consider myself to be a Marxist, guided by the concept of historical materialism. Marx didn't invent anything. He just discovered a way of explaining it.

The discipline of observing behavior should not come from the behavior but should start with the concrete historical condition, antedating the behavior. The man becomes the embodiment of the event. The event is not the embodiment of the man.

S.M.: What do you mean by that?

T.N.: In the material world forces gather and break in on a personality. Sometimes he thinks he caused a situation and blames himself for it but this is not true. The events work on him and recreate him—so much for the better or worse, that he thinks that he created it. Napoleon was supposed to have lost the battle of Waterloo because he had a belly-ache but it wasn't the belly-ache that lost the battle, it was the emergence of the battle that made the belly-ache.

S.M.: Can we talk some more about the specific conditions that motivate your art?

T.N.: It is a current critical fad to think that life is full of ambiguities and is therefore impossible to define. I reject this because I feel that you should start and not end with ambiguity. It is the ambiguity that sets me off—the dissonance of two or more disparate factors like a bad chord on a piano. My instincts as an artist drive me to resolve this. By letting this dissonance work on my head—causing me to throw out innumerable lines of resolution—only to find the dissonance magnified. I find at last a way of bringing it to resolution and clarification.

But every dissonance has the seeds of a further dissonance which energizes itself in a new situation and so the artist runs the whole gamut of those dissonances until finally, the ambiguities are wrung out and he knows that he has brought this energizing situation to its logical end. It just runs down like a watch.
S.M.: But there is always a new conflict emerging?
T.N.: Yes. But it always comes under a certain head or assumes a certain trajectory that reaches its greatest height and starts to lose force and comes down and that is its artistic wholeness because art must have segmental completion. It has to be a piece of itself. It has to have its borders. It has to be recognizably related to itself.
S.M.: The creation of the problem, the seeing of the problem, is in this respect every bit as creative and significant as the final resolution.
T.N.: Yes. But if you are talking of an artist in my sense, you are talking about someone who is constantly trying not to put his own anxieties and ambiguities into an art form—beginning and ending with himself. I am concerned with the artist who is concerned with liberation, or in the marvelous phrase of Anatole France, describing Zola: "His life was a moment in the conscience of mankind."
S.M.: Yes, but the so-called egocentric artists like James Joyce, Sylvia Plath and Jackson Pollack who deal primarily with their own experience in their art would perhaps argue that there are certain universal qualities to their private experience that others can identify with.
T.N.: That fact is, and it is tragic that this is so neglected in academic circles, there is a whole pantheon of artists who directed themselves to conscience problems of an epoch rather than the problems of an individual or themselves, and these artists have a permanence that is indisputable. There is no reason to oppose the artist of conscience with the artist of consciousness so that one or the other has to go down—a process that seems to be taking place today. The examination should come not altogether on the social value of their work but on their creativity itself—how long it lasted and how strong it remained throughout their life. For example, Verdi was a highly political artist who was creative into his eighties. Hawthorne, a great artist, lost his creative vigor because he became in fact alienated from the people and the situations that could have maintained it. I am only saying that the political artist is constantly confronted and triggered

by ambiguities and dissonances in the human condition that renew his task.

S.M.: Most people in our society look upon tension as trauma.

T.N.: Yes but the artist has to commit himself to a range of themes. There are many different kinds of tension. You can say that a big tension makes a big theme; a small tension makes a small theme; a political tension makes a political theme; a personal tension makes a personal theme; and so forth.

S.M.: To what extent then is tension a motivating force?

T.N.: There are those artists that I describe as 'the beat and shit boys' or 'the scab-pickers'—they see humanity as having scabs. They call attention to the scab wounds and pick at them and while they bleed, they feel they are having a great art experience. Some of them are fine artists—for example, Tennessee Williams. But you see, bleeding does not resolve tension—only with the grave. The tension that has grandeur—that is a tension that involves a large segment of humanity—needs grandeur in its working out. In this way you get into a particular form of art that involves the creation of larger than life human beings.

It is important to realize that we all look at the world differently. My mental index is one of the 19th century—the 1850s and the work of Emerson, Thoreau, and Melville—and I bring this mental set to all of my art. I realize that I cannot be judgmental about the mental indexes of other people. I feel though that they have to be legitimate as artists and not deceivers who prostitute their art for money; who vacillate with the desires of the people around them; and who use their art as a fraud. The goal of my work is to free people from disparities between each other. I am working toward an egalitarian world in my art which takes down the barriers between people and which *sensitizes* people to each other. This must become a continuous process.

S.M.: Would you call yourself a Romantic?

T.N.: No, because Romanticism implies a falseness and subjectivity. I want to write prophetically and prophesy must be based on the real world.

S.M.: Do you have role models?

T.N.: Yes, I am committed to a role model who in his person actually transforms his community and who is larger than life, not in the romantic sense, but in the sense that he is the embodiment of many, many people who each have a piece of him.

S.M.: Like who?

T.N.: Like John Brown. He embodied the same function as the criminal who by a violent act against society takes away the guilt of those conventional medium-sized people for not doing anything about the wrongs that society is committing in the name of right.

The greatest figures in literature, Raskolnikov in *Crime and Punishment*, Pierre in *War and Peace*, and in a more comic sense Don Quixote, all went up against society in a legally criminal way in order to transform it for its own good.

S.M.: Yet you do not commit crimes?

T.N.: No, I don't have to. I do not have to look for crimes to commit. I go to crimes against humanity in history. Dostoevsky had to create a crime to get his role model because he was not an historian. Tolstoy, a consciously ethical man, used Napoleon's historical occupation of Moscow to trigger Pierre's criminal desire to kill him.

S.M.: Who are your personal role models?

T.N.: Those writers oddly enough that conform to Aristotle's definition of great art in his *Poetics*. The artist who is more talented and more representative than others (talent really consists of the ability to represent many, many states of consciousness). He creates a figure who has a tragic flaw which in the end destroys him and others before he is destroyed by time/natural death and who ends his life as Eliot puts it "with a bang instead of a whimper." The writers I admire are those who give up a segment of their lives deliberately to act politically—Tolstoy, DeFoe, Milton, Sean O'Casey, Yeats. . . . There is an unending list. But oddly enough when you chart a litany of today's writers you see practically nobody standing at the barricades. The response that the writers of the past got was dependent upon the responsiveness of their particular epoch. The kind of artist I admire went on with his work whether or not he got a response. This persistence indicates to me that the person is first of all an artist who cannot deviate from his art. The artist who talks prophesy in a time of cynicism and despair—a voice in the whirlwind—has to be more purely an artist than someone talking directly to more approving masses. So in the end it is the art alone that saves him and redeems him.

S.M.: Have your role models motivated you?
T.N.: Yes, I feel that a great artist should be a great man or woman. I would like to be a great man and a great artist without separation. To me a role model is not someone I admire but someone I want to replace with equal value and status.
S.M.: A competitor?
T.N.: No, just a replacement. You cannot compete because their moment in history is gone. They have crossed the river. There are different waters coming down now so when you cross the river it is different. You study the role model first, for his consistency; then for his courage; pig-headedness; and the source of his energy. In all of my studies I have only found one man with a totality of consistency and that man is John Brown. Consequently, the bulk of my work has been taken up with his delineation.

The greatest art experience in the life of Western man is the four gospels. I see a parallel here with the life of John Brown. When describing the details of his execution in my book, *The Old Man*, I realized that everything about his death lent itself to great art. It was a natural epic. You cannot tell the story any other way. It is the kind of situation that the greatest artists try to create. The greatest liberating experiences for people in history are the greatest art experiences.
S.M.: Would you like to be considered with John Brown in history?
T.N.: We would all like to die a hero's death. It is bred into us by the greatest of role models, Jesus Christ. Christianity, the greatest mass movement, along with Islam, is nothing but role modeling and it is very curious that people feel the imposition of Jesus Christ on their consciousness no matter what religion they are.

Once again "I am sicklied o'er with the pale cast of art" (Hamlet) in that I want to manufacture a replica and so I become self-conscious about it and so it will never happen that I will be a great man like John Brown. You cannot observe yourself being a great man. It won't work if you do. Artists become great men by accident.
S.M.: Do you have any female role models?
T.N.: No, and it is unfortunate. In my realm, which is one of revolution, of overthrowing existing governments by force, there is not an abundance of female role models. This is not chauvinism. It is just an historical fact. You have the Countess Markievicz in Ireland; but gen-

erally, women have not participated in the actual vanguards of the revolution.

S.M.: Where do you get your reinforcement?

T.N.: My work is reinforced by my self-comparison to my role models.

S.M.: I assume that you can do this in isolation?

T.N.: Yes, that's right. As long as you have a library you have validation. What emerges from all of this is the fact that I have a massive ego—which is good.

S.M.: Do you need this to keep going?

T.N.: Yes. It is armor and it is a generator. There is a certain kind of ego to whom defeat is trauma—that disintegrates—and dies a little. The massive ego convinces himself that the abrasion of defeat hones and burnishes him.

I want to be judged as a man of genius. All of my books are ruthlessly purged of any conscious crowd pleasing or meretricious aspects or sentimentality and never will I let the will take the place of the imagination. You cannot will art any more than you can will love—it has to come from the spring. I have to feel in my bones that my circuits are working of themselves—that the flow is genuine.

A writer like myself who is writing emotionally is walking a tightrope. You have to be so careful of melodrama when your compulsion is to elevate man so that he can exult in himself and redeem himself.

Robert Frost once said that: "I want to have a few things that they cannot get rid of." The only way that you can make your message permanent is to make good art.

If I did not receive validation of my competency from my critics, I would not be going from one book to another. *Art is very much like a machine. There are a lot of parts that you put together and the emotion that you inject makes it run.* So the artist is like a mechanic in this sense. He has to be competent. *So competency is absolutely essential. You have to put the forms together in such a way that there is an emotional charge. There has to be a meeting of form and content.* The ultimate thing for the artist-writer is to have a complete unity of time and place.

S.M.: Why do you want to be judged a genius?

T.N.: Because only then can I be judged a carrier of the broken and/or hidden continuities that order and renew my life. I have convinced myself that this is the purpose of my life.

S.M.: And what about the approval of the people around you?
T.N.: I have enough. My book, *The Torture of Mothers*, actually got six young blacks convicted of murder out of a life sentence and out of prison after a series of trials in which the book was their most substantive defense mechanism. Also a guy in the Sorbonne wrote a thesis about me. Max Geismar, the critic, feels that I am the last of my time. W. E. B. Du Bois praised my work. Sean O'Casey has done the same and has written me to send his admiration. A friend recently saw Ho Chi Minh's desk in Hanoi, which is kept exactly as he used it last, as a perpetual memorial, and one of my books was on it. These are the men that I tried to imitate and they accepted me into their company.
S.M.: Is that still a great source of motivation?
T.N.: Yes. Who could ask for anything more?
S.M.: Were there other significant people who supported your art over the years?
T.N.: Yes. Let me speak more personally of how that relates to me. My father was a barber and very poor. My mother was a strong woman who consistently supported me. We all seem to have a strong woman behind us somewhere. I was working in the factory at the age of forty in Lynn, Massachusetts, when I wrote a poem called "False to King Ahab" which I sent into Little, Brown Publishers in Boston and they asked me to do something else with it. At that time I went to a meeting where F. O. Matthiessen, author of the *American Renaissance*, spoke. He said that the man who meets the ultimate challenge of life is the one who can be with the oppressed against the oppressor. The first real books that I read were by Proust and D. H. Lawrence and they helped me to realize that art is not always something that makes you feel happy but something that makes you feel perplexed. So I decided to work in this way as a result of their influence and my natural convictions. How was I at forty, married, with two children, to deal with my then constant aesthetic impulse?

I decided to write to Matthiessen, who was then at Harvard. I was very class-conscious and introduced myself to him as a factory worker and told him that I would pay him to work with him at Harvard. As you know I left high school before graduating and had never attended a university. Matthiessen agreed to meet with me and discuss my work. I began to write my first book, called *The Sin of the Prophet*. I could only meet with him on Sundays—my only day off and my wife's only day off—she also worked in the factory. Every night I would leave work at four and go to Boston Libraries to do research for the book. My wife was beginning to hate me. I got a $2,500.00 advance from Little, Brown which enabled me to finish the book. Matty liked it and said that he would review it in the *New York Times*. Shortly afterwards he was dead after jumping out of a window. He had been called to testify before a McCarthy committee and could not handle the situation. He presented himself in a very apologetic way and kept saying "I am a Christian." If he could only say: "Fuck you Jack!" He just was not strong enough.

I decided to dedicate the book to Matthiessen but began to wonder if the work was good enough for such a great man. I then went to Harry Levin at Harvard and asked him if the book was good enough—was I being presumptuous? He said that it was a good book and praised it highly. He said that it was the best book written that year.

So I walked out of the factory.

S.M.: So what was the effect of your relationship with Matthiessen on your writing?

T.N.: There is one thing that we have to know about creative people. They have to have constant validation. That is the role of the teacher. You have to validate people's desires and dreams. Without this validation I could not have made it.

So I was left without Matthiessen. And a hostile critic, Perry Miller of Harvard, a bitter personal enemy of Matthiessen, reviewed the book in the *Times* and blasted the shit out of me.

S.M.: Your personal history documents the growth and development of art out of an adverse environment.

T.N.: It depends on what kind of art you are interested in. I am a pre-revolutionary artist. If a revolution had taken place and I was asked to extoll it, I might not have been too good at it. Oppression turns me on, combat excites me—it gives me euphoria.

S.M.: How come?

T.N.: Because I have great gifts of vituperation and abuse which are drawn out in these situations. I feel excited by this. I find it Shakespearean. The literature that molded my mind was a literature of dissent and upheaval—of eloquence and combat.

S.M.: So where do you stand now?

T.N.: I am now sixty-five and applying for social security. My monthly stipend will be one hundred and forty dollars. This could be devastating to think that my ultimate income is so little. My only recourse outside of my writing is welfare which would bring it up to two hundred dollars a month. But I feel honored by this. I am proud of the fact that I have contributed eight revolutionary books without feeding any profit back into the system. A French-Swiss philosopher that I spoke to once exposed me to a philosophy of selflessness in which you do not weigh things in material calculations. There is just enough art in my work to convince a publisher that it might make money but there is enough morality in it to piss-off the aesthetes. When you have a sense that you have responded to the need of the epoch then you feel that you have locked into some kind of useful function. People have come to me and have said that I have changed them. I do not want to be overly modest about this because changing people has been the purpose of my life. It is interesting that you were talking on the telephone to Robert Coles when I came in this morning. He has made himself useful to society in the manner that I have described but I assume that people have a difficult time going to him and seeing him—possibly out of their own fear that he is too busy for them. I think that this applies to me too. I am waiting for people but they do not come. So while I am waiting I write. I have a purpose—this is of course a nineteenth-century concept but it is valuable and should not be disparaged. I am not overly sensitive to criticism. I tend to be arrogant. I have what I call revolutionary obtuseness. It means that you do not sit down and get petty about your problems. This enables me to keep going. It is like John Brown at Harper's Ferry before his attack saying to two young men: "Are you with me? Are you going to go?" They say: "No," and he says "All right. I will go alone." When you think about your work solely as a socially acceptable product, you lose the fuel that makes it run.

(April 1976)

T.N.: The exuberance of perceiving life as art can be maintained under any conditions. The need is that you have to tell somebody what is happening to you. By the time you have become my age the canons of art have been engraved like mosaic tablets on your mind so I have to go through certain circuits and make it all come out in the form of art and not a complaint. Complaints are not art. Personal agonies per se are not art. My canon of art is that comedy and tragedy exist together in every phase of our lives.

S.M.: Can you say at this point that the ultimate art motive is the need for the affirmation of the self?

T.N.: The Old Puritans used to say that if you are an artist, you can put your own glosses on life. The strength of the Puritan movement was their belief in the right to put their own individual interpretation on the meaning of the Bible. In this way the individual had control over the Bible; he had control over history; and in a way he had control over God because God was what he made him to be. The idea of God being made in man's image was an important part of the Puritan movement.

I hate to say this because we have been so corrupted by cynicism but I wanted to bring joy to people; to bring pleasure; to bring a smile to people. It is a very powerful motive but you just cannot talk about it today because it is considered to be old-fashioned, nineteenth-century stuff. But I tend to look in someone else's eyes for a little light and some kind of response. Putting it negatively, you cannot get love unless you give it. You cannot get sympathy unless you arouse it. The positive side is that there is a feeling of joyous satisfaction in the consciousness when you transmit and bring sensual listening pleasure to people that you are talking to.

S.M.: As we move deeper into your analysis of your motives, there seem to be many different themes that emerge. There is the dissonance factor that you described so well; there is also this burning desire to communicate—not only revolutionary morality and heightened states of consciousness but simply a communication of yourself to other human beings. All of these motives seem to run together. You have started to describe your unconscious motivations. Can we move now into an analysis of the extent to which your motives are conscious or unconscious?

T.N.: This becomes a problem in what we might call middle-class morality in that people feel sometimes that if you arrange your thoughts consciously that you have made a false construct. It's hard to answer this question because my response is determined by my age, training and character. Since I have been storytelling for so long people will say that I cannot show the cries of anguish, fear and defeat that come up in every human being. The Freudians will say that what is outside is a construct which is not the real person and that underneath there is a yawning chasm of defeat, envy and despair that the artist covers with these constructs—with a kind of surface tap dance. But you see it isn't true because I know that what is underneath is on top too. I think that there are people who are the same on the inside as they are on the outside.

S.M.: You say then that there is a continuity between what is underneath and what comes out and that you are in touch with your motives on every level.

T.N.: People say that you can never tell a book by its cover. Maybe among madmen there is a perfect consistency between inside and outside because they have lost the self-censorship and falseness that society seems to require. I have found people who are the same on the inside and the outside and I want to celebrate them. However, I am criticized for this because no one wants to believe that. Now, I believe that Garrison had this inner and outer continuity along with John Brown and others. What happens though is that writers come along and say that people like Martin Luther have some kind of mixed up things in their lives that make them the way they are. I think that it is dishonest to represent a person in this way.

S.M.: There is this tendency in art interpreters to reduce motives to something psychopathological and the process seems to be motivated by the interpreter's need to be omniscient and to feel that he knows more about you than you know about yourself. How do you respond to this, Truman?

T.N.: Well, I find this to be the malaise of the age. It is a return to medievalism and the "spirit witness" where you ascribe an unconscious or conscious motivation to somebody and you treat it as gospel. The effect of all of this is that we can never believe what is; we can never see what is right in front of us; we can never listen and believe. We listen only to a question: "What do they really mean?" This mucking about with the unconscious is a return to spirit witnessing and judging motives on the basis of some subconscious desire which is the opposite of my belief in historical materialism; in proof; in evidence; believing in substance; and in believing in continuity. So I try to avoid this search for deep, arcane and secret motives. In my last book, *The Old Man*, I simply wrote down what John Brown did at Harper's Ferry in its enormous complexity and you see a mind planning in great detail and with a clear sense of strategy rather than the mythical notions of John Brown being deranged with voices coming to him from God.

S.M.: So he was very much in control and quite conscious of what he was doing rather than being motivated by hidden forces in his psyche?

T.N.: Yes. This retreat to the inexplicable and unknowable is a thing which really brings defeat. Because then one has to knuckle under to elements beyond his own power and his own destiny.

S.M.: How do the present literary trends that you have described affect you?

T.N.: They frustrate me. This morning on the "Today" show they had a woman on who had been sick and while she was in bed she would look out the window and watch the pigeons and in watching them she resolved her own problems and she wrote a book about this and how delightful pigeons are. And here I am taking up the great themes about the history of our lives and I've never been asked on the "Today" show or any other such media event. Obviously people prefer to read about the pigeons. And of course there is the direct suppression of my work because of its political orientation—when you attack society, you cannot expect it to exult you.

S.M.: And as you said before, the rejection feeds you?

T.N.: Yes, it feeds me by example. For instance, I know that Dr. Du Bois, who was called the Lenin of Africa, the greatest man in Africa, the father of the African Revolution, lived at 16 Grace Court in Brooklyn during the beginning of the African Revolution in Kenya with Jomo Kenyetta. Do you know that the news people never once put in a 10¢ call across the river. Nobody called him and he was sitting there waiting for them to call him. Now I know that was deliberate and that I am not being petty in saying that to a certain extent the major communication networks have ignored me in this way.

S.M.: If you don't mind, Truman, I would like to discuss a motive that we have not paid much attention to yet. To what extent is your sexuality and your sexual drive connected to your art motives? I ask you this question in full view of your physical vitality. Do you see a connection between your sexual motives and your art motives?

T.N.: Oh, yes. Of late I have been able to talk about my sexuality and I never used to be able to. I am a sexual person but I get a little afraid when I hear some writers say that when you are writing you shouldn't fuck because it comes from the same source and you're cutting down on your creativity. I don't know if that is true. Sometimes I have tried to operate in that way but I have no real proof of it.

S.M.: Sometimes you purposefully abstain from sex?

T.N.: Yes, I have said to myself "If I spend the night fucking I won't be able to do my work the next day," —and I feel guilty. But sometimes I don't do a day's work the next day without doing anything the night before—so it doesn't prove anything.

S.M.: How does all of this relate to your art motivation?

T.N.: I have great sex at my age and I find that I have the same drive in art. The advances that you make toward a woman in bed with you are the same as those that you make in storytelling—you have to make it last; you have to build to a climax; you have to bring in little varieties; and so forth. You tell a story with body language by evoking past sexual experiences; you promise those of the future; and you give those of the present—and my concentration in both art and sex is intent upon pleasing the other. Both sex and art have to be evocative. A story has to be chordal in that it has to ring on several different levels and good sexuality has to be like that. You can't just go in and "bang, bang" and go to sleep.

S.M.: Then your storytelling and your art making are directly connected.

T.N.: I think it's what I said earlier. If you can somehow arrive at the simple human methodology of knowing how to give art or love in an unselfconscious way, you will receive something in return. In both art and love I like to work on one project at a time. I can't be constantly shifting gears because the architecture in both is so complex and I do not want to mar the lines.

S.M.: Is your art always a sublimation of your sexuality? Is all of your art motivated by sexual drives?

T.N.: I can't separate them. My sexuality is the same as my storytelling because they are both in some way constructed processes in which you are always looking and checking with the other person to see what is going over, what is working. It is controlled and not blind ecstasy. And again sometimes I get fearful and feel that I have to live like a priest and save all of my energies for my work. So my sexual motives and my art motives are in this respect one and the same. It is a person rather than a reader that I am writing to. And sometimes I get a sexual response from the people I write to. My book *The Torture of Mothers* is a very passionate book but there's no sex in it—it's nothing but pure anger, pure protest. This woman in New York who happened to be quite liberated came to me and said that the emotions in the book were so strong and so raw that they really turned her on and she then said that she would like to go to bed with me. She had in this way turned my whole political and humanitarian thrust in the book into an erection. And I couldn't do it to her because I did not know her—I had no form; I had no creative plan; I had no scenario to work on with her. I just couldn't go to bed with her because she had the attributes of a female and I had the attributes of a male.

S.M.: In general what do you think of our talk together?

T.N.: You are performing an important function for me. You are addressing yourself to the perception of me that you have had for a certain number of years so that you can zero in, and in this way you are flattering me. I liken this to what happens when I read a very good book and I am motivated to write down my thoughts in response to the author's statements. For example, when I read Tolstoy, I often sit at the typewriter and we carry on a dialogue with each other. But this interaction with you is better because you are relating directly to me. The interviewer should meet the person on a level where the person feels that he has to strain himself a little to answer. It is a dialectical process where there is work involved and you cannot read a good book without working. When you ask these questions which come out of your knowledge of psychology, many of my answers are perhaps recognizable to you in relation to the literature in that field but they are not recognizable to me as psychological ploys. They are recognizable to me as half of a searching dialogue. Now I am putting a lot of work into this and I find it true of my make up. So instead of Tolstoy asking me his questions that I have to pit myself against, you are asking me my own questions.

(May 1976)

Bibliography

Compiled by Garrison Nelson

Books

The Sin of the Prophet. Boston: Little, Brown and Company, 1952.
The Passion by the Brook. Garden City, N.Y.: Doubleday and Company, Inc., 1953.
The Surveyor. Garden City, N.Y.: Doubleday and Company, Inc., 1960.
The Torture of Mothers. Boston: Beacon Press, 1968. Originally published by The Garrison Press, Newburyport, Mass., in 1965. Published in Germany as *The Long Hot Summer* (Berlin: Seven Seas Publishers, 1967), and translated into Turkish (Istanbul: Yucal Yaymevi, 1973).
The Right of Revolution. Boston: Beacon Press, 1968.
The Old Man: John Brown at Harper's Ferry. New York: Holt, Rinehart and Winston, 1973.

Books Edited

Documents of Upheaval: Selections from William Lloyd Garrison's The Liberator, 1831–1865. New York: Hill and Wang, 1966. Reissued in 1969 in the First American Century Series.

Unfinished Works

God in Love: The Sexual Revolution of John Humphrey Noyes. Under contract with W. W. Norton, Inc., New York, N.Y.
Revolutionary Morality: The Lives of the World's Great Thinkers as Judged by Their Revolutionary Content. An examination of the writings of Tolstoy, Machiavelli, Lord Byron, Giuseppi Verdi, and Sean O'Casey.

Pamphlets

People with Strength in Monroe, North Carolina. Monroe, N.C.: Committee to Aid the Monroe Defendants, 1963.

Plays

The Torture of Mothers. Adapted and directed by Glenda Dickerson, Back Alley Theater, Washington, D.C., December 1, 1972.

Films

The Torture of Mothers. Directed and produced by Woodie King. Narrated by Adolph Caesar. New York: Black Filmmaker Foundation, 1980. Broadcast on Public Broadcasting System, WNET-TV, New York (1982).
John Brown in Kansas. Directed by Steve Schmidt, produced by Fred Whitehead. Lawrence, Kans. (1981).

Articles

"Theodore Parker: His Bricks Were Books." *The Christian Register* 133 (January 1954): 11–12.
"John Brown Revisited." *Nation* 185 (August 31, 1957): 86–88. Reprinted in *A John Brown Reader*, ed. Louis Ruchames, pp. 406–10. New York: Abelard-Schuman, 1959.
"W. E. B. Du Bois: Prophet in Limbo." *Nation* 186 (January 25, 1958): 76–79.
"Shores of Strife." *New York Times Magazine*, April 27, 1958, pp. 78–79. Reprinted in the *Emerson Society Quarterly* 4 (Spring 1958): 8–9.
"Walden on Trial." *Nation* 187 (July 19, 1958): 30–33. Reprinted in the *Emerson Society Quarterly* 4 (Spring 1958): 10–12; and in the *Western Humanities Review* 12 (Autumn 1958): 307–11.
"The Walden Pond of R. W. Emerson." *Emerson Society Quarterly* 4 (Spring 1958): 6–8.
"The Matrix of Place." *Essex Institute Historical Collections* 95 (April 1959): 175–86.
"John Brown—The Man Who Is Still There." *National Guardian* 11 (October 26, 1959): 5–6.
"John Brown's Brain." *Mainstream* 12 (December 1959): 17–25. Originally presented to the John Brown Convocation at the University of Minnesota on the Centennial of the Raid on Harper's Ferry, Minneapolis, Minn., October 1959.
"Theodore Parker as Revolutionary Moralist: From Divinity Hall to Harper's Ferry." *Proceedings of the Unitarian Historical Society* 13, Pt. 1 (1960): 71–82.
"The Battle of Walden Pond (Part I)." *National Parks Magazine* 34 (December 1960): 4–6.
"The Battle of Walden Pond (Part II)." *National Parks Magazine* 35 (January 1961): 4–6, 14.
"The Conscience of the North." *Freedomways* 1 (Fall 1961): 259–74. Originally presented as an address to the Community Church of Boston, March 12, 1961.
"A Case in Point." *Bay State Librarian* 52 (July 1962): 3–4, 13.

"A Society Not Yet Formed." *Liberation* 8 (April 1963): 23–25.
"The Cuban: A New Kind of Man." *Independent* 138 (October 1963): 1, 4–5.
"A Plea for Unity." *Freedom* 1 (April 13, 1964): 6.
"John Quincy Adams and the Revolutionary Temper." *Ramparts* 3 (December 1964): 20–27.
"W. E. B. Du Bois As a Prophet." *Freedomways* 5 (Winter 1965): 47–58. Reprinted in *Black Titan: W. E. B. DuBois*, ed. the Editors of *Freedomways*, 138–51. Boston: Beacon Press, 1970.
"The Liberator." *Ramparts* 4 (November 1965): 20–29.
"Thoreau and the Paralysis of Individualism." *Ramparts* 5 (March 1966): 16–26.
"The Torture of Mothers." *Ramparts* 5 (July 1966): 16–27.
"The Pacifist 100 Years Ago." *Boston Globe Magazine*, September 18, 1966, pp. 18 ff.
"Pacifist, Moral Crusader, Newspaperman: His Liberator Hammered the Slave System to Pieces." *Boston Globe Magazine*, September 25, 1966, pp. 40 ff.
"Man of Peace Finally Accepts Solution of Force." *Boston Globe Magazine*, October 2, 1966, pp. 33 ff.
"It Happened Before: Today's Youth Underground." *Boston Globe Magazine*, March 12, 1967, pp. 32 ff.
"The Puritans of Massachusetts: From Egypt to the Promised Land." *Judaism* 16 (Spring 1967): 193–206.
"Mr. Emerson Buys a House for Impoverished Mr. Alcott . . . 'the most refined and most advanced soul we have in New England. . . . '" *Boston Globe Magazine*, July 2, 1967, pp. 9 ff.
"How the 20th Century's Classic Revolution Was Made." *Boston Globe Magazine*, October 22, 1967, pp. 32 ff.
"An American Tragedy: The Decline and Fall of the Nonviolent Movement." *Boston Globe Magazine*, April 21, 1968, pp. 38 ff.
"On Creating Revolutionary Art and Going Out of Print." *Triquarterly* 23/24 (Winter–Spring 1972): 92–110. Republished in *Literature in Revolution*, ed. George Abbott White and Charles Newman, pp. 92–110. New York: Holt, Rinehart and Winston, 1972.
"Waiting for Melville." *Quindaro* 2 (August 1978): 9–12.
"Address to the Community Church of Boston, November 16, 1980." *Quindaro* 12–13 (1982): 27–33. Translated into Russian and reprinted in *I Believe in Humanity* (Moscow: Raduga, 1986), pp. 556–63.

Chapters in Books

"The Resistant Spirit." Introduction to Robert F. Williams, *Negroes with Guns*, edited by Marc Schliefer, pp. 17–36. New York: Marzani & Munsell, Inc., 1962.
"An Introduction," to *Puritan Paths from Naumkeag to Piscatagua*, by Law-

rence Green Dodge and Alice Cole Dodge, pp. xv–xvii. Newburyport, Mass.: Newburyport Press, 1963.
"Introduction," to *Documents of Upheaval: Selections from William Lloyd Garrison's The Liberator*, ed. Truman Nelson, pp. ix–xxii. New York: Hill and Wang, 1965.
"Thoreau and John Brown." In *Thoreau in Our Season*, ed. John H. Hicks, pp. 134–53. Amherst: University of Massachusetts Press, 1966.
"No Rights, No Duties." From *The Right of Revolution* and reprinted in *The New Left: A Collection of Essays*, edited by Priscilla Long, pp. 72–86. Boston: Porter Sargent Publishers, 1969.
"Introduction," to *The Gift of Black Folk: The Negroes in the Making of America*. by W. E. Burghardt Du Bois, pp. vii–xx. New York: Washington Square Press, 1970.
"Introduction," to *The Souls of Black Folk*, by W. E. Burghardt Du Bois, pp. ix–xxv. New York: Washington Square Press, 1970.

Published Interviews

"Writes Novels In His Head," by John Mason Potter, *Boston Post Magazine*, March 9, 1952, p. 7.
"Tense: Present Imperfect," *North Shore* '66, 1 (October 8, 1966): 2, 5.
"Causes Without Rebellions," by the editors of *Underground* 1 (October 19, 1966): 3–4, 6.
"The Angry American '68," by Bill Plante, *North Shore*, a supplement to the *Newburyport* (Mass.) *Daily News*, May 25, 1968, p. 20.
"The Harlem Six," by Angela Terrell, *Washington Post*, December 6, 1972, pp. D1, D12.
"Staging Politics With Lyricism," by Robert Buchanan, *Washington (D.C.) Evening Star and Times-Herald*, December 13, 1972, p. B1.
"Truman Nelson: A Regional Author," by Dorothy Patten, *Haverhill* (Mass.) *Gazette*, March 27, 1973, p. 8.
"Truman Nelson: An Interview," by Shaun A. McNiff, *Minnesota Review* 10 (Spring 1978): 72–86.
"Panel on the Frontiers of Language," with Meridel LeSeuer, Jack Conroy, and Tom McGrath at Second Midwest Cultural Conference, Kansas City, June 3, 1979. Published in *Quindaro* 8–9 (1981): 27–34.
"The Revolution Is Not Over," by Barbara Walsh, *The Current* 5 (January 28–February 10, 1981): 1. *The Current* is a supplement to the *Haverhill* (Mass.) *Gazette*.
"The Artist Can Never Be Defeated Because He Gives His Best," by Nanette Morin, *Anemone* 2 (Winter 1985): 6–8.

Book Reviews

"The Poor and the Dull." *Saturday Review of Literature* 35 (April 12, 1952): 23. A review of Richard Hagopian, *Faraway the Spring*.

"History Stood on Its Head." *National Guardian* 13 (May 8, 1961): 9. A review of Robert Penn Warren, *The Legacy of the Civil War*.
"Du Bois' Epic of the Negro." *National Guardian* 13 (July 17, 1961): 8. A review of W. E. B. Du Bois, *The Black Flame*.
"John Brown's Shining Example: A Noble 'Insanity,'" *National Guardian* 14 (February 12, 1962): 6. A review of Louis Ruchames, *A John Brown Reader*.
"Abolition History." *National Guardian* 14 (May 14, 1962): 9. A review of Dwight L. Dumond, *Anti-Slavery*.
"Remember Hiroshima." *New World Review* 31 (February 1963): 54–55. A review of the Japanese Council Against Atomic and Hydrogen Bombs, *Hiroshima-Nagasaki Document* (1961).
"The Real John Brown." *National Guardian* 15 (February 14, 1963): 8. A review of W. E. B. Du Bois, *John Brown*.
"Henry James De-Idolized." *National Guardian* 16 (November 7, 1963): 10. A review of Maxwell Geismar, *Henry James and the Jacobites*.
"Delinquent's Progress." *Nation* 201 (November 8, 1965): 336–38. A review of *The Autobiography of Malcolm X*.
"Clarion Call on Civil Rights." *Boston Globe*, September 7, 1966. A review of Francis L. Broderick and August Meier, eds., *Negro Protest Thought in the Twentieth Century*, and Mary T. Clark, *Discrimination Today*.
"Higginson's Platform." *Boston Sunday Globe*, February 11, 1968, p. A-37. A review of Howard N. Meyer, *Colonel of the Black: Thomas Wentworth Higginson*.
"From Prison—A Unique Document." *Boston Sunday Globe*, March 24, 1968, p. A-27. A review of Eldridge Cleaver, *Soul on Ice*.
"A Life Style of Conscience." *Nation* 206 (April 29, 1968): 574–75. A review of *The Autobiography of W. E. B. Du Bois*.
"Che Guevera Reminiscence Real Swinger." *Boston Globe*, June 27, 1968, p. 34. A review of Che Guevera, *Reminiscences of the Cuban Revolutionary War*, trans. Victoria Ortiz.
"Guerrilla of the Mind." *New York Times Book Review*, October 13, 1968, p. 16. A review of Julius Lester, *Look Out Whitey! Black Power's Goin' Get Your Mama!*.
"A Question of Equality." *Boston Sunday Globe*, November 16, 1969, p. A-44. A review of John F. Kain, comp., *Race and Poverty: The Economics of Discrimination*.
"Scholarly Gallimaufry." *Nation* 210 (January 19, 1970): 56–57. A review of Eugene D. Genovese, *The World the Slaveholders Made*.
"John Brown Biography Disputes Fanatic Image." *Boston Globe*, July 27, 1970, p. 8. A review of Stephen B. Oates, *To Purge This Land with Blood: A Biography of John Brown*.
"'You Have Not Studied Them Right,'" *Nation* 212 (March 29, 1971): 405–8, 410. A review of Stephen B. Oates, *To Purge This Land with Blood: A Biography of John Brown*.

"Wrestling with John Brown." *Boston Sunday Globe*, April 4, 1971, p. B-67. A review of Jules Abels, *Man on Fire.*
"Garrison's Letters." *Boston Sunday Globe*, September 19, 1971, p. 61. A review of Walter M. Merrill, ed., *The Letters of William Lloyd Garrison*, vol. 1, *I Will Be Heard!* 1822–1835.
"Garrison: Revealing Letters." *Boston Sunday Globe*, April 16, 1972, p. B-48. A review of Louis Ruchames, ed., *The Letters of William Lloyd Garrison*, vol. 2, *A House Dividing Against Itself*, 1836–1840.
"A Protest of Conscience." *Boston Sunday Globe*, March 25, 1973, p. 75. A review of Jack Nelson and Ronald J. Ostrow, *The FBI and the Berrigans.*

Unpublished Addresses

"The Guardian of Our Conscience." A speech at the Eleventh Annual Dinner of the *National Guardian*, New York City, November 18, 1959.
"The Transient and the Permanent in Man." A speech delivered at the Community Church Forum, Boston, May 23, 1960.
"Ghana—Black Man's Miracle." A lecture and discussion based upon a visit to the Summit Conference of African Leaders before The Friday Night Forum, Newark, N.J., February 18, 1966.
"On Revolutionary Separatism: The American Revolutionary Experience." A presentation to the Society for the Humanities of Cornell University, Ithaca, N.Y., March 8, 1968.
"The Counter-Revolutionaries We Teach." A paper delivered before the New England College English Association at the University of Massachusetts, Amherst, May 4, 1968.
"The Preservation of Revolutionary Morality in a Time of Reactionary Engulfment." An address presented to the Community Church of Boston, September 28, 1986.

Unpublished Manuscripts

"The Ballad of Faneuil Hall: A Play." On file at the Widener Library, Harvard University, Cambridge, Mass.
"Theodore Parker and Our Business Civilization." 1952. On file at the Essex Institute, Salem, Mass.
"A Corpus of Work, 1950–1960." On file at the Essex Institute, Salem, Mass.

Biographical Sketches

Library Journal 72 (February 15, 1952): 354.
Saturday Review of Literature 35 (February 16, 1952): 20.
Wilson Library Bulletin 37 (April 1963): 37. Written by Jane Maddox Hatch.
Dictionary of International Biography, ed. Ernest Kay. 12th ed. Cambridge, England: Melrose Press Ltd., 1976.

International Authors and Writers Who's Who, ed. Ernest Kay. 7th ed. Cambridge, England: International Biographical Centre, 1976.
Contemporary Authors, new revision series, vol. 1, ed. Ann Evory. Detroit: Gale Research Co., 1981. An earlier version appeared in *Contemporary Authors*, 1st revision, ed. James M. Ethridge and Barbara Kopala. Detroit: Gale Research Co., 1967.

Literary Assessments

Doucette, Rita. *Parallel Lives: A Comparison of Henry David Thoreau to Truman Nelson*. Salem, Mass.: R. Doucette, 1964.
Mayfield, Julian. "The Legitimacy of Black Revolution." *Nation* 206 (April 22, 1968): 541–43. A review of *The Right of Revolution*. Also published as "White Man in the Black Revolution." *Boston Globe Magazine*, May 5, 1968, pp. 24 ff.
Llorens, David. "Note on 'The Conscience of White Folk.'" *Negro Digest* 17 (August 1968): 97–98.
Schafer, William J. "Truman Nelson: Heeding the Voices of Revolution." *Minnesota Review* 7 (Fall 1976): 66–82.
Meyer, Michael. *Several More Lives to Live: Thoreau's Political Reputation in America*. Westport, Conn.: Greenwood Press, 1977. Pp. 168–71, 188–89.

Acknowledgments

It was at Truman Nelson's seventy-fourth birthday party in February 1985 that this book was developed. More than a decade had passed since Nelson's last major novel, *The Old Man*, had been published and those of us at the party were concerned that he might not publish again in his lifetime. His latest manuscript, *God in Love*, dealing with John Humphrey Noyes and the Oneida Community, had been slowed by the onslaught of arthritis and other debilities of aging. It was our hope that the return to print would enable him to work through the pain and complete *God in Love*.

The original conception of *The Truman Nelson Reader* belonged to Fred Whitehead, an English professor, welder, and social activist from Kansas. Building on Whitehead's conception, the new compilation made more use of Truman's literary essays in order to give emphasis to both his intellectual and his political contributions.

Sharon Hollis of Newburyport put together the original collection of Truman's essays and Shaun A. McNiff of Lesley College worked with Truman on excerpting the novels for their inclusion in the *Reader*.

I became involved in the manuscript in September 1986 after Truman's initial choice of an editor left the project. It was at this time that Professor Bill Schafer of Berea College in Kentucky took over the editorial responsibilities of the *Reader*. Truman, Bill, and I worked very closely on the book, cleaning up excerpts, gaining republication permissions, and compiling the only complete bibliography of Truman's extensive writings. We all knew that time was short although none of us would speak of it.

302 ACKNOWLEDGMENTS

It was my hope that Truman would live to see the publication of *The Truman Nelson Reader*, but it was not to be. He held the manuscript in his hands and he knew what was to be included. And on our last day together, I was able to present him with his bibliography, a list that exceeded more than one hundred titles of books, articles, and speeches. An impressive feat for any lifetime, but one even more remarkable for a high school dropout who was forty-one when he first entered print.

The publication of *The Truman Nelson Reader* has been facilitated by the diligence and commitment of Richard Martin of the University of Massachusetts Press. His steady encouragement to Truman, Bill, and me kept us focused on the project and I cannot thank him enough for his support.

Others who I wish to thank are those friends of Truman who contributed financially to the book, thus guaranteeing its completion and, we hope, its wide dissemination. They include: Sharon Hollis and Glenn Richards, Jean Alonso, Christine Morton, Maraia Govignon, Randa Dore, her daughters Robin and Beth, David Christy, Judy Johnson, Anna Smulewitz and Alan Schutz, Nancy Creamer, Elaine Wing, Carol and Chris Kent, Leslie Bartlett, Ted Polumbaum, Bette Keva, Peter Lenz, George A. Billias, Dr. Bernard Lown, Albert Finn, Dian Barrett, Dr. Daniel L. Leary, J. Frank Raley, Al Santoro, Caroline Ramsay, Joyce DeBacco, Joanne Purinton, Lynn Frothingham, Charles L. Newhall, David A. Gass, Maureen Regan, John Kitchener, Susan and Patrick Fitzgerald, Peter Valaskatgis, Harry and Lee Rosenthal, Patricia Gozemba, Angus Cameron, Dr. William Alberts and the Community Church of Boston, my sister, Abigail Nelson, and my children, Shyla A. and Ethan Nelson.

Garrison Nelson
Colchester, Vermont